PRAISE FOR ELLE MARR

Lies We Bury

"A twisted mashup of *Room* and a murder mystery, Marr's *Lies We Bury* is a story that creeps into your bones, a sneaky tale about the danger of secrets and the power the past holds to lead us into a deliciously devious present. Say goodbye to sleep and read it like I did, in one breathless sitting."

—Kimberly Belle, international bestselling author of *Dear Wife* and *Stranger in the Lake*

"Dark and compelling, Elle Marr has written another atmospheric and twisted thriller that you don't want to miss. *Lies We Bury* delves into the darkest of pasts and explores the fascinating tension between moving on and revenge. This is a fly-through-the-pages thriller."

—Vanessa Lillie, Amazon bestselling author of *Little Voices* and *For the Best*

"This haunting and emotional thriller will keep you up at night looking for answers."

—Dea Poirier, international bestselling author of *Next Girl to Die*

"A clever, twisty murder mystery packed full of secrets and lies that will keep you turning the pages way past bedtime. *Lies We Bury* hooked me from page one and kept me guessing until its dramatic conclusion."

—Lisa Gray, bestselling author of *Thin Air*

The Missing Sister

"Marr's debut novel follows a San Diego medical student to, around, and ultimately beneath Paris in search of the twin sister she'd been drifting away from. Notable for its exploration of the uncanny bonds twins share and the killer's memorably macabre motive."
—*Kirkus Reviews*

"[A] gritty debut . . . the intriguing premise, along with a few twists, lend this psychological thriller some weight."
—*Publishers Weekly*

"Elle Marr's first novel has an intriguing premise . . . The characters are well drawn and complex, and Marr's prose offers some surprising twists."
—New York Journal of Books

"A promising plotline."
—Library Journal

"*The Missing Sister* is a very promising debut—atmospheric, gripping, and set in Paris. In other words, the perfect ingredients for a satisfying result."
—Criminal Element

"Brimming with eerie mystery and hair-raising details . . . A chilling read that shows the unique bond of twins."
—*Woman's World*

"This thrilling debut novel from Elle Marr is a look into the importance of identity and the strength of sisterhood."
—*Brooklyn Digest*

"An electrifying thriller. A must read—Karin Slaughter with a touch of international flare. Just when you think you have it all figured out, Marr throws you for another loop and the roller-coaster ride continues!"

—Matt Farrell, *Washington Post* bestselling author of
What Have You Done

"A riveting, fast-paced thriller. Elle Marr hooks you from the start, taking you on a dark and twisted journey. Layered beneath the mystery of a twin's disappearance is a nuanced and at times disturbing exploration of the ties that bind sisters together. With crisp prose, a gripping investigation, and a compelling protagonist, *The Missing Sister* is not to be missed."

—Brianna Labuskes, *Washington Post* bestselling author of
Girls of Glass

"A gripping thriller. *The Missing Sister* delivers twists and turns in an exciting, page-turning read that delves into the unique bond that makes—and breaks—siblings."

—Mike Chen, author of *Here and Now and Then*

LIES WE BURY

OTHER TITLES BY ELLE MARR

The Missing Sister

LIES WE
BURY

ELLE
MARR

THOMAS & MERCER

Published by Thomas & Mercer, Seattle

www.apub.com

Amazon, the Amazon logo, and Thomas & Mercer are trademarks of Amazon.com, Inc., or its affiliates.

ISBN-13: 9781542026192
ISBN-10: 1542026199

Cover photograph by Lara Rossignol

Cover design by Shasti O'Leary Soudant

Printed in the United States of America

For Caden, who took my world from grayscale to color

Unexpressed emotions will never die.
They are buried alive and will come forth later in uglier ways.

—Sigmund Freud

Row, row, row your boat
Gently down the stream
Merrily, merrily, merrily, merrily,
Life is but a dream

One

Secrets never stay buried for long. Photography won't allow it, for one thing. The shutter of a camera captures moments that would have otherwise gone unseen—like that photo of a lone Jewish woman staving off the Israeli Army before they nearly trample her. Or that shot of a man jumping, falling, from the World Trade Center. If a camera snaps long enough and in the right location, anything can be unearthed, documented, and preserved for all time.

In my case, I needed only seven years before I came to light. Images of me trembling in a torn blanket and too-small shoes were plastered across newspapers, then the internet—hair washed but matted because I had just woken up, eyes wild like the feral animals so many compared us to in the headlines afterward. I had been born in captivity, unbeknownst to our neighbors who, in interviews, said we had the nicest lawn on the street.

Secrets have a way of breaking free. But when they do, their shame lingers—like the smell of rotten meat sauce. Even some twenty years later.

I brush back a strand of hair that's come loose from my messy bun. Green pine trees in the distance sway against the rolling breeze, creating a natural horizon between Portland's city blocks and the suburbs over the hill. The trees were the first thing I noticed upon moving here two weeks ago from the flat, dry desert of southern Oregon.

"Claire?" A woman with short, tight curls stands at the double doors of a white brick building, the *Portland Post*. "Are you Claire Lou?"

I step forward as though I've always answered to this name. Cross my fingers that—this time—my secrets might last a while. "Yes, hi." Claire is my middle name, and I changed my last name to my grandmother's maiden name when I was eighteen.

Self-inflicted cigarette burns—failed adolescent attempts at exerting control—peek from beneath my pushed-up sleeve. I tuck my inner elbow into my left side to avoid the woman's notice.

She shakes my hand. Red lipstick amplifies the lines framing her mouth. "Thanks so much for your quick help, Claire. Our regular photog is out on PTO this weekend, and no one bothered to set up coverage for him. I'm Pauline, editor in chief. We spoke on the phone yesterday."

She ushers me past an empty lobby and through another door. Desks with stout cubicles occupy the floor, while two offices and a stairwell line the back wall. Pauline heads into one of the offices. She slides behind a plain beige laminate desk, then motions to the cushioned folding chairs in front.

"I'll cut to the chase. We're swamped with local events coming up, and you've got an eye for wide shots. The work you did at Firenze Winery in Newberg was good. Think you can manage this list at the Rose City Parade tomorrow morning?" She hands me a sheet of paper.

I nod, reviewing the shots they're looking for. Pauline expands on what journalistic style the editorial team prefers as a cramp forms in my stomach.

Landing a gig with the *Portland Post* is a jackpot; I know it. But I'd immediately gotten cold feet after answering their job listing for photographers on a major freelancer website. Pauline must have been desperate, because she emailed me an hour later, ignoring the glaring lack of live-event coverage in my portfolio. A voice inside me insisted that I wasn't good enough, that I would disappoint this industry professional and burn a potential bridge—but for once I let optimism take over. If I could get in good with a news outlet like the *Portland Post* and work up a steady income, I might be able to stop sneaking into Costco to fill up on samples with the expired membership card I found behind my apartment.

Pauline leans back and places her hands flat on the desk. Money details are up next; I always recognize when someone is about to stiff me. "Given your limited experience with this kind of event, I'd be willing to offer you a dollar per photo, however many we decide to buy from you. Does that work?"

"I . . . my usual freelance sessions are significantly—"

Pauline clasps her hands together. "That's the best we can do right now. And I had several photographers respond to my ad. If you want to think about it, I can schedule other appointments—"

"No, that's fine. I'll take it." I plaster a tight smile on my face, then fold up the shot list. A dollar per is so much less than I was hoping for, especially given the scowl that the property manager lobbed at me when I was leaving the apartment complex today. He's been trying to get the last $200 of my security deposit. I promised I would pony up after I borrowed money from my sister—unbeknownst to Jenessa. We have a coffee date after this meeting, but she thinks it's to catch up, since we haven't seen each other in years.

Pauline walks me to the front door. On the way out, we pass a dusty bowl of fruit, and I pocket an orange out of pure habit. Heat flushes my neck as a man looks up from a nearby cubicle; his brow scrunches. I hurry to exit the building before anything else goes wrong, like Pauline offering me less money or this guy recognizing me—if anyone would, it would be a reporter.

I return to my car and begin the slow drive through downtown, considering all the ways in which tomorrow's photo shoot could go wrong. Rarely do I wake up that early on a Sunday, so I'll have to set two alarms tonight.

At a red light, I scan the storefronts along the sidewalk. A chalkboard outside a bar advertises cheap happy hour, and next to it in the alcove of a brewery entrance sits a stuffed animal—a black-and-white penguin that used to star in a children's animated TV show during the late nineties and early aughts. One arm is missing. A red stain covers its throat.

I blink, willing my eyes to focus, to make the details that shouldn't be possible disappear. Is that—

The car behind me honks. I pull forward through the green light and park at the curb a half block up. Craning my neck to look behind me, I fumble in the well of the back seat until my fingers land on the thick strap of my camera case.

I walk the hundred feet back to the brewery where the penguin sits propped against the brick wall. The second arm is nowhere in sight, and the red stain looks suspiciously like pasta sauce—exactly like the Petey the Penguin I owned as a child. A chill ripples across the exposed skin of my forearms. Before I think better of it, I reach out to touch the toy. The material is soft yet flat in spots. It's been used. Loved. Lifting it up, I scan its bottom and spot a name written on the tag in permanent marker: BARRY.

A wave of illogical relief sluices over me. Not the same plush I asked my mother to grab twenty years ago when she, my sisters, and I escaped Chet's basement, and which the police probably have stored as evidence in a cardboard box. Something about the penguin, seated outside the glass doors of a brewery, seems poetic—thought provoking. Like innocence contrasting adulthood. Who we were then and who we are now. Who I was then and the functioning ball of self-loathing I am now.

I step back to the curb's edge. Raising the Canon I saved up for by working four different jobs concurrently for three years, I angle the lens another fifteen degrees off-center until the light strikes the scene perfectly. The toy occupies the corner of the alcove, beneath writing on the window: LIVE MUSIC STARTING AT 7PM BLUES AND BREWS FOR

Cool Kids Only! Switching to a wide shot, I frame the entire entryway, capturing the silhouettes of patrons inside.

I pull open one of the glass doors, prompting the chime of bells, and step into a slender hallway. Tables and chairs occupy space on each side, and a fireman's pole descends from the ceiling, adjacent to a winding iron staircase. Air-conditioning ruffles a stack of napkins on the bar counter.

The bartender looks up. He brushes a floppy curtain of black hair from his eyes. "Welcome to Four Alarm. Get you a table?"

I shake my head and lift my camera in response. He returns a confused smile before someone calls him from down the bar. I snap a photo of the dining area. The light streaming through the tall bay windows looks better suited to a church—peaceful.

After a few more clicks, I check my phone. Shit. Jenessa has already texted me twice. Where are you? and Coming? I'm at the coffee shop. Another glance at the penguin outside makes my skin feel grimy, like I'm back in the cramped, musty tomb of my birth and now all I want to do is go home and take a shower. Why does seeing a stuffed toy feel so visceral? This year marks the twentieth anniversary of our escape, and I'm probably on edge because of it.

I text a reply: Sorry for the late notice, but the interview went well. I need to prep for tomorrow. Can we reschedule? Asking to borrow money from my holier-than-everyone sister can wait for a day when my ghosts aren't clawing to the surface.

The door chime sounds as I exit the brewery, while the bartender's voice trails me onto the sidewalk: "Stay safe out there."

The next day, a crowd jostles at the curb to snap photos of the parade on their cell phones. Sunday traffic from my apartment was lighter than yesterday, but I still got lost on downtown's one-way streets and showed up later than I wanted; the sidewalk real estate I managed to carve out is a fraction of what I normally work with. A man beside me steps into my field of view, again, and I resist the urge to elbow him in the ribs.

"Go Raptors!" he bellows.

Raising my camera, I focus on a passing teenage girl. Fat brown curls, tied and separated by two ribbons, flank her jaw; the sweet throwback style juxtaposes her heavy chest and the tight T-shirts the students wear in this April humidity. The man claps extra hard as the girl bends down in a dance move, and I watch him from the corner of my eye; he shifts toward her, turning as she moves five, then ten feet ahead.

Rows of smiling high school students file forward in matching color-guard outfits. Gymnasts cartwheel diagonally across the cordoned asphalt, while families and adults (some waving red plastic cups even at this early hour) shout encouragement. I step into the street, hiking my backpack higher, and snap photos of the oncoming float. Papier-mâché roses cover its platform, leaving only twelve inches of windshield for the driver of the truck to see through. White flowers clustered together on the side of the float spell out ROSE CITY.

I check my counter. Three hundred and eighty-six images this morning, and I've only been out here since eight. Not bad. Pauline should be pleased I grabbed all the shots on her list, at least a dozen of each.

I turn, shouldering my way through the crowd's enthusiasm until I reach an empty bench. Standing on it, I'm heads above the swath of bodies. A gust from the nearby Willamette River swirls my hair in a black cloud at my shoulders, and I lift my camera. Orange shifts through the frame as the man who was beside me walks forward, following the teenage girl's knee-high march down the street. Zooming in, I can see that she's no longer smiling. I press the shutter, capturing the dip of the man's head as he inclines toward her chest for a better view.

Freelance photography has its pros and cons. Disgusting moments of human nature that people would rather forget become fixed on film, snippets of time that would otherwise disappear from memory. Then again, since I gave up waitressing at run-down diners, headshots and wine-country landscapes have covered my expenses—first in a college town a few hours south, then here for the last two weeks. My camera has always been a safe haven. A way to experience the world from a distance, when so many unwanted admirers were intent on observing my every move. Portland is only the third city I've lived in, but I've broken a lease more times than I can count.

I used to get angry when I thought about the residual effects of the horror Chet inflicted on us and how I'm still living out the consequences. Now, a pack of cigarettes inside my backpack reminds me I'm not subject to him or anyone anymore—I'm no longer a teenager, hiding in my locked bedroom from one of my mother's catatonic spells. I'm in control.

The storefronts are quiet the farther west I travel, away from the river and the parade. My path doesn't take me by the brewery where I saw the stuffed animal yesterday, but I don't need to see it again. I can recall every detail of the penguin's languid expression and stained fur. I went to bed imagining the last time I held Petey the Penguin in my arms, and I fell asleep crying tears that I didn't fully understand.

Police sirens are wailing from somewhere close by when I reach my car. The sound prickles my skin as I hurry to unlock the door. I place my camera in its case in the back seat, then notice the folded piece of paper tucked beneath my windshield wiper. A letter *M* is scratched out, with *Claire* scrawled beside it.

Suddenly, I'm conscious of how blithely I walked through a crowd of people today, then left without once checking over my shoulder to see if someone was taking an interest in me—simply because it was Sunday morning.

Sunshine doesn't mean protection. The worst crimes can happen in the daylight.

I remove the paper from beneath the wiper. With shaky hands, I unfold it. The sirens are louder now, a tense soundtrack. A dog barks nearby. Sweat gathers beneath my arms as I hold the page at eye level.

Four alarms have been shot.

Twenty years. Twenty beers. All named for leaders.

Find the name I most admire and you'll find the next one first.

SEE YOU SOON, MISSY.

My hand claps to my mouth, a strangled cry muffled against my palm. I snap my gaze to the bus stop across the way, but it's empty of anyone watching, threatening me. The words—typed out on computer paper—sink through my skin and root around my guts. The burn scars on my inner elbow tingle.

I scan the page for any markings, smudges that might contain fingerprints, a signature to tell me who this note is from. My first initial—my real first initial, *M*—glares from the reverse side.

Someone knows who I am. Where to find me.

They know the twentieth anniversary of our escape is this year.

My eyes skitter away. Fear licks down my calves. Portland was supposed to be a fresh start. A place where I could stay awhile—remain hidden in the biggest city in Oregon.

Opening my backpack, I fumble until my fingers grasp the plastic wrap of the emergency cigarettes. I get in the car, then jam the key in the ignition. With a jerk of my thumb, the round lighter in the center console engages.

I push my sleeve up to my bicep and wait for the coil to glow red.

Two

Outside the *Portland Post*, I park my car and look across the street to the food trucks. The windows of both vehicles are still dark. I head inside the building. My inner elbow throbs from the cigarette burn, but it restored my sense of reality and control in a way I used to seek out regularly, and which I've managed to cling to for a year or so now. Well, managed. Past tense.

As I walk through the first floor of the office, a radio on a desk sputters with the garbled jargon of police dispatchers. Pauline's door swings open. She throws me a smile before her brown eyes widen. "Everything all right, Claire?"

No, nothing is all right. Nothing is fair or makes sense, and I have no good response to give. "Yes, fine," I manage to say, willing my face into a neutral expression. I withdraw my camera from its case, and the strap trembles against the shaking of my hand.

Pauline watches it, then raises an eyebrow. "Well, let's see what you got," she says and steps back inside her office. I take a seat as she rounds the square table to a mesh chair. She holds out a palm.

I stare at her—not only because residual shock is slowing every movement I make but because when I was first beginning photography, I might have simply ejected the camera's memory card and dropped it into her hand. Eager to please, I wouldn't have realized that she could copy all its contents to her desktop in three clicks.

Instead, I remove my laptop from my messenger bag. It's even older than my car, with scratches along the gray shell, stickers from an attempt to blend into a college town, and a chipped corner where hardware is visible. I pop the memory card into the slot. A grid of excited faces appears on the screen.

"These are great," Pauline says. "May I?" She lifts a finger to the touch pad, and I nod. She scrolls through, making little affirming noises. *Mm-hmm. Mm.* "I'll take the first fifty. Nice work."

"Only fifty? I took over three hundred. You don't want to see the rest?"

She shakes her head. "I only need a handful for the Local Happenings section. Fifty photos means fifty dollars—per our conversation yesterday," she adds when I balk.

"Okay." Not seeing another way, I try to get a grip, to resume an impassive face. I want to escape, to run screaming from this town, but I also need the *Post* as a client.

"Okay," I repeat, focusing on Pauline's white nail polish. "Thanks for your time. Where do I pick up the check?"

Pauline doesn't say anything. She looks at my laptop, pausing on the chipped corner, before heavily mascaraed eyes flit to my face. "What else do you have?"

I hesitate, knowing that the rest of my Recents folder contains senior portraits from high school students. Navigating to a different folder, I double-click and pull up the brewery and Petey photos— images that, in hindsight, given the note I found on my windshield, might be more than my PTSD fixating on a stuffed toy.

In a wide shot at the beginning of the series, the brewery's name, Four Alarm, is clearly stamped on the glass door. The note's typed phrase surges to mind: *four alarms have been shot.*

I bite my cheek, watching Pauline as she scrolls through the exterior, then interior galleries. Landing a consistent client would allow me to save up another nest egg. Get enough money to start over. Just go.

Move up to Seattle or maybe Vancouver. Canadians are supposed to be nice.

"Those are from yesterday, that brewery on Fourth," I say. "I don't know what you could use these photos for, but if you're doing a feature on local businesses, they might—"

Pauline holds up a hand. "Hey, Elliot, get in here!" she shouts out the door.

A man runs in, older, midfifties, svelte around the middle of his blue cotton shirt and jeans. He pushes wire-framed glasses higher onto a prominent nose.

"Four Alarm Brewery is the one you just heard about on the radio, right?" she asks.

As a child, I was surrounded by women who all shrank before the single man I encountered—they never gave orders, only accepted Chet's with downcast gazes. My mother whispered into my ear on a daily basis, *Good little girls do as they're told by the man. They stay alive.*

Elliot nods. "Yeah. You hear anything else?"

Pauline licks her lips. "This photographer—Claire—was there yesterday. She took photos of the entryway, inside the foyer, and all the patrons having their afternoon stout."

Elliot's mouth falls open. He turns to me. "The police called in cars to that address about ten minutes ago. A body was found there. Probable homicide last night or late afternoon."

Pauline leans in, a wild sparkle in her eye. "I'll buy all the images you took at this location."

"All of them? That's around one hundred."

"You got it. We'll use some in tomorrow's physical publication and our online channel. I'll contact you if we need extra photographers again."

"I . . . okay." As we both stand, I nod again because I'm stifling a happy scream.

Outside the building, a freshly written check from the *Post* in hand, I withdraw the anonymous windshield note from my pocket. Petey the Penguin, a well-known part of my childhood, was sitting out front of a brewery where a murder was committed. The note mentioned that four alarms had been shot. "Shot" could be a reference to my photos, but maybe it means "shot with a gun." Was Petey meant to grab my attention, to draw me to that building?

My eyes catch on the second-to-last line: *Find the name I most admire and you'll find the next one first.* Phrasing that I thought was nonsensical gains context to become coherent instructions and stops my breath.

Find the next one first.

This note's author *wanted* me to take photos of that crime scene. Then provided a clue to the next location. Was I just handed a riddle to a murder?

"Claire? Everything okay?" Pauline pauses beside the solid double doors.

My heart is clanging against my bones. Claire would nod. Claire would smile and thank this woman again for buying her photos, not start babbling that a killer might be following her, laying a twisted scavenger hunt at her sandaled feet. And this isn't my first stalker.

I slip the folded square into my back pocket. "Everything's fine," I say. "Is there a place I can grab a croissant nearby?"

Pauline directs me to a bakery around the corner, where a line stretches ten feet down the sidewalk across the street. I sigh, letting my shoulders drop. I really wanted a place to sit a moment, eat something buttery, to still the ping-ponging of my thoughts. Maybe spend more than a dollar on breakfast, knowing I can cash the *Post* check tomorrow.

"Hey."

I turn toward the assertive voice. A young woman leans against the wall of an adjacent clothing consignment shop. Farther down the block, teenagers are seated against the brick, wrapped in dirty blankets and ponchos. Plastic bags cover shopping carts beside them. One of the boys hunches over a stout camping grill, plumes of smoke curling skyward.

"You looking for something?" the woman asks. She eyes the still-fresh burn on my inner elbow, and I wonder whether Pauline noticed, too. Brittle, white-blonde hair with dark roots touches her shoulders. Her round face appears flushed and clear of makeup. The only details that suggest she's homeless are the numerous holes in her sneakers. Red socks poke through in a macabre pattern.

"Ah, yeah. Do you know where I can find a bakery not packed with people—"

"Not food, darling. Something else," she interrupts with a smirk. She glances at my elbow again, then flicks dark-blue eyes to mine. Across the street, people stare into their phones or talk in pairs, oblivious to any drug deals occurring opposite.

"Oh. No. Thanks."

She shrugs. Slender hands dip into the pockets of her cargo pants. "Suit yourself. You change your mind, ask around for Gia."

Without any comfort food or comfort beyond the residual sting of air against my wounded flesh, I scurry back to my car. As I slide into the driver's seat, the windshield, empty of additional threats or riddles, feels like a middle finger to my initial hopes upon moving here—a sure sign that just when I think life might be going my way, the past isn't through with me yet.

Three

Sisters are the absolute worst. They take your favorite book, wear your good pair of shorts, and sit in your corner of the basement, which has been your corner since forever—since way before Mama Nora left and before Mama Bethel left the earth. Mama Rosemary always says Mama Bethel went to heaven where the rooms have no walls and the ceilings are see-through and the air-conditioning is called "wind" instead. Mama Nora went outside a few years ago. Maybe outside and heaven are the same?

I told Twin this and she said *There is no outside, duh*. Mama Rosemary smiled then and explained what a metaphor is. She was pretty smart before the man took her.

Sisters are supposed to be my friends and be everything to each other and supposed to tell each other secrets—but we don't have any secrets. Not in a two-room basement. I remember once when I was six I tried to save an extra piece of toast for myself behind the tub in a washcloth and Sweet Lily found it in minutes and almost choked on it. I got yelled at.

Sisters are supposed to keep our secrets but Sweet Lily was too little to realize. I don't know what Twin's excuse is.

Sometimes sisters aren't so bad. The three of us like to play castle together and war battles. I always want to be the king but Twin won't let me—she's always King and I have to be Queen or Knight. I like those pretend roles fine but just once I'd like to be King. When I say this to Mama Rosemary she says, *Wouldn't we all?* I don't know what she means by that.

Once I asked her if we could have a brother and Mama Rosemary got angry. She shouted, *Don't even think such a thing!* Then burst into tears. I felt really bad after and remorse filled me from head to toe just like in *Anne of Green Gables* when Anne accidentally got her friend Diana drunk off wine instead of raspberry cordial.

So no brothers for now. Only sisters—two of them. The basement didn't feel so cramped when we were all little. But now I can't step sideways without bumping one of them.

"You're in my seat." I stand with my hands on my hips the way Mama Nora used to do and point at Twin. In the first room we have plastic bins for storage and a table with four chairs and a bathtub and a frigerator and the Murphy bed in the wall. The potty sits in the corner. The walls are decorated with drawings that Sweet Lily and me made. Mama Rosemary always says *we are packed to the gills in here* so there's not enough room to start taking people's seats. "Move," I say again to Twin.

She looks up from the Game Boy game she's playing. Mario is jumping from pipe to pipe and she's hunched over it like it's one of our birthdays and she's guarding her slice of cake. Her pink tongue pokes from the corner of her mouth. "What?"

"You're in my seat."

She's not really my twin but that's what all the mamas call us since we were born in the same year. *Irish twins* they said. "Irish" describes people from Ireland which is another part of the world that exists in books. Mama Rosemary has black hair and she would be from China in one of our books if she weren't from a place called Boys-y. Me and Twin look alike since Mama Nora has black hair, too. Mama Nora would be from a place called India and that's where Mowgli is from. Mama Bethel had yellow hair and yellowy skin and no one knows where she'd be from. Me and Twin were the same height before she grew two inches.

Twin juts out a foot and kicks at my shin but she misses. "Don't gotta." She reaches out and pinches my knee.

"Ow! Mama Rosemary!"

"Girls, don't fight, please. I'm working on something, and I need you to be very good while I am. Okay?"

"Yes, Mama Rosemary," we say together.

"Good girls. Now, what did we talk about earlier? What is today?"

"Escape day," we answer eyes wide, still not really sure what that means. Mama Rosemary has been distracted for days talking to herself, writing stuff down then ripping it up and flushing the pieces in the toilet. After, she goes to the bed room and gets real quiet. She stares at the wall with tears on her face but she won't talk if I talk to her. That's how I know she's in the Dark Place and I should leave her alone. Sometimes Twin goes and sits with her and doesn't talk. I think Mama likes that.

"Mama Rose?" Sweet Lily pipes up. She's three years old and not much bigger than a baby. Mama Rosemary still treats her like one anyway. "What is escape?"

"What *does* escape mean. It means we're going to get out of here, sweetheart." Mama Rosemary picks up our youngest in her thin arms and twirls her around until Sweet Lily's face breaks into the smile we love. It doesn't happen so often but when it does it makes all of us stop what we're doing and be happy together. My sisters and me and Mama Rosemary.

Mama Rosemary puts Sweet Lily back on the ground then touches her finger to Sweet Lily's nose. "Escape, my love, means we're going to be free."

Four

As I pull into the boxy parking lot of my apartment complex, a car zips past me to exit, narrowly missing my side-view mirror. When I lock eyes with the driver, he gives me a dirty look like I've done something wrong.

I park in one of the uncovered—free of charge—spots, then watch the entrance for any other aggressive drivers barreling through the narrow opening. Someone else might be in a hurry to take out the plot of peonies growing on the corner, or someone may be more focused on slipping unseen into my neighborhood. Watching. Waiting for me to feel comfortable and safe again. Before they note exactly where I live and how to get inside while I'm sleeping.

Stop it. No one is coming to get you. The note suggested a location in Portland, and no one is driving out to the 'burbs to give me a scare.

Paranoia has been a constant since my twentieth birthday, when I turned the same age as Rosemary when she was abducted. But while Rosemary was carefree before that day in 1989, I had my first stalker at age fifteen. Someone keen on *revisiting Chet's legacy,* according to the notes they tucked into my school locker.

Grabbing my backpack, laptop bag, and camera case, I shimmy out of my car, being careful not to ding the sleek, freshly washed sedan beside it. As I near my first-floor apartment, footsteps approach from behind, and I whirl to face my attacker.

"Claire. So glad I could catch you." The property manager, Derry Landry, stares at me with a self-satisfied grin. His blond buzz cut gives him the illusion of a halo against the morning sun. "You left in such a hurry yesterday, I couldn't ask you about the final deposit amount."

"Yeah, sorry about that." I sling the camera strap around my neck. "Once I cash a check tomorrow, I'll have a hundred and fifty. I should have the last fifty dollars soon."

If the *Portland Post* sends more work my way, I won't have to borrow money from Jenessa.

"Hundred dollars. The corporate office tacked on a fifty-dollar late fee," he says.

"Wow. That's, like . . . a thirty-three percent increase."

Derry maintains a stoic mien, as if I withheld the cash from his grandmother. "Not my problem."

He steps toward me, and his hand grazes my elbow. "You know, I was excited when you moved in, Claire. Thought it would be nice to inject some young blood into the neighborhood." Gray eyes the shade of the community garbage bin seem to drink me in. He leans forward, using the extra six inches he has on me to block out the sun. The shadow on his face makes him appear more aggressive, and I briefly wonder whether he has the spare key to my apartment or the corporate office does.

I step away into the carpeted hallway. "I'll make sure I get that hundred dollars to you."

"When?" he asks, closing the distance between us again. His breath smells of milk, like he just finished eating cereal. I turn away and grapple for my key.

"Very soon. Thanks for the heads-up on the late fee." After closing the door behind me and locking the dead bolt, I watch him through the peephole. He lingers a moment longer, swearing something inaudible.

He runs a hand over his head, hesitates, and actually lifts his fist to knock on my door. Then he walks toward the parking lot, out of sight.

I turn and lean against the cool wood. Across the room, the digital clock of the kitchen oven glares the time: barely eleven. I peel myself from the door and place my stuff onto the love seat. The laptop bag is old, with cracks in its leather, but an aluminum plate beneath the handle shines with my initials like Rosemary had it engraved yesterday—*MCM*. The Sweet Sixteen gift was meant to see me through college, but that plan (and those initials) didn't last.

A quick glance confirms the studio is exactly as I left it: a bowl rests on the tile countertop of the kitchen nook, stale toast peeking from beside it; the sheets of my full-size bed, rumpled in a ball, are nearly off the mattress in the corner; and a broad coffee table, rescued from a classifieds website, serves as the room's centerpiece. The flat-screen television—my one splurge, bought with the money I saved from a lucrative senior-portrait season a few years ago—enjoys the place of honor on a grocery crate.

I grab a glass of water from the faucet, then survey the room; it's better than the last shoebox I lived in. Its main redeeming quality is the view, ironically hidden by the blinds. Anyone could see inside without them. Beyond the parking lot, an open field leads into the thick forest of a nature preserve—a view of uninhibited space that's the perfect way to end any day. Access to photographic, idyllic scenery is a major reason why I stayed in Oregon and moved to Portland. When foot traffic dies down for the night, and there are fewer ins and outs through the parking lot, I'll turn off my lamps, raise the blinds, and gaze out on the trees, illuminated only by moonlight.

Voices pass outside the window, and I stiffen by instinct. The note folded in my pocket resumes pulsing, announcing my brief reprieve is over. I take it out.

Four alarms have been shot.

I retrieve my laptop from my bag, then begin a flurry of internet searches. *Portland news* brings up an article about the top five best places to live in the country. *Portland murder* results are dominated by updates on a domestic shooting. The *Portland Post* is the only website that's reported on the suspected murder at Four Alarm Brewery. The photos I took yesterday are featured throughout the story.

A thrill of excitement registers, seeing my work on a leading news outlet, before sobering anxiety resumes its grip. Someone set me up to take those. But was it an obsessed fan of Chet's or a more sinister stalker? *See you soon, Missy* could be a threat, and one intended to do more than expose me. Did the author of the note kill the victim in the brewery?

According to a *Post* article written by an Oz Trainor, the Four Alarm victim was a local exotic dancer. She was employed at one of Portland's many strip clubs and had been reported missing last week. The time stamp shows the article was published about thirty minutes ago; the final paragraph notes that the story will be updated as information becomes available.

What did this woman, this dancer, do that she deserved to die? The truncated sentences don't elaborate. The body was found in the brewery's basement. No cause of death has been identified yet, and the article doesn't say whether she was killed there or moved to the location afterward.

Most importantly: given the hand-delivered note I received today, what does she have to do with me?

> Find the name I most admire and you'll find the
> next one first.

Suddenly filled with more questions, I open a new browser tab. Searching the words *Portland brewery*, I get dozens of results—features

on local favorites, top-ten lists, and national statistics regarding breweries per capita.

Twenty years. Twenty beers. All named for leaders.

The phrase *Portland brewery leader names* provides just as many
links, leaving me feeling more overwhelmed than hopeful. I jot down
the addresses of three breweries that seem like a possible fit: McHale's
Brewery, Patriot Brewery, and Bridge City Brewpub; each of their websites boasts a list of beers that seem to be named for real people.

Navigating back to the tab with the *Portland Post*'s home page, I hit
"Refresh." No updates on the Four Alarm murder. By now, two hours
have gone by since I locked the dead bolt.

Anyone with access to the internet could dig up the photo of me
as a child outside the hospital, clinging to Petey. The author of the note
must have known I would see it at the brewery entrance and stop. Then
again, the toy was weathered, dingier than mine, since Rosemary was
factidious about our cleanliness belowground; it could have been there
for days or weeks.

I hit "Refresh" again. No updates.

A woman cackles from the parking lot outside my window, and I
jump.

I can't stay here waiting for—anticipating—another threat to slip
under my door, to wake up later tonight at the sound of my window
being jimmied open by practiced, calloused hands.

Grabbing my keys and the list of breweries, I head out. A quick
glance through the peephole confirms no one is hiding in the hall.

The drive back to Portland passes quickly. Most drivers stay to the
far right, allowing me to zip along the ten-mile distance with barely
enough time to wonder what the hell I'm doing.

Blue uniforms and blazers stream in and out of Four Alarm Brewery.
A crowd forms across the street; yellow police tape ropes off the block,
making it inaccessible to cars. I park on the next street south. A plain
brick structure, Four Alarm is located in a part of downtown nicknamed

the Pearl—a suggestion among Portlanders that there's hidden treasure inside despite outward appearances. Watching law enforcement cross the threshold now, the word FORENSICS emblazoned across certain jackets, the irony is too fitting.

A trio of teenagers stands at the corner observing the scene. One of them clutches a sleeping bag and wears a sweatshirt with a retro Mickey Mouse design from the nineties—same as the one I used to own. With a jolt, I take a step toward the group as white-blonde hair turns the corner and joins them. Gia.

"Hey, do you mind?"

A man whose path I crossed gestures toward the brewery. "I'm working. You just stepped into my line of sight." He returns to scribbling in a palm-size black notepad.

"Sorry." I keep moving to the right, nearly colliding with a woman who's stopped walking her dog.

"Hey," the man says again from behind me. I turn. Recognition lightens his brooding expression as he points a finger at me. A flash of cold douses my neck.

He knows who I am. Shit.

"Claire. Right? You did those photos for Pauline—the photos of the brewery. I'm with the *Post*. Oz."

Oz Trainor. The journalist whose article I read at home. Styled sandy-brown hair complements hypnotic green eyes that focus on my mouth, and suddenly I feel nervous for a different reason.

I release the panicky breath I'd sucked in. "Uh, yeah, that's me. Are you covering this all day, then? Have the police confirmed other details?"

The woman with the dog looks our way, and I'm aware that mine isn't the only inquiring mind.

Shouts come from the interior of the building, and Oz squints toward the noise. His gaze flits over our audience. "Just what you find on our home page," he says, his voice raised.

To me, he shrugs. "I'm supposed to interview the chief of police in a bit, but she keeps pushing me and the other press reps off. Come to think of it"—he clicks his pen—"you would actually be good to interview. Since you saw Four Alarm the day before the body was discovered. Did anything look unusual to you?"

Several heads turn to us. Heat flushes my cheeks.

"Ah, no. Nothing did. Everything I saw you now have in the photos that Pauline bought. If she needs anything else, she knows how to contact me." Spinning on my heel, I walk toward the corner, the teenagers, and Gia. Oz's curious stare seems to drill into my back, and I hurry away from the throng of law enforcement and the possibility of actually being recognized, of being called a different name than Claire.

Gia is gesturing to a guy facing away from me. Her eyes widen; then she scans the sidewalk and the clumps of police in front of the brewery. She says something, but the guy raises his arms. Sunlight glints off metal. A shot rings out, scattering homeless kids and blue uniforms, and I don't hesitate—I sprint back to my car, away from the scene. As I pass Oz, I see he's hunched over, scribbling notes furiously, the only person not looking for cover.

What the hell was that?

It's not until I arrive at the address for McHale's Brewery that I catch my breath. My hands have relaxed enough that the color is returning to my knuckles, but I still can't grasp what I just witnessed. Why did that boy fire a gun? Was it something Gia said?

I land a spot directly out front. McHale's has the typical Pearl-area warehouse exterior, and reviews I found online highlight its twenty specialty beers. Adrenaline hums through my limbs as I cross the street toward the first location on my list that might fit the note's clue regarding *twenty beers. All named for leaders.*

The closer I get, the more anxious I become, until I'm at the curb and able to read the sign in the window:

**AFTER FIFTEEN YEARS OF BUSINESS, MCHALE'S SADLY
CLOSES ITS DOORS.**

A laminate banner above the glass entryway announces that Tia's Taqueria will open for business in a month. Frustration punts the hope in my chest: this can't be the author's intended location.

I face my car, debating my next move.

Across the street, someone is staring at me. A man, wrapped in a quilt and wearing swim trunks that reach his knees. We lock eyes. Another moment passes; then he picks up a reusable shopping bag stuffed with clothing and walks to the corner, turning out of sight.

Five

As a child, post-captivity, I was always aware that we were different. We didn't have a father or a regular nuclear family—we had all the game pieces, but they were spread out. Chet was in prison; Rosemary raised Lily and me after Lily's mother, Bethel, died in the basement; Jenessa was raised by her mother in the Portland metro area. We were like cousins who saw each other a few times a year, and the ache of not growing up with both my sisters began to weigh on me after only a few months.

Kids in school, once they learned about our sordid past, were merciless. They teased me, calling me Bad Blood, and pinched Lily whenever a teacher wasn't watching. But I was. Whenever I could get away with it, I made sure to kick those brats in the shin or groin, and I expertly applied burns by gripping their small arms and twisting my hands in opposite directions. I learned at a young age that people assumed the worst of us, due to our origins; I learned to leverage that fear, if that meant safety for the ones I loved.

Too rattled by the day's events and the closure of McHale's, I headed home to the safety of my locked door without visiting other breweries. This morning, sunshine streams through the blinds of my east-facing windows. Mrs. Henley's dog paws around the corporate flower beds outside, snorting as he goes. Rumpus lost a nasal passage to cancer, leaving him with the phantom smell of a treat always just out of reach. He pads insistently around the pansies every morning until Mrs. Henley tugs him away. I've taken to leaving him cooked chicken among the flower roots.

Although I only recently moved in, I've tried my best to make this studio feel like home—maybe not my home but, rather, a safe space. From my love seat, the framed photos I've kept over the years perch on a shoe-rack-turned-display-shelf: an image from my hometown, of Arch's downtown shopping scene, which always struck me as charmingly normal; a photo of half-drunk coffee cups on a table stained with brown rings; and a shot of the treetops lining the University of Oregon campus, a scene both eerie and tantalizing, suggestive of being unmoored, running loose in this world. An art gallery owner I was trying to sell prints to commented that each image suggested a fascination with the mundane. He didn't buy any. No doubt he smelled my desperation for both validation and money.

The only nonphoto in my collection is a framed drawing Jenessa sent to me when we were nine years old of a flower in bloom. Beneath its pretty pink-and-yellow petals and its single green leaf, she wrote in messy, little-kid handwriting, *Miss you, kiss you, see you soon!*

On the shelf beneath the frames sits a cardboard box. Scribbled on the side are the words *Wasted $50. Don't be this dumb again.* I kept three dozen of the business cards—out of nostalgia? Fear that someone else might find them and plaster them all over the internet? I'd ordered them out of a foolish desire to advertise my photography business around the college town. Foolish, because within a week of my distributing them to coffee shops in the area, a man with a full gray beard began showing up to the diner I worked at. When he sat at my table and addressed me as *Missy*, my terror made delight stretch his lined features. He said he'd researched family names on Rosemary's side—Lou seemed as good as any—and found the website I had created. Said he helped people find their family members on lineage platforms and called himself an *adoption angel*. He'd used a computer program to age me from a photo that was published when I was seven. More importantly, he said, I carried myself like a dog that had been kicked too many times—probably why I sympathize with Rumpus so well.

After dumping lukewarm coffee—the diner's specialty—on him, I quit my job. I knew then that any paper trail gave people like him the power to out me, to expose me in record time as Missy Mo, one of three children born of false imprisonment. I shut down the website immediately. Then I returned to each of the coffee shops and dining halls, gathered what was left of the business cards, and threw them into a box. It took me another year to save up enough money to move to Portland, but I knew if the adoption angel could find me, more like him would follow.

Scrolling through the internet on my laptop, I see that other news outlets seem to have caught up to the *Post*. KGTV 8's and the *Portland Metro Times's* websites dedicate the most space to details of the Four Alarm death, with the *Portland Post* now coming in third.

According to the *Times*, the body was discovered not in the basement but in an adjacent tunnel. The infamous Portland Shanghai Tunnels, once thought to be used to kidnap men at the turn of the twentieth century and force them into labor aboard steamer ships, lie about a mile east; the *Times* suggests this tunnel beside the brewery may be a forgotten passage.

Jesus. Shanghai Tunnels?

The victim's identity has been confirmed, but family is still being notified. The cause of death has been preliminarily called a homicide, due to the restraints found near the body. This woman was held against her will, then left to die—or killed—in the darkness belowground. I sit, glued to my computer screen, struck by the similarity of her end to my beginning.

At the same time, without more details, it's hard to speculate how her death relates to the note I received. Although she was killed around the time I took photos of Petey the Penguin, and the note suggests that her death is the first of at least two, the author doesn't explicitly claim responsibility.

A slow curl of tension tightens my stomach. Memories of scratchy blankets and the white noise of a television tiptoe around the edge of my senses. Blurry happiness slides forward to wrestle with vibrating fear.

I slam my laptop shut. I can't do this. I can't presume we're to blame—I'm to blame, somehow—for this woman's death. I can't create some relationship to this victim where there's none. If the killer is the author of the note, it's coincidence he saw me taking photos and recognized me.

My phone buzzes with an unknown number. I let it ring another three times before I hit "Accept." "Hello?"

"Claire, it's Pauline Adebayo of the *Portland Post*. Do you have any free time today? We need new staff portraits, and I was hoping you could assist."

"Uh, yeah. Sure, I'm free," I reply, eyeing my framed photo of the treetops. I agree to meet at the office in an hour, then hang up and grab my keys.

Monday morning traffic puts yesterday's to shame, and I sorely underestimate the drive time. When I finally find a spot on the street about six blocks over from the *Post*'s building, I make a mental note to research nearby parking garages.

The ground floor is crammed with people when I walk in—"Mostly interns," Pauline says, weaving through the room—and the low current of laughter and phone calls feels like a college dorm hall, from what I've seen in movies. As we approach the stairwell, we pass desks that were empty on the weekend, now occupied by people, stacks of folders and paper, and breakfast food wrappers.

"Hey, Claire," a voice calls. Oz Trainor waves at me from beside two young women. His smile is relaxed as his eyes trail down my neck and chest. "Good to see you again."

I lift a hand in return, then follow Pauline up the stairs.

"So the digital marketing team has an influx of new hires, and they all need headshots for our internal website. That is your specialty, right? Headshots?" she pauses on a step to ask.

"I do a little of everything," I lie.

"Even better." She turns onto the second-floor landing and down a hallway lined with framed newspaper pages. At the end, we continue straight into a conference room. A long white table occupies half of it, while tall bookcases filled with binders, videocassettes, and books take up the rest of the space. A woman with a topknot and natural curls sits in a deep armchair near the mini library.

"Claire, meet Amanda, our marketing director. If you could start with her, she'll send in the next person to be photographed until we get the whole team's gallery completed. I'm looking for business casual, not too stuffy. I don't think it should take more than a couple of hours or so, and I'll pay you five dollars per portrait. I want some light retouching to make everyone look their best. Sound good?"

This new rate is still not ideal, because retouching can be painstaking work if you're a perfectionist like I am, but I don't have any bargaining power. Hopefully it's enough to cover my apartment company's late fee. "Yeah, that's fine. Thanks again for thinking of me."

"You got it, Claire. Oh, and here's a TriMet pass for getting around the city while you're doing work for us. Just one of the many *Post* perks." Pauline hands me a card with a bus in the foreground.

"Ah. Thank you."

"Thank *you*," she says, as though the extra emphasis will nourish me the way an increase in wages might. She smiles before walking out the glass door.

From among the book spines, I find the brightest ones in the collection—Crayola red, Egyptian blue, and spring green—then move them to a shelf by one of several windows along the back wall for the best lighting. I ask Amanda to stand in front of my makeshift backdrop, and she automatically adopts a charismatic smile. Not her first photo shoot, either, apparently.

"So what do you do for digital marketing?" I ask, snapping two test shots. "Can you tilt your head forward a bit?" There's more shadow in the room than I'd like, and I narrow the aperture of my Canon for a sharper image.

"Like this?"

"You got it."

She switches to a more subdued, pensive smile. "I lead a team of three marketing specialists and four college interns."

"Sounds like a full plate. Can you cross your arms and hug your elbows? That's great."

"Yeah, it's a lot. Luckily, I live and breathe social media, so it doesn't feel like work." The laugh tumbles out of her like it's too big for her throat. "Our job is to make sure Portland readers know where they can find reliable and accurate news."

"Is that a problem, generally?"

"Not exactly. I mean, most of the news that outlets are reporting is all from the same handful of sources: the police, eyewitnesses who want their five minutes of fame, or government officials. For that reason, it's about building brand loyalty with readers versus trying to be the first ones to report. There's no way you could know what to report on first, every time, unless you were the criminal." She grins again, lifting an eyebrow.

"That makes sense. Let's do a series of profile shots. Then I think I have everything I need."

Amanda gives me her left side and smiles at a shelf in front of her.

I lift the viewfinder to my eye, but her words roll through my head again. *No way you could know . . . unless you were the criminal.* If anyone knew I took photos of Four Alarm before it was a crime scene, would I be a suspect?

When I don't click the shutter, Amanda turns back to me. "Uh. Claire, right? Everything okay? Should I do something different?"

"No, you're good. The focus was off," I mumble. "I read on the *Post* website about the Four Alarm death. Has the brewery staff been cleared of suspicion?"

"Too early to tell. Word on the street is that one guy is being looked at for having ties to the S&M community, but no one has been arrested."

"Sadomasochism?"

Amanda meets my eyes with a smirk. "Right? As if being into a little kink means you're into murder."

I nod, then snap another three photos. "Any other crimes like this recently? Or similar crimes in the past? A woman being held underground and then killed." Speaking the words feels wrong, as though I might out my origins accidentally. *Remember that one guy who held three women underground and made them bear children?*

"Or killed and then moved underground—there have been a few," Amanda says. "From years ago. Three others that all involved bunkers or basements or something weird going on belowground. The crime team has been trying to dig up those details since the weekend, but they're short on help."

"Lots of people on PTO, huh?" I ask, remembering Pauline's explanation for the last-minute coverage of the parade.

"That, paternity leave, and someone else quit out of the blue."

A midmorning shadow slides down the window, followed by a rumbling noise. An airplane dips low, probably landing at Portland International Airport, and obstructs the light for a final shot. Unease seems to paint Amanda's face in the gloom of the cavernous room. Then the airplane's engine fades into the distance, and the sunrays return.

I snap the shutter button and tell Amanda we're done. She leaves, promising to send the next subject upstairs. I remain at the window, digesting her words, waiting for the sun's warmth to energize me. Instead, a cold, clammy feeling persists along my skin.

When a man knocks on the glass, I jump and almost drop my camera to the floor.

"Claire? You ready for me?" The man Pauline called Elliot peers at me from the doorframe. He runs a hand through gray-threaded black hair, then tucks a thumb into his belt loop. Although he must be nearing fifty, his shirt buttons strain against the muscles of his chest. "I got Kasey covering for me on the police scanner for the next twenty minutes."

"You're with marketing, too?" I ask.

A conspiratorial gleam enters his eyes. "Newspapers run pretty lean nowadays, so I'm on three different teams. The interns find it funny that the old guy is in marketing—as if social media and publicity are just for kids. What can I say?" he adds. "I surprise people."

Glancing down at Amanda's wary expression on my screen, I clutch my camera closer. "I know the feeling."

Jenessa's phone goes to voice mail as I cross the river to the house she rents in North Portland. She hasn't invited me over since I moved here, but I have to speak to her. There's no one else in the city who will understand the panic blurring the white dashed lines of the asphalt. If there is a link between this victim and me, there's only one person I can speak to freely about it. My sister.

Hurtling over the bridge at a speed too fast, I pass individuals standing at the thick-beamed railing, alone and seemingly deep in thought.

Are they contemplating jumping right here and now or planning out a return visit under cover of darkness, as I would?

The city Rosemary moved us to after we left Portland didn't have a major river that would assist a suicide attempt—only a lazy one that wound through the desert town. Despite our torrid beginnings, my mother didn't even own a gun, too terrified that one of us, herself included, might do something drastic. She wasn't wrong. Although the obvious means of hurting myself were out of reach, I never let that stop me.

I merge onto another freeway and swerve onto the shoulder to avoid a car ambling forward. Breezy. Calm. Carefree.

A sign for Jenessa's exit looms around the corner, and I hit my blinker with a shaking hand. Following the directions the navigation app on my phone provides, I turn right and pass a pet hotel next to an Asian grocery outlet.

I park my car in front of a bungalow with yellow trim. Before climbing the stairs, I look in each direction to see if anyone else just parked, too, or might have followed me from downtown.

"Jenessa? Open up—it's me." I knock again on my sister's door, then press my ear to the peeling paint of the wood. No footsteps come to greet me. An ambulance siren howls from the next block over. "Jay, you home?"

"Marissa? What are you doing here?"

I turn and face my sister's surprised expression where she's paused on the cracked sidewalk. Worry lines mark her forehead in the direct sunlight, and her jet-black hair appears wiry. She's aged since the last time I saw her (when she graduated from rehab again), but so have I. A bag of groceries digs into each of her thin shoulders before she sets them on the ground.

"I'm sorry to drop in on you like this after I canceled yesterday," I begin, feeling myself sliding into old patterns with her. Always apologizing. Always the one at fault. "I need to share something with you."

She stiffens. "What's wrong? Is everything okay? It's not Lily, is it?"

I shake my head. "No, nothing to do with Lily. As far as I know, she's fine. It's something else. Can we talk inside?"

Jenessa picks up her grocery bags, then sniffs. "You'd think Lily would figure out cheap international calls at some point. Isn't Switzerland supposed to be more advanced than us? All those electronics and watches?"

We pause at the door while she digs in her pocket for keys. Wild roses bloom along the sidewalk plot in a thick hedge, mostly red but some yellow. Jenessa inherited her mother's green thumb. Nora often sent us photos of Jenessa posing beside Nora's latest prizewinning hydrangea or rhododendron, but Jenessa never looked too pleased in those photos. In each picture, she always had both hair and makeup done for the occasion. She was Nora's pliable doll until she hit adolescence.

"Good thing I went shopping. You hungry?" she asks. "Did you drive all the way out from the suburbs? You could have called."

"No, downtown. Work for the newspaper I told you about."

Jenessa smiles, the first time, as she opens the door. "That's right."

She kicks off her shoes, and I do likewise. A quick tour of her two-bedroom house confirms she lives alone—no pets, no nosy roommates. She explains that the creaking I hear with each footstep is the house's invaluable "charm."

We settle into a worn couch and armchair in her living room. A bookshelf sits against the wall opposite, and I can make out a few titles on the spines. *Getting Right in a Wrong World. When Horrible Things Happen Again.* Wedged in an empty spot is a framed photo of the three of us—me, Jenessa, and Lily—the only photo in the space. We must have been fourteen; Lily, ten. The photo captured a moment of joy when we discovered a kitten behind the rear tire of Rosemary's car. Lily holds the kitten, triumphant, above her head.

"So can I get you anything?" Jenessa asks, sinking into the couch cushions. "What was so urgent that you came directly here?"

"This." I withdraw yesterday's folded piece of paper from my pocket and lay it between us. Jenessa reads it, her eyes widening with each line. She lifts a hand to her mouth, as I did. As much as I don't like thinking about who links us, the genetics we share can't be denied.

"What the hell is this?" she whispers. "What the fuck is this?" She leaps to her feet and backs away from me, nearly tripping over her coffee table.

I inhale a breath, try to keep us both calm. "I found it on my windshield."

"Well, what do you think it means? Why four alarms? Why aren't you freaking out?" Jenessa's eyes dart across the page as she rereads it.

"That's a brewery." I do my best imitation of a woman's elevator voice: cool, measured, collected. Even as I remember all the times Jenessa threw wild temper tantrums growing up, the peaks of her mood swings, and that she may just be getting started. We have that in common, too.

"There was a murder committed there Saturday. A body left in an underground tunnel. I don't know, it's all—" I pause, searching for the right words, for her confirmation that this is as bad as it feels. "This person knows who I am."

Jenessa rubs her arm where I notice she's broken out into hives. We each look down at the paper again. The last time I felt this anxious was three years ago when a middle-aged woman followed me to each of my four jobs for a week—then drove an hour to appear on Rosemary's doorstep under the guise of selling beauty products. She said she wanted to be friends with our family and that she had survived a terrible upbringing, too. Judging from her lack of boundary recognition, we weren't interested.

"You know what?" Jenessa taps the page with a gray lacquered nail, still standing. "I think I know who wrote this."

"What? Who?"

She begins to chew on a fingernail, reading again. "Last week, I was approached by someone. He called out of the blue—no idea how he got my number—and pitched me this book idea, wanted me to act as his source. Offered me a grand up front to do it."

"Wow. I'm assuming you said no?"

"Are you kidding?" Her nose wrinkles. "Reporters and bloggers have been chasing me for years. More so than you or Lily. Something about rehab making me the most interesting sister," she grumbles. "The very last thing I'd want is to give those bastards more ammunition."

I tuck my legs underneath me. "This is all so crazy. Why me? Why now?"

Jenessa pushes a thick curtain of wavy hair behind an ear. "Isn't it obvious?" she asks in a small voice. "It says so right there. Twenty years. The author wants to capitalize on the anniversary. Drum up more publicity by getting you involved. It's probably that writer."

"Mm."

A thousand dollars. Would I have accepted it had I been approached? The idea of exposing myself, my family, more than we already are feels awful, but my empty wallet would be tempted. Even though a small voice within me is wondering why Jenessa was approached and not me, I'm glad I didn't have to make the decision she did. Sibling rivalry be damned.

I tear my eyes from a book entitled *My Sister, My Friend* and turn back to Jenessa. "You think the note has nothing to do with the killer? It's just someone trying to manufacture an association between our case and this new crime?"

"I mean, yeah. Doesn't that make more sense? If it is the writer who contacted me, and he wrote you this note to grab your attention, I can see how your involvement would benefit him. Help sell more books. Why would this killer share information with you otherwise?"

I glance down at the page, wanting to believe. But the police didn't learn about the body until the next day. "I don't know. I just want this to go away. Maybe it will."

She laughs, then runs a hand down her face. "God, it's so like you to assume things will just *go* your way. Everything will work out because it always has for you. Been that way since we were kids."

I stiffen. "What is that supposed to mean?"

"Come on. That time when we were eight and you were watching the class guinea pig and it just died overnight? Rosemary made sure to tell everyone it choked on a pellet."

"It did. Why are you bringing that up?"

"Marissa—"

"Claire. I go by Claire now."

"Whatever. It was found with pellet mush coming out of its mouth. You fed it to death, like that scene in the movie *Seven*."

My cheeks flush, embarrassment tightening my chest. "He was hungry, and I didn't know their stomachs were so tiny or that the pellets expanded once they were eaten. It was an accident."

Jenessa rolls her eyes. "Whatever the intention, Rosemary cleaned up your mess like always."

"Whoa, do you really think I killed my pet?"

"I think it annoyed you with how often its cage had to be cleaned."

We're both silent a moment. The words we just exchanged hang between us like noxious fumes. To say I'm disappointed would be an understatement, but I guess I didn't think our first visit in two years would spiral so quickly. Or that she thinks I would hurt an innocent animal.

I love my sister. However, as adults, we've always disagreed about the past.

Jenessa offers up a tight smile. "Look, I'm sorry. I don't know why I brought that up." She gestures toward the table. "About the note? I think anyone can type and lead you down a wild-goose chase. The world has shown itself to be hard. Self-serving. And it treated us like circus freaks. This"—she holds up the paper—"is another example of that. If there really is another body, it will get found with or without you. Right now, it's none of your business, and I would try and keep it that way."

Due to her rehab stints—both of them—for drug addiction, the world hasn't let its grip on her loosen. I've visited the websites dedicated to her progress or regression and seen the annual updates on her sobriety, given by "caregivers in the know." Vultures, all of them.

"I feel like we've barely had a chance to connect again, and I've already brought this brick into our lives," I say. I fold up the paper and tuck it into my jeans pocket. "What are your plans today?"

She straightens, fixing me with serious brown eyes. Of the three of us, Jenessa inherited Chet's stern jawline and sharp cheekbones—but her coloring is all Nora. Thick, wavy hair; tawny skin tone; full lips; and lengthy eyelashes make her the beauty of our trio of outcasts. More than once, as a teenager, I wondered whether I would have gotten into equal trouble with drugs and the wrong boys, were I deemed as attractive.

"I'm off from the doughnut shop today. I had planned to get some work done in the garden, actually."

"That's great. Are you still staging the shop front? I imagine it's a nice way to be creative." I peer past her at a framed watercolor of Mount Hood that Lily painted for me. "Hey, you still have it?"

Jenessa follows my gaze. "It's the only real piece of art I own."

The peak of the inactive volcano sits dead center in a cerulean blue sky, with pine trees cascading down its slopes, fresh snow decorating the branches. Our youngest sister is surprisingly talented—surprising when one considers that I can barely color within the lines. While I acted out in my own private ways and Jenessa engaged in more public forms of self-harm, Lily exercised her angst in earth-friendly, artistic behaviors: painting, sculpting, writing poetry, and protesting industrial practices with hunger strikes. Moving around the last few years, I didn't feel like I could care for Lily's artwork the way I should, and Jenessa agreed to hold on to it. Irony of ironies: the addict sister is the most stable of us all.

My lips purse. "Well, thanks for allowing me to drop in on you like this. Can I help in the garden? It's probably the least I can do, after you trucked around the painting all this time."

"I could use some slave labor," she quips. "Thanks."

In a modest backyard overflowing with plants, Jenessa proudly presents the tomato vines she's grown along the perimeter and the flowers sprouting beside them. Nora's green thumb, all the way. From beside the porch, she produces a tray of iris bulbs and shows me where they should be planted.

"How's Nora doing?" I ask.

Jenessa pauses beside a bird-of-paradise flower. "Good. She's taken a back seat at the floral shop and is traveling more. Seeing more of the state lately."

"Do you spend a lot of time together?"

Jenessa hands me a trowel, and I use it to form a shallow pit in the moist earth. The first bulb I grab feels damp in my palm.

"Enough."

I nod, needing no further explanation. After years of alcoholism and prescription-drug abuse, it sounds like Nora's finally found balance—at least outwardly.

We finish depositing the last bulb. Jenessa walks me back through the house to the front door.

"You want to grab a late lunch at Patriot Brewery?" I ask. "Their sandwiches are supposed to be stacked. Extra fries."

She brushes hair from her forehead—"Sure"—and says she'll meet me there. Although she advised against pursuing the note any further, I can't see the harm in checking out another brewery while I'm in the area. I lean into her shoulder and get a lungful of her fruity shampoo scent. She pulls away, holding me at arm's length. Her grip on my shoulders is firm.

"Don't want to get lipstick on you," she says.

"No." The tension between us has always been there. But she's family. I recognize myself in the quick way she strikes out, then recoils—burrows—back inside herself to safety. Seeing her now, I have to wonder what drove me to remain so aloof for so long from the only people who could possibly love and understand me.

As I turn to leave, I pass a bowl of bananas, apples, and nectarines within reach on an end table, but I tuck my elbows in and refrain from pocketing any.

Six

THEN

Mama Rosemary pats Sweet Lily's head again. Stroking her hair like she would a little doll in her lap. Just like always. Never mind that I've been practicing my alphabet all morning while Mama Rosemary said she needed time to think. I taught a new song to Sweet Lily, too, but all Mama Rosemary cared about was whether Twin had memorized the speech she gave her for articulation practice. I huff in my corner, now that it's finally free of Twin and I'm able to sit. She left a Mars Bar wrapper on the ground, saved from her birthday back in April. Caramel sticks to the baseboards like yucky snot.

Sweet Lily starts to hum the theme song from *SpongeBob*. She twists her little neck side to side on each word. *Sponge-Bob-Square-Pants!*

"Sweet Lil, do you want to come sit with me? We can play patty-cake." I move over to make room, but not much is needed for the littlest of us. "Lil?" I pat the ground.

She raises blue eyes as big as marbles to me. I think she's going to say yes when her favorite toy—a fire truck— erupts in a long siren.

"Wanna play with me, Sweet Lily?" Twin stands up and makes the truck *vroom vroom* around the room all giggly. Sweet Lily's face breaks into a smile and she slides off Mama Rosemary's lap.

"Girls, will you please? Your sister is not a plaything. You can share her attention. Lily, you don't have to play with either of them if you don't want." Mama Rosemary sighs.

Sweet Lily hesitates between me and Twin, then points to the fire truck in Twin's hand. "Truck." She joins Twin in the bed room that someone dug out way way back and the mattress creaks as they jump on the bed.

Mama Rosemary places her hand on my shoulder. Her hair almost touches the ceiling and the paper we looped together to form a chain dangles from the pipes and hits her head. "Sweetheart, why don't you help me choose what we should bring with us?"

A tear falls from my eye and piddles on the frayed rug. Like Courage the Cowardly Dog piddles on the rug in his house. Sadness pokes up beneath my T-shirt and I start to hiccup a cry. Mama Rosemary rubs my back until I get it all out. I sniffle then rub my nose with my sleeve.

"All better?" she asks.

"Mm-hmm."

She takes me over behind the cupboard where she pulls out a plastic bag. She dumps it on the rug. I recognize one shirt for each of us, one pants for each of us, our toothbrushes and the last box of crackers that Mama Rosemary made us stop eating.

"Can we have more now?" I point to the crackers. Round buttery and crispy circles. I suck on them until they dissolve in my mouth. Yum.

Mama Rosemary shakes her head. "Not yet, honey. We're going to need these, depending on how this evening goes. Come help me make more rug." She points to the small table that fits only three of us at a time and rips off a strip from an old sheet. Stains cover one side left over from when Sweet Lily was born and which Mama Rosemary always hated. Said it reminded her of bad times, and Mama Bethel leaving for heaven. I never understood that because Sweet Lily being born was a good time but I wasn't allowed nearby. I was only four.

She wraps a knot around the middle of a strip then sets it aside. "What do you think? Can you help your mama that way?"

I try one out myself and beam at her when I line ours up side by side. Mine is almost the same as hers but the knot is more lumpy.

"That's okay," she says, putting her hand over mine. "They don't have to be perfect." She pauses and leans over the wrinkly sheet on the table. "You don't have to be perfect, either. You're pretty great as is."

Sisters squeal and laugh about something from the other room. "But they won't play with me."

Mama Rosemary smiles. "They will, honey. One day, all they'll want to do is spend time with you. Trust me."

I slip my hand into hers and her skin is warm. "Can I get in your lap?"

"Oh, baby, you're a big girl. I'm not sure—"

But I already climb onto her knees and curl up under her chin. She wraps her arms around me and starts humming a song about rowing boats down streams.

"Why are you humming that song, Mama?"

She kisses my head and I feel all safe and squishy. "To remind us to keep going, baby. Even when it's upstream."

Seven

Jenessa waits out front of the brewery, her face twisted up in exaspera-tion. "How did I beat you when you left before me?"

Opaque walls beside her reveal nothing of the interior. The reviews online suggest it's a great place to grab a pint and brush up on American history. Maybe American leaders? I withdraw my camera from its case and frame a shot of the door to include **Patriot Brewery** in Gothic cursive above.

"I'm still not great at navigating these one-way streets," I reply, lowering the lens. "Sorry."

She huffs, then pulls the brass door handle open for me. I slide inside first, wondering whether I should have invited her. Jenessa under normal circumstances can be terse, while Jenessa *hangry*—hungry and angry—is something to be avoided.

Most summers growing up, we spent two weeks together when she came down to Arch, to—as Nora put it—*give her mom a G-D break*. One visit, Jenessa went four hours without eating when we went to a movie marathon at the local theater, then threw a fit in the parking lot as we were leaving. I was shocked, but Rosemary later told me I was guilty of the exact same moodiness; she often kept a bag of almonds with her in case hunger struck.

Jenessa and I settle into a high-top at the bar with a view of the advertised thirty-plus beers on tap—not the twenty that the note suggested would be at the next location. Maybe only twenty beers relate to leaders.

"Have you been here before?" I ask, still waiting for my sister's icy layer to crack.

"First time."

The bartender comes by and takes our order. He returns with a Diet Coke for Jenessa and an Aaron's O'Duel for me, the only nonalcoholic beer available; I have another stop after this and want to be alert.

He drops off a basket of unshelled peanuts. Jenessa grabs a handful and tears into them. She chews and swallows the first two, then breaks into a smile. (H)anger abated.

I scan the names on the tap handles behind the bar: Jefferson Ale. Adams Apple Cider. Hamilton Hops Summer Wheat. "So how is working at the doughnut shop? You've been there—what—six months?"

Jenessa pauses between bites. "A year."

"That's right." I shake my head. "I remember."

None of the beers on tap stands out to me. None of them seems related to either Four Alarm Brewery or the murder—or myself, for that matter. Without knowing anything else about the note's author, I can't guess what their favorite might be or where another dead body may be, waiting to be discovered.

A barback arrives and sets our plates on the table. The scent of french fry grease instantly makes my mouth water.

"Are you okay?" Jenessa pauses in wolfing down her toasted tuna sandwich. "You look flushed, and I know your beer isn't to blame."

"Yeah, I'm fine." I lean back in my seat. She resumes telling me about a guy she's seeing, whom she met on a dating app. Apparently, he starts singing immediately after sex, and she's not into it. I take a bite of my BLT, but I'm too distracted to enjoy it.

A giant American flag covers the wall behind Jenessa. The bartenders hit an imitation Liberty Bell each time someone orders a Betsy Ross

Saison—the thirty-fifth beer on the menu. The ambience is festive and seemingly without any connection to the note.

Jenessa advised me to ignore it. But what if I could stop another death by pursuing this message? Aren't I obligated to try?

The thought in and of itself rings hollow, the fresh influx of money in my wallet from Pauline countering my supposed altruism. I do have an ulterior motive in this, if Pauline keeps paying for pictures. What if I arrive at the next crime scene first—before it's an official crime scene—and take photos of the space? Will there be another paycheck in it for me?

Just the idea turns my stomach. I'm not an opportunist. I want to help prevent another murder, someone else losing their life, for God's sake.

Then again, if I really think the note is a threat or a clue, why haven't I told the police yet?

Years ago, I went on a date with a cop. We hit it off and saw each other a few more times. I really liked him. When I hinted at my difficult background and childhood, he looked happy about it—no, elated. He said he was into researching the *gory details* of Oregon crimes that make national news and was aiming to become a detective one day. When I understood he was more excited by my parentage than by me, I cut him off—but that didn't stop him. He abused his connections in the police department to access archived files on me, to get the *real story*, as he later put it when he asked me to confirm some of what I'd said in police interviews when I was seven.

I don't trust the police. I don't trust anyone.

All around us, glasses clink together. People savor their meals, mumbling through conversations. Afternoon patrons, jammed in at each of the available tables, swell the noise level in the room and make the shallow ceiling feel even lower.

Two women at the counter discuss the Four Alarm murder. Seems I'm not the only one ravenously consuming its details.

"You sure you're okay?" Jenessa asks. She eyes me over our split check. "You've taken almost your entire sandwich to go."

"Yeah, I'm fine. I ate a late breakfast. Thanks again for hanging out."

"Sure thing. Next time, I'll bring you a voodoo doll doughnut if you promise to finish your lunch," she says with a motherly finger wag. The shop she works at is famous for its oddball doughnut shapes and designs—a reason I suspect my normally atypical sister enjoys working at a place with health insurance; we've only ever felt comfortable occupying the fringes of society.

"Yeah, I'd love that. Thanks."

"Hey, do you remember when we were kids—before"—and I know Jenessa is referring to when we were belowground—"and you ate my entire birthday cake slice? You had yours and then mine, on *my* birthday. You've always had a sweet tooth."

She laughs, but I return an embarrassed stare. "No way. I don't remember that."

"Seriously? I was so pissed, I cried in the bedroom for an hour. Rosemary made me another 'cake' out of toast and mayonnaise." Another laugh. "You really don't remember?"

"Absolutely not." I smile, shaking my head. "Although I wouldn't be surprised. We were always at each other like that. Didn't you eat an entire container of gummy vitamins once, just to spite me? Rosemary was worried you had overdosed."

She shrugs. "I don't know. Water under the bridge. I was just . . . reminiscing. It's funny in hindsight. I mean, we were all hungry."

We stand awkwardly, remembering.

"I'm sorry about earlier," she says. "I think I snapped at you back at my house."

"No, it's okay. I didn't set us up for success—first, bailing on our coffee date yesterday, then surprising you at home today with the weird note I received. It hasn't always been like that between us." I offer up a smile that Jenessa doesn't return.

"Hasn't it, though?"

I shake my head. "What do you mean?"

"C'mon, Mar—I mean, Claire. Case in point, the birthday cake memory. Even back in Chet's basement, we were at odds."

"We were four people shoved together in two ten-by-ten rooms. Everyone was."

Jenessa stares at me, like she's unsure whether I believe what I'm saying. "Well, there was a lot going on then. If we were at each other, I don't think anyone would judge us for it."

Outside the brewery, we hug each other goodbye. Jenessa gets in her car to return home, while I head down the next boulevard.

Five blocks east toward the river and the site of yesterday's parade, I arrive at the third brewery I found online that bears some connection to beers named after leaders, Bridge City Brewpub. Inside is less packed with people than Patriot Brewery, probably because food isn't served here. Take-out bags like my own cover most tables. At others, plastic baggies of snacks crowd the pints of beer and sampler glasses.

A chalkboard menu above the aluminum tap handles lists the twenty-two beers available—twenty-two for the number of bridges and pedestrian walkways in Portland, according to a plaque on the wall. None of the first few beer names stands out to me—Walsh, Ergo, Smythe, Berren, Nguyen.

"Excuse me." I wave at the bartender as she wipes down a glass with a dish towel. "Who are all these beers named after? Owners of the brewery?"

She laughs and tucks a blonde curl into her loose fishbone braid. "That would be a lot of owners. They'd all kill each other if there were that many. No, beers are named after local people who helped build Portland. You've probably seen them as streets."

Walsh, Ergo, Smythe, Berren, Nguyen. I look through the front window, past the patio table and chairs, and duck down to view this corner's intersecting street signs. Nguyen Street and Ninth Avenue.

My heart beats in my throat, fearing and anticipating being so close to my goal. "Okay. So what did these people do?"

Twenty beers. All named for leaders. Find the name I most admire and you'll find the next one first.

"They were politicians. Tedrick Berren pushed through the first law outlawing prostitution, but I forget what the rest of them did." She taps her finger on the bar. "Can I get you anything?"

"A Walsh Wheat. Thanks." While she pours, I whip out my phone and do an internet search on each of the names on the chalkboard. Every man or woman was involved in local government or grassroots efforts to regulate Portland vice—not the people I assume a killer would admire.

I take a sip of my beer, stumped. The liquid is cool, light but full bodied against my tongue, and slows my pulse. It leaves me with a slight buzz and nothing more substantial that might confirm this location hides a dead body.

After I pay for my beer, I slide into a chair beside the glass wall and take out my camera. Positioning the viewfinder so that the street signs of Ninth Avenue and Nguyen Street are both captured, I wait until a couple vacates the crosswalk, then click.

※

Vanilla air freshener stings my nose upon entering the apartment housing office, and I'm reminded why I never come here and always wait for Derry Landry to track me down. Crisp white napkins are folded into cranes beside a plate of chocolate chip cookies. A tall fake plant in the corner enhances the showroom atmosphere—clean, uncluttered, secure: the exact opposite of how I lived growing up with Rosemary.

"Claire, good to see you." Derry winks at me from behind a white oak table. A stack of lease agreements sits aligned with the table's edge. "What can I do for you?"

"Here's the rest of what I owe." I hand over the remaining hundred dollars, earned from this morning's photo sessions. Air-conditioning chugs through the ventilation duct above and adds to the sick feeling in my stomach.

"Excellent. What are you doing later?" he asks in a low tone as he writes out a receipt.

I face him, annoyed that we can't interact without him flirting. His gaze travels down my tank top; then he looks at me from beneath dark eyelashes. "I get off at five if you feel like a beer. You like beer, right?"

My skin prickles at the question—the subject of my thoughts the last day and a half. "Why do you say that?"

I wonder if the Walsh Wheat is noticeable on my breath from this far away.

Derry shrugs. "You carry out a lot more beer in your recycling than wine bottles."

He points a thumb over his shoulder to the window behind him. With the shades open, his desk has a perfect view of the path from my apartment to the complex's dumpster. He's been watching me.

"Thanks for the receipt." Before he can say anything else unnerving, I leave, pocketing a cookie as I pass the front table.

Safely behind the dead bolt of my apartment door, I sink into the cushions of my love seat.

My phone rings. Pauline's phone number flashes across the screen, and my stomach knots, fearing she's calling to tell me about another murder. "Hello?"

"Claire, hi. I have a proposition for you. How would you feel about becoming our resident photographer?"

I sit up and move to the edge of the couch. "That would be amazing. What for? I mean, what department at the *Post* needs coverage?"

Papers rustle in the background, and a woman shouts something. "I know you've never done this before, but you seem to handle each assignment I give you easily. Tatum is going to be out for another six weeks, because the idiot went for a late snowboarding trip and broke his damn leg, and—"

"You want me to cover live events?"

"Hold on." Pauline muffles the phone and bellows something about a deadline. "Madison, victims never cooperate with us after the fact. They're unpredictable. I need a better variety of sources, got it?" She uncovers the phone, and the sound becomes clear again.

"Sorry about that, Claire. The crime beat. We need someone on call during this business with the brewery murder. The police don't usually allow this much media access to live sites, but they're desperate to find the culprit. This is something that's usually seen in Seattle or San Francisco, and we need to take advantage of that urgency. So what do you think? . . . Hello?"

"Yes, I'm here." Sweat breaks out across my neck as I try to marshal my thoughts. Get a grip. Process what she's suggesting. "What kind of—what would you pay me to be your crime photographer?"

I hate negotiating. I always get nervous and psych myself out, certain that the other party will tell me I'm not worth whatever price I'm asking. But I've had enough experience with law enforcement, violence, and criminals for a lifetime. For me to accept a role in which I must be physically present at these sites, in the thick of the chaos of police personnel and up to my neck in crime details, I'd need to be offered a solid sum.

Although she is offering to pay me for what I'm already doing on my own. And recalling the two dead-end breweries I visited today—someone's life may depend on it.

Pauline clears her throat. "The same rate as before. How does that sound?"

I lean onto my knees, hugging the phone to my ear. "For me to be your sole crime photographer . . . I think . . . it's not great."

She makes a noise, and I can't tell if it's good or bad. I wait for her to hang up, to tell me she's going to call someone from the ad that she placed on the freelancer website.

"Fine. I'll double it," she says with a sigh.

Double? To two dollars per photo? Even the retouched photos cost her five dollars each. I take a deep breath.

"I'll need my normal rate. One hundred dollars per hour of work." My headshot sessions actually amounted to more than that—but this rate will narrow the gap. And allow me to buy more than a sandwich for lunch and Cup Noodles for dinner.

Pauline clicks her tongue. "All right. Come back to the office to sign the paperwork. We're already a day behind, so I need you to go and capture images from the brewery's basement today."

"Like . . . right now?" The panic in my voice makes me wince.

"Is that a problem?"

Flashes of memory snap forward at her words, and I recall climbing Chet's crooked stairs, leaving the darkness beneath. The metal door he kept us behind was painfully cold on one side, subject to the house's air conditioner that was on full blast during the summer heat. Rosemary told me not to look back, but I did; the dim space of our home, where I had spent the first seven years of my life, hungrily returned my gaze. Suddenly it was a monster, nipping at my heels and eager to keep us in its belly.

My insides twist, but I form the words with my tongue anyway. "No. Be there in twenty."

Eight

Lunch comes and goes with Mama Rosemary whipping up pasta with red sauce—my favorite! All our favorite actually. We get to slurp the spaghetti like *Lady and the Tramp* and Mama doesn't yell at us.

After we clean up and me and Twin do the dishes and Sweet Lily lays down for a nap Mama Rosemary breaks out the chalkboard.

"Even today?" Twin whines.

Mama nods wiping off the last of my drawing of a boat. "Especially today."

We review our math first and add up all the macaroni that we have. I count seventy-two pieces of macaroni and Twin gets the same number so we're happy. "Good job, sweetheart," Mama says to me patting my hand.

"What about me?" Twin asks.

"What about you?" I mumble.

"I'm not talking to you!"

"Ow! She bit me!"

"Girls! We need to focus," Mama says. "Bodies to ourselves—you know that."

Mama says something nice to Twin but I know she meant it more to me.

Next we do geography. Mama draws a map of America and we have to point out where Oregon is. I point just below Washington and Twin points at the middle which Mama always says has names but she doesn't remember them. I laugh behind my hand. Next Mama erases her lines and draws the outline of Oregon. Oregon always looks to me like a square waving its arms. *Look at me, America!* People don't like it when others try to take all the attention by waving their arms or jumping up and down. We have to wait our turn to speak.

Mama draws a straight line up and down and a straight line side to side—our road. "What street is this?" she asks.

"Redding Street," we answer. We've been asked this one before.

"And what is the cross street?"

"Cross street? Like a cross?" I make the sign of Jesus's cross.

"No, the intersecting street. The one that meets Fir Street. Anyone?"

Twin and me think for a minute before I remember. "Pouch Street!"

"Yes, but it's pronounced 'pooch.' Not 'powch.'"

Twin sticks her tongue out at me.

Mama wipes down the chalkboard again and takes a seat at our table. One chair is empty—it's really a crate but we call it a chair—because that's Sweet Lily's spot. She's still napping. "Now, once we're out of here, what do you do?"

"Mama?" I ask raising my hand just like she taught us. "You usually write it down on the board when you ask us. So we can look at the answers. And tell you them."

She shakes her head and long hair falls into her face. She pushes it back behind her ears. I push my hair back behind my ears, too. "Not today, honey. Today, I need you both to remember the next steps on your own. Can you do that for me? We've been talking about it for a week."

"But why does it have to be today?" Twin's eyes get all big and she looks like Sweet Lily for a second. "Can't we go tomorrow?"

Mama leans over and says, "Hush now. I know you're scared, but we can't stay here any longer. The man is going to bring someone else here to live with us soon, and we're too big for this place. Look around us. There's no room!" Her voice gets all high like a seagull's. She watches us to make sure we understand.

"But. The outside. You said it was scary and we shouldn't want to go. That bad monsters live outside and we were safe in here." Twin's voice rises to match and I stay quiet. I agree with Twin.

Mama lets her head fall in her hands. "I know. I know, you're right. I'm sorry, okay? I didn't know what to tell you when you started asking . . . I didn't know what to say to make it okay . . . to make this . . . okay. But I'm going to need your help tonight."

Twin stands up and pushes back from the table. "You said what happened to Mama Bethel can happen to you or to us. You said it!"

Mama looks at Twin all sad. She reaches out a hand to touch her but Twin yanks her arm back. "I know I did. And that's true. People do die out there. But we all do. We'll die in here if we stay."

I start to cry. Dying is for old people. We're all young people. Mama Rosemary doesn't have any gray hairs like old people.

She takes my hand and reaches across for Twin's hand and Twin doesn't move away. "We have to leave, girls," she says in a soft voice. "You're getting bigger. He's already starting to notice you."

"Notice how?" I ask.

Mama looks up like she sees something on the wood beams. Twin yanks her hand away and Mama's voice is rocky. "Like the man notices me."

Nine

Outside Four Alarm, navy slickers clump together in the misty rain—
police officers and a forensics team. From what Pauline told me in her
office, day two of the investigation is progressing at the rate of day
one—slowly, and with the police maintaining guarded secrecy against
the public. Those not in uniform who are granted access are watched
like shoplifting teens—which won't bother me any. My sticky fingers
were good at grabbing makeup and accessories, but it was only a phase;
I was glad to turn eighteen and leave a midsize juvenile record behind.
Now I limit my thievery to fruit.

Around me, policemen and a few people in suits speak in quick
sentences. No one appears as lost as I do.

"You think this started on the dark web? Another murder-for-hire
plot?"

"Oh, come on, Reynolds. Don't start that crap again. You think
everything's the dark web. Besides, we don't know enough about—"

"Dude, I just had a life-changing doughnut this morning. You got
to try the . . ."

The conversations run together. I finger the thick camera strap
around my neck. The yellow press pass lanyard lies flat against the cotton of my long-sleeve shirt.

"Claire Lou?" a man grunts as he approaches me. His pale skin is flushed pink. "Sergeant Yann Peugeot. I'll show you to the area we're allowing the media. Follow me."

We enter the narrow vestibule I stood in two days ago. Exposed pipes I didn't notice before are suspended from the vaulted ceiling above the winding iron staircase. Peugeot's auburn crew cut bobs a few feet ahead. Past the restrooms and through a black-painted door, we descend stairs to the level below. The steady bass of a man's voice carries from somewhere nearby. "Haven't heard of anything like this for twenty years."

I suppress the urge to look over my shoulder, to confirm no one is looking directly at my ponytail. "Sergeant Peugeot?"

"Yes?" He sidesteps a man carrying a bulky trash bag. Dark eyebrows tent on his wide forehead—*five-head*, my middle school classmates would have snickered—as he holds open the door at the end of the hallway. A faint orb of light shines from the cellar, and a response chokes in my throat.

We've already traveled underground. One more level deep shouldn't scare me; I've been in storage units, walk-in closets, and other confined places that should remind me of my time as a child, locked in the interior compound Chet built to contain his secrets, but they don't; I always deemed myself lucky to not have that part of my life incapacitate the rest. Even as I learned from my classmates that I was the zoo animal no one would ever stop pointing at. *Missy Mo, bred in captivity.*

But here. In the darkness below, where anyone could whirl on me and recognize the fear of being discovered and the self-loathing stark across my face, it's different. The fear is visceral. Alive. Like a towering creature with stank whiskey breath that might jump into my skin and commandeer my body—blurt out the truth, unleash the ugliness I know resides within me. I haven't been inside a cellar since we escaped. The smells of burned toast and fresh urine rise from my memory, along with the nagging feeling of shame.

"Ms. Lou?" Peugeot's gruff expression drops. "Hey, Claire. You okay?"

Chin up. Shoulders back. *Don't let anyone know your past,* my mother's voice warns in my head. *They'll reject you for it. Be scared of you.* "Fine. Thanks."

He hesitates, then steps down and out of sight. I follow him. Aluminum racks stand against the concrete squares of the walls. Sacks of flour and grain and plastic containers of spices and sugar line the shelves. The cellar extends longer than it should, past the building's foundation, making the air cold—damp—the farther in we go. Construction lamps placed along the walls offer better light than the weak bulb hanging from the wooden rafters. I avoid a stack of plastic patio chairs covered in cobwebs and identify a hole in the back along the wall. Broken wooden boards lay piled on the cellar floor.

Rosemary's voice again: *Chet is a light sleeper, baby.*

"Hey! Hey, don't touch that!" Peugeot yells to someone. At the end of the cellar, he turns left into the hole, stepping clear of the steel organizer shelf pushed to the side. Quickly, he pivots back into the storage space and levels a finger at my chest. "Stay here." He disappears.

A woman in a black dress shirt punctuates something on a clipboard with a stab of her pen, then ascends the steps into the restaurant. I'm alone.

My pulse throbs in my fingertips where they clutch my camera. I lift the lens and snap a few images of the shelves, the containers of rye, the weak light above, and the gaping cleft in the wall.

Pauline said they were desperate for new photos of the brewery that no one else has. It's after four o'clock on the second day of this investigation. What photo could I possibly get that hasn't already been taken?

Voices come from the hallway above, and before I think better of it, I tiptoe to the opening and slip inside. More construction lamps illuminate the space. An alcove precedes a tunnel that continues straight, before another tunnel veers diagonally to the right. A group of uniformed officers stands around three small orange cones that form a triangular outline.

A dank smell sinks into my lungs. I've seen a dead body before. Once, as a child. But this is my first time being so close to the site of a murder. Metal hooks protrude from the wall at hip level along three-foot intervals.

"Anything else?" Peugeot speaks to a woman wearing a slicker.

She folds her arms. "The bartender who found her was the only person to go into the cellar on Saturday after two p.m., and we're still trying to track down where the restraint materials came from." She waves a manicured hand at the extending paths. "Chains along the walls and some blood splatter across the dirt there."

"How'd the bartender find this place?"

"Says he came down per usual to check on the garnish he was pickling and saw the hole where it was boarded up previously. When he waved his phone's flashlight into the space, the body was visible."

"Right. So gunshot to the head. But Lew said possible fatal force. Was there bludgeoning before the gunshot?"

"Looks like it. Pretty sloppy. I'll keep your guys posted on any new conclusions we come to."

While Peugeot gives her his full attention, I snap one, two, three photos of the cones, the metal hooks, before I turn and slide back through the wall. The dry goods appear as I left them. The door to the restaurant opens with a flush of warm air, and I casually lean against a sack of flour. A man descends the stairs.

Peugeot reenters the cellar through the hole in the wall. "Get what you needed?"

I lift my camera in response. "Yup."

"Good. Pauline Adebayo better stop bothering me now."

"Hey, Sergeant." The man who just arrived jerks his thumb toward the restaurant hallway. "Chief is looking for you."

My guide rubs his chin. "Looks like we're going to cut your visit short, *Portland Post*."

We head back upstairs. A serving tray of cups filled with steaming coffee is out on the bar counter beside a plate of pretzels. I wrap three of them, freshly baked and still warm, in a dinner napkin and stuff it in my coat pocket. I'm a nervous eater; I can never help the urge to squirrel away food in case bad times hit.

Outside the brewery, back in the afternoon rain, Peugeot turns to me. "Good to meet you, Lou. I guess we'll be seeing more of you around here."

My stomach clenches. "Why would that be?"

Peugeot narrows blue-green irises. "Because you're the new crime photographer for the *Post*. Right?"

"Oh. Yeah, I'll be seeing you."

He glances at me from the side of his eye, then approaches a woman in an orange poncho.

I walk down the street to where I parked, goose bumps percolating along my skin. As if someone's gaze traces my form, settling on the shoulders I always thought were too narrow, inherited from Chet.

"Excuse me," a male voice calls out.

I turn. Behind me, a man in a leather jacket and glasses smiles. My muscles instantly tense. We're the only ones on this side road, and some instinct tells me to keep walking.

"Hey, excuse me," the man says as I resume a quick pace. "Missy, I just want to talk."

I stop dead. A knot of anger forms in my belly. Climbs my chest and swells into rage.

It's the person who left me the note. Hearing that nickname for the first time in Portland reinforces my desire to run, but not before I kick this man in the groin and make him sorry he stopped and spoke my secret aloud. Even as my self-preservation instincts wonder whether he could be the killer.

"What do you want?" I ask.

He steps backward, taking in my expression. Slowly, he retrieves a business card from his jacket pocket and offers it to me. "Ms. Mo. Or do you prefer Ms. Lou? I'm sorry to sneak up on you like this, but I didn't think you'd appreciate me approaching you at the brewery. I'm a journalist."

Shit. "You say that like you're proud."

Brown eyes so dark they could be black widen behind thin frames. "Ah, more importantly, I thought you might need someone to talk to."

I scan his tentative mien, the square temples that loosely resemble a LEGO, and can't help thinking it's not fair. I've worked hard to establish a normal life. I just moved to start fresh again. Who is this guy that he's found me so quickly? My fingernails curl into my palms, piercing the thick pads of my skin, and I focus on the sweet bite of pain.

"Not interested." I turn on my heel. I'd love it if he followed me just past the stop sign and down the hill to the secluded copse of trees I parked beside, where I can test my bottle of pepper spray.

"Missy, you've got a lot to consider with this year being the twentieth anniversary of your escape, and—"

His footsteps nip at my heels, and I reach into my shoulder bag, my fingers fumbling for the aluminum tube. "Leave me alone!"

"I just thought, with Chet's release next week, you might be interested in sharing your feelings."

I freeze. Shift my feet in a circle until I face the man again. "What?"

"You didn't know? This year was also the first time Chet was eligible for parole. The parole board granted it."

I stare at him. His off-center nose, the thick eyebrows, and the mouth that keeps moving, making words I don't quite grasp. The traffic on the main thoroughfare a block away dulls to a murmur.

"If you change your mind, here's my card." Handwritten on the back is an address and a time. "I wasn't sure whether to leave this on your car, so I wrote down a meetup location for tomorrow. If there's another one that suits you better, I'm flexible."

I gape at him, not knowing what words to speak, what phrase would be appropriate upon learning my captor-father will be released in mere days. Terror slides across my mouth in a metallic film. Chet was sentenced to life in prison with the possibility of parole after twenty years; I didn't connect that the twentieth anniversary also meant his potential release.

When we turned eighteen, Jenessa and I signed up for the victim notifications from the court system. Did Lily? I haven't received anything, but I also just moved here, and mail is still being forwarded from my last city.

Does Rosemary know?

"Well, I can see I may have delivered some surprising news. I'm Shia, by the way. Shia Tua." He extends a hand, but I don't take it. "So if you're free tomorrow, I'll be waiting at that address."

I watch the gray backpack he wears bounce up the road, then over the hill toward the brewery. Shadows from the building across the street reach my chest as the wind picks up.

While I don't know what Chet hopes to do on parole, I know he wants to see me. He said so in the few letters he wrote over the years and that my lawyer forwarded. He's also been hell-bent on rehabbing his image, granting interviews and recording his "side of the story" during the first several years of his incarceration. If he succeeds in locating me, he'll bring the cameras, and everything I tried to leave behind—Chet's basement, the pain of adolescence, persistent strangers and the danger they pose—will catch up to me in an instant. No one will let me near their high school senior for a photo shoot during grad season. Chet will have taken everything from me all over again.

A drop of rain slides down my ear, and I jolt from my trance, breaking into a sprint toward my car. The wind whips against my face as I jam my key into the driver's door, flinging it open. I slide inside, breathless, then hit the "Lock" button with a shaking hand.

When I uncurl my fist, the ink from Shia's card marks my palm. His handwriting—messy, pointed—is smudged but legible, and I'm able to read the address of tomorrow's meeting.

Ten

The last time I saw Chet was when we escaped. Rosemary was asked to testify against him in court, and she did, but all the adults involved, to their credit, agreed to spare us children further trauma. The prospect of seeing Chet out in the open for the first time left me wide-awake until around three in the morning. My need for coffee is real.

Of the café's patio tables, only one seat remains vacant during this Tuesday midmorning, opposite a lone man. Shia Tua peers at me, and he hasn't stopped staring since I turned the corner from where I parked. The last time someone approached me out of the blue, I had just turned eighteen. A tabloid magazine suggested I pose topless, and despite the pitiful sum, I considered it.

"Ms. Lou," he says, standing and extending a hand. I take it, and his skin is warm, moist in the cool temperature. "Or should I say, *Missy Mo*?"

He offers a flirtatious smile, speaking the alliterative name the press loved to use as I ventured past puberty, then into adulthood. Missy Mo Learning to Drive! Missy Mo All Grown Up! Missy Mo Models New Swimwear! The final headline was a complete lie. Some idiot blogger took a photo of me on their phone while I was floating downriver in my hometown.

"Claire." I take a seat and clutch my cross-body bag in my lap. The man doesn't appear to have any weapons handy. Nothing to knock me out with, although how he'd do it in plain sight with ten witnesses beside us, I don't know.

"Of course. Thank you for meeting me. Coffee? This place is kind of Portland's answer to Starbucks." He leans forward, fidgeting with the sleeve of a too-small jean jacket and placing a cup with a lid in front of me. "The brew here is amazing."

"Thanks." I wrap my hands around it but don't drink.

Shia's probably in his early thirties, was around twelve or thirteen when our story broke. The local papers were horrified that something like our captivity could have occurred within their polite, sleepy city. A place where the running joke is that if four Portland drivers arrive at a four-way stop at the same time, they're still there, insisting the person to their left goes first.

Shia tucks thick black curls behind an ear. Olive skin glows beneath the overcast sky.

"You left me a note," I say. "A threat."

The pair of women beside us pauses their conversation to eavesdrop. Shia shifts forward and angles his body away from our neighbors—not the kind of self-assured comportment I would expect from a stalker or killer after brazenly suggesting we meet in public. He grips his paper coffee cup.

"I'm confused. I only wrote you one note, on the business card I handed you. Did someone threaten you?"

When I don't reply, he inhales through his nose.

"Actually, I've been following your story since I was in high school. Along with the rest of the country. Since college, I've focused on writing nonfiction, some editorial, but mostly true events that I believe were pivotal to the American consciousness."

He pauses as if waiting for me to challenge him. The women beside us resume discussing the latest tsunami, which struck Indonesia last week. "What does that have to do with me?"

He leans forward onto the wooden slats of the table. "The thing is, I've been offered a major advance to write a book. On your family. Your . . . whole family."

A chill sweeps down my chest. Of course he has. This is the writer who spoke to Jenessa. Maybe he is the author of my note, the way she suspected, or maybe he's not. Either way, he's still trying to manipulate me for his own gain. Vultures. All of them.

"You don't know us," I say. "How can you write a book on us?"

"That's exactly the point. We know very little. Just the facts. Yet your experience stuck with everyone for years. People want to know what happened from a firsthand perspective."

The fine lines on Shia's forehead, around his mouth, and the scruff that caps his square jaw—even the long, unruly hair—seem familiar. Like the type of predatory men I've tried to avoid my whole life.

"How did you find me?"

Pink colors his cheeks, and he takes a moment to chew his lower lip. "I found your sister first. Jenessa. She refused my offer over the phone, so I was . . ." He takes another sip of coffee, as if gathering his will to confess.

Understanding dawns on me. "You were out front. Of her house. You followed me." It's not hard to find a person online using basic information. Jenessa has lived in that house for the last three years; she's had the same cell phone number since she was seventeen.

Shia sucks his teeth as though caught in a lie. "I followed Jenessa to the brewery where she met you; then I followed you home. I was getting ready to knock on your door when you left again and went downtown. I followed you, then approached you outside Four Alarm. Now I'm just pleased you decided to join me today." He spreads his hands in a deflated *ta-da* gesture.

"I don't understand. How did you know it was me?"

"Ah. I hate to break it to you, but there are whole websites devoted to speculating on what you look like as an adult. Here." Shia types something in his phone's browser, then slides the screen around so I can read. A dozen different sites claim to offer images of me—What Missy Looks Like Now.

Childhood photos of me have been manipulated to age the little girl in the pictures into a woman who isn't far off from my actual appearance: medium-length black hair, light-brown eyes that tip upward at the outer crease, and a round nose that—shudder—I think Chet and I have in common. The main differences seem to be that my eyebrows are actually thicker than the theorized version, my face is thinner overall, and I have a dimple in my chin. A few other pictures show up toward the bottom of the results page, which I remember were snapped outside a grocery store when I was twenty-two, five years ago, and wearing sunglasses. These websites seem to use the same technology that the adoption angel described when he tracked me down at the diner.

"So you see, Claire. I got very lucky in finding you, but the internet has been tracking you for some time."

His words fly like casual bullets, puncturing the anonymity I had aspired to. *My name is Claire*—a trite story line.

I was naive. So dumb to think I was being covert. That I would ever be able to fully leave behind what I never chose to begin with. It's only a matter of time before the rest of this city finds out, and they'll look at me as strangely as my grade school classmates. Pauline will write stories on me, featuring updates on what sandwich shop I frequented this week. Refuse to pay me, because as she said, victims are unpredictable. Fear and ogle me, knowing what darkness my genes contain. Jenessa's story about my guinea pig will be only the beginning of what surfaces.

This Shia person clutches his coffee, awaiting my reply. Full eyebrows form a steeple between strained brown irises. A writer who enjoys research. No doubt, meticulous. Ambitious.

I tap the side of my cup, then take a deep gulp. Too much sugar. "So what is your goal here? Are you saying you'll expose me if I don't help with your book?"

"Not at all." He leans forward. "I only want to make sure the truest story is recorded. If you agree to a few interviews, I'll share the advance with you."

"Define 'share.'"

"A hundred thousand would be yours. I'd get it as soon as the manuscript is accepted." Shia sucks in a breath. "And I'll wire you a thousand of my own money now if you agree, as a show of good faith."

One hundred thousand dollars. That's way more money than my settlement portion. I could live on that for years.

I could put a down payment on a house with that.

I could buy a whole new identity with that.

The last thing I want is to expose myself to further poking and speculation, but a sum of that size would buy me stability. Allow me to navigate building a solid photography portfolio. Give me my first bridge to ordinary in ages. Hell, even $1,000 up front is a dream come true.

After Chet was sentenced to life in prison, an attorney approached Rosemary and offered to file a separate lawsuit, pro bono. Said he'd work to ensure we received adequate recompense for our pain and suffering. Since Chet abused company funds to build out his compound—our living quarters—in the basement, the civil suit would name both Chet and his employer as codefendants. Six months later, we received a settlement—money to cover our initial medical bills, relocation costs, whatever we needed to move on.

Rosemary's settlement money went mainly to housing, as she held only sporadic jobs afterward and permitted a few paid interviews. My share was depleted five years ago—the price of pursuing normalcy without a steady income proving higher than I planned. I did my best to replace it with wages from restaurant jobs, online proofreading gigs, and easy nannying that didn't require more than a driver's license. Before I turned to photography, the topless tabloid offer from when I was eighteen crossed my mind more times than I'm proud of.

Jenessa's disapproving scowl flickers to mind, reminding me that she didn't even return Shia's call when he reached out to her. She wouldn't like me accepting now.

"The publisher is keen for a draft as soon as possible, given that this year is the twentieth anniversary of your escape, and Chet's parole is next week. The market is dying for details."

I only nod. Sweat breaks across my chest at the thought of that monster being out in the world, trying to contact me.

Lily and Jenessa will be distraught. What about my mother? How will Rosemary react to seeing her captor grabbing groceries in the same city as me?

"Claire?" Shia says in a low voice.

A thousand dollars right now. I could use the money. And it seems I still have some issues to work through, if the bitter taste of anxiety I felt in the brewery cellar is any indication. More importantly, if the note I found on my windshield is linked to the twentieth anniversary, answering Shia's questions may offer information—some details of my childhood that I've admittedly never explored as an adult. Working through those issues could lead me to the next body indicated in the anonymous note, and maybe someone else won't have to die.

If I learn the killer's identity before anyone else and before Chet exposes who I am, Pauline will have to keep me. My past will be an advantage.

"So I could be a 'source'? I wouldn't go on record. And you wouldn't reveal anything about my location or jeopardize my privacy in any way."

Shia regards me with hopeful, droopy eyes and something else. A spark. A flicker of excitement before it dies like an ember I'm not sure I saw. "Sure. What do you say, Claire?"

We agree to meet tomorrow at the city library for our first session. I leave the coffee shop feeling hopeful for the first time in days—resolute that this is a way forward, even as my stomach clenches, ties itself into a series of loops.

Leaving downtown, I brake my car to a hard stop as a man jaywalks across the street. A blanket covers the shopping cart he pushes, so I can't tell what it carries, but he sees me looking. He lifts a hand wrapped in a scarf and points to me over one—two—three seconds, proud aggression tightening his features. Curiosity makes me lean over the steering wheel and watch him complete the path to the sidewalk.

Four alarms have been shot. Twenty years. Twenty beers. All named for leaders. Find the name I most admire and you'll find the next one first.

Leaders. Who would the note's author most admire? What would he protect? The first victim was a woman, a stripper, restrained and held underground for several days from what the news reports. She likely died from bludgeoning, according to the medical examiner I overheard with Peugeot.

I tried to look up local Portland leaders related to breweries and didn't get anywhere. The killer wouldn't admire law enforcement or politicians.

Pulling over at the next stop sign, I park at the curb. A quick search on my phone of *killers + beer* sends me to a concert listing.

Twenty beers. All named for leaders. I search the phrase *leader brewery*, but the results return another series of top-ten lists. Four Alarm turns up, along with an announcement that the victim is named Eloise Harris.

I try again. *Serial killer + twenty beers* provides a dozen links to irrelevant websites, but the third page down, I find one that fits: The Stakehouse Brewery and Gentlemen's Club. A strip club serving beers named after homicidal men.

Tapping on my passenger window tears my attention from my phone. The homeless man has pushed his cart up the street to where I parked. He points to the steel signpost beside me and says, "No parking," the admonishment audible through the window.

I nod and shift my car into drive. It's past time I got moving.

Eleven

Ranger Mo scans the horizon searching for children and injured animals who need her help. She raises a hand to her eyes to protect from the high-noon sun.

A little animal—a Lily frog—ribbits across the desert town with a limp! Poor little Lily frog, with no crackers to eat or spaghetti to slurp—

"Wait a minute. Frogs don't live in the desert." Twin stands pouting against the far wall of the bed room. She didn't want to play a few minutes ago when Sweet Lily and I started.

"Why not?" I ask. Frogs live in a lot of places on television. Land *and* water. "Horses live in the desert . . . and . . . and snakes?"

Sweet Lily gives a fast nod. "Turtles."

"And turtles! They live on land and water, right?" I look from Twin to Sweet Lily but only Sweet Lily smiles. Red sauce from our pasta lunch still covers her chin.

Twin scoffs and throws her hands up as if I've just said the dumbest thing. "Yes, *they* all live in the desert, but not frogs. *Frogs* need water. What you're playing doesn't make sense. Sweet Lily can't be a Lily frog in the desert." She rolls brown eyes like two poops up toward the ceiling.

Sweet Lily looks like she might cry, lower lip shaking and blues getting all shiny. A fat tear rolls down her cheek.

"Hey that's okay. Why don't we play Lily turtle in the desert? I'll be Ranger Mo still, and I'll find you all tired from your long journey from a mountain—"

"Turtles don't live in the mountains!"

"How do *you* know?"

Mama Rosemary pops into the doorway. "Girls, what is going on here?" Her hair sits on her head. Like a black hat. A turban. "You're supposed to be doing arts-and-crafts hour. Where are your bracelets?"

We hold up the one we did together.

"You've been in here for forty-five minutes and that's all you've made?"

We nod.

Mama Rosemary makes a face. "All right, well, let me see you make two more. You each need one. One for each sister."

"I forget the song though," Twin says all whiny. "Why are we doing this? How much longer do we have to?"

"Less questions, more bracelet braiding. I'm sure your sisters can help you. Right, girls?" Mama Rosemary looks at Sweet Lily and me. So I know she really means me.

"Right," I say. I scooch over to Twin and hold the three threads in my hand. Twin takes them and spreads them out then she looks at me not sure what comes next.

"The baker goes for flour." Twin moves the left one over the middle one.

"He's gone for an hour." She moves the right one back over the first two.

"He bakes what he wants." Twin takes the new right one and puts it in the middle again.

"A big fat croissant." Then she takes the left one and puts it back in the middle.

She holds up her end of the bracelet and it's exactly like Mama Rosemary taught us from her Girl Pouch days.

"We made a croissant!" I laugh then stop laughing. "Mama Rosemary, what's a croissant?"

Her mouth moves up and she looks happy. "It's kind of like a buttery bread . . . treat. When we get out of here, you'll all have one."

"Three croissants?" Twin asks.

She nods and looks sad again. "One for each of you to match your bracelets. Now, hurry up with the last one so you can nap. You need rest for tonight."

We finish number three and singing the song. Then Twin and Sweet Lily get into the bed and I get in beside them. Sweet Lily is in the middle. I always like to sleep on the left side not touching the middle where the big brown stain is. Mama Rosemary tried to scrub it off years ago but it's still there. After a minute both sisters' breathing turns to easy and deep. I slip out of bed. I walk into the main room where Mama Rosemary is sewing a hole in my pants.

Each of us has two pants that we wear three days a week then we switch to the other pants for four days. Our shirts are more between us because we all share T-shirts. I like Mama Rosemary's old shirt to sleep in that's a pattern she calls *plaid*. I have five underpants to wear. But pretty soon I'm gonna have to give them to Sweet Lily because they're getting so small and hurting my thighs. Mama Rosemary has a lot of laundry to do but now I help because I'm big enough. Twin has been helping for a while longer because she grew faster than me and could lean over the bathtub without falling in.

"What is my sweet girl doing out of bed?" Mama Rosemary whispers. She lifts her eyes to mine and smiles but raises a finger to her mouth. So I know to keep quiet.

"I want to help you," I whisper back. We both stop and listen if the other girls woke up any. Twin is snoring.

"You should be sleeping," she says and lifts me onto her lap. "Oof. You're getting too big for this, you know." But she doesn't make me get down. Instead she tucks a finger around my hair and kisses my head.

"We've got to make the most of our time left to us. Who knows what the world will be like once we get out there?"

I shiver and huddle into Mama Rosemary's neck. "Do you think someone . . . a man . . . will take me away from you?"

She pulls back to look at me. She lifts my chin with her pointer until I have to look up, too. "That's not going to happen. I won't let it." Her voice is almost like she's angry but her eyes get wet and shiny. "I won't let it. You believe me?"

I believe her.

"Good. Now, how do you think your sister managed to tear a hole in the front *and* the back of the knee of her pants?" Mama Rosemary wipes her eyes then picks up the jeans she's sewing.

I shrug. Leaning into her neck again I feel safe. Like nothing could tear me from this spot. "I don't know. Twin is always making trouble."

Mama Rosemary makes a soft sound and I don't recognize her usual laugh. *Heh-heh.* "Your twin is a rambunctious one—full of energy, I mean," she adds when I lift my head again.

Last week Twin kicked and kicked and kicked the dirt wall screaming and crying because she wanted to go upstairs to the outside and away from the man. He only visits three times a week at night on Monday, Wednesday, and Friday, and always to see Mama Rosemary and the Murphy. Sweet Lily and I just covered our ears and looked at each other while Mama Rosemary had to rock Twin in her arms like Twin was a baby for an hour afterward.

"That's for sure," I whisper in a grumble. "And she's always asking too many questions."

Heh-heh. That same laugh again. She touches my nose. *Boop.* "All right, let's get down to work, shall we? If you're awake, you can help me finish the rope. You're almost as good as I am at it."

I smile so big my ears jump. "Yes, Mama."

She pulls out the ball from behind the sink, all squished against the wall. "All right. Show me how you add on to it."

I let it roll on the ground until I find the end. "Sheet?"

"Oh yes." Mama pulls out the Mama Bethel sheet from where it's flat under the storage bin. Mama Rosemary says it's cut to ribbons and bits. What's left of it looks like long hair or fingers waving hello.

I rip off three long bits then tie them to the rope ends. I do the over-under, over-under that Mama Rosemary taught us for making bracelets. Only, the rope has to be tight tight. I'm the best at making bracelets.

"Mama, I'm gonna make jewelry when I grow up. And different kinds of bracelets for you and Sweet Lily and Twin. Necklaces, too, like your Before necklace."

"I'd like that very much, baby."

"When I grow up, can we have another bed? Maybe a Murphy? I don't think we can all fit together when I'm fully growed." I stop and think. "When we're all fully growed."

Mama only breathes heavy. In and out. In and out. In out.

"Mama Rosemary?"

She makes a throat noise. "Yes, baby. Very soon, we'll each have a Murphy bed of our own."

Twelve

Trash litters the quiet street. Industrial big rigs are parked next to sedans with tinted windows. The neon silhouette of a woman's writhing body sways side to side as the image shifts along two tracks of light bulbs, enticing customers at noon on a Tuesday.

The vertical bar of the front door is sticky when I grasp it and pull. My shadow stretches across the dim interior of the strip club, and a mirror behind a bar reflects bottles of cheap liquor lining a shelf, a string of vanity lights enhancing the visual. No one occupies the barstools, but two dancers in sequined costumes lean against the far end near a small, round stage. Must be break time. A wiry-looking man in a T-shirt and jeans is talking to them about "new marketing strategies." The trio lifts their heads toward me, toward the daylight infiltrating the space, and I step inside, letting the entry fall again to blackness.

A stout bartender squints as I approach. "What can I get you?"

"Coffee. With Baileys," I add when he raises a pierced, bushy eyebrow. Behind him, beer taps line up in a row. The handle closest to me is labeled *Charles Manson*. Another: *John Wayne Gacy*. There are a few I don't recognize, like Dayton Leroy Rogers, but I'll bet he didn't save kittens from tall trees.

The bartender snorts. Light reflects off his bald head. He turns toward the mirror and fills a mug with thick, dark liquid from a sputtering machine. He slides the full mug over to me with a grimace. Despite the Baileys, I empty four containers of half-and-half into my cup and succeed in lightening the color to a dull mud shade. Yum.

The dancers in the corner laugh, pounding their fists on the bar's red leather border. They appear to be young, maybe in their early twenties.

"What's with strip clubs in Portland?" I lean forward, then recoil when something wet touches my arm. "They seem as common as brunch spots."

The bartender smirks. "Not from here, huh?"

"Three hours south."

"You like beer?"

"Yeah."

"Strip clubs are like beer in Portland. They're as much a part of local history as craft brew, and Oregon has been protecting them since the 1800s." He plants two hands flat on the bar top as though giving a sermon. "Free expression or something. We actually have more than anywhere in the country. They're more embedded in Portland's culture than a lot of outsiders realize."

I slug back some of my tar and feel the Baileys beginning to do its job. A hazy feeling settles over me. "Is the strip club community pretty close-knit, then? Did you know Eloise Harris?"

Instantly, he straightens, then looks over my shoulder. He licks his lips. "Are you a cop?"

"Definitely not." I clasp my hands around the mug. "Just moved here and trying to get a feel for the local dance scene. I saw that she died recently. I'm a dancer, too."

Dark-blue eyes sweep down my neck and flat chest, then flick back to my makeup-less face. "You don't look like a dancer."

I take a sip, offer a self-deprecating smile. "The scene is less glamorous where I'm from."

He gives a slow nod. "Yeah, Eloise was a sweetheart. We worked together over at El Cody's. Real shame how she died. I'm still trying to wrap my head around it."

"Yeah, crazy," I mumble. "Has there been any news on who killed her?"

"Not that I know of. She volunteered at an animal shelter on Tuesdays—had a big heart, that one. We haven't spoken in a while, but I can't imagine anyone would want to hurt her."

"Any aggressive boyfriends or—"

"Oh. I mean, I don't know." He scratches the back of his head. "I haven't seen her in a bit. Although one time, we were ending the late shift together, and a big, angry white dude came in, wearing fur everything—I remember that, because, right?—and demanded that she pay him for her last bump."

"She did cocaine?"

His eyes widen, and he glances to the dancers to see whether anyone heard. "Uh, you sure you're not a cop?"

"Would I be—"

"Nah, forget it. I shouldn't be talking poorly of the dead, you know? I don't know why I said anything; it's all hearsay anyway. None of my business. Did you want something besides Irish coffee?" He grabs a dish towel and starts wiping the spotless counter.

If Eloise Harris was into drugs and she owed that man in the fur, maybe she racked up a much larger bill in the time since my bartender last saw her. Was her murderer punishing her for not paying?

I scan the tap handles behind him and note the anxious way he watches the door. Waiting for blue uniforms to come charging in, no doubt. "Who's Dayton Leroy Rogers?"

The bartender wrinkles his nose. "One of Oregon's finest. He killed seven women during the eighties. Pretty gruesome for the Northwest."

"And Pierre Arktiq?"

"Kept a family of four in his basement. Hey, you're not going to say anything to anyone about Eloise, right? I feel terrible I even mentioned it."

I stare at him. At this man's double chin and the deadpan way in which he recounts what could be a summary of my childhood. "Say that again? About Pierre."

He wipes the inside of a shot glass. "Arktiq? The guy was nuts. After getting naturalized from Canada, he broke into a family's home and made everyone, the teenagers and parents, get in the basement. Made them gorge on fast food for a week, tried to fatten them up, so that he could eventually eat them."

Raucous laughter erupts from the women as one dancer takes the stage for the empty room. Music begins to blast through the stereo system. I lean in closer. "What happened?"

The bartender shrugs. "Just what you'd expect. The teenagers' friends came calling, and the parents' coworkers stopped by when they didn't come to the office. Arktiq was found out and arrested—but not before he shot the family; he prepared one for dinner but didn't get to enjoy the meal." I shudder, and the bartender notices. "Pretty creepy, right? We've got more stories than that." He waves a chubby palm at the rest of the beer taps.

Find the name I most admire and you'll find the next one first.

Pierre Arktiq, murderer and basement lover. Just like Chet. Just like the Four Alarm killer.

I lay a few dollar bills on the counter. "Bathroom?"

The man points down the hall. "Hurry up, though. You'll want to see Candy's set, and she's on next."

I head down a narrow hallway, but instead of going left toward the women's, I pause outside a door marked EMPLOYEES ONLY. Before I can second-guess myself—wonder what the hell I'm actually doing here—I lean into the door, and a messy kitchen is revealed. Dirty dish towels are slung across a wooden table while a plastic bag of frozen steaks lies on the tile, mostly thawed in a puddle of watery blood. Above the wide basin of a porcelain sink, a professionally printed canvas sign reads **BEER BREASTS AND STEAKS TO DIE FOR!** Past a wide refrigerator, another door leads down two steps into a cellar. I descend them. The floor here is smooth, flat concrete, matching all the walls except for the farthest one from the door. Potato sacks, stacked three high on each shelf, are the major commodity here, but as my eyes adjust to the semidarkness, I see plates and glasses, tubs of glitter, tubs of chalk, containers of rye, and cartons of light bulbs occupy steel trays. All the essentials. At the very back of the cellar, a walk-in cooler aligns with one wall, nearly touching the ceiling.

Voices carry from the kitchen. "What the hell happened to the steaks? Are you freaking kidding me?"

I freeze, not daring to take another step. The stocked shelves leave no hiding place large enough to fit me. My heart clamors against my chest. The bass of the dancer's set list muffles the conversation, but the voices become louder, heading my way.

I grip the handle of the cooler, then slide inside and pull the door shut. A light switch is already flipped on. Stainless-steel kegs are stacked upright on tracks along the floor and the ceiling. Puffs of hot air form beneath my nostrils as the grooves of the aluminum handle dig into my palm, and I brace for someone from the other side to wrench it free. Seconds go by. The handle doesn't move.

I turn to take inventory. The first row of kegs slides out, like from a drawer. The names of the beers—of serial killers—are written above each row in black pen on laminated paper. The label on the keg beneath "Charles Manson" reads COORS LIGHT.

"Classy move, Stakehouse," I whisper. Removing my camera from my case, I position the lens at eye level and capture the cooler's stock in two frames.

Moving from row to row, I search the labels. Adrenaline spurts through my veins, warming me, as I pass each row, each killer, until I'm only three labels out from the end.

Two rows of Pierre Arktiq beer are stacked two high, the letters *P.A.* on each face in curling font. Behind the last keg lies a bunched black mass—a trash bag. With human legs. Sticking straight out against the tracks of the mobile rack and concealed by the final row of kegs. A body.

Acid climbs my throat. I stare at the legs, terror locking me in place. My mouth goes dry as I imagine the limbs moving, twitching, this person rising and pulling the bag off its own head.

Does rigor mortis set in immediately? Is it already well set in if the body has been here since Sunday morning, when I received the note directing me here? Practical thoughts boomerang in my head, shock taking over and stifling a scream inside me.

A normal person would run. A sane person would alert the police.

With an unsteady hand, I lift my Canon. Raise the lens to the corner. *Click.*

I step backward and at an angle to capture the space between the stacks of beers, a slivered view of what should be the body's bagged head. *Click. Click. Click.*

The screen of my camera displays the most recent shot. Bright colors decorate the body's wrist. Slowly, I lower the camera to view them directly. Around the left hand is a bracelet made from three strings. My stomach clenches as I identify each color: red, green, and blue. Me, Lily, and Jenessa.

Gooseflesh ignites along my arms. This bracelet is the second item plucked from my childhood to be placed at the site of a murder.

Another thought freezes my movements: Did Chet know about these bracelets? We made them only the one day, the day we escaped, but did he see them when he came downstairs?

I inch closer and get down on my knees. I'm eye level with the trash bag. The feet. The bracelet that resembles those we made during arts and crafts with Rosemary.

Suddenly, the body slides, falls, then bangs into the back wall, and I scramble away on the cold floor, expecting it to reanimate and beg me to take it out of here. The trash bag has nearly come off the person's head. Tears pool in my wide eyes, watching the body. Waiting. Anticipating.

With a trembling hand, I pull up the tip of the plastic bag until a face is revealed. I don't look. I can't, not directly.

Lifting my camera from around my neck, I focus the frame on sallow skin and a round jawline. Then I press down on the shutter button with my thumb.

Click.

I zigzag among cars on the freeway, not sure where I'm going until I spy the exit I took this morning. Outside the same coffee shop, Shia raises his head, a shaggy mane of black curls, from over a journal as I approach. A puzzled smile breaks across his face. "Claire. Back so soon?"

Standing at the same spot that I left only hours ago, I feel numbness flood through me. Shock. Fatigue. Confusion.

After wiping the handle of the cooler, then sprinting through the kitchen of The Stakehouse, I slowed my walk through the club and ignored the bartender's announcement—*Candy's onstage! You're leaving?*—barely making it to my car before the shaking began.

Part of me wanted to be wrong about the location—wanted the killer to be wrong about me. I didn't have some special insight into a killer's mind or riddles, just because I was born into a situation normally seen in horror films or because I share genetics with Chet.

But he wasn't wrong; neither of us was. I did find the body. Now I have to wait until the strip club staff and the police find it beneath that specific beer.

Pierre Arktiq. Pierre *Arktiq.* If I roll the name around in my head with an American accent, it sounds like—

Arctic. Pierre Arctic. Peter in French. Or Petey.

In that cartoon from my childhood, Petey the Penguin lived in the Arctic.

"Claire?" Shia looks at me with pinched eyebrows. "I asked if cash would be okay. I already went to the bank." He lays a hand across a white envelope on the table. Crisp one-hundred-dollar bills peek from the top of the open flap. From the looks of Shia's Boy Scout concern, I'm willing to bet there are ten of them without counting.

"That's fine. Thanks."

"Are you okay? You look pale."

My tongue feels thick. I thought the Petey stuffed animal was there to lure me to take photos of Four Alarm. At no point did I think it was meant to serve as a clue to the next location—a bridge between the first dead body and the second. And if that's the case, what does that bracelet I saw in the cooler mean?

"I need to ask you something," I say and slide into the chair opposite. A barista approaches us, and I order another coffee, eager to blame my nerves on something normal like caffeine. "Do you know anything about a bracelet or some jewelry? I mean, one that would be significant to my childhood?"

Shia checks the clock on his phone, then closes his laptop. "I don't think so. Describe it."

"A dinky little braided thing. Three strands, different colors. We made them during arts-and-crafts hour the day we escaped."

I study the arch of his eyebrows and how they rise nearly into his hairline.

Two details from my childhood have now appeared at separate crime scenes. What I don't know is whether the killer is obsessed with Chet's legacy or imitating these aspects out of some secret motivation. There are already two victims to this person's resume. If I can somehow determine his next move and limit the casualties of his nostalgia, I have to try.

Shia stirs his coffee, his eyes never leaving mine. "Yeah, I don't recall. Maybe we can have our first interview session now, and you can tell me more about it."

I return his stare a moment longer. He doesn't know. If Shia, self-appointed archivist to our lives, isn't aware of that detail, what does that tell me about this killer?

"Why don't we discuss the basics?" he continues. "What do you know about Chet, his family history, or how he came to those violent . . . impulses?"

Unless—Shia doesn't want to share the extent of his knowledge up front. Why do I feel like he's gauging mine? "As much as anyone. The media covered it back when he was being prosecuted. Shouldn't you already know this?"

He presses his hands flat on the cast-iron folding table. "I'm looking for information that outside parties didn't capture. I want your firsthand observations or details you heard from Rosemary while down below. What do you know?"

"I told you. Nothing that isn't already public knowledge. I did a deep dive on the Internet when I was fourteen and read everything available on Chet at the time. There was nothing damning that I found—he was an only child born to a frail mother and a young father who abandoned them to pursue a musical career that probably ended in a heroin overdose. Chet was raised by his mother and an alcoholic stepfather. If anything has been published on him since then, I don't know about it. Besides, does any of that matter? I thought you wanted a day-by-day accounting of my childhood abuse."

My tone is sharp, biting, and I'm not at all sure why. My mother didn't spank me, and Chet was interested only in my mother.

Shia opens his journal. He flips backward; page after page is filled with notes, scribbles crawling up the margins. "Chet was a fairly normal kid—played sports with the local neighborhood kids, got okay grades in school—but his teachers recall him hoarding food, toys at his desk, pens, and attempting to keep his friends to himself. Twice, Chet tied up a classmate with jump rope and tried to keep the boy hidden in the field next to the schoolyard. When asked why he did that, Chet replied he didn't want the boy to leave him."

I raise my eyebrows at this anecdote as the barista drops off my coffee. "Disturbing, sure. It speaks to Chet's abandonment issues."

"You would think. However, his father reportedly came back into Chet's life when Chet was thirteen and attempted to have a relationship. Chet's mother gave an interview to the police department when she filed a complaint against his father."

"How do you have access to police records?"

"It was a public complaint at the time. Akin to a noise complaint nowadays. Or a public safety complaint that she filed on behalf of her son to get Chet's father, Jameson, to stay away from them. As far as we know, Chet never reestablished a relationship with Jameson."

I sip my coffee, savoring the froth and sweet caramel at the top of the mug. Today's temperature is brisk, but as additional clouds grow in size overhead, the humidity thickens to match. "Interesting. What does this have to do with my childhood and what your readers are interested in knowing more about? Why would they care?"

Shia bites the tip of his pen, revealing straight white teeth. He twists the blue plastic in his mouth, as if savoring my question. "Because, Claire. Your grandfather Jameson knew about you."

I pause from wiping whipped cream with my finger. Shia takes in my shocked silence, looking pleased he had information I wasn't aware of. He bobs a quick nod. "Jameson knew about you, maybe all of you. Inside your basement, the police found a cardboard box underneath the mattress with a return address from a children's toy store and originally mailed to an address different from Chet's. I found it by zooming in on digital photos of the room and of various items that were taken the day you escaped. Then I did a public search of the residents registered at that address twenty years ago. It was him. Your grandfather."

A car passes by too close to the curb and splashes gutter water onto the sidewalk beside us. I don't move. "Someone knew we were down there."

"I know it's a lot to take in. I would be pretty flummoxed, or whatever you may be feeling, too. But yeah. It seems that way. No matter how I look at it, someone at that address purchased toys for children, then hand delivered them to Chet's address, where the box ended up in your basement."

"What kind of toys?"

"What?"

"The toys that this person . . . Jameson . . . purchased. What were they?"

Shia shakes his head. "I don't know. The only way to know that would be to search Jameson's purchase history with that company— Yeltsin, I mean. The company I know, at least, was Yeltsin."

The megawatt toy engineer during the eighties and nineties. They sold every kind of toy imaginable and were behind all the Christmas hysteria for whatever doll or remote-controlled car was the best seller that season. As the major toy company, Yeltsin was also the chief merchandising partner for the era's kids' television shows—*Undercover Spy*, *Princess Angels*, and *Petey the Penguin*.

Memories swim before my eyes as I recall the stuffed Petey's fluffy chest and what would become a faded yellow beak. In the cartoon, Petey always sang songs about friendship and family, and I would sing them after every episode.

"I understand this may be hard for you." Shia interrupts my thoughts in a small voice. "But what was your interaction with Chet like? Do you think he ever showed any kindness to you, the way that Jameson might have? What is your first memory of Chet?"

Footsteps. The heavy impact of his weight on the steps directly above, in the alcove he built, before punching in the electronic code to the metal door. Then his gait passing into the basement, the creak of the boards as he moved down the stairs and into our world. Once, he tried to play with Lily when she was a baby, and Rosemary flew at him, struck him across the face. He returned the blow, his fist crashing into her cheek. After the pair huffed and puffed and stared at each other another moment, he grumbled something and trudged back upstairs.

There was another time that they fought, really brawled, and Rosemary came away with a black eye. I don't remember why—only that he said he would kill us all if he didn't get something he wanted.

"Fear. Violence. Anger." Speaking the emotions that Chet generated in me as a small child, I internally register how often they come to me as an adult. My own post-traumatic stress disorder mental prison, in which I feel the impulses of fear, violence, and anger all the time. Did I ever have a shot at escaping that?

Shia nods, writing in his journal. "Okay, let's go back. What do you remember before your half sister Lily was born?"

"Sister. They're my sisters."

"Right. Sorry. Any memories of before she was born?"

I think back on those early years and remember only being happy, blissfully unaware—happy to play with Jenessa and to feel my mother Rosemary's attention was wholly centered on me, even as she and Nora did their best to give both us girls the care that we needed in such a dank environment. I remember realizing, for the first time, that we had no windows after seeing some in a cartoon. The thought didn't bother me—in fact, it seemed like an advantage to enjoy; I could nap as long as I wanted or sleep as late as I wanted without being woken by a bright, intruding beam of sunshine. "None that's fully formed, exactly. Just being cared for by my mothers and playing with Jenessa."

"By your 'mothers,' do you mean Rosemary, Nora, and Bethel?"

"No, Bethel wasn't there yet. This was before her."

"Got it." Shia makes another scribble. He looks up, dark-brown irises contrasting the blue of his pen. "It seems like you recall a pretty normal, easy time growing up—at least initially. Is that right? Would you say that the experience of being born in captivity, underground, was more or less damaging than any other childhood?"

I stare at him like he just suggested organ harvesting as a viable business model. "No, it was damaging. It was fucked up." The adjacent table's conversation pauses, the anger in my voice filling the space. I lean closer. "The first few years, I was naive and a child. My mother sheltered us from the knowledge that she and the others were assaulted and sometimes beaten a few times a week by a man fifteen years older than them in a two-room space with no windows. It was when I became older that I began to notice Rosemary's haggard fatigue, her restlessness, and my own."

"Did you help plan the escape?"

"No, I was seven. I couldn't plan anything, but I recognized the same tension in myself that my mother had been exhibiting for years. I knew Jenessa felt it, too, when we were big enough that we started knocking into each other, then hitting each other. There was no more space. Either more people had to die or we had to get out."

I take a moment to gulp back the rest of my latte while Shia writes something else. He looks up and watches me; I see it from the corner of my eye while I examine the tables around us. A couple leans back in their chairs, each typing something on her phone while their feet touch underneath; a woman in a long, wraparound scarf reads a book; and a male student hovers over an open textbook displaying an anatomical depiction of the human body. Through the window of the coffee shop, I see people lining up to place their orders, the queue stretching back to the front door.

"How do you think being born into that situation affected you as an adult?" Shia asks.

I sigh, recalling the feeling of being belowground, in the two different storage spaces this week. "I don't know. Badly?"

"More specifically. Can you recall when you decided that being belowground was negative? How did your mother react to it? Your sisters?"

"What do you mean?"

"As in, how did Rosemary manage being kidnapped as a twenty-year-old, being thrown in with another woman, Nora, then eventually watching the third woman, Bethel, die in childbirth? How did she deal with it, and how did you and your sisters deal with that trauma in such close proximity?"

An image from my childhood returns, of Rosemary crying in a corner after trying to do something, I don't know what. "I . . . I can't remember." Flashes of running from one end of the compound to the next, of racing Jenessa, then Lily, back and forth, rise in my head, then disappear as quickly as they came. A frame, as if from a movie, snaps forward, of Chet looking at me, no more than a foot away. He reaches for me with something like hunger in his gaze, and Rosemary flies at him, clawing him across the face. He beat her then.

Their fights weren't only about him playing with Lily.

I stand up, pushing my chair backward. "I . . . I can't handle this. It's too much."

Shia stands, too. "Let's take a break. Five minutes?"

"No, I can't right now. I'm at my max. I'm sorry." I grab my shoulder bag, withdraw my keys, and begin walking. It takes me another two blocks before I realize I started off in the wrong direction and have now completely turned myself around. My knees buckle, and I sit down on a nearby bench advertising a real estate company.

Sitting with Shia for twenty minutes and answering his simple questions is more time than I've spent thinking about my childhood in years.

Recalling his bombshell about Jameson—did Rosemary know someone else was aware of our existence? I do the math. Jameson would have been about sixty when I was born. Is he still alive today?

The spidery fear that crawled across my skin upon seeing the bracelet on the body in the cooler returns. Could Jameson be the one leaving these details behind at crime scenes? If he sent me the original stuffed Petey, desiring a relationship with us, he could be sending a signal that he desires one now. The person leaving me messages and clues is responsible for two murders. Chet had it in him—the violence, the disregard for human life. Maybe Jameson does, too.

My phone vibrates in my pocket. Pauline is calling me.

"Claire? I have more good—I mean bad—news. What's the soonest you can get to The Stakehouse in North Portland?"

Thunder rumbles overhead, drowning out the rest of her words. Without waiting for the address, I hoist my bag onto my shoulder and walk in the direction of my car.

Thirteen

Shouts rise from the interior of the strip club, and all heads outside the building turn toward the sound.

Oz and I exchange a look.

"Think it's another body?" he asks. A crime reporter's dream. Bright-green eyes squint together, and full lips turn up at the corners. Naturally dusky skin gives him the appearance of an omnipresent tan.

I don't answer. Instead, I stare down at bullet points about my family, which I scribbled on a notepad not unlike the one Oz was using outside Four Alarm. Knowing I couldn't arrive too quickly and reveal I'd already been to The Stakehouse, I sat in my car two streets over, researching local news stories from the last twenty years on my phone. Tried to ignore my camera and the horrifying images it now contained.

Everything I found on us was in order: Chet abducted and held a woman, Nora, for two years before he decided to take my mother, Rosemary. Nora then gave birth to Jenessa. No doubt disappointed at the limited inventory, with Nora being out of commission postnatal, Chet saw fit to introduce a third woman, Bethel, to his harem. By Rosemary's account, Bethel was a slight woman, and the stress of imprisonment particularly affected her; her hair fell out in clumps. After Rosemary gave birth to me and Nora to Jenessa, Bethel eventually died on the same mattress giving birth to Lily.

No mention of Jameson at Chet's trial. According to archived newspaper articles online, there was plenty of speculation about what kind of rearing Chet had, but no parents came forward at the initial hearing or at the full trial, and Chet hadn't been born in the area. It was only after Chet was in prison that the family history I discovered online as a teenager came to light: Jameson abandoned his wife and young son. She remarried, and Chet's stepfather beat them both nightly.

While part of me is satisfied that I did glean and retain the correct information at fourteen years old, another is disappointed there isn't more to analyze. Shia's publisher's enthusiasm for this book makes all the more sense.

The forensics team strides inside the building, passing the medical examiner on his way out. I recognize the man with salt-and-pepper hair from Four Alarm. Turning to Oz, I find him consulting his notes. "Has there been any progress on the brewery murder?"

He inhales through his nose, as though it pains him to say. "Yeah, the chief of police is looking at two people."

"Who?" It's only been two days. I haven't come close to identifying someone, and I may have more clues than Chief Bradley.

"A nineteen-year-old homeless girl named Gianina Silva and the bartender who found the body at Four Alarm, Topher Cho."

An image of a tall man with thick black hair and a friendly voice rises to mind from when I stepped into the brewery and took photos. *Stay safe out there,* he had said. Was that Cho?

"Wait, what does Gia—Gianina—look like?"

"I don't know." Oz shrugs. "Haven't seen a photo of her—I just know she's young and known for drug dealing downtown."

The petite blonde with brittle hair and dark roots looks me up and down again in my memory. *Ask around for Gia.* "Why her?"

Oz blows air from his cheeks. "Did you hear that gunshot at Four Alarm yesterday? It was right after you left. The kid who pulled the trigger was waving it around like an idiot when it went off. Apparently it was Silva's, and she doesn't have a license for it. It also matches what the M.E. believes was used on Eloise Harris."

"The first victim. The stripper."

"You got it."

"But a teenage girl? She doesn't strike me as a killer." I think back to our chance meeting in front of the bakery and the way in which she eyed the cigarette burn on my inner elbow. Maybe she's an opportunist in that she thought I was high—but a murderer?

Then I recall my conversation with the Stakehouse bartender. Did Eloise Harris owe Gia money?

"Nope. And that's what's frustrating," Oz says, flipping his notepad closed. "I did some digging on Silva, and she had straight As before she dropped out of high school. She seems to be like any other kid you see on the street. They're all runaways or drug addicts, or both, and the city doesn't do enough to help them, so they piss off the rest of us by hanging out in downtown, and we all demonize them." He takes a breath, catching my surprise. "Sorry. I . . . my brother was homeless for a while."

I give a slow nod, remembering the teenager at Four Alarm wearing the Mickey Mouse retro hoodie. Most of the group around him appeared dirty and tired but harmless. "What about Topher Cho?"

Oz resumes a more curious expression. "Cho . . . now he's someone who might make more sense. He's got a misdemeanor from a fight with an old girlfriend—apparently things got physical between them, and she filed a complaint. He's a bartender-slash-actor and been trying to get an agent from some hotshot agency since he moved to Portland. A murder where he works could, in theory, provide more publicity. Get him more attention as the guy who found the body first. It's a stretch, but it fits better than a nineteen-year-old with no priors."

"Interesting."

"Yeah, I don't understand it, either. But we're just the news team, right, Claire? They've gotta keep the wheels of government moving."

"What are you saying? Have they both been arrested? That seems preemptive."

Oz smirks. "Officially, Silva and Cho are still only persons of interest, but I'll bet the cops are getting serious pressure from the upper brass to publicly name suspects. I haven't seen them this worked up since I've been at the *Post*, or the *Gazette* before this." He nods toward the groups of officers and concerned employees.

Candy, the dancer I saw earlier, left about five minutes after I arrived, and the bartender I spoke with is gone, too.

"A lot of angst seems to be going around, not the least of which is Chet Granger's parole next week. Tell me you know about that guy, at least." His gaze narrows to examine me, likely evaluating my worthiness of being on the "news team."

I shift my weight onto my heels. "Yeah, he imprisoned women and children underground."

Oz scoffs. "More than that. The *Post* archives show that only four underground incidents occurred in the state over the last thirty years. One, an oddball case of a woman attempting to create herself a crypt for beloved pets; another, a man dug himself a bomb shelter in the event of nuclear war; creepier, a mother and father kept their child, a deformed twin brother, belowground in an extended wine cellar while the other twin was raised aboveground as an only child. You'd think that would be the winner for the most messed-up cases, but no. There's the Granger case. The guy kept amassing women, forced them to dig out his basement and expand it, to have children by him; then he kept his own kids there until they were, like, ten."

"Seven. They—the oldest were seven and the youngest three."

Oz smirks again, sugary-sweet. "Aw, you do know more than the average photographer."

I swallow the pooling saliva in my mouth. Force a smile. "I stay up to date."

"Anyway, nerves are running high. The timing of these deaths so close to Granger's parole is not great for morale. Mayor's up for reelection this year, and detectives are being pushed for progress—plus the discovery that the basement passageway at the brewery and the one here at The Stakehouse could be connected to the Shanghai Tunnels. All of that amounts to a very on-edge police force, and they are dying—pardon the pun—to make an arrest."

Someone calls for Oz, and he tucks his notepad in his pants pocket. "I'm on. We should get a drink afterward. Since we're colleagues and all."

I shake my head, trying to organize the information Oz so easily rattled off. "How do you know all this?"

"Like any good reporter, Claire, I have a source." He turns his face away, a teasing grin just evident. "Why? What does a photographer care about solving a case?"

If I had access to records, archives, and police hearsay, I might get ahead of the author of the windshield note. Could Oz be my source? Or better yet, I could figure out the identity of Oz's source and go directly to that person.

He watches me, alert green eyes admiring my mouth. A shiver skates across my arms as I try to remember how to flirt.

"I've always thought crime reporting is an exciting career." Tentative smile. "Maybe I could intern with you, in a way?"

Delight mixes with pride as he runs a hand behind his neck. "Might be fun. See you at the next crime scene, shutterbug." He winks, then crosses the street and joins a woman in a starched blazer with rolled-up sleeves. She begins speaking while Oz withdraws a handheld recorder and holds it between them. Something he says makes her erupt into giggles.

If I weren't already suspicious of men, I would be after seeing this police official lap up Oz's charm. He wields it like a weapon to get what he wants. I could learn more than crime scene details from him.

"Lou!" Sergeant Peugeot waves at me from the front entry, his red hair a beacon. The wrinkles on his forehead appear deeper than when we met yesterday. A man stands beside him wearing a yellow press pass and holding a camera nicer than mine. "Media has five minutes, and then the crime scene is police only."

"Sergeant, I know the *Gazette* is just finishing up at a municipal campaign around the corner," the man says. "Do you want to wait for their photographer?" Next to his press pass is a second lanyard with the logo of the *Oregon Times*, the biggest newspaper in the region.

"Nope. You snooze, you lose around here. Clock's ticking."

The two of us follow Peugeot inside. Overhead lights are turned on, removing any mystique or sexy ambience from earlier today. Without cover of darkness, the bar top, tables, and stage seem worn and depressed instead of sexually liberated. I click through a dozen frames, taking a few more of the beer taps for my own records, then follow Peugeot through the kitchen. The puddle of bloody steaks has been cleaned up. As we traverse the spotless tile, fear spikes through me: I could have stepped in it with my shoe, tracked blood to the cooler, and left some evidence of my foreknowledge of the body.

I look up toward each corner of the ceiling as I trail the pair of men. No security cameras. Some of the tension leaches from my arms, but not by much. It was foolish traipsing back here alone earlier—no hat, no disguise. Idiot move. Impulsive, per usual.

In the storage area, two men in matching black shirts with the word POLICE across the shoulders stand beside a hole in the wall that wasn't visible when I was here before. Large plastic tubs of rotini seem to have been covering it. Peugeot approaches the men as I snap photos of the pasta. One of them explains how The Stakehouse has one of the oldest foundations on this block and was rebuilt twice in the last century. I reach for the handle of the walk-in cooler.

Peugeot turns. "Not in there," he barks. He strides over to stand between the entry and me.

The *Oregon Times* photographer stops what he's doing to watch us. "Isn't that where—"

"Police only. Media isn't allowed." He crosses his arms as if to punctuate the point. A woman in all-white coveralls exits the cooler carrying a yellow, opaque plastic bag.

"Okay. Sure. No problem." I move to take photos of the potato sacks and try to put some space between us.

". . . string of social workers tried to get her into a halfway house, but she never stayed sober and never held down a job. She disappeared about a year ago, off our dashboard at least, then shows up about six months back. This time Silva's throwing lavish get-togethers in a warehouse by the river and hosting line parties."

The second man makes an affirming noise. "I picked up a guy who went to one a few months ago. Buyers come, party, and buy drugs before leaving."

I pause beside two kegs stacked on their sides, trying not to make it obvious that I'm listening.

"Yeah, well, one of Four Alarm's employees said she was caught living in the basement underground."

"Which employee?"

"The bartender. Detectives thought he might have something to do with it, since he found the first body, but now they're not so sure. He's still being questioned at the station."

"Why not?"

"From what they tell me, the guy has been a mess since he was brought in."

Mess?

"Ready, *Portland Post?*"

I turn to face Sergeant Peugeot's stern mien. Fear shoots through me again, wondering how long he was watching me eavesdrop, not taking photos. "Yes, I think I have everything I need."

As he escorts me back through the club, I wrap my arms around my elbows. I thank Sergeant Peugeot, then head down the street. Oz is nowhere in sight. Traffic should have died down at this point, and an alluring image of an unopened bottle of wine I have at home pops into my head.

"Missy?" A woman's voice carries from behind. Adrenaline rises, frothing in the back of my throat. I whirl, hoping I misheard, that it's just nerves getting to me, but a woman with a muscular frame stands ten feet back, wielding a smartphone and a cautious smile directed at me.

Peugeot is still standing outside, speaking to the strip club's general manager. I can even make out Peugeot's voice saying, "We'll need to speak to that person." We're not a full block from the latest crime scene—from the earshot of authorities who let me into not one but two, without realizing the liar I am.

I need to get out of here. I start walking, almost jogging, willing the woman's insistent voice to fade away in the nearby freeway traffic.

"It is you, isn't it? Missy, please, can we talk? I'm a reporter with *Tru Lives*. I'd love to know how you're faring for a Where Are They Now piece. This year is the twentieth anniversary of your escape."

I reach the corner and realize if she sees my car, my license plate (if she hasn't already), she'll probably be able to find me again. Everything Oz already knows about Gia and her high school transcript is an example of the connections reporters have. This woman could learn where I live.

Slowly, I turn and face her. Her hand flinches like she might slide open her camera app and take a photo of me, but she doesn't. Instead she watches me like I'm a feral animal, unpredictable and potentially hostile.

"How did you find me?"

A crease forms between brown eyebrows tweezed within an inch of their life. "Your friend Serena Delle suggested I could find you here.

I wasn't sure I'd recognize you from those photos years ago, but you've grown up beautifully."

I stare at her. Try to ignore the cold ripple of air that skims my back. This woman doesn't seem like a psychopath, with her coiffed brown waves and the tattoo of a peace sign on her forearm, but why else would she be in contact with the girl who stalked me during high school and, for a time, followed me to another city? The smell of the roadkill Serena would find and leave me like an offering in Chet's name is still singed into my nostrils. For a long time, I couldn't get the heavy-set girl's ghostly blue eyes out of my head, always seeing them in large crowds, whether or not she was present—until the day my restraining order went through. Then she stopped following me in her yellow Mini Coop and disappeared. "How do you know Serena?"

The woman squints, dark eyes disappearing into thick eyeliner, and cocks her head. "I don't. I received a letter with this address and instructions to come here every day this week. It was signed by a Serena Delle."

"Signed, like written?"

"Typed."

Of course it was. Maybe Serena Delle has turned from leaving dead animals for me to leaving dead bodies. She could have killed the person in The Stakehouse, then left a note that she knew would bring me here eventually—and this reporter would be waiting to further torment me.

"Listen," I begin and take a step toward her. "Why don't you feature a different subject for your story? You work for *Tru Lives*? Your show is notorious for always going after celebrities who have lost weight or had a breakdown. Why not focus on something even more interesting?"

Her curiosity piqued, she doesn't move as I inch forward. "I'm not sure what that might be," she says. "People have been asking about you for years, wondering how you and your sisters are doing, but mostly you. You seem to be the anomaly—out of the spotlight, relatively okay as far as we can tell. Jenessa, poor thing, in and out of rehab, and Lily, the wild child, never with more than a dime in her pocket thanks to all the surgeries on her foot. Our viewers want the real story, Missy. They want to know who you are. And what you're feeling right now."

I shake my head, allow my gaze to fall to the side, lulling her into a false sense of safety. "The story shouldn't be whether I'm surviving all right. Or maybe . . ."

"Yes . . . ?"

I bite my cheek, now within a solid foot of this woman—this reporter. Unsuspicious in her throwback Care Bears T-shirt and jeans. Blending in like any other Portlander enjoying their weekday.

"Maybe the story should be about something more exciting. Something relevant and universal." Within this woman's personal bubble, bravery stark across her excited expression, the smell of onions is thick on her breath. In my peripheral vision, I see her thumb drag along her screen, then press. Recording me.

"What do you suggest?"

"How about . . . a woman fighting for her privacy?"

I grab her phone and throw it as hard as I can across the road, over the chain-link fence and onto the freeway below.

She stares in the direction her phone flew, then snaps back to me. "Do you have any idea how many notes, what kind of files, I had on that? That's destruction of private property."

I meet her furious glare with a cool shrug. "Which is about the equivalent of stalking and harassment. Next time, leave me alone."

Without looking behind me, I walk toward the corner at an easy pace, then turn right and jog to my car, my heart pounding in my ears so thick and fast, I can barely breathe.

I check the rearview, half expecting to see Peugeot running toward me, open handcuffs in his grip, or Serena Delle herself marching closer. Instead, an empty road stares back at me. Hollow relief spreads across my chest, though I know that might change at any second. As I merge onto the freeway, the gloomy cloud coverage rolling in mirrors my unease.

Fourteen

Twin didn't sleep the whole hour. She got up and stumbled into the front room and complained that me and Mama Rosemary were doing something important without her. We were but that was beside the point.

But Sweet Lily did—she slept the hour and then some. While we helped Mama Rosemary sort through our things and pack an item for each of us Sweet Lily kept right on in bed barely moving. When I went to check on her she was hot like a fever. I ran and told Mama Rosemary. She said "Shit" and then ran and got a washcloth and wet it under the sink and pressed it to Sweet Lily's head. She looked so small and just like a doll curled up in the very middle of the bed on the brown spot. The place she came into our family.

Mama Rosemary was upset. She sat by Sweet Lily and started to cry. Big tears fell on her face, made her skin all pink. When she saw me and Twin watching from the doorway she sat up straight. She gasped and ran into the kitchen tripping over the old rug she made from a towel that got blood on it when Twin cut herself falling down the stairs. Noise came from the bin next to the sink that we use as a chair sometimes. Mama Rosemary held up pillboxes and medicine jangling them like toys then throwing them back in the bin.

"Mama, is everything all right?" I asked in a whisper.

She threw both hands down and leaned forward like she might be sick. Her whole body shook and she was crying again. "We were so close. So close," she kept saying.

I went and put a hand on her back and she didn't move. "Is Sweet Lily gonna be okay?"

Mama Rosemary turned around. Her face was still wet but she wiped her nose then rubbed her hand on her sleepy pants. The loose ones that are her favorite. She pulled me into a hug on her lap. Twin came over and squeezed in, too.

"Your sister is going to be just fine, girls. It's her little toe again. Without treatment, her whole body starts to feel sick sometimes. You remember what having an extra toe is called?"

"A congent . . . ?" Twin mumbled.

"Congenital . . . birth defect," I finished for her.

"Very good. You girls really are like twins sometimes. Not just Irish twins." Mama Rosemary's head was above ours and I couldn't see her but I heard her smile.

We were quiet a long while.

"Mama Rosemary?" I asked. "Are we still doing escape today?"

She sighed and didn't answer so long I almost asked again. Then she said: "I'm not sure, darling. With your sister sick, it's going to be much harder to maneuver everyone out safely. I was counting on you all being able to run."

Twin stood up. She looked at the bed room then back to us and said, "When I'm not feeling good a hug always makes me feel better. Maybe we should go hug Sweet Lily?"

Mama Rosemary's voice got all heavy again. Like she was sick, too, and I got scared for a second. What if Mama Rosemary got sick and left us? Just like Mama Nora and Mama Bethel? What would we do for food? We couldn't eat cereal all day. The stuff the man gave us always made me sleepy and happy but gross afterward. But I eat it anyway because it's sugary and yummy before it makes me feel gross. I eat it and Mama Rosemary says it's good for us and will make us relax. She calls it Lith-yum. She asked the man for it one day to help us all be calm together.

"I think that's a wonderful idea," she said. We stood up and all crawled into the bed around Sweet Lily. I didn't want to touch the brown spot but then there was no more room and I did. I didn't like it but I wanted to be near Sweet Lily. She was hot like she just took a bath and sweating like she just finished exercise hour.

Twin fell back asleep first and her breathing got all patterned and quiet. Then Mama Rosemary fell asleep. Her breath was the same only deeper.

I stayed awake.

I'm still awake.

Everyone has fallen asleep and left me alone and awake. The only one. All by herself.

For a second my toes curl up and I get scared again. What would happen if I was all alone and no one in my family was here with me—if I was in this bed and had both rooms to myself? I wouldn't like it. I would be so lonely.

The thought makes me cry but Mama Rosemary doesn't wake up. Twin neither.

I poke Twin with my finger. Poke poke. Poke. She doesn't move still sleeping.

There's a brown-green-yellow spot on her arm. I poke that and she jumps like my finger was a needle. It's a bruise.

I sit upright fast rocking the bed and Mama groans but keeps sleeping.

Someone has been hurting Twin.

Fifteen

My phone occupies the countertop of my kitchen—the only item on the counter after a morning of stress-cleaning, dusting, and doing dishes I haven't touched in days. With each plate I towel-dried, I thought about recent events, and my two visits to The Stakehouse yesterday. Reflected on all the surprises that have jumped out of the ether in less than a week. Each of them meant to capitalize on our story or force me to do something I may regret.

The handheld device appears hostile. Capable of blowing up the apartment complex if I input the wrong combination of numbers. I unlock my phone, clearing the image I took of the adjacent forest of trees, and dial.

"Nine-one-one, what is your emergency?"

My tongue feels thick in my mouth. "I—not an emergency, exactly, but—I have something to tell the police."

It takes emergency dispatchers less than a minute to pinpoint a caller's city and street, down to the exact location within a few square feet. In the event that the call is disconnected, the police can go to that address and verify the caller is safe. According to my phone, I've already been on the line for sixteen seconds.

"The Four Alarm murder is linked to the Stakehouse murder. The killer admires leaders relating to—" I scan the words I wrote on a pad of sticky notes. Saying the next phrase, *The killer admires leaders relating to*

Chet Granger, feels more incriminating than it did an hour ago when I crafted my five-sentence anonymous message to the police. I was hoping that by offering up what clues I have, I could wash my hands of the information and let the police do their job—step back and stop involving myself, despite the killer's interest in me. But staring at the words in front of me, I realize the only fact I've supplied points directly back to Chet—and to me.

What else can I say exactly? *The killer left me a note outside of Four Alarm, baiting me with a stuffed animal from my past, which led me to The Stakehouse, where a body was wearing a bracelet like one I used to make with my sisters*? Sharing those specifics would only lead the police to add me to a list of possible suspects. Why else would I have that information unless I know the person behind this—or worse, am committing the murders myself?

"Ma'am? Are you still there?"

Thirty-seven seconds have elapsed. My fingers grip the phone as I debate my reply.

Forty-one seconds. "Yes, I—I'm sorry to waste your time; I have to go."

Panic jolts through me and I hang up. I shouldn't have called. Calling was a mistake. Why didn't I think that through better?

My phone rings—an unknown number. Do the police automatically call back?

My hand shakes as I slide the answer bar right. "Hello?"

"Marissa!" a woman squeals into the receiver.

". . . Lily?"

"Yes!" The word dissolves into a throaty laugh. "I'm back from Switzerland, and I'm dying to share some news with you in person. Are you free now?"

"What? Like, right now? When did you get back?" My kitchen clock says eleven thirty, and I scheduled another interview session with

Shia for the afternoon. "Yeah, I'm free for a few hours. Holy crap, Lil, are you actually home? What happened? Is everything okay?"

"Fantastic. Everything's great. Do you still have the Find-My-Family app we downloaded on our phones before I moved?"

"Oh, yeah. I guess. I didn't remove it, at least." She was so insistent she wanted to be able to visualize where Jenessa and I were while she was abroad. Said it'd help her feel more connected.

"Perfect. You can navigate to my apartment with it. See you soon!"

I hang up in a daze. The police haven't called by the time I grab my keys and unlock the door. Before I turn the handle, I check the peephole. No uniforms waiting in the hall.

※

A woman sits on the curb when I arrive at a modern apartment building in the middle of downtown. Petite and towheaded, she taps some game on her phone. Narrow shoulders hunch forward, and her feet point together in ballerina flats. Hearing my approach, she lifts her head, and a smile breaks across her heart-shaped face. Lily stands, opens her arms, and reveals a bulging belly in a high-waist dress.

"Happy to see me?" The bright-blue eyes that always made her seem so innocent as a kid now seem to glint with mischief.

"You're pregnant?"

Disregarding the question, my little sister crosses to me and wraps me in a hug. I shift my hips backward to make room.

"I'm so happy to see you. But what are you doing here?" I laugh into her hair. "You didn't want to share you were moving home, and with an extra human?"

She pulls back to look at me as a cloud of hurt passes down her face, ending in a pout. "Once we decided to move home, I thought it would be a fun surprise. And I didn't want to promise anything, in case plans changed."

Free-spirited Lily went rogue after deciding college wasn't for her. She and her then-brand-new girlfriend, Bianca, decided to move to Europe. Lily has been quiet these last few months, replying to my texts with stunted answers, and she stopped accepting my video calls. I thought she was going through a phase, or maybe that she and Bianca had broken up, as relationships during your early twenties often do. I guess I was half-right; the phase should last about nine months.

"How are you?" I stare down at her belly, then back up to Lily's beaming face. Full cheeks suggest the time we've spent apart has been good to her, and she seems happy about the baby. "Are you a surrogate?"

She giggles, a husky sound, just the way I remember it. Warmth spreads along my limbs, and I can't deny how good it is to see her.

Here. In this city. During this week. Did Lily return home for the anniversary, too? Is she here, knowing about Chet's parole and intending to . . . do something next week? Doubt and concern mingle together as I search her face for that glint that sparkled upon my arrival.

"No, I'm not a surrogate. Jesus, Em." She rolls her eyes, then crosses her arms beneath a swollen bosom.

I lift both palms up. "Hey, I've thought about it. It's a handsome check at the end of it, and you're helping someone, right? No judgment."

Lily's smile fades. "Actually, Bea and I got a sperm donor over in Geneva. We wanted to start a family. Realizing I was going to have my own family made me want to come home to Oregon. For good," she adds. "You're here now, so we figured Portland was a good spot to settle down."

"And Jenessa."

"What about her?"

"Jenessa is here, too."

Lily pauses. "Oh. Well, all the more reason." She resumes a broad grin. Since Lily and I grew up separately from Jenessa, I sometimes forget that the pair of them never really bonded. Of the seven years I lived in Chet's compound, only three of them were shared with Lily; she remembers less of it with Jenessa than I do.

We enter the lobby and pass a potted lily of the valley, lush with its green leaves and white bell-shaped buds, which my sister points out with pride—her first addition to the space. As we take the elevator to her fourth-floor apartment, I wonder whether I should have waited for Jenessa to visit with me. To share in this welcome home to our little sister. When the elevator stops, Lily takes my hand, swinging it back and forth as we walk down the hall, limping with the uneven gait she's had almost her whole life.

Calling Jenessa on the drive here didn't earn me a return call—I tried, at least. When we were kids, she and I couldn't help fighting over Lily like she was a toy, at times pulling her between us until Rosemary made us stop. We would often try to lure Lily to play with one of us individually, by dangling either her favorite toy or the prospect of a game; the winner would get five minutes of uninterrupted play time with Lily before her attention fluttered elsewhere, or indeed, the older sister got bored. We even called her Sweet Lily, because Rosemary and Nora were always commenting what a sweet baby she was, despite losing her birth mother.

In hindsight, we had such limited sources of entertainment—and even affection—that I don't blame us for treating Lily's love as a trophy.

The fourth-floor hallway is peaceful, empty it seems, on a Wednesday at noon, and I wonder whether anyone else—the media or Rosemary—is aware Lily's returned.

Pauline wired payment for the hour I spent at The Stakehouse yesterday and the two hours last night that it took to touch up the *Post* employees' photos. As I was selecting images from The Stakehouse that I thought might be of interest to her, I made sure to exclude photos of the body—trash bag over its head, behind the kegs and undisturbed. Revealing that I was there in advance of the police would start an avalanche of questions—even as Pauline would, no doubt, pay top dollar for something that unique and which only the *Portland Post* could offer readers.

The gray-painted apartment door already bears my sister's signature decoration: several pots of her favorite flower, the Stargazer lily, flank each side. Vibrant pink, black-freckled, narrow petals lean forward as if they sense my anxiety.

"Ready?" Lily turns to me with a smile, limping from the tight rotation. She reaches for my hand, and I help to steady her. "Sorry. Pregnancy has really thrown off my balance. The old hitch has flared up again."

"No problem. And yes. I can smell the muffins from here."

Once we were out in the world, medical professionals ran all the tests and suggested all the expensive procedures to make us whole—*As if you weren't born underground,* they said with self-assured nods. They would fix us, mostly using Chet's insurance, which a lawyer argued should be extended to us as his biological children. Rosemary didn't want anything to do with him once we were free, and she initially went hysterical at the lawyer's proposal. Then the doctors sat her down and laid out our medical needs as they saw them; she relented. The vitamin D deficiency I had was treated with therapeutic drugs for six months until my biochemistry normalized, Jenessa was given braces to correct a painful overbite (although Rosemary saw to it with our daily flossing that none of us had any cavities), and Lily was granted a pro bono surgery on the congenital defect that had left her with an extra toe.

As an infant, it wasn't an issue; she crawled everywhere on her knees. When she started walking, she complained of increasing pain that led her to favoring the other foot. One surgery turned into two, then a third when she was a teenager and past her final growth spurt. The last I heard, her foot ached when it rained very hard, like a meteorological barometer, but the pain was minimal. The medical bills beyond that first pro bono surgery, however, were not, and both Rosemary's and Lily's settlement money went quickly.

Lily opens the door, and stacks of boxes greet us at the narrow entryway. "Welcome to our home," she says.

"Bonjour, ma belle!" French rings out from the kitchen; then Bianca peeks around the corner wearing a chef's apron. Lily had texted that fresh baked goods would be waiting for me, and I knew that Bianca, first as a baker in Portland, then as a culinary student in Switzerland, wouldn't disappoint. She strides forward and kisses me on both cheeks; I stop myself from flinching backward. The girl who instigated Lily's disappearance from my life when she suggested they pack up and leave the country has never earned a cozy place in my heart.

"Bianca is super content to see you, if you can't tell," Lily says with a grin.

"Oh my God, you did it again." Bianca moans, shaking wavy brown hair at her shoulders. "Just stick to one language, honey. Or, you know, maybe skip talking at all."

I hold my breath. Lily gives a feeble cough. "Did what, babe?"

"Thought in French in your head and translated it to crappy English. Only eighteenth-century maids are 'content to see' anyone." Bianca's smile is cramped, and I wonder if I interrupted a fight by arriving when I did.

"It's fine—I knew what you meant, Lil." I reach for her hand, but she pulls away.

"No, Bianca's right," she says, her voice hoarse. An overhead light fixture makes her eyes appear glassy. "My American mannerisms and slang have dipped. Being immersed in Swiss culture for five years, speaking French, and learning some German and Italian with Bianca, I went all in, I guess."

"Of course you did. You were living abroad," I say.

Bianca glances over her shoulder. "Try living with her now." She heads back into the kitchen.

Lily rubs her arms and turns her face to the wall.

Is this always my little sister's life? Or just the tail end of a passing tiff? I touch her elbow, upset by this welcome from Bianca.

"I did go all in; she's right. The new continent and culture made me feel like . . . like I could escape everything, you know? Create a new identity for myself." She looks past me before meeting my concerned gaze.

The number of times I've wished that is probably in the thousands by now. "Yeah. How successful was that? Did you pick up any wigs or adopt a thick accent?"

The left side of her mouth tips up. The angst pinching her eyes lessens, and some of her normal warmth returns. Her hands find the top of her belly. "I was pretty close."

We walk into the kitchen to find a tray of a dozen freshly baked muffins cooling on a tile counter. The layout flows into a small sitting room with an L-shaped sofa that occupies the corner, beneath a broad rectangular window. Natural light streams into the space, notably absent of Bianca. Floorboards creak from the neighbors overhead. I pause by the oven and breathe deep. "I'm starved. Can I?"

She nods. I reach for the closest muffin. It's still hot when I begin peeling back the wrapping, and I wait for it to cool enough to eat. "So why did you really come home?"

Lily tenses, her delicate features tightening. "What do you mean? I told you. I wanted the baby to be close to family."

"Sure, I understand that. But why now?" I've always been direct with Lily. Call it the result of having only a small circle of people to trust.

"I don't know what you mean."

"Lil, I—you do realize this year—next week is—"

A loud crash sounds from down the hall, where I assume the bedrooms are. Lily grabs a muffin and bites off a mouthful, then another, despite steam still rising from the nooks and crannies. She inhales through her nose as she chews.

"You know, I'm so glad you got to see the place. But I think maybe we should grab lunch another time this week. Can we do that?" She plucks another muffin from the tray and places it in my hand. "I've got loads of boxes to unpack still."

"Are you sure? I'm happy to stay and help."

Lily casts another glance behind me. The apartment is quiet. "Well, we do have a stupid amount of to-go containers to organize. I hate that job."

"Perfect. I'll find which top goes with which plastic bowl. Point me to them."

She limps to a stack of cardboard filing boxes. "Thrilling stuff."

I settle onto the floor and get to work, separating the round covers from the square ones. In truth, I loathe mismatched plasticware; it's never apparent which lid goes with which bottom, and I usually toss what comes with my Thai order after I've finished eating. But if this eases something about Lily's tense afternoon, I'm all for it. Lily measures out shelf liner, then begins cutting identical copies for the cupboards.

Once I've stacked her three dozen containers according to size, Lily rewards me with the first genuine grin since she announced my presence to Bianca. "Thanks so much, Em. You're a lifesaver."

Hearing the nickname she always had for me—my first initial, *M*—fills me with a sense of home. "I'm happy to help," I reply, genuinely meaning it.

She walks me to the door. Once I'm at the elevator, I wave goodbye to Lily, who stands beside her potted flowers.

"Tell Bianca I said thanks?" I lift the now-cooled muffin.

Lily nods, too enthusiastically. "Of course."

I return her forced smile, then step inside the elevator. Whether it's pregnancy hormones or something else, the way Lily seemed so broken when Bianca was in the room was disheartening. Overprotective sister or not, I don't like it, and I have to wonder whose idea it was to move home—maybe one of them wanted to return and the other didn't, and that's what's causing tension. Or the fact that they're about to welcome a baby into their lives. Or maybe I'm just on edge about everything, about this year.

Outside the building, I take off toward the boulevard. A dog barks from a patio restaurant to my right, and I recognize two of the greatest words in modern English visible in the bagel shop window: *Free Wi-Fi*.

Finding a seat at a raised counter overlooking foot traffic through the window, I order a coffee and unwrap my second muffin. Shia and I agreed to meet in another hour, and I could use this free time to research whoever is behind these murders.

Using my phone's browser, I type in the phrase *serial killers*. Truthfully, I should have done this yesterday or the day before, but I've been so distracted with reunions and remembering things about my childhood—finding myself humming songs that I used to sing with my sisters that I haven't thought of in years, imagining footsteps coming from outside my bathroom door while I'm showering, waking up recalling the bland taste of spaghetti and red sauce with no salt or pepper—that I haven't made the time.

The internet doesn't disappoint. According to a website called Serial Killer Basics, modern murderers are likely to be white males, in their midthirties, with a penchant for violence and two or more kills. Statistically, that's the most common profile in metropolitan areas, although institutional biases may have led criminologists to overlook serial killers of other ethnicities. So my killer could be anyone. Great.

Whoever is behind the appearance of these two dead bodies—be it Topher Cho, Gia Silva, or someone else—they are linked to the author of the note I received. That person seems intent on drawing a connection between my childhood and these present-day deaths. Although Chet might fit the physical bill of a serial killer, the only death I know he made happen was Bethel's when he refused to take her to the hospital when she was hemorrhaging after giving birth.

Tabbing over to the *Portland Post*'s web page, I find the latest update on the Four Alarm victim, the dancer. According to the medical examiner, she died from fatal force to her head and not the gunshot subsequently fired—confirming the speculation I overheard in the brewery. The bruises she sustained are consistent with being forcibly abducted and restrained. No sign of sexual assault.

If Petey the Penguin was actually code for Pierre Arktiq, mass murderer, what does the braided bracelet mean? I haven't received a new message from the killer since leaving The Stakehouse, unless I count that reporter's sneak attack.

Immediately after I drove away, I felt a wave of regret at throwing her phone onto the freeway. Not only because the phone may have landed on a moving car and hurt someone but because I just proved them all right. I'm no better than Chet when he would snap and begin beating Rosemary. The anger issues I've worked haphazardly to subdue, the rage that percolates beneath my skin and marks me as Chet's perverse offspring, align exactly with what people think of me—that I'm damaged. A wild animal. Not to be trusted. I proved them all correct in that moment.

What else would this killer do? What will his next action be? Is he going to attack someone at an arts-and-crafts store, where people engage in activities like the bracelet- or rug-making Rosemary made us do our last day? The connection between flimsy thread jewelry we braided and this latest dead body should be clearer, but I can't recall why a bracelet might be important. I need to understand him better. His choices. His victims.

I remember the shoes on the most recent body—loafers whose soles were worn smooth. The ghost of the cooler's chilled temperature burns my nostrils, and my stomach clenches against a sudden urge to vomit. Accessing my camera's recent photos on my cloud server, I pull up images of the victim's face. In the moment, I couldn't bring myself to examine him without the protection of my camera lens. Now, and in the safety of the bagel shop's warmth, I can fully confront the details.

A naturally long face appears rounded at a slackened jaw. Pale pink lips are open, revealing the tip of a dark-red tongue within. Reddish-brown whiskers dot his mouth and chin in uneven patches sprinkled with gray. This man was likely in his midforties, maybe early fifties.

A rush of cool air enters the bagel shop as a woman opens the door and crosses to the counter. A child, somewhere behind me, asks her parent for more schmear, and I hunch over my screen, keenly aware I'm gazing at a cadaver in public. I type *reverse image search* into a new browser tab, then upload a photo of the man.

The results are all insurance related. This victim, Gavin Nilsson, was an insurance agent, and pretty successful, earning a Salesperson of the Year award last year. The prize was a trip to London. Happy images of him in front of Buckingham Palace cover the insurance company's "Events" page. I return to the search results and click on an art website. He also painted landscapes of the Pacific Northwest. From the looks of his tableau of the Columbia River Gorge, he was talented. I scroll through lush green mountaintops and towering waterfalls, wishing I could draw more than stick figures.

Do the police know all of this about him? What does he have in common with the stripper found in Four Alarm's basement? I search *Eloise Harris art*, but the web results lead to an octogenarian living in Berlin. How does any of this relate to me?

Shia's words from the coffee shop return to mind. *People want to know what happened from a firsthand perspective.* Hell, I want to know. So much of what I've recalled since he proposed interviewing me have been details without any apparent significance. Freezer-burned vegetables. Games that Jenessa and I used to play together. The scratchy feeling of the blanket I liked to wear as a cape.

I map directions to the location where Shia and I agreed to meet, and find I'm already running behind.

The city library appears ominous under the afternoon's gray skies. Zigzags made by last night's rainstorm streak the stone face. The neoclassic design common to so many buildings around here reminds me that these neighborhoods are old by West Coast standards.

Across the street, a tent town that sprouted up on the greenway bustles with activity. A few men and women shake out blankets and cook food over an open flame rising from a metal trash barrel. I skim over the burning yellow and orange ribbons, never allowing myself to focus too much on them.

Inside, in a spacious atrium, readers sprawl in plush armchairs near bookshelves along the perimeter. Shia is seated at a table. He withdraws his phone and a journal from his backpack, then places them carefully at nine and three. He looks around him as though energized by the locale, lamplight reflecting on his glasses. Seeing me, he breaks into a lopsided grin.

"We gotta stop meeting like this." He rises from one of a dozen tables on the ground floor. "How was traffic?"

"Fine, I was in the area. Are we allowed to talk in here?" I take a seat and try to ignore his stare, the feeling that the seven other people scattered among the neighboring tables are listening. Although I'm sure this is the right way forward, all things considered, it still feels dangerous confiding in a stranger.

Shia's pen is poised over a yellow-paged journal. He taps a button on his phone to record, and a wavelength undulates across the screen. "Yes, but only in the community room. As I said yesterday, my publisher is anxious for a draft, given Chet's release on Monday. I've been up all night outlining chapters and possible subjects that I'd like to get your thoughts on." I nod, and he winces. "I'm sorry, but could you try and speak your answers or comments aloud?" He glances down at the phone.

"Oh. Yes. Sorry. Yeah, I'm . . . ready to give my thoughts."

"Good." He smiles and flips to another page filled with writing. "Let's start from the beginning. Please state your name."

Although I knew this would likely be part of giving interviews, I balk. "Why? I mean, I thought I was going to be an anonymous source. Why would I be recorded saying my name?"

Shia flushes, then clears his throat. "Okay, you don't have to state your name. This recording is only to facilitate my note-taking so I don't miss anything. Let's try another question. What is your earliest memory?"

Lily. My first memory is about Lily, and suddenly the impact of what I'm about to do—share intimate details to every hungry rubbernecker in the country—feels wrong, and not at all my story to tell. She's barely returned home, pregnant and dealing with problems in her relationship.

Then there's Jenessa. How would she react if she knew I was itemizing our past for this person? Especially after she turned down his money.

Instead of my first memory, I recall watching my sisters huddled together beneath a blanket on a hospital bed as we waited to be examined by a nurse the night that we escaped. Shame roils through me.

I stand and sling my messenger bag across my chest. "I can't do this today. I'm sorry."

Shia's mouth falls open. He pushes his glasses higher onto his nose. "What? We just started. You're not doing anything wrong here, and I already gave you cash. You agreed," he adds in a low voice.

"No, I know. I'm just . . . I'm not feeling well. And we already had a mini session yesterday, right? Let's try again tomorrow. Or the day after."

"Claire." Shia drags the word out through gritted teeth. "How can you know where you're going unless you examine where you've been?"

I grab my sunglasses and haul ass out of there. The woman at the welcome desk looks up when I burst through the doors of the lobby, but I don't pause. Today, after a failed call to the police and a failed visit to warn my little sister about Chet, the last thing I need is to inflict more damage.

Sixteen

As a child, I always felt an obligation to make sure the others were okay. I knew the cadence of Rosemary's antidepressants the first several years post-captivity, and I kept an eye on her outgoing mail to confirm utilities wouldn't be shut off. I kept a stash of Spam and rice in the bottom corner of the kitchen pantry, and the number for the church food bank was on speed dial, just in case. Down in Chet's basement, it was a regular thing to see Rosemary slide into a catatonic state, but I never wanted to be at the mercy of her emotional voids again.

As the oldest of my sisters—albeit with a head start on Jenessa of seven months—I felt responsible for them, worried about them, as much as a nine-year-old could. I tried to take good physical care of Lily by ensuring her hair was shampooed and she bathed every few days, whenever Rosemary became too *distracted*, as she put it, and needed to change her dosage. It was harder with Jenessa three hours away in Portland, but I wrote her letters, knowing that Nora was not as consistent as Rosemary in paying utilities like the telephone. I don't know if Jenessa received every letter, and I never held it against her when her reply wasn't prompt. She'd write back sooner or later.

It was an abrupt shift after our escape, ceding one of my sisters to a stranger, to the woman I knew as Mama Nora. I once read somewhere that humans can get used to anything.

Well, I never did. I don't think Lily or Jenessa did, either.

When I look up from my phone, the sun is shining off-center in the sky—finally, a clear blue. I shrug off my jacket into the passenger seat of my car and allow the warm beams to bathe the skin of my forearms. My most recent burn has taken on a dark-red color as the wound heals. Faded scars flank it like grave markers, poised to welcome another to their dead ranks.

I lock my phone, rest my cheek against the glass, and close my eyes. Just for a second.

Poring over bookmarked websites feels redundant, but I don't know how else to approach this search. I found articles about the other underground incidents that Oz mentioned, but I don't see a clear link to the current murders or to me.

My eyes snap open. With everything going on, I forgot to ask Jenessa whether she knows about Chet's release. Crap. I type out a message on my phone.

> Hey! Did you know that Chet will be released on parole on Monday? Just wanted to check.

I shake my head. Erase the message, then try again.

> I have some bad news. Chet will be released on parole this Monday. Did you know?

Still awkward. Still a terrible text. Although there's probably no easy way to write this.

> Bad news that deserves a 1-hour phone call but I want to ensure you know ASAP: Chet will be released on parole Monday. Did you receive the victim notification?

After dropping in on Jenessa earlier this week with news of a possible murderer and his apparent interest in me, I've gone and delivered another bombshell. I should have called her, but I also need to beat the evening dinner rush. And just the idea of discussing Chet's release shortens my breath. How selfish and self-preserving of me, to choose my own comfort over Jenessa's.

I purse my lips, noting these instincts, and step out of my car. The three blocks to Four Alarm, to where it all began for me, are clear of foot traffic. Without a sure path forward, I'm crossing my fingers that something will stand out at the brewery, something I may have missed during the last frenzied visit under police supervision.

Door chimes announce my entry. Topher Cho looks up from wiping a glass behind the bar counter.

"Welcome to Four Alarm," he says. "Table?"

A current of déjà vu sweeps down my back. I shake my head as I cross to him at the bar. Tables that were nearly full last Saturday are now peppered with customers, spread out and speaking quietly.

"When did you guys reopen?" I ask, sliding onto a swivel bar chair. The question I want to ask is, *When did the police release you from questioning?*

He grabs the handles on either side of a keg and sets it down by the flap doors to the kitchen. It's impossible not to admire the muscles of his back, evident through the thin cotton of his T-shirt. A man pauses in eating his burger to watch, and a tomato splats onto his plate.

Topher returns to pour me a glass of water. "Yeah, we had a pause of two days. But things are back up and running."

"You mean, this was a crime scene and you were forced to shut down."

Dark-brown eyes narrow. "You read the news, huh? We're all hoping Four Alarm is done being examined now that the police have moved on. Have I seen you before?"

I lean an elbow onto the counter and rest half my face on my palm. Things would go from bad to worse if Topher recognized me from my visit on Saturday, before he discovered the body. "Ah, maybe. I was there—or, here—when police were still investigating in person. I'm the crime photographer. Claire."

Topher stiffens. His eyes dart past me to the street, probably looking for blue uniforms. If Topher had admitted anything damning to the police, he would have been formally arrested—not back at work. But he might still have insight that could lead to the killer. If I ask the right questions.

I throw him a big smile. "Everything okay?"

His laugh is a machine-gun chortle. "Yeah, yeah. Fine. I just didn't realize you were with the police. I've already told you guys everything I know, about how I found her, and—" He gulps. "How frightening the whole thing was."

If Topher believes I'm with Portland PD, all the better. I am a crime photographer. Only not for the police. "Of course. I'm just the shutterbug, so I'm not here to interrogate you or anything. I . . . plan on doing some promotional stuff for the department and need models. You're an actor, right? Do you model, too?"

He relaxes, running a hand through his hair. "I've done some print work."

"Bartending is a side hustle, then?"

I really want to ask Topher all the details of his misdemeanor and what went down between him and his ex. Knowing that won't happen in the light of day while he's working, I'll settle for chatting him up. Form my own conclusions about his personality.

Topher grabs a dish towel and begins cleaning the same pint glass he had when I walked in. "You got it. I moved down from Washington last year because Portland's film scene was booming. All kinds of great shows were being shot here, but lately auditions have been slower. But hey, you never know what's around the corner, right?"

He looks up wistfully before resuming eye contact. "I mean, I'm not desperate or anything for things to change. I'm very happy at Four Alarm. It's a great place to work."

"It seems like it." Remembering my conversation with Oz, I say, "You been signed by an agency yet?"

Topher shrugs. "Nah, not yet. I'd like to be."

"You've got a great look; I'm sure it'll happen."

He beams.

"How'd you decide you want to be an actor?" I ask.

The smile makes his brooding features magnetic. "I guess I've always thought that relationships are what's most interesting in this world, you know? It's not exactly who you know—more like how you make people feel. And acting is all about tapping into emotion like that."

I nod. "Seems like you know your stuff. Any agency is wrong not to give you a chance."

He shakes his head, floppy hair falling artistically across his face. "Man, I keep sending my headshot and YouTube reel, trying to get their attention. I think my stuff gets lost in their inbox."

"Wow, you have a reel?"

The pint glass sparkles in the sunshine slanting through the bay windows. The woman next to me licks her finger, having finished her burger and fries.

Topher places the glass on the bar. He withdraws his wallet from his back pocket, then removes a card. "Yeah, I mean, if you want, you can check it out here."

"Thanks." I take the square. "Hey, random question for you. Are there any good strip clubs close by?"

He lifts both eyebrows.

I shrug up to my ears and throw him another smile. "Strippers are great background in any law enforcement shoot."

He grabs the dish towel again. "I mean, we know the victim was a stripper, if that's what you're getting at . . ."

"Do we? I'm not following the investigation right now. I get in, take pictures, and get out. But hey, if you don't feel comfortable answering, I get it. I'll keep you in mind for our next photo shoot." I rise to stand, and he rushes to speak.

"No, I'm not—yeah, I mean, I've been to a few. The Drive-In is a fun spot."

"And El Cody's?"

He shakes his head, and more black hair flops. "Never been. I've heard it's fun, though. That's the vegan strip club."

"Thanks. And thanks again for the card."

He straightens, like I'm departing military. "Thank you . . . uh . . . Officer."

I lift a hand in a wave, then hightail it onto the sidewalk before any real uniforms arrive.

My phone buzzes, and I realize I missed three text messages from Jenessa. The first one contains only "mind blown" emojis, but she says she did know about Chet's parole:

Victim notification arrived two weeks ago, yes. Did you get yours? I've been trying not to think about it, honestly. You?

I exhale the breath I'd been holding, my whole body deflating. Relief and annoyance mix together—annoyance that Jenessa didn't tell me about the notification but mostly relief that I didn't just deliver another bombshell of unwanted news. At least she will be prepared for whatever happens come Monday.

Sweat forms underneath my arms and the backs of my legs as I walk the blocks to where I parked. My interaction with Topher went better than expected, even earning me a card with his contact information. He didn't seem to recognize me—not the response I would expect if the murderer was the same person who left me the anonymous note—but I can't help feeling the police aren't wrong to identify Topher Cho as a person of interest. A desire for fame, for notoriety, for extra followers—those are motives for murder. John Wilkes Booth was a respected theater actor before offing Lincoln. Now he's a household name.

When I arrive at my driver's side door, I startle at coming face-to-face with two sculpted dogs I hadn't noticed in my hurry earlier. No, not dogs—Chinese dragons. Stone jowls part midway in a roar or as if readying to eat me. I step back, one foot in the street to fully absorb the scene.

They're guard dragons, protecting Portland's Chinatown district. Crouching on either side of the road, they flank an ornate archway painted red and gold—colors meant to bring good luck, and which I recognize from when Rosemary first tried to teach us girls about our respective heritages.

My phone vibrates in my back pocket. An unknown number. I raise it to my ear. "Hello?"

"Claire Lou? This is Juan Montoya from the *Portland Gazette*. Are you the one who took photos recently for the *Post*? At Four Alarm Brewery."

"Yes, that was me."

"Excellent. Do you have any others of that crime scene? I'd like to feature some of them in the *Gazette*'s online channel."

"I can't." I shake my head, ruing the one-page contract I had to sign before Pauline handed me a check. The exclusivity clause said I couldn't supply photos to any of the *Post*'s competitors for six months. "I wish you would have called me sooner."

There's a sigh on the other end of the phone. "I thought as much. Pauline and her damn lawyers." The line clicks dead.

I stare at the phone until noise carries from farther down the narrow road, from past the storefront signs displaying Chinese characters in neon lettering. Music. Laughter. Glasses clinking. I follow the sound around a corner and find a door propped open. Hanging in the front window, a sign in English with characters beneath reads BEIJING SUZY'S.

Framed war-propaganda posters decorate the interior walls, evoking another time and place. As I step into the bar, I recognize a photograph of a student facing down a military tank in Tiananmen Square. Beside it hangs a frame of Bruce Lee from the movie *Enter the Dragon*, while a photo of a bowl of egg flower soup hangs above a trio of arcade machines.

"What'll it be?" A woman with electric-blue hair leans over the counter in a lace tank top. Behind her, a sign on the wall advertises Tsingtao beer, the green color clashing with her hair.

"I'm good. Thanks."

"You here for the Shanghai Tunnels? The entry is in the hotel across the street. Group tour is about to leave."

"Wasn't planning on it." But this isn't the first time they've come up. "What's so special about them?"

She snaps a bubble of pink gum. Heavy eyeliner emphasizes deep-set features. "They're Chinatown's claim to fame. But you don't have to wait to get a peek in, if you want. We got our own tourist attraction." She lifts both eyebrows and nods toward the wall.

"The dartboard?"

"What? No. Look down."

I follow her gaze to the floorboards. A square is cut into the wood directly beneath the bull's-eye. "Is that a trapdoor?"

She grins. "You betcha. Anyone tells you basements around here were only for rationing dry staples, they're either lying or they've never gone looking for the facts. Used to be there was a table and chairs over there, around the 1910s, 1920s, when this was a speakeasy. A man would get drunk enough, and the owner would hit a lever, having made a deal with some ship captain earlier in the day."

"A deal to what?"

"Hoodwink a drunk fool into working aboard a ship to China. But the man had to be drunk enough that he was about to pass out and wouldn't fight down below. He'd wake up a few hours later and try to leave—only to find he was barefoot and surrounded by broken glass." Purple lips pucker to the side. "Pretty sad, but pretty neat that the evidence still lives today."

"I thought that was all urban legend in Portland. That the practice was more in San Francisco or Seattle?"

She shrugs. "Depends who you ask."

I bend down over the square and touch the outline of the box shape. The edges of the door are worn, with several coats of paint, probably meant to match the rest of the black floors, becoming thick and uneven in the splintered cracks. My stomach tightens, touching a tool used to inflict such unusual punishment, imagining what it must have been like—plunging into the darkness and for a brief moment having no idea where it ended.

Beside me, a man plays the pinball machine in the corner, but we're the only ones in the bar on a Wednesday afternoon. I straighten, then turn to the bartender. "These aren't still used . . . are they?"

"Honey." She slides a hand onto a sharp hip. "Do I look like I need to trap a man?"

I thank her for the history lesson and promise to be in for a drink soon.

Back at my car, I step into the street. I lift my camera and angle upward. Framing the shot to capture both dragons' gaping mouths, I imagine hot breath upon my face, the sharpness of their teeth, before jaws snap shut around my neck.

Seventeen

An hour later they're still sleeping. I couldn't take lying there any longer, trying not to move, so I got up and went into the kitchen and tried to be helpful quiet as possible. Quiet like a mouse or a cockroach which Mama Rosemary says aren't my friends.

Mama Rosemary is upset again. On TV we see mamas who hug their babies and say everything will be okay. That they shouldn't worry and she'll fix whatever is the problem. Mama Rosemary can't do that sometimes because she's too sad. I tried telling her those things while she was sleeping but she didn't wake up. Only cried more in her sleep.

I sat still and wondered what happened to Twin's arm. Did she knock into the sink? Or did Mama Rosemary grab her when she was asking another question? I poked Twin again in her bruise. She woke up and hit me with her good arm but now she's back asleep.

First I sewed up the hole in my T-shirt under the sleeve. Then I closed up the rip in Sweet Lily's underpants. I even managed to get Twin's sock to close up at the toe so she doesn't have to go around with cold air getting in and biting her feet. All in all I only poked my fingers with the needle twice—once on my pointer finger and once on my tummy when the needle slipped.

"Sweetheart." Mama Rosemary stands in the doorway. "What have you been up to? I thought you were napping with us."

I show her everything I did and she's not sad anymore.

Sisters wake up and start moving around. Sweet Lily sits up in bed while Twin brings Sweet Lily water in a sippy cup. Mama Rosemary says that's okay because then water won't spill on the mattress.

Twin and me turn on the television and sit real close to watch cartoons. Mama Rosemary only lets us watch one hour per day and we already got our hour in the morning but she's sitting at the table writing something. She doesn't say anything when we turn the volume up. A dog runs around a glacier and says *Awesome-sauce!* Me and Twin start laughing every time.

"Awesome-sauce," I whisper. Emmy and Max walk in a green place. A forest. Then they're trapped with their dragon friends in a mountain house. A cave. They talk about escape to get back home to their beds. Max ties a rope around the rock blocking the exit then ties the other end around him. He pulls real real hard and everyone helps and then the rock moves and Emmy and Max and the dragon friends get out.

Twin wraps her hand over and under my hair and yanks. "Ow!" I say.

"Move over, you're too close."

I don't move because I'm mad and Twin pulls my hair again harder. "Ow!"

"Hey, you two, knock it off. I'm trying to think." Mama Rosemary looks at the paper still.

"Mama?" I ask her and rub my head. My hair still hurts so I pinch Twin's leg. She makes a face and I think maybe I gave her the bruise on her arm. "Are we still doing escape today?"

Twin hits me again then looks at her, too.

Mama Rosemary takes a second to reply. I think maybe she's forgotten my question. "Are we still doing escape—"

"We have to. There's no other way around it." Mama's voice is low and she stares at the table in front of her. "We can't stay here, and we can't risk him changing the code again."

"What code?" Twin asks. Mama Rosemary looks at me and doesn't talk.

Twin was asleep the last time when the Murphy was done squeaking but I was awake. The man went up the stairs like always only this time he needed help because he was too drunk. He's drunk a lot when he comes to visit. Mama had to help him and I could hear the stairs extra loud then and thought they might break. The man entered the code—*beep beep beep beep beep-beep*—then he was gone. I came out to say hi and good night to Mama and she was writing on a paper. When she saw me she said *Go to bed!* and looked all scared and scary. She said not to tell my sisters what I saw or heard. I did not.

"Never mind, sweetheart. We just have to leave."

"What code, Mama? What code? Tell us what code!"

Sweet Lily moans from the next room. Twin's mouth sours like that time she ate a rotted apple.

"But Sweet Lily is sick again and she can't ever move when she gets like that. We have to wait for her. We can't leave her!" Twin's voice gets high and I look to Mama's face to make sure Twin is wrong, that we would never leave Sweet Lily.

Mama inhales a deep breath. She stares at one of Sweet Lily's drawings on the wall. "It's been done before. And sometimes, it's the right call. To leave someone behind while the rest of us try and get help, to make it possible for everyone to get out, not just one or two of us. We could go fast. Have the police back here in twenty minutes."

Mama's words leave me feeling cold. Sweaty like I'm the one with a fever. *Leave someone behind.* Her voice is the same warm but her words make me feel sick. Worse than when I wake up screaming thinking someone is touching me.

"We can't do that to Sweet Lily," I whisper. Not sure whether the littlest of us can hear. "Not gonna do it."

"But I don't wanna stay either," Twin says. Her eyes go big and round.

"Baby, look at me. Look at me, both of you," she says again when I won't. Slowly I raise my head to her neck. "No one wants to leave Sweet Lily alone, but think of each other. What about your Twin, hmm? We need to leave."

Twin makes a squishy sound. "But . . . Sweet Lily."

Mama Rosemary thinks for a second. "It's not going to be easy, darling," she says to her. "And you'll need to be brave."

The way Mama Rosemary looks at Twin makes me nervous. Like Mama wants something from Twin. Just like everyone else. I start to get angry. Frustrated that Twin is the center of attention again. But then I see Twin's face. It's pale. Empty like she's already reading Mama's mind. And knows exactly what Mama is going to ask.

Eighteen

It's not exactly who you know—more like how you make people feel.

How can you know where you're going unless you examine where you've been?

Create a new identity.

Snippets of conversations from yesterday reverberate in my head. A deep need swells within me to be done with this and to put our never-ending saga to bed. To move on. The well-meaning words of advice I've been given fail to consider that I've already tried normal methods of coping—being a considerate person, doing self-reflection and therapy, and trying to leave the stigma behind haven't worked. I'm still here, trudging through life with this target on my back, courtesy of Chet.

In order to figure out the murderer's identity before Chet is released in four days, I need to be more intentional with my sources. Neither of my sisters is going to pluck the exact memory from their childhoods and adulthoods to point the finger at the asshole harassing me. The police have released only the bare-minimum details on the dead dancer and the insurance salesman, not mentioning at all his side hustle of selling his artwork.

No. If I still have a chance in hell of figuring out what's going on before someone else is hurt, it's going to be by asking the hard questions face-to-face.

From where I stand outside the chain-link fence topped with barbed wire, the state prison is already crowded with visitors. I get in line behind a woman with a wide-brimmed turquoise hat, bearing an actual plume along the band. Words are hushed except for one family in the front, who whoops and squeals that today has finally arrived; their person is being released. Their glee continues as guards inspect identification, then wave each person through a gate in the fence and past an armed guard brandishing an automatic rifle.

The signs that pointed to the visitors' parking lot a half mile down also directed me to a shuttle waiting to ferry passengers to the main security gate. Thursday afternoon—apparently the perfect time to engage with your incarcerated loved one. I stepped off the yellow school bus to anxious memories of arriving at elementary school as a child. A similar taut feeling coils in my belly now, like a garden hose ready to burst.

Ten minutes pass in line before I'm admitted into a stuffy waiting room. I take a seat and try to blend in. A soap opera plays on a boxy television mounted on the wall.

After another half hour, my name is called, and I'm ushered into a rectangular room with four people who all seem to be visiting the same inmate. We step through a metal detector, then into a long hallway with flickering lighting panels overhead that give off the ambience of a psych hospital in a horror movie just before the power goes out in a thunderstorm and all the patients run loose to exact their revenge. The air is dense with body odor.

We turn left into a shallow hallway. Another armed guard grants us entry into a room where a wall of Plexiglas bisects ten visitor booths. Each cubby comes complete with a landline phone. Beige is the central theme, accenting the walls and the chair I lower myself into. Inmates enter the other side of the room and spot their visitors with a grateful smile, a laugh, or a somber meeting of the eyes.

Emotions churn in my belly, a cesspool of hate mixed with terror, but I sit still. I jam my hands under my thighs and, for some reason, feel relieved I chose a high-neck dress.

He can't hurt you.

You're not a child anymore.

You can leave now, and no one will know you were here aside from the lobby clerk.

I clutch the strap of my shoulder bag and rise to exit the way that I entered when a man walks to the chair opposite my own. Handcuffed, knobby knuckles curl over the metal seat back. The top two buttons of an orange jumpsuit are undone, revealing a white shirt underneath. Scraggly beard hairs punctuate a pudgy face. Deep lines mark the skin around tired brown eyes. Chet takes a seat, then slowly lifts the telephone from its cradle. Hesitation gives way to curiosity, and I see his gaze take in my face, my neck, my chest, and my hands, before flicking back up to my eyes. It registers that he's never seen me before; he doesn't recognize me. Rosemary, I know, has never come to see her former captor, and I know my sisters wouldn't dream of it; I don't know if Nora has been here.

Strange feeling, given that I memorized photos of him when he was somewhere around the age at which he abducted my mothers. I had just turned ten years old and gained more understanding of what had happened to us, and I wanted to know what he looked like. The occasional tabloid cover story over the years featured photos of him in prison looking depressed and disheveled.

He can't hurt you. Mustering every ounce of strength I have to not run away, to not run screaming from the past as I have done my whole life, I imitate his movement until I have the receiver to my ear. "Hello, Chet."

He hesitates at my voice. Then a smile lifts his cheeks. "Marissa. Nice of you to come all this way."

A shudder ripples across the thin fabric of my dress. "You know who I am?"

He nods, pleased that I wasn't expecting this. "I've tried to keep up with you online. There was a snapshot of you a few years back that I think still looks like you."

Nausea boils in my stomach, realizing that all these years I was worried someone was watching me, maintaining a record of my mistakes and self-involved loathing, it was Chet. I grip the leather of my bag, digging my nails into the thick material.

"Chet, I came to ask you a few questions. Not for some kind of reunion." My tone is gruff, loud, but people beside us continue their conversations, untroubled; witnessing someone yell in this room is probably a square on the prison-visit bingo card.

Chet leans in closer, pressing the phone to his face. "What kind of questions?"

I inhale a deep breath. Try to wrap my head around this moment and that it's actually happening. That through the coiled wire of the phone, winding along the plastic rings through the glass barrier to Chet's receiver, we are physically connected. The thought makes me gag.

"I'm working on . . . a photography project."

He sits up straight, his thin eyebrows lifting into his hairline. Something like excitement passes across the gray stubble around his mouth. A new wave of revulsion coats my body; that's the same way Lily reacts when she's intrigued by something.

"How can I help?"

I pause, savoring withholding something from him for once. His face is open and eager from behind the glass, and the urge to rise up and leave without another word, just to make him wonder and wait and wait and wait, returns to contract the muscles in my toes.

"There's a killer committing murders underground, or transferring the bodies underground afterward. I'm taking photos of the crime scenes."

According to the *Post* update I read in line outside, the body in the cooler at The Stakehouse, Gavin Nilsson, was restrained in the adjacent tunnels before being moved behind the kegs. After his throat was slit. When I read that, my gasp drew concerned looks from the strangers beside me. It's probably for the best that I didn't examine the body more closely on-site.

"How many?"

"Two. So far."

He shifts the receiver to his other ear, his handcuffs knocking together. "What else?"

"The victims are an exotic dancer and an insurance salesman."

"Interesting pairing. What links the victims together?"

"The police don't know yet."

"Ah. They're working on that part while you're profiling the killer?" A smile forms on Chet's mouth—hinting at pride or mocking me, I can't tell.

I purse my lips and glance at the guard behind Chet. He's preoccupied with another inmate who's getting riled up at the far end of the room. "That's all you've got? Nothing about you sharing obvious psychology with this killer, since you both kept your victims underground?"

The smile drops like a mask. "I'm not a killer, Marissa." His voice is stern, as if he's doing an impression of an angry father.

"You let Bethel die."

Shia's eager face at the coffee shop flashes to mind, recounting his research of the toy company listed on the cardboard found beneath our bed. "Who else knew about us? Who else knew you were keeping us imprisoned, our mothers imprisoned, for years?"

Chet stammers, opens his mouth, then closes it. He tries again. "What makes you think anyone else knew?"

I stare at him, will my eyes to bore holes into his head and force some kind of pain to travel through these six inches of barrier. "Jameson.

Your father. He knew about us." Chet begins to speak again, but I talk over him into the phone. "He knew, and yet he did nothing, too."

I spit the words, and I wonder why I bothered to come here. What the hell I expected to unearth by confronting this man for the first time. How desperate I was to believe something productive might come from this visit.

As I stand, Chet lifts his palms, pleading for me to stay and listen. I grudgingly bring the phone back up to my ear.

"Marissa, there's nothing I can say . . . that might undo what I've done. I'll grant you that. But I've spent twenty years thinking about my actions. About the sickness that told me to keep you all to myself. Your killer would be hurting people—keeping them underground—for the power of it, too. He'd enjoy flexing that control over his victims. Maybe as a punishment? If I had to guess, I'd say it comes down to whatever the victims have in common. That's where you'll find your killer."

I allow myself to consider his words and sit back down. Despite wanting to chalk up everything he says to a waste of air—he could be right.

"Why should I listen to you? You're not a psychologist."

"No, but this is a state prison. I've been surrounded by the worst of the worst for two decades. Believe me when I say I know more than I'd like."

I fix him with a blank expression and watch for any tic that might give him away. "Are you involved in these murders?"

What if Chet is partnering with someone? What if, driven by some personal stake, he's the one leaving clues from my childhood around Portland? If I could prove his involvement in these deaths, Chet would be locked up forever. I'd never have to see him or worry about my sisters seeing him again. The thought brings a smile to my face, and Chet mirrors my expression, encouraged.

"No, Marissa. I am not."

I stand again, done with this conversation.

He lifts another hand. "Please," he says. "I'll be released on parole Monday. Once that happens, I'd like to see you. And your sisters. I know Jenessa is in town, but does Lily live nearby—"

"What makes you think I live in Portland?" I snap, racking my brain trying to recall whether I let that information slip.

Chet fixes me with a stare. "Do you?" I don't answer. "You do, don't you? You wouldn't have driven all the way up from southern Oregon or anywhere else for this conversation. You live in Portland, because it's only two hours away and the risk of wasting your time and energy is small compared to the possible benefits."

Dumbfounded, I stutter, "Wh-why . . . what—what makes you think that?"

He's perfectly at ease on his side of the room. "Because it's how I would assess whether or not to come here."

Disgust burns through my limbs, outrage at his suggestion we're so alike. "I don't care what your plans were, don't come near us," I hiss into the speaker.

My anger balloons at the thought of him loose—tracking me down like that *Tru Lives* reporter, bothering Lily when she's eight months pregnant.

Speaking into the phone and towering over his hunched shoulders, I seethe—feel myself coming unglued. "Stay away from us."

"Marissa." His voice is calm. The exact opposite of my shaking frame. "I loved you girls in my own—"

I slam the phone down. Marching to the door, I bang my fist against it. The guard on the other side opens it and lets me pass, her arm poised on her firearm. I stalk back down the long hall, no longer bothered by the noise of male inmates shouting somewhere in the building, and retrieve my two forms of ID and pepper spray from the lobby clerk.

"Can I help you with anything else?" the man asks. His clip-on tie skews off-center.

"Nope, all set. Thanks," I say, still fuming. Then my eyes land on the sign-in sheet and my messy signature. "Hey, could you tell me who has been to visit an inmate? It's my . . . father."

The clerk raises an eyebrow.

"I'd like to make sure my grandmother has been in to see him over the last month. She's got Alzheimer's, and her recall is spotty."

The eyebrow lowers. He taps a few keys on his keyboard, then clicks with his mouse. "Over the last month, he's had Karin Degrassi and Shia Tua come to visit. Are either of those your grandma?"

My face goes slack. "No. Nana must be confusing things again."

Outside the prison, fresh air swirls my hair, loose at my shoulders, while my stomach tightens in knots. I raise my camera to eye level and snap a photo of the concrete entrance. All the better to compare to the nightmares sure to come later tonight.

Climbing the steps of the shuttle bus back to visitors' parking, I look down as a sharp pain registers. "Miss? You all right?" the bus driver asks.

Blood dots from my palm as I uncurl my fist and release the aching flesh. "Just fine," I reply.

The driver sees what I've done, and she hands me a tissue that feels like sandpaper. "Family can be complicated, miss. I promise you ain't the only one that feels that way."

I take a seat in the first empty row I see and keep my gaze straight ahead. The gray mass of the prison slides by my peripheral vision.

Shia lied to me. Or rather, he didn't have to—he omitted the fact that he'd paid Chet a visit.

Once in my car, I navigate eastern Oregon's major freeway on autopilot; the drive home passes without conscious effort. Seeing my exit at the last minute, I cut hard across a lane of traffic.

When I finally trudge up to my doorway, my eyes feel heavy beneath the weight of my afternoon and more revelations than I care to remember. The flower bed below my window is in need of watering, and beside it, bird poop is caked on the concrete edge of the walkway. A stick from a discarded lollipop lies a foot into my hallway.

I stop dead. A white piece of paper peeks from the corner of my doormat.

The hall is empty. Scanning behind me, there's only a neighbor across the parking lot unloading mulch from his truck.

Clutching my keys like a weapon—pointed ends first—I bend down and grab the square. The message reads:

Lucky number three
Depends on you.
Find and photograph the location
Before I get tired of waiting.
THREE MORE DAYS, MISSY.

I unlock the door, maintaining a white-knuckle grip on the note, and head straight for the kitchen. After uncorking a bottle of wine, I pour myself a pint glass, then lay the note on the kitchen counter.

Three more days, Missy. Chet will be released in three days. That fact, paired with this author's use of "Missy" leaves little doubt: whatever his reason for killing these people, it's related to my family.

The red liquid hits the back of my throat with a satisfying twinge, the black-cherry currants rolling along my tongue. The beginning of a haze settles over me, along with a thin film of clarity.

Although I've avoided my past—thinking about it, coming to terms with it—for as long as life would allow me, I can't stick my head in the sand anymore. For some perverse reason I don't yet grasp, this person has fixated on me more so than a fan might, and in order to solve this next riddle before someone else dies, I have to start exploring my memories instead of suppressing them.

I need to be honest with myself—about everything.

Nineteen

Drunk patrons dance and sing along to a retro jukebox occupying the corner of Ezra's Brewery and Restaurant. Shia waves his hand in front of my face. "Claire? Should we go over this again?"

I shake my head. "No. I mean, yes. Yeah, say it again."

I spent the rest of the afternoon in a daze after seeing Chet, then reading another threatening message, this one delivered right to my door. I sat on my couch and began searching listings online for any brewery location associated with luck, lucky number three, or the number three. Or bracelets. Jewelry shops selling items made by children.

Nothing made sense. I began reviewing the photographs that I took at Four Alarm and The Stakehouse, rereading this second message again and again, its meaning becoming increasingly potent with each review: someone else may die depending on how fast I solve this clue. Someone has already been chosen as the next victim.

This was different than the first note. At Four Alarm and The Stakehouse, the victims were already dead, decaying to some degree when they were found. The realization that the killer has linked me to the fate of this third person seized my chest and made me sit forward on the couch cushions to hyperventilate between my knees. When I was able to catch my breath, I downed the rest of my pint glass.

Shia called me, asking to meet up for one of his sessions, and suggested Ezra's. I wanted to hang up on him right then and there, but the envelope of cash hidden beneath my mattress and his promise of another, much larger paycheck kept me from being rude. Instead, I showed up thirty minutes late.

He takes a deep swig of his stout ale, then plucks a thick-cut french fry from our basket. Our new meeting point definitely has advantages over the library's community room.

"Okay. We're trying to determine what did Marissa, the child born in captivity, experience that no one knows about, what wasn't reported on the news or already beaten to death by human-interest pieces over the years?"

Excellent question. Others might be: what does the killer think he knows about me, and why does he keep looping in details from my early years? Why did Shia go to visit Chet but not tell me about it? My initial fear that Shia is the note writer returns. Scanning the wall behind him, I locate the glowing green letters of the emergency exit sign. Just in case.

Lucky number three depends on you. Three more days, Missy.

"Claire?" He pushes thin glasses higher on his nose. A black ink smudge covers the bone of his wrist.

Although he was drafting his manuscript before we met, Shia has been working day and night to make progress faster. He's already one hundred pages in.

He leans across the tall bistro tabletop. "Think hard. I'm sure it was normal in a lot of ways, but how was it abnormal, knowing what you know now? Try and remember what it was like, being a five-year-old underground."

My legs dangle from the chair as I weigh his prompt. "I was generally happy for most of it. We were like any kids in tight spaces, bumping into each other, playing games, and retreating to our separate corners when we needed space; we didn't know what we didn't have. Rosemary allowed us to watch television, and at first, she said it was all make-believe—that the people we'd see on there weren't real. Then when we got older and started asking questions, she said some things were real—people on talk shows—while other things were just make-believe and for fun—like cartoons and movies. Nora was there for the first few years before she escaped, and I remember her telling me that ice cream was real when I was about three years old. Rosemary was so pissed because she thought that would start the landslide of questions from us girls. And she was right. I sympathized, even as a small child, but I was also beyond curious to know what it tasted like after that and what else was real that I thought was a game or make-believe."

Shia slides his phone closer to me, recording my every inhale and crunch. "Where is Nora now?"

I shrug and wipe my hands on a paper napkin.

"Don't know. She seemed enthralled with the florist shop she bought with her settlement money. I haven't heard from her in years, but I know she's taken up traveling recently." My voice drops off, hearing my sadness at not having contact with a woman who was so involved in my life at the beginning. "Jenessa actually asked to live with us after we were out. It was a big thing between Nora and Rosemary."

"Wow, I'll bet. How did that turn out?"

"I think the courts kind of decided? I felt terrible for Nora after that. She went through rough phases of depression and was in and out of psychotherapy. I know she was on some medications, and Jenessa said there were a few months of dissociation, too. No one really processed our time in captivity well."

"Except you."

I pause in wiping the beads of sweat from my beer glass. "What does that mean?"

"You're the only one who managed to adjust to outside living, to deal with all the emotional baggage of your past. You made it. Whereas everyone else, all the other women, and Chet included, have struggled to get by."

Shia looks at me with something like arrogance. Part of me wants to throw his drink in his face and then smash the glass on the warehouse floor. "You don't know me. You don't know how I've processed anything, and you sure as hell can't judge me against my sisters or mothers."

He nods and uses my moment of ire to take another sip. "Fair enough. I overstepped. Let's talk about your mothers. Was that ever weird calling them all Mom?"

"Mama," I correct, still huffy. "They were all Mama plus their first names."

"What was that like, having multiple mothers? Did you feel more affectionate toward one or the other?"

Mama Bethel used to braid my hair before bed, and I would lay my head on her belly and wait for the baby to kick. "They were so young, and all of us were desperate for comfort and kinship. I would say no. It was like one big commune. Everyone cared for each other, regardless of who birthed you. We were all connected anyway."

"You were all connected by tragedy and circumstance?"

"You could say that."

Shia writes something down. He looks up. "What was your interaction like with Chet?"

The question stiffens my back. "I went to see him. Earlier today."

He lays the pen on the page. "Really? What was that like?"

For a moment, I debate keeping my knowledge to myself. But I doubt the snarl on my face will allow that much longer. "I found out you went to visit him."

His face blanches. "You did?"

"What were you doing there?" Heat climbs my neck. "Why didn't you tell me?"

He sits forward. "I went to speak to him, just like I asked Jenessa and you to speak to me. Chet didn't want to see me, though. So I left without even a face-to-face."

I cross my arms. "Is that supposed to make it okay?"

A smile slides across Shia's mouth. "This is my job, Claire. I was trying to get sources for my book. I'm sorry if I gave you another impression."

"You didn't," I snip. We sit awkwardly for a minute while we both digest that I thought Shia was better than seeking out the monster who ruined so many lives.

"Who is Karin Degrassi?" I ask.

Black eyebrows draw together. "No idea. Should I?"

"She was Chet's other visitor this month."

"Huh." He chews his pen a moment. "Sounds familiar. I'll do some digging and let you know if I find anything. Do you want to talk about your visit to him? Your impressions of Chet?"

"He was exactly what I thought he might be. Self-involved. Presumptuous."

"What were his spirits like, days before his release?"

I shrug, and the white envelope underneath my mattress returns to mind, pressing me to earn my paycheck. "I mean . . . it was my first time seeing him. He seemed . . . secure. Expectant. Assured of his freedom."

In truth, he was a sad, longer version of what I once knew him as: a terror, a resident player in my nightmares, although I'm not sure I could have picked him out of a lineup before this morning. The way he used to look at me as a child would send me crawling into my mother's lap, covering my ears, waiting for her shouting to die down and for him to return upstairs. I'm not sure I even remembered that until now. Or maybe I did but tried to excise anything related to him from my mind. Being honest with myself, as I vowed I would be, might be painful.

I flag down our waiter for another beer. Wheat. Citrusy. Big. The smell of something deep fried wafts from the next table over.

"What else do you remember of him from when you were a kid?"

I look down at my hands, tan with knobby fingers. Other scars from my adolescence mar the wrists and knuckles in white lines, matching the polka dots of my inner elbow and its still-healing scab.

"The way he walked. His footsteps always seemed heavy, foreboding, coming down the stairs. In hindsight, that was probably the floorboards being old and him owning a Victorian. His footsteps were the first sign that he was on his way, and it was a three-times-a-week ritual. It was never a surprise, those heavy steps. The reaction they elicited in us was one of stress."

"What would he do once he was down there?"

"Once a month, he would inspect us. Inspect the women first. Rosemary later told me her theory was that Chet was ex-military, but it turned out he's a germaphobe; despite us being insulated from any serious diseases, he wanted to make sure we were all clean and well cared for physically. So it was first the women, then us girls."

"How did he inspect you kids?"

The words lodge in my throat. I blink back tears. "When we were very small, we were running around in diapers all the time, so it wasn't unusual for us to be naked. When we started wearing clothing more consistently, we would have to undress." My cheeks flush, speaking my childhood shame.

The waiter returns with my beer, and I whisper a grateful "Thank you."

Shia watches me a moment. He doesn't try to lighten the mood or sympathize or say something utterly trite that people think will make things better when it can't. When I feel in control of myself again, I exhale a deep breath. "I haven't thought about our day-to-day in a long time."

"Normal." He squints at me with a reassuring smile. "And you haven't been interrogated by police on the minutiae in a while. You have a lot of darkness to navigate but nothing to be ashamed of."

His words trigger another memory, more recent than the ones we're diving into—a theory. From a conversation I overheard outside the brewery and a thread I saw on an online forum for Portland crime lovers: the murders were committed for fun; anyone can hire someone to provide that kind of fringe sport if you know where to look. "Have you spent much time on the dark web?"

Shia pauses his sip of beer. "Isn't that a bit of a non sequitur?"

"I mean, a little. But I'm not the only one with darkness. I heard someone talking about . . ." Although Shia is aware that I'm taking photos for the *Post*, I don't want to advertise that I'm eavesdropping on law enforcement. "Well, what is it? The dark web."

Shia drums his fingers on a laminated menu. "It's part of the regular web. An overlay network that uses the internet, but you need certain software to access it. Because it's encrypted, there are a lot of offbeat activities that go on there."

"And how do you know about it? What's a mild-mannered journalist doing, poking around there?"

Shia examines me. My suspicion. "To be honest with you, a lot. I weighed theories about your family—your locations, your backgrounds, what went on in your basement—against what other people had dug up over the years. A lot of conspiracy theorists, and those interested in your family, are users. They think the government knew about Chet's secret family."

"Fantastic." Sarcasm steams through my words. Knowing now how dedicated Shia is to this book, he probably knows some of these users by name.

Shia sinks into a deep nod, folding his hands across his flat belly. Curly black hair falls from behind his ear. "Claire, I want to be candid with you. I can tell it's not always easy to explore these moments, particularly if you weren't aware of certain details or if you've repressed them. Are you getting something out of this arrangement? Is it helping you the way you thought it might?"

The more I learn about his tenacious research, the less I view Shia as some wide-eyed creative. But after a beer and the wine I drank at home, the anger I felt upon coming here shifts to indifference. "I mean, it's bringing up a lot of stuff for me, sure. Did I tell you about the stuffed animal?"

He shakes his head.

"Off the record." I lean forward.

Shia cocks his head at me, as though not fully trusting this potential gift. A black tattoo—a spiral fern—is visible on the left side of his neck, the kind I've seen on rugby players from New Zealand. He clicks the recorder to pause. "Of course."

"I think the Four Alarm killer knows me. Like, knows who I am and my background as Chet's offspring. Do you think other people may have tracked my steps like you did? Could someone else do the same thing?"

"I mean, it's possible." He cringes, as though speaking a truth he's not sure I'm ready for.

I'm ready. I've been aware of the perverts and weirdos since I was thirteen. I've always known they're out there. Just didn't realize they'd all find me at once or become so frenzied around this particular anniversary. "What are you getting out of this? Besides your publisher's paycheck."

Shia crosses his arms and leans backward. "Isn't it usually my job to ask the questions?"

"Tit for tat today."

He purses his lips into a thin line. "Okay. Like, did I grow up in a basement also?"

"Let's start there, sure."

The thin line breaks into a small smile. "The high-level summary is, I grew up atypically, too. My mother dumped me off at a fire station when I was a year old, and I shuffled through the foster-care system my entire childhood. As a result, I think I've always been attracted to stories that demonstrate resilience. That we aren't defined by our beginnings or by the choices our parents made for us. We can define ourselves. I think that's what you've done, and I want to highlight that."

"That . . . was not what I was expecting."

Shia lifts his pint to me before taking a drink. "Happy to surprise you."

A moment passes between us, the tenuous trust I felt with him growing. He's got some darkness, too.

"I have a theory," I resume. "At the first crime scene, there was a stuffed animal outside the entrance. It was the same as my stuffed animal in the basement; at the second crime scene, the body wore a bracelet like I used to make with my sisters. Knowing that, let me rephrase: Do you think the killer knows *of* me, the way that you do, or does the killer *know* me personally?"

Thick eyebrows glue together. "Stuffed animal? From your childhood? What one was that?"

"You don't know?" A sinking sensation floats in my belly.

"Wait. It's not . . . what was his name . . . Peter the Pelican?" Shia looks at me, his upper lip raised in doubt.

"Petey. He's called Petey the Penguin."

"That's right. You were photographed holding him in the hospital. I remember now."

Relief swims across my eyes. "Okay. Whoever's behind this could be a tabloid fan or someone who has a personal connection to me. So that doesn't narrow down the pool."

"No, I guess not."

We're silent a moment, and the brewery's patrons, the music, laughter, and clinking glass, seem to rush forward. A clamor incongruent with our discussion, with what is driving each of us to meet.

Shia pays for our meal, insisting that he'll write off the expense later. We agree to dig into the activity hours that Rosemary established to provide us with routine in our next session.

On the drive home, exhaustion pulls like weights on my eyelids, but Shia's words rebound in my head. Despite his suggestion that he can use my memories, capitalize on my history just like the other grubby vultures, he is providing context for the many people emerging from the woodwork. And speaking to Shia about meeting Chet gave me the idea for a plan tomorrow.

After stunted, failed attempts as a teenager to gain clarity from Rosemary, to get specifics when I asked questions about my origins, it's time to try again. This week—this killer—doesn't really leave me the option.

Twenty

The next day, rolling hills sprawl before my windshield on the winding road to Arch. Spruce firs and pine trees, my friends growing up, line the road as if welcoming me home. There weren't many trees around where our house was located in the desert of Oregon, but the few there were felt like wise caretakers watching out for us, vigilant throughout time and able to confirm that whatever crisis was occurring, whatever we had already lived through, would pass.

Along the highway, patches of black earth from a recent wildfire interrupt the greenery in sporadic bursts, marking the areas where firefighters were unable to succeed in subduing the flames. Seems I'm not the only one who acquired new scars.

I didn't want to come home, let alone remove myself so far from Portland, where the *Post* could call at any minute with a request for coverage. The update this morning on the "tunnel murders"—what the Four Alarm and Stakehouse crimes are now being called—was less than encouraging. Gia Silva continues to be the chief person of interest, while Topher Cho, on the other hand, has been cleared of suspicion. Having taken the liberty of scrolling through Topher's social media posts, I have to agree. The mix of selfies and inspirational quotes about achieving one's dreams didn't strike me as belonging to a killer, even one who's interested in boosting his acting career.

Meanwhile, Gia's got a history of living on the street, of drug use, and of ties to local drug lords who've committed serious crimes, including murder. But as a nineteen-year-old girl, she's only ever occupied the periphery of those incidents. Counterintuitively, the police seem to think that's why she's the ringleader—the brains behind it all. And at one point, she was found sleeping in the tunnels below Four Alarm—a direct link between Gia and the first victim.

Without more to go on, I'm returning home and hoping for some big reveal in Arch. Following bread crumbs of details I'm remembering with Shia is the only thing I've done that resembles progress. Rosemary's recollections of a time when so many of my own experiences were a blur may be the light bulb I need.

Downtown Arch is picturesque. Shadows from today's overcast skies cut the painful glare of the river that runs through the town. Boutiques and some larger, corporate shops have replaced family-owned standbys, reminding me that life continues to roll forward even when I wish it would stop forever and Monday would never come. The ice-cream shop run by the Wilkinsons still pulses; a few early-bird customers enjoy a cone beneath the store's awning, searching for relief from the region's dusty, dry air.

I pass the elementary school where I attended grades three through six. After a year of adjusting and minimal homeschooling as she had done with us underground, Rosemary was told I had to transition to public school and a normal life. Wounding emotions limp to mind, recalling the way other kids avoided me for months—they had all heard I was demon spawn and born of incest. I was isolated that first year, until Lily joined me when she was admitted to kindergarten.

A new plastic jungle gym lies in place of the old metal one that used to stand in the sandbox. A phantom itch tickles my chin as the road veers left and I drive on by. It was there that Vera Hutchinson called me a dirty mutt while I was hanging upside down on a bar. Startled by the insult, I slipped from the metal and split my chin open on the ground.

The houses age as I make a right, becoming smaller in size. Chipped paint and dilapidated sideboards warped by the arid heat signal that I'm almost there. A lone dog trots beside the road, balancing to avoid the ditch. Uneven mange is visible from my driver's seat as I pass, but the dog looks alert—on the hunt for something besides trashed leftovers. He pauses to pee on a discarded Christmas tree, brown and brittle in April. Despite all the updated fixtures and new businesses thriving in downtown Arch, not all of the town's neighborhoods have changed for the better.

Outside a faded yellow house with a modest front porch, I put my car in park. Before I can consider turning around and grabbing some liquid courage at the local liquor store, the front door opens, followed by the screen door. Rosemary steps forward, her hands folded beneath her ample chest and wearing a smile that matches. Straight black hair that hasn't faded with time is piled in a wild bun, and she wears sweat-pants stained with something dark. Her solid red shirt reminds me of when I was twelve and she slept in that exact outfit for a week, unable to rouse herself to change or bathe.

"Hi, Rose—" I stop myself. "Hi, Mom." I step from the driver's seat and leave the door unlocked. No one followed me all the way out to Arch, and everyone already knows who I am here. They wouldn't let me forget it.

Rosemary darts a look for any spying neighbors, then waves me forward. "Come, come. Let's get inside."

The urge to roll my eyes pulls upward like a magnet. I focus that energy into a tight-lipped smile. "Mom, when is the last time you were out of the house?"

She tucks a strand of hair behind her ear, as if genuinely worried someone might see her this way, then shrinks back into the shadows of the porch roof. Her thin skin is more papery in appearance than I remember it. She's turning fifty this year, but dark circles beneath her dim brown eyes and those deep lines at the corners peg her as closer to sixty. "Hurry up—it's going to rain."

As if on cue, thick clouds clap overhead. Drops of water find my head, my shoulders, and then I'm walking quickly into the house I swore I would only return to when someone died. Internally, I note the irony: someone did.

Musty air enshrouds me like a veil the moment I pass over the threshold. The shag carpet from the 1970s that I always felt was akin to Mary Poppins's bag—you never knew what you might find in its thick fringe—was old when Rosemary purchased the house back in the early 2000s. We bounced around from apartment to apartment in Portland, trying to find the right spot, before realizing we couldn't remain where we'd been imprisoned. We moved to Arch when I started school, and Rosemary found this one-story. She used as little of the settlement money as possible, as she knew she might never work a real job again. And aside from the year she dished out ice cream on Main Street when Lily needed a new surgery, she hasn't.

"Lemonade?" Rosemary calls over her shoulder. She walks past the front room that's filled with cartons and has been since I turned sixteen. Labels across the cardboard tops identify the supplies she uses for her Etsy embroidery business: yarn, needles, a loom, and various colors of thread. When it was clear the money was running out, Rosemary turned to the skills she learned as a kid, and she tried to teach me, too, however terrible I was at it.

"Sure." I move a box that reads SHIPPING SUPPLIES written in permanent marker.

"You talked to your sister lately?"

"Which one?" I murmur.

"What's that?" Glasses clink from the kitchen, and I can picture her reaching up to the highest shelf in the cabinet to the left of the sink for what she deems the Good Cups—actual glass instead of the plastic kind we used growing up because we kept breaking everything.

"I said, which one? They're both in Portland."

Rustling in a drawer stops, and I know she's paused in riffling through all the drink-mix packets she's stored up over the years. She walks back into the front room where I sit wedged between cartons and a stack of coats she laid across the headrest of the couch. "Lily's back? From Switzerland?"

Rosemary's face lights up, then drops like a sheet. Lily didn't tell her—that she was returning home or that she was already here. I'll bet she doesn't know that Lily is pregnant, either. My heart actually hurts for Rosemary a moment, watching her alternate between joy and sadness as she processes what this news might mean. Then a corduroy jacket brushes my cheek, a reminder that Rosemary loved her things, her comforting possessions, more than us—more than providing us with a clean home where clothing was put away and boxes didn't fall on kids when they were studying on the floor. The feeling of pity goes away.

"Yeah, she is. Just a week ago or something. Recently. You haven't spoken to her?"

Rosemary purses thin lips. "Not yet. She's a good girl, though. She'll call."

Lily—my free spirit of a sister—call, because it's the right thing to do? Not likely. She's always lived by her own rules. While the rest of us have felt encumbered by our history, Lily seemed liberated by it. *We already lived the worst there is in this world,* she'd say. *What are the odds of something like that happening to us again?*

The rustling in the kitchen resumes, and I take a moment to admire the number of storage bins Rosemary has managed to fit in the rectangular space. The couch and love seat that have occupied this room since forever haven't moved, only now they come with a blanket on the cushions—presumably to cover the wear and tear of twenty years.

"Do you think it's time for new furniture? This couch is ancient." A spring digs into my left cheek, as if protesting my critique.

Rosemary returns with two glasses of swirling opaque liquid. Thunder growls outside in the distance. "Too expensive. These are perfectly fine. Besides, there are good memories on them." She goes to place our lemonade on the wooden table, but finding no space available, she nods to me. "Can you?"

I move the closest box to the floor, and she puts down our cups. Her hands free, she moves another carton from the couch to the floor beside her, then props her feet up on it.

"It's gotten pretty bad, hasn't it?" She looks around the room. Beneath the cardboard boxes are plastic containers. Through the side of one, the spines of binders I used in the fifth grade are visible: SCIENCE, READING, and SOCIAL STUDIES. Adjacent boxes are labeled in Rosemary's square handwriting—BAKING WARE, BROKEN DISHES, LILY'S TRAINING BRAS, MARISSA'S DENTAL EQUIPMENT. During middle school, I had to wear a head guard while I slept. In my defense, everyone grinds their teeth at that age—twelve years old is a stressful time, especially if you're called Pissy Missy.

Rosemary heaves a deep sigh. "I should probably get rid of some stuff. You want any of it?" She waves a flat palm like she's on a game show, showcasing product.

"Afraid not."

"No, I get it. I probably wouldn't give it to you, even if you said yes." She laughs, a hard sound. "Difficult to part with things you've grown used to seeing. Once you've had them taken away at one point, that is."

I don't know whether she's referencing being imprisoned by Chet or the furniture company that came a few years ago to repossess a dresser she'd bought online after she failed to make the final payment. I sip my lemonade instead of commenting. My mouth automatically sours as the drink's sugar lights up my tongue.

"Oh! Do you want to see the changes I made to your bedroom?"

I follow her down the hall. A thin layer of dust crests the framed photos of Lily and me decorating the walls. We pass Lily's room, still swathed in baby-pink everything. By the time she got old enough to find she preferred other colors—bright creams and sunny yellows—Rosemary had given up trying to find a job in between her intermittent bouts of depression; she didn't have the money to buy us new bedroom decor. However, when Lily and I each turned eighteen, we did receive the money set aside for us from the settlement: $40,000. We could have decorated our rooms in crushed velvet if we wanted, but by that point we were ready to move out.

I turn in to the last door on the left, opposite Rosemary's master bedroom, and face the scene of my adolescence. Stark white was always my style from the time I was allowed to choose things for myself. White bedspread, white drawers, white binders. The only color visible is the blue marker I used to decorate the binders, still stacked on the pale wooden desk, and black circles where I accidentally dropped cigarettes while blowing rings out my bedroom window. My arm tingles, and I absentmindedly touch my scars.

Looking back, I was fascinated with fire as a child. The first time I saw a live, flickering candle, I was almost eight. A flame seemed so powerful, potent in its capacity to destroy. Which is exactly how I viewed myself.

"What do you think?" Rosemary beams at me from the doorway. I touch the desk with a finger and it comes up clean.

"What am I looking at, exactly?"

She makes a face. "There are no boxes? Hello? I cleared them out for you so you could stay the night. What do you think?" she says again.

That's why there's no dust. The desk used to be a holding pad for whatever supplies she carried for baby announcement T-shirts or embroidery items reading HOME SWEET [Insert City]. "That's very nice, Mom. Where'd you put all of it?"

"Oh, I know you'll say I should put things away more fully and organize them properly and all that, but I just threw them on my bed for now. I'll sleep around them."

Her bedroom door is the only closed door that we passed. No doubt steeped in towering boxes, just like the front room. Years ago, I tried to convince her to throw out the comic books that I collected as a kid—none of them valuable—and blankets stained from a failed science experiment, but she's held on to them.

"Actually, I have to get going after this. I told you about doing photos for the *Portland Post*, right? That's why I came down here."

Disappointment lengthens her narrow features, and my chest pinches with that persistent pitying feeling. And guilt that I know I shouldn't allow in.

"But I haven't seen you . . . in ages. Not since last June."

When I don't answer, she hugs both her elbows tight.

Restricting our time to an annual visit is hurtful, I know. Especially considering I've been only two hours away for much of the last year. But I also know what I missed out on all that time: watching Rosemary bury her life in scraps of fabric from clothing we outgrew and expired packages of macaroni and cheese, because it was a favorite of hers as a teenager and she never wants to go without it again.

In my head, I understand her compulsion to amass possessions after everything was taken from her during a morning run when she was twenty; I get it. But watching her wither away to a woman who scurries past her own front door to avoid the neighbors or any other sign of life that might take away her mac and cheese again—that has been painful to watch. Once Rosemary had made some friends online and joined some virtual book clubs, I told myself I didn't have to maintain regular visits anymore.

"I know it's been a while. I'm sorry about that, but we call each other on the phone, right? We video chat? I do need your help," I add. "Can we talk on the couch?"

Her face brightens a little. "Okay."

We settle back into our respective spaces among the memory-laden containers. Rain taps against the front windows. It makes the inside of the house feel even stuffier, but I know better than to ask to turn on the air conditioner.

"Remember how I said I'm freelancing at crime scenes? Well, it's complicated. It seems like someone involved in the crimes knows about me. About us."

Rosemary's eyes widen. "Is that so?"

"More than that. I think they're leaving me notes to . . . to threaten me. To goad me."

"I don't like this."

"So I did something else. Something drastic."

I don't know if Rosemary is aware of the anniversary or that Chet will be released on parole soon—mostly, she focuses on getting through the day and on to the next. "I went to see Chet in prison. To see if he could help me profile this killer, whose mode of operation seems very similar to his."

Rosemary's mouth opens, then closes. She spies her glass of lemonade and drinks half of it in one gulp. She stares across the room a moment, then sets the cup back down. "You know he's getting out on parole Monday. Did you get the victim notification?"

I shake my head. "I think my mail is delayed while it's being forwarded from my last address."

"Well, I don't think you should be working on anything crime related, Marissa. It's too close to home. Promise me you'll ask to be reassigned somewhere else."

"I can't do that. I'm brand-new to the *Post*, and I need this steady income."

She shakes her head again. Her eyes drift to my shoulder, glazing over; I wonder what she's seeing.

"Mom?"

"All your life," she whispers, "you handled it differently from Lily or me, and I think better than Jenessa and Nora, too. Nora, she's . . . she's had some trouble. Bad stuff. When she emailed me at Christmas, she was switching to new antipsychotics. I've struggled with depression; we all know that. But when Nora escaped, she went to her family and was shunned. They said she allowed herself to be kidnapped and then assaulted. She hadn't even told them about Jenessa being born. At least I didn't have any family to break my heart once we were free."

I take in Rosemary's wide eyes and the crease that sits between them. She was the only child of two immigrants from southern China, who died from carbon monoxide poisoning while Rosemary was spending the night at a friend's.

"You've never told me that about Nora before."

She shrugs. "It wasn't mine to share. However, if you think working on this murder plot is a good idea, I'll tell you everything I know. It hasn't been easy for you, and I don't want you to get caught up in this. To live out more pain."

"What do you mean? What 'it'? Our captivity? I'm past that. I've done the work; we all have; we should all be past it." Panic whose source I can't identify surges in my throat.

"Babies, you know? They come into this world, and no matter where life takes them, they always exhibit some personality at birth. They take that spark of themselves throughout life, and it grows and evolves, assuming different shapes. But it's always there."

"Mom. What are you talking about? You sound like a fortune cookie."

She sits forward and clasps my hands in hers. Long fingernails I hadn't noticed before cut into my skin while she looks me in the eye. "I want you to get as far away from this case as possible, Marissa. You handled our family's origins . . . differently from the rest of us. You've been angry, rightfully so. And there is documentation of that anger. Most of it we know is sealed in school records, but I have pink slips from principals here in these boxes, too. God only knows what you got into off the record. But if anyone is trying to implicate you in a case that's similar to ours, to make it look like you're repeating something that Chet did—"

Her hands move to cup my face. Her skin is cold against mine, and the shock of her body temperature in this heat steals my words. "Run. You run away from those crime scenes and that case as fast as you can. Do you hear me? Take up a job as a checkout clerk—do whatever you have to, run away. Promise me you'll stay far from this case. Promise."

I slowly pull her hands back. I had hoped Rosemary would impart some obscure fact about my upbringing to direct my next steps. Instead, she's given voice to the same fear that's been tingling at the back of my mind—that the killer may be setting me up. "I hear you. I'll . . . I'll find something else to do at the *Post*."

Rosemary exhales, then sinks back into the couch cushions. "Good."

I sip my lemonade, grateful for something to focus on. Out of the corner of my eye, I watch her. She stares straight ahead, as though exhausted.

When I hug her goodbye, she feels limp in my arms. "You'll come visit again soon?" she asks.

I want to know when was the last time she left the house—whether all her food is delivered by drone or delivery service as I suspect it is—but I can glean the answer by the darty way she peeks through the curtains before unlocking the front door.

The drive is much longer on the way home.

When I was fourteen, I went digging in one of the boxes Rosemary had only begun to accumulate. Photos of a young woman with thick black side-swept bangs were protected in a shoebox; she was sunning herself on the beach while surrounded by friends and admirers.

That woman was kidnapped by Chet. Her carefree spirit died in his basement compound.

The courts said that Bethel was the only one who died there—*only one woman*, the male defense attorney said, as if that demonstrated care on Chet's behalf and deserved leniency. But I knew better. Rosemary left whatever shred of herself that remained below when she climbed the eight steps up to the main floor of Chet's house—with not simply the daughter she birthed but three girls in tow.

Twenty-One

Mama Rosemary rushes around pulling out books and medicines and forks and spoons I haven't seen in years and years. She opens all drawers looking through everything again and again. She turns and sees me watching her instead of *Arctic Adventures* with Twin.

Lily is still lying in bed but she's not sleeping anymore. She's humming a song now but I don't know what it is. "Row Row Row Your Boat"? No more like "Can You Feel the Love Tonight" from *The Lion King* maybe. That movie is the best. I'm like Simba the leader of the kids. Twin thinks she's Simba but she's wrong. She barely does her chores and instead lies around all depressive. Just like Mama Rosemary sometimes.

"Have you girls seen my necklace?" Mama Rosemary looks at us.

I nudge Twin in the elbow and she looks at me all sharp. "Hey!"

"Girls," Mama says again and her voice is mad. "My necklace?"

Twin picks at the hole in her sock. "Maybe Mama Nora took it with her."

My eyes are still on the TV. Petey the Penguin slides down a snowy mountain on his belly and I lay down on my belly, too. His friends Sasha the Sea Lion and Heathrow the Husky are missing and he knows it's his responsibility to find them—even if it's dangerous. It's our duty to the people we love. To help. Especially when we're scared.

"Or Mama Bethel?" Twin asks.

"No, honey, Mama Bethel didn't take it. Mama Nora, though. There's a thought." Mama goes into the bed room and a drawer opens, then closes. Another one opens and closes.

"Dude. You guys!" Her voice is long and whiny like Lily's when she's cranky. "Who taped my necklace to the side of the nightstand? Jesus." Mama makes a frustrated noise—like *Auuuughhhhh*.

A loud noise from the bed room. *Crash!* I look to see if Mama needs me if she's upset and crying again but it's quiet. Then the mattress squeaks and Mama's gotten on the bed to check on Lily. Soft voices talk.

I don't answer Mama because I saw Twin tape the necklace last week after playing in the Before Clothes. She said she wanted to keep it for her own because she has to share everything here. Mama keeps all her Before Clothes in the bottom drawer the biggest one because she says it makes her sad to see them. All our clothes are in the top two drawers and a plastic tub by the kitchen sink and we can go in there and see them all the time if we want. But Mama Rosemary says her Before Clothes we're not allowed to touch. Twin went in and played while Mama was resting the way she does with her eyes open for hours staring at the wall. Sometimes when I stare at the wall I try to make shapes in the dirt with my mind and see a hidden dog or a cat.

Twin put on the necklace and the stretchy pants that made her legs look even littler. And the stretchy top over her head. And the headphones Mama says play music if you have a battery in the little square plastic player. Twin put Mama's running shoes on her feet and those were too big, too. Then she danced around like a dummy pretending to be Whitney Houston the woman in the tape inside the plastic player. We both sang without singing out loud. *Ohhhhh I wanna dance with somebody! I wanna feel the heat with somebod-AY!*

Twin asked for a little dog once—another word though—a puppy—and Mama said there was no room. Which I thought was wrong because Mama Nora left already a year ago then.

There's barely room for the four of us! Mama said in her high voice. Twin mumbled *But it could protect us* and Mama just said *It's time for geography lessons.*

"Girls." Mama Rosemary stands in the doorway without a door. "I need you to choose one toy to take with you. Can you do that, please?"

When we were five years old Twin asked Mama Rosemary *How come we call that doorway between this room and the bed room "a door-way"? There's no door. The only real door is the front door above the stairs that the man always uses and we're not allowed to use. So why is that a door-way?* She looked at her and said *Be quiet please.*

Both me and Twin get up and go to our toy crate. Mama calls it a *toy box* but it's not a box. There's no lid. We each pick out a toy and hand it to Mama. I choose Petey the Penguin my Christmas gift two years ago.

"Thank you, girls. Now hurry up and get dressed for bed," she says.

"But whyyyy?" Twin asks.

"Because I said so, please."

I run and put on the long-sleeve nightgown Mama made from one of Mama Nora's old T-shirts. The nightstand is moved against the wall because Mama kicked it. Twin comes in the bed room and tugs the nightgown off my shoulder. "I was gonna wear that!" she whisper-yells. It sounds like a whisper but her face is yelling.

"Well, I got here first," I whisper back. I push her hand off me and finish buttoning up to my neck. The nightgown hangs all the way down to my knees and I feel like I'm in a big bag of cozy.

Something heavy knocks my head and I see white spots. I look around for a brick but only see the words book that Mama Rosemary makes us memorize sometimes. I touch where it hurts and my skin goes *bump bump* like the clock's little hand. Twin stands away from me her face all angry.

"Mama Rosemary," I yell. "Twin threw the . . . the dictionary at me again!"

"Hey." Mama Rosemary pokes her head in. "I need you two to behave. Now and after we leave here if we want to stay together. Do you want that?"

"Yes. But I didn't do anything!" I say.

"Then hush now." Mama Rosemary disappears.

Twin only makes a face like she might cry. Her eyes get all big then they snatch around the room looking for something. She goes to the top drawer of the nightstand but Mama hasn't made us all nightgowns yet. Twin pulls out a regular shirt and loose shorts that we have to tie with a rope that Mama Rosemary taught us how to braid. She fiddles with the rope then climbs into bed. I climb in beside her careful not to touch the brown stain that peeks through a hole in the sheet.

Footsteps come from overhead near what I know is the front door. The real doorway. Then the door song begins and I realize that's what Lily was humming earlier—the up and down sounds of buttons being pushed from outside and upstairs. Mushed together they sound like a song. *Beep beep beep beep beep-beep.* I hum it back to myself. *Hum hum hum hum hum-hum.* Twin kicks me beneath the covers and my head goes *bump bump* again.

Voices come from the front room. Mama Rosemary says something in a low tone.

"We'll get to that. I want to see them," the man says.

The man breathes through his mouth when he steps into the fake doorway. He smells like the whiskey Mama says makes people not themselves. I don't understand that. And he smells like the time Mama Rosemary forgot about our toast and the bread burned in the pan and smoke filled the front room. Both rooms smelled awful for days.

My heart beats in my chest like a scared bunny and I shut my eyes tight.

"Sleeping already?" he says.

He never comes into our room. When we do inspections it's always in the other room.

When he comes to visit we stay asleep or pretending to be in bed while he and Mama Rosemary pull down the Murphy in the other room. The Murphy squeaks and makes groaning sounds like when I jump on the mattress. Then the man leaves. Why is the man not leaving? Why is he standing over us? He's closest to me and my stomach squeezes. My heart is so loud I think it might wake Lily who's lying between me and Twin.

Footsteps move. The man walks to the other side of the bed. To stand over Twin. I open my eyes just a little.

His face is covered in gray hairs—like old people I've seen on the television. His head hair is cut like Barbie's boyfriend Ken and his eyes are brown like mine. He reaches out and pulls the blanket from Twin's shoulder. I stop breathing. His fingers hover over Twin's arm uncovered in her T-shirt and move down her skin like he's painting. She shivers and we don't have to be real twins for me to know what she's feeling. I look at his face again then my stomach twists and I feel sick.

"Ready?" Mama Rosemary's voice comes from nearby and it sounds mean. Not her voice she uses with us. I shut my eyes again.

No one talks. No one moves. Then the footsteps walk back slowly toward the doorway. The Murphy creaks down. And it begins to squeak.

Twenty-Two

My phone vibrates, clatters, dances from the surface of the moving box I'm still using as an end table and falls to the floor with a *bang*. I move from my kitchen, coffee in hand, and scoop up my phone just in time to swipe right. "Pauline, hi."

"Claire? We need you down in Northwest as soon as possible."

Instinctively, I look through the blinds of my window to my car. The windshield is free of any threatening notes. "Sure, I can do that. What happened?"

"A third body. I'll text you the address, but the place is called Trois Croissants."

"Trois . . . ?"

"Yeah, *trois* means *three* in French. It's some family-owned bakery, and it's being swarmed by police and our competitor outlets as we speak. Get there as soon as you can."

She hangs up, and I dive to my bed, where I stacked the notes I've received, and Shia's business card, in a pile. The most recent one, which had been wedged under my doormat, is on top.

Lucky number three depends on you.

Horror mounts in my chest as I realize my error. While I went traipsing down to Arch to gain some form of insight from Rosemary—and what did I leave with exactly?—I missed the deadline. It hasn't even been two days since this note appeared, but the killer took action. Someone else is dead because of me.

Crowds pile onto the sidewalks of Northwest Fir Street for Saturday morning brunch. A line winds out the front door of a glass-walled restaurant, forcing me to dodge bodies and weave between emphatic gestures. I sidestep a laughing woman despite the impulse to freeze and take her backhand against my head.

I'm responsible for this. I'm to blame.

After the six hours of driving yesterday and the abrasive ringtone of my phone so early this morning, my whole body is achy. I crack my neck to release the dull pain. Music blasts from a passing car stereo, and I step into the crosswalk before the red hand symbol changes to white.

Behind the officers standing guard at the perimeter, a green-trimmed window advertises fresh baked goods daily. Police are visible through the glass, taking notes, speaking to witnesses, examining the site for evidence.

Lucky number three depends on you.

As I stand beneath the sign TROIS CROISSANTS, another memory surges forward: *The baker goes for flour. He's gone for an hour. He makes what he wants. A big, fat croissant.* Rosemary made us do arts and crafts for an hour the day of our escape, and we made braided bracelets using that rhyme as directions.

We made three bracelets that day, one for each of us. "Three croissants," I whisper, remembering.

The image of the second body in the cooler and the bracelet he wore flashes to mind. It was a clue meant to lead me to this bakery and the dead body waiting inside.

Black hair comes into focus from around the corner. Shia.

"Hey, Claire." He lifts a hand in hello.

I cast an eye for Oz or anyone else I know from the *Post* and see only nondescript police officers whom I haven't met yet. "Hey. What are you doing here?"

Shia shifts his weight and looks down at the sidewalk. A spray-painted stencil filling one square of concrete says KEEP PORTLAND WEIRD!

"I was in the area, and I saw all the excitement. I thought it might have something to do with . . ." His voice trails off as my expression hardens.

"You were in the area?"

He shuffles his feet. "Nearby, yeah."

"You're here way too promptly. You have a radio scanner, don't you?" I shake my head. "One that monitors police communications, so you know when and where a crime has occurred. Is that right?"

I stare at Shia with a mix of surprise and resignation. For some reason, I believed he was a purist when it came to journalism or writing or whatever he does—I thought he genuinely wanted to share the facts, versus being the first one to share them. Disappointment number two, counting his visit to Chet. He's like the rest of them, desiring to report on the most blood and gain the most profit from a tragedy. Teenage recollections of reporters waiting outside my high school jolt forward and fuel my distaste now.

Shia, for his part, looks embarrassed. "Isn't that what you're doing here? As a freelance photographer for the crime beat?"

"It's different." I sneer before I remember I'm supposed to be simply Claire in this space—sweet, hardworking photographer with nothing to hide.

"Look, I thought maybe this murder had something to do with your fa—with Chet. Do you think it does?" He drops the remorse and peers over my shoulder to the scene behind me.

I shake my head again. "I don't know. I have work to do."

"See you Monday?" Shia's voice trails me as I step around someone shouting into a loudspeaker—*Move back, respect the police tape*—and slide beneath the yellow barrier. I flash my press badge to a cop, then slip into the bakery's interior.

Pauline made me take a photo for the badge after I finished the marketing team's headshots. With wide eyes and tense cheeks, my portrait looks every bit as uncomfortable as I feel now.

"Hey, it's my favorite intern," Oz says to me. "Good of you to join. You're late." Bright-green eyes flick below my collarbone in an appreciative glance.

A few heads turn at the scolding, but I ignore them. "What happened here?"

"The owner went downstairs this morning looking for his grandson's baseball mitt. He got more than he bargained for when he went poking around the boxes in the basement."

"Ms. Lou. Ready? *The Oregonian* is already below." Sergeant Peugeot appears from a narrow hall, clutching an extra-large paper coffee cup. Without waiting for an answer, he turns on his heel.

"Be right back," I say to Oz. A few men pass Peugeot, carrying clear plastic bags containing fabric. Beside a cramped counter, a display case presents rows of neatly arranged golden croissants, chocolate croissants, tarts, other pastries I don't know the names of, and sandwiches. My belly grumbles.

The baker goes for flour. He's gone for an hour.

We head into the hallway. A pair of bicycles is propped against the side wall, a child's baseball hat dangling from one of the handlebars. Beside them is a crepe maker, something I recognize from an old Belgian movie I saw at an indie theater. Tape across the top of a plastic bin reads, WINTER COATS.

Peugeot pauses to speak with a slight man who reaches the sergeant's shoulders. I get closer and realize they're speaking French. Peugeot says something to interrupt the man, then waves me forward. He leads me through a door that's been propped open, then continues downstairs. A moldy smell rushes my nostrils. Dull light emanates from the corner.

Police personnel crouch along the ground, where the concrete cedes to earth, shining flashlights into crevices, searching for something. Handheld lamps are placed along the perimeter of the dug-out enclosure, and a quick glance ahead shows that it leads to a longer path—to the network of underground passageways. A body lies on the ground with a tarp over it. Beside it are a can of kerosene and a burned match, each accompanied by a plastic number, likely placed by forensics, and something else: a blanket—the white kind with stripes that's usually given to newborns at the hospital. Chet gave one to Bethel when Lily was born. I adopted the blanket for my own and slept with it from ages four to seven. I climbed out of Chet's basement clutching on to it, and the image was memorialized in a photo snapped by someone at the hospital later. When someone searches my name online, that's the first image that pops up.

I suck in a sharp breath, recognizing the scratchy material. I wore the blanket as a dress, played with it like a cape, ate with it, carried it across the two rooms and back again during exercise hour, and loved it so much that I was devastated when the seams of one of its hems came loose and a hole ripped through the middle. Although Rosemary tried to sew it back together, my blanket was never the same. I couldn't look at it without recalling my own carelessness. I had ruined something I loved.

"Turns out," Peugeot now says to another officer, "the bakery owner also owns the property next door. It's his family home. The passage extends from below his kitchen and partially under his business."

Straightening, I take in the layers of dust on each item stored in the basement, the old rug covering the cement floor, and the lack of intended entryway to the next cell, where the body was found. "Did the owner know about the passageway? Was it boarded up before?" I ask.

Both officers turn to me like I just sprouted horns. "Ms. Lou." Peugeot glares at me. "Time to take your photos so you can leave."

The photographer from *The Oregonian* pauses in the corner, where he snaps pictures of baking paper, then resumes clicking faster than before.

I nod.

Peugeot and the other officer continue discussing the victim. He was burned, hence the can of kerosene, but the medical examiner is still determining the cause of death. My camera is heavy as I withdraw it from its case and sling it around my neck. Although Sergeant Peugeot warned me not to take photos of the body, I sneak one of the blanket.

The two officers continue speaking at low volume. "He did know about the passageway. Detectives are questioning him in his home right now."

"You think he's involved somehow?" An extra bar above the second officer's badge reads LIEUTENANT.

Peugeot shrugs. "The fact is we now have three bodies left in or near this underground set of passages. We need someone to confirm what else we should know about these tunnels. Lou. Jankowski." He turns to me and the other photographer. "Let's go."

Back outside the bakery, several onlookers snap photos on their phones and record the storefront activity. A car honks at the crowd spilling onto the road. I pull my hair from my ponytail and try to hide behind it as Peugeot says something about the utmost confidentiality and respect being shown to law enforcement when I'm invited to a crime scene. He makes me show him the photos I took inside, as if eavesdropping on one conversation shot my credibility.

As he flips through the three dozen pictures, relief courses through me. I just cleared my memory card last night, and I make it a habit each time I download images to my computer. If someone saw the photos I took of the body in The Stakehouse's cooler, it would be apocalyptic on all levels.

Peugeot lifts his eyes to mine. "All right. You're free to go." He hands back my camera, then heads indoors.

"Sergeant Peugeot?"

He pauses, already past the threshold. "Yeah?"

My tongue slides between my lips, hesitates.

"Spit it out, Lou. I've got things to do." He turns sideways to allow another officer to pass.

"Right. I was just wondering—is Gia Silva still a person of interest in these murders?"

Peugeot's eyes narrow. "Yes, she is. You can follow the updates on any local news website. Now, if you'll excuse me—"

"She's not it," I blurt out. "She's not your murderer or your ring-leader. She's too young, and she couldn't have . . ." Words pointing out the low likelihood of her knowing as many facts about my family as the killer does die on my lips. But as Peugeot takes a step toward me, good sense replaces the momentary impulse—the desire to save someone else from the prejudgment I've struggled against. Sharing my rationale would only expose me before I've got anything to offer the world in my defense.

"How's that, Lou? You were saying she's not our murderer. Who is, if not Gia Silva?" Peugeot crosses meaty forearms.

I slide my hands into my pockets, place my weight on my heels. "I've just been reading the news reports and trying to wrap my head around it all. The police obviously know more than I do."

He doesn't say anything but continues sizing me up. Then he turns and walks back into the bakery.

Oz bumps up against my elbow, startling me. "Just finished inter-viewing the deputy chief. They got fingerprints off a pair of dog tags the victim was wearing."

I release a breath, feeling my pulse throb in my neck. Why suggest any kind of theory that contradicts the police? Drawing attention to myself outside of being a crime photographer will only cast suspicion on me, exactly as Rosemary worried.

I rub my jaw. "Dog tags? Was he military?"

Oz seems to dance, shifting his feet in excitement. "No, the ones you buy for five ninety-nine at an accessories shop. Nothing unique about them, except a fingerprint that doesn't match the victim's—or the fingerprints found on the other bodies." Oz widens his stance. "Apparently, none of the prints found on the three victims matches the other crime scenes, and there's no record for any of them in the database."

"Not even a misdemeanor? No prior infractions?"

Oz shrugs, looking almost gleeful. "It's not often that criminals surprise me, but this one—these criminals—did. I think it's a coordinated gang. Plus, don't forget juvenile records are sealed. It's possible these guys did break the law, but we just don't have visibility."

"Ah, yeah, I hadn't thought of that." I have, in fact, been thinking of that my whole life, ever since I became an adult and left the dark years behind me—legally, anyway.

However, the rest of Oz's logic doesn't add up. "Though, just because these people don't have a police record and the fingerprints are inconsistent doesn't mean there's some network of bad guys out there. Maybe this guy knew enough not to leave prints."

He scoffs. "I thought you wanted to intern with me, Claire?"

"Oh, c'mon, I—"

"No, no. If you feel like you have a better grasp on crime scenes—this being, what, your third—please enlighten me on this criminal's profile."

I roll my eyes. "Fine. Your theory is possible. I'll give you that."

"I accept your apology."

"Well, what else did the deputy chief say? Does this third body have anything in common with the others?"

The first was a stripper; the second was an insurance salesman who also sold original paintings. If this latest victim knew either of them, there might be some pattern.

Oz scratches his stubbled chin. "The victims all seem distinct. No obvious link among them. I'm just glad the police are finally looking somewhere besides a street kid."

Something shifts in Oz's frame. Emerald eyes half close, augmenting the bedroom stare he seems unable to switch off with women. A dog walker with short, wavy hair sashays past us, momentarily distracting Oz before he resumes his seduction. "What are you doing later?"

"Why?"

He licks his lower lip. A smile spreads across his pointed jaw, and he could be straight off a red carpet somewhere or in a candlelit restaurant on a date. "You see, Claire, that reply is exactly why I'm intrigued. It's not just the no-nonsense attitude I enjoy or the schoolmarm way you think leaving two buttons undone on your shirt is casual. It's that fire that says you want a proper welcome to Portland as much as I want to give it to you."

"Wow, Oz. Sexual harassment went out of style in the nineties."

He laughs a big, confident chuckle, self-assurance still intact. "When are you going to let me take you out? I've tried to be subtle, but I think you'll notice it's not my strong—"

I lift a hand to stop him. With Chet's release Monday, my thoughts have been a mass of distractions. I don't have the time or energy to deal with Oz's lack of boundaries. Attractive or no.

"Rain check. Maybe we can invite Pauline, then."

Oz grabs my hand as I turn to leave. "If you change your mind, I'll be hanging out at Beijing Suzy's later."

I nod, recognizing the name of the bar I explored in Chinatown with the trapdoor. His touch is calloused, warm against the brisk morning air, like he runs hot. This close to him, my stomach tenses. The appealing sensation moves lower to curl around my thighs.

His thumb strokes the back of my hand before I pull away. "Good to know," I say.

As I walk back to my car, clearing my head of Oz's pheromones, my phone rings. *Jenessa* scrolls across the screen.

"Hey," I answer, dodging a teenage couple. "What's up?"

"Marissa, have you seen it?" Her voice is taut with panic. Hairs on my neck stand alert.

"No, what is it?"

"I sent you the link via text. It's bad. It's going viral right now. You need to see it."

I switch her to speakerphone with shaky fingers and open our text messages. We haven't exchanged more than ten since I got home. Tapping the link is easier than it should be for what I fear awaits. YouTube pops up in my browser, and the video's headline stops my breath: Missy Mo: Pissed and All Grown Up.

"Um? I mean—Claire!"

"What the hell is this?" My voice mirrors hers now. I can't tear my eyes from my own frozen image—hand raised and preparing to throw the *Tru Lives* reporter's phone into traffic. "Who did this?"

Typing comes through the speaker, and Jenessa must be researching the video from her desktop. "The poster is anonymous, some dumb pseudonym with numbers after it. It was uploaded this morning, and I just saw a hashtag about it on Twitter. The good news is you can't see your face, since it was filmed from behind."

"But everyone already assumes it is me—that the headline is true?" My words are shaky, and I feel ashamed of how much I hope she answers *no*.

"Yeah, I'm sorry. But we only see your back. Hard to tell who it is from that angle."

I click the "Play" button and watch my own antics from last week—so self-righteous, enraged. I approach the woman, lure her in with my calm appearance, then snatch the phone and heave it onto the freeway like a maniac. The number of thumbs-downs vastly outweighs the thumbs-ups in the comments section.

Run. You run away from those crime scenes and that case as fast as you can.

"I look insane," I murmur, holding the phone at my chin. "Can we tell anything else about the poster?"

Jenessa types more through the phone. "Not that I know of. This is the only video uploaded by the account. What were you doing anyway? Who is that woman?"

"She's a reporter. For some TV show. She caught me off guard."

Jenessa snorts. "Is that why you threw her phone?"

I lift my eyes toward the low-hanging clouds. "I threw her phone because she was going to record me and expose me, and I didn't want her to follow me again. And I was pissed."

"Just like the video's title."

"Shit," I moan. "Who was filming from around the corner? She mentioned she received a letter from Serena Delle with directions on where to find me."

"Who's Serena Delle?"

"A high school classmate. It doesn't matter." I lean against a steel lamppost, run a hand down my face. "Who would benefit from this video being published? A clip of me acting like a violent jackass but which clearly has some traction with people . . ."

Jenessa is silent on the other end, and the answer comes to me.

"I gotta go."

"What? Who did it? Who do you think?"

"I'll call you later." I hang up, wishing I had another phone to throw.

The drive across downtown is quick and gives me just enough time to visualize all the ways I'm going to kill him.

Shia taps away on his laptop in the window of his favorite coffee shop, Stump City, the one he first suggested we meet at, where he shared he *always comes to write*. I park across the street, then march up the walkway. Flinging open the door earns me a hard look from the cashier. People texting on their phones—or maybe watching a certain viral video—look up at the brash jangle of the entryway's bells. Shia remains engrossed in his screen.

Get a grip. Relax. Skewer him with words, not fists. Don't prove the video right.

"Shia," I say, standing over him.

He tears his head from his laptop with a start. His face melts into a smile, and he tucks hair out of his face. "Hey. We should have carpooled from Trois Croissants."

I slide into the empty seat at his table and close his laptop. "Why did you do it?"

His eyes narrow. "Do what?"

"Record me with the reporter. Upload the video to YouTube." I dart a glance around us to make sure no one is listening. One man catches my eye. I lean closer to Shia. "I don't know why you used a high school classmate's name to sign your letter, but you would have known all about Serena Delle and thought she was a good cover. You told that reporter where to find me, and who I am, so she could antagonize me. Then you recorded me smashing her phone."

"What?" He scoffs; then the humor fades from his expression. "You think I would sell your location to someone? Why? What's in that scenario for me—a *more* guarded and closed-off Claire?"

Two men enter the coffee shop, initiating the jangle of the door handle's bells. More people to take note of our terse conversation. People who may be following me, hoping for another round of internet fodder. Coffee brews from behind the counter, and the smell is heady, filling the air, giving me the illusion of a caffeine contact high, adding to my adrenaline and nerves.

"Because it'll help your book. Because if you drum up more interest from the public, your book will sell better when it's released and your publisher will be even happier with you. It's the same reason you use a police scanner to show up at crime scenes you think are relevant to my story."

Shia stares at me without speaking. Sudden doubt punts my anger and replaces it with the feeling that I'm wrong and I am making a jackass of myself.

"You think that of me?" he asks in a low voice.

"I don't know you," I reply. We've only had four meetings so far, all of them around or under an hour and within the last week.

On a basic level, I know he tips the server 20 percent because he says he remembers how challenging the service industry can be; he stops recording our conversations whenever I want to speak off the record; he's shared insight on my family, details I never knew; he's shared that he grew up in the foster system and had an awful start, too. All these facts, while endearing maybe, don't explain what truly drives him—why he's obsessed with my story the way that he is and why he's better than any of the other bottom dwellers out there seeking to exploit my life for their amusement.

Shia scowls as he leans over his laptop. "I did not collaborate with anyone, least of all some scummy reporter who surprised you somewhere. I haven't seen a video, and I'm not sure it would help my book if you're painted as an unhinged person, destroying private property."

Outside, through the window, someone stares at us across the street beneath a leafy tree. The man walks closer, and I prepare to stand and run when he pauses at the entry. He points a finger at the wall and examines the menu posted on the brick. I inhale a shaky breath.

"You have motive. You have a reason to get all that you can out of our interaction and my presence in this city."

Shia shakes his head side to side, and the outrage dissipates from my frame, leaving me feeling weak and foolish.

"You're paranoid. You know that? All I've ever desired to do is help you. Yes, that leads to a profit for me—both financially and in my career—but they're not mutually exclusive. I can help you and myself at the same time. It's what I've tried to make clear since first meeting you. Seems I've failed there."

"Look, someone is following me. I can't explain it, but it's true, and I have to look for who would have an obvious reason to do that, don't I?"

He slides his laptop into his gray backpack, then stands. "I'll see you Monday if you're still up for it. I hope you get some rest, Claire. It must be exhausting assuming everyone is out to get you."

Clouds roll in, replacing the tentative sunshine of the morning. On the drive back home, Shia's words replay in my head over and over: *You're paranoid.* The assertion rankles me, grates at my pride and the certainty that I've succeeded in dodging the prescribed fallout of my origins—what the professionals all suggest I should spiral toward. The certainty that I've avoided going down the same path as Jenessa—drug addiction, dead-end relationships, and a few nights in jail after an alcohol binge during which she broke a storefront window—or, in a lesser form, the apathetic attitude of Lily, who's never seen value in pursuing a career, savings, or a stable address. Although maybe that will change now that she's about to have a child.

If I'm being fair, Shia's not wrong. I never keep male friends; I don't trust men. Rosemary never dated or married after we joined the rest of the world, and her visceral anxiety whenever a man approached our brood in a supermarket, the bank, or our elementary school wriggled its way into my chest, shooting stabs of fear to my stomach. I thought I outgrew that instinct.

If Shia is right—and I do have some paranoia, toward all men, not just Chet—I may have been wearing blinders to certain facts, and it's possible I missed something in my analysis of the killer's profile. I'm no closer to identifying this person than when I first started. Chet's parole and the end of the life I've built for myself crawl closer every second—while another innocent person has died.

My apartment smells different when I walk in the door. Not musty. Not stifled because the humidity seeped through the window when I neglected to lower the blinds this morning.

Fresh. Clean, like the scent that lingers ten minutes after a shower. Some instinct makes me pause on the threshold and flick on the light switch before entering. Everything looks normal. The cardboard box I use as an end table is exactly where I left it. The half-finished cup of coffee on the counter sits in the same dark ring stain I keep meaning to wipe away.

I exhale a breath. Throwing my messenger bag on the couch, I head to the fridge and retrieve the bottle of vodka I added to the freezer last night. The clock above the two-burner stove says I have another hour before good breeding deems liquor acceptable. Not falling into that category, I withdraw a tumbler from the cabinet. The label covering the side suggests IT's 5 o'CLOCK SOMEWHERE.

I pour myself a half glass, neat. I never understood ice in a drink. Since I was a teenager, I've been taking mine straight—albeit the kind with which you could probably remove nail polish. Rocks only dilute a drink's true purpose: numbness. I lift the drink to my mouth, then taste that fresh, thick scent again.

I stop moving. Stop breathing. I wasn't imagining the smell.

Setting my drink on the counter, I grab the knife from my cutting board and walk to the bathroom. The floorboards creak beneath me. The bathroom door is slightly ajar, the bathroom itself dark. Nudging it open with a toe, I hit the light switch with my free hand. As I step inside the cramped space, the air is dense, like I forgot to turn on the dehumidifier after I showered this morning and the door was stuck closed all day, trapping the moisture inside.

But I showered last night.

My heart pounds against my ribs, and I yank back the shower curtain to reveal the empty square basin with only enough room for someone to stand. My gaze swings to the right, to the benign wooden cabinet. Slowly, I raise my eyes to the mirror above the sink, and my hand flies to my throat. The message written on the steamed glass has almost faded to nothing, but it cuts into me like the knife I drop to the floor:

TIME TO COME CLEAN, MISSY

I grab the knife and run back to the front entry, tear open the side closet door. I thrust my hands among my coats, looking for someone hiding and waiting for strong arms to jerk out and pull me in.

Panting heavily, I survey the apartment. The studio I tolerated but which felt like mine now seems to vibrate like a living animal, having been violated by an intruder. I return to the bathroom and take a photo of the message with my phone. Evidence.

My contacts list is relatively small at this point. It takes only two swipes to find the number I want. Loud music and laughter reach through the phone before Oz's voice of surprise registers against the din. "Claire? You coming to Suzy's?"

Downing my vodka, then grabbing my keys, I allow a full shudder to ripple across my back. Someone gained access to my home and might return while I'm sleeping, to plant items from my past here as they continue to do at the crime scenes. Or simply to gut me from clavicle to navel. I fumble in my backpack until I find the pack of cigarettes.

"Obviously," I say, angry at everything. Then I remember I've been avoiding men and assuming the worst of them without looking at all the facts, and check my tone.

I wipe my mouth with a shaking hand. Try for a smile that he can hear through the speaker. "I could use a night out."

We hang up, and I cross to the kitchen stove. My shoulders tense, passing the bathroom.

The front burner ignites, and the cigarette pressed between my thumb and forefinger follows suit. Sharp, acrid tendrils rise to the smoke alarm. The sour smell curls my toes as I quickly lower the lit end to a new circle of flesh.

Twenty-Three

Anger pulses beneath my skin most days. I used to take note of it and attempt to talk myself down, to diminish the fury, as if my internal thermostat had broken and all I needed was an adjustment down a few degrees. But I was a lost cause, as I was told by my tenth-grade school counselor after a boy I knew fell down the stairs and broke his leg.

No matter that the boy had cornered me in the girls' restroom and tried to stick his hand down my pants. I'd punched him in the nose then, which resulted in his family bringing assault charges against *me*. A month later, after I was allowed back at school, the boy broke his leg, and I happened to be nearby. No one, not even Rosemary, I think, ever believed that he slipped on his own. *Physical violence breeds physical violence,* the entire town seemed to whisper.

Though I may appear outwardly calm now, the thrum of rage continues to boil on low. A childhood therapist I saw—before Rosemary's money ran out—suggested that anger was a secondary emotion to fear, that I was, underneath it all, afraid of something. I didn't know what to make of that at the age of ten. But I knew at sixteen, when that boy cornered me, that I was afraid of being touched in an unwanted way.

It's why I feel an effortless peace only when I'm behind the camera, snapping photos of the world from a safe distance that no one can cross without my notice.

Drums beat on the inside of my skull, pounding away at my feeble, remorseful, regretful brain.

No, not drums. My pulse. My own bewildered and disoriented heartbeat. I reach out from underneath flannel sheets and press both palms to my temples. Jesus. Flannel sheets?

Why did I have that fifth bourbon shot? Why didn't I go home last night after meeting Oz for one drink and working through my next steps in the safety of a very crowded, public bar?

I open my eyes. Blackout curtains reveal little in this bedroom, but the outline of a stout, cheaply built dresser and an unframed poster of the movie *Police Academy 4* on the wall tell me enough. Sitting up in Oz's bed drains the blood from my head and brings on a new wave of dizziness and images from last night: that final shot of whiskey, kissing Oz on the mouth, leaning on him as we walked to his car, clumsy hands as he tried to take off my shirt on his couch, then me growling at him to leave me alone because I was tired. Although I committed a little too hard with the excessive drinking, my plan worked: I didn't sleep at home last night.

I roll onto my side, and a square of paper greets me at eye level.

Morning! Went into the office.
Coffee is brewing on automatic setting.
Thx for a fun night.

—Oz

So he's a morning person. And extremely trusting to leave me alone in his apartment.

Bumbling on the ground for my phone, I note the fresh scab newly formed on my arm. Did Oz see this last night? It throbs a *yes* in response.

I search the web for local locksmiths and find pages of options. Derry Landry said he'd handle anything needing fixing in my apartment; then we'd negotiate the division of financial responsibility. In this situation, I don't care how much it costs, and if it requires the rest of Shia's $1,000, I'll pay it. I can't go back to my studio knowing someone has a key or can pick the lock. I call the only company that's open at 7:00 a.m. on a Sunday and make arrangements to meet the locksmith at my apartment this afternoon.

An electric coffeepot finishes sputtering somewhere in another room. I swing my legs over the side of the bed, bringing myself to a seated position. The room sways.

Yesterday, someone was in my home encouraging me to confess, as if I'm the murderer. Navigating to the photos app on my phone, I absorb the image of my fogged-up mirror. *Time to come clean, Missy.* In preserving the evidence of harassment and stalking, am I doing the killer's work for him? Did I just record another implication of my guilt, one that otherwise would have faded with better ventilation and disappeared from my future court transcript?

I press the back of my hand to my forehead, willing my hangover to go away like that mirror message likely has. Prior to seeing it, part of me was still debating whether the anonymous author could simply be an obsessed fan, killing as a tribute to Chet and wanting me to embrace my identity. And now?

Using the nightstand for balance, I almost knock over a red cup filled with water, two aspirin beside it. Oz is more considerate than I gave his grabby hands credit for.

Opposite the bed, paperwork is stacked on a dresser. What else is Oz meticulous about? Does he bring his work home with him?

Creeping from the bed in case he's still lurking somewhere or has a roommate, I tiptoe to the pile. A manila folder contains bills from Portland General Electric. Loose papers beneath seem to be old concert tickets printed at home. A magazine on the Portland real estate market rests atop a small spiral notebook, and I pause. The notebook is like the one I saw Oz writing in outside Four Alarm and The Stakehouse. I flip it open.

Slanted box letters take up two rows on each page, with sporadic dates marking every few pages. It's hard to know where one entry begins and another ends, but it seems this notepad was first put to use back in February. A March protest staged at the Portland Art Museum consumes twenty pages, so I flip to the end and search for the latest date. April 4. One week ago.

At the top of the final page are the words *F.A. Brew*. I hold my breath as I scan Oz's notes from the day we met. His writing is hard to decipher in the dim light, but the words *Suspect Woman* are underlined.

Someone laughs nearby, in this apartment or the apartment complex, snapping me out of my daze. Using my phone, I take photos of the last several pages, front and back, then take a picture of the closed notepad. Two can be meticulous here.

In a box on the floor beside the dresser sit a dozen identical black notepads, each individually wrapped in plastic.

I grab my wallet, pocket my phone, and slip on my shoes. The walls of Oz's short hallway are empty, while the front room contains a leather couch, a glass table, and a nice television displayed on an entertainment center I recognize from IKEA. A nanny cam below the television offers a complete one-eighty view of the apartment. Not a leaf of greenery in the place. Very bachelor chic.

Glorious coffee aroma fills the open-kitchen floor plan, but I shouldn't dawdle when I've got stolen intel on my phone to analyze. I leave the apartment and walk down the carpeted hall toward where hazy memories recall climbing the stairwell.

Working from Powell's, Portland's largest bookstore, allows me to get lost in the white noise of people coming and going. I still have a massive headache, despite my breakfast of pain blockers.

Most of Oz's notes confirm what I already knew: the Four Alarm victim was thought to be killed sometime Saturday afternoon or evening after being held in the underground tunnel for an undetermined amount of time; Chief Bradley was looking into all brewery employees; Topher Cho, bartender/actor, discovered the body and was being questioned. No mention of any specific woman, aside from Chief Bradley. *Suspect Woman* doesn't make any more sense than it did in Oz's apartment. However, next to notes about Topher are tiny box letters: *YT.*

While these notes aren't a map to the killer, I don't regret spending the night. I'd presumed, accurately as it turned out, that once drunk, Oz would want to discuss the murders. Topher is still his chief suspect. But, regarding the identity of his source among the police, he turned out to be a locked safe. I kept pressing, but he stood firm.

A stabbing fear suddenly grips me. Did I say something to him as we were drinking last night? Did I use my real name or let it slip that I'm one of the freak-show Granger kids?

"Hey." Jenessa stands beside the line of people waiting to order coffee from the café.

"Hey." I rise, pushing my chair back. "What are you doing here?"

She gestures away from the crowded space, down an aisle of books. I follow her, confused. I had texted Jenessa my location when she asked for it, but I didn't realize she was coming to meet me.

"Are you okay? What's wrong? Did something happen at the doughnut shop? Aren't you working right now?"

She shakes her head, then turns to me, her face serious beneath the ceiling-height shelves. "Someone left me a note." She withdraws a wad of paper from her pocket and hands it to me. I smooth it out and read:

Time to come clean.

My breath catches in my throat, and I can't speak, can't move or tear my eyes from the box letters. "Where did you . . . what is . . . ?"

"I found it this morning on my car windshield. What do you think it means? I've been consumed with it since then, and lunch is the first time I've had a break. Freaking weekend rush has been crazy."

The memory of my fogged-over bathroom mirror fills my mind. "Someone knows where you live."

"I know. It's pretty scary, right? What do you think it means?" she asks again in a small voice. When I meet her tight gaze, I see the sister I've hurdled through life's obstacles with, whose triumphs and defeats I've witnessed; I see the little girl I was imprisoned with and the woman who struggled to leave the consequences of that beginning behind.

"No idea. I received the same message—in my apartment."

Jenessa's eyes widen. "Like, in . . . ? Where? How?"

I shrug, then lean against a row of nonfiction. A man yells from several aisles over that he found the book he needs. "Don't know. I have to believe I forgot to lock the dead bolt that morning and only locked the doorknob, which would be easier to pick. A locksmith is coming today."

Jenessa crosses her arms, then stares down at the tile floor. "This is crazy. This is unlike anything I've experienced before. I mean, during my second rehab, I had a guy follow me everywhere for a month once I was discharged. He was determined to catch me falling off the wagon, I guess. What are we going to do?"

The fear in her eyes pains me, makes me rack my brain for something to make her feel better. It's the least I can do; the killer seems to be interested in me specifically. Why would he loop in Jenessa, if not to make it clear he can reach past me to people I love?

I point to the paper and hold up my phone. "Can I?" She nods, and I take a photo. Now that I think about it, the box letters—so different from the typed notes I've received before—seem roughly similar to Oz's messy script. Maybe they're shorter, a little neater. Still, I'll zoom in and compare the two later.

"We aren't going to do anything. You are going to stick to your normal routine and job. Have you connected with Lily yet?" We exchange a glance. "She's home. I hope this guy hasn't reached out to her, too."

Tailored black eyebrows knit together. "No, I haven't. She called me, though. I just haven't had time to call her back. It's been months since she returned my texts or calls, and now that she's home, she's desperate to see me and tell me something."

I check my watch. Twelve thirty. "Listen, I've got to get going. I'm actually going to see her now. Do you want to come?"

"I have work. I only ran over here to show you the note."

"That's right. Sorry. But you should call her. She's got big news."

The corner of Jenessa's mouth twitches. "She already told you?"

I nod. "Just call her, okay? I'll walk out with you."

"Actually, I'll stay here. Give her a ring before I get distracted again."

"Sure."

She pulls me in for a hug. Her nails dig into the skin at my elbows, and I flinch. "Thanks for always being such a good sister," she whispers.

I give her a pat on the back. "Hey, you got it." Taking a last look at Jenessa among the rows of books, I feel a pang of nerves strike my chest—for leaving her here alone, for not telling her about Lily's pregnancy, and for inadvertently involving her by not solving the third clue fast enough to satisfy its author.

Lily's red-splotched face and watery eyes make her appear younger than her twenty-three years. I clear my throat, then pat my sister's hand. Her massive belly looks out of place beneath her smooth, round face, virtually unlined and unchanged since before she moved abroad.

When she called me after my first cup of coffee, I scrambled to silence my phone before the other bookstore patrons kicked me out of the building. I answered with a breathless, "Hey." Lily had smiled through the phone and explained that she wanted to chat in person. This afternoon. Knowing the locksmith had agreed to arrive after three, I said that worked, but was there anything I should know before then? The tone of her quivering voice suggested there was.

Bianca had left her—high and dry and eight months pregnant, Lily, my stoic emotional tank of a sister, had calmly explained. Bianca didn't want to be back in Portland or the United States; she had purchased a ticket to return to Geneva and flown out on this morning's first flight. She had said she wasn't ready to be a mother.

Although I had offered to come over right then and there, Lily insisted she needed the morning to get some affairs in order—pack up more of Bianca's things and also set up the baby's crib. When the elevator doors opened onto the fourth floor of Lily's apartment building, she was waiting for me with muffins she'd purchased, this time from around the corner.

After an hour of analyzing where she went wrong with her partner of four years, Lily stacks her hands across her swollen belly. "Well, I guess that's life, isn't it? Or my life, at least. People fail you, and the only choice you have is to move on."

A better, cheerier person might have scoffed at the cynical statement, but I know better. "Move on or wait for them to come back around when you least expect it."

Her hands clasp tighter. Light-blue eyes become pinpricks. "What does that mean?"

"Nothing."

"Right." Her smile fades. "No, really. What is it?"

I scan my sister's high forehead and plump cheeks, wishing I had more of a filter when I'm stressed. "Do you know what is happening tomorrow?"

She returns a blank stare. Her shoulders creep up to her ears. "Should I?"

She had no idea about Chet—about any of it. In all Lily's worrying about her relationship and its effect on the baby, the issues of Chet's parole tomorrow or this year being the twentieth anniversary of our escape were the last two things on her mind; she didn't sign up for the victim notification. When I finish explaining my new freelance gig for the *Portland Post* and the notes that I've received relating to the crime scenes, Lily, to her credit, doesn't become hysterical. Instead, she rubs her stomach in a circular motion.

"Can I see them?" she asks. "The notes."

"I . . . I don't think so."

"Why not?" The rubbing stops.

Shame presses in on my frame. "It's not a good idea."

She laughs, the same wind-chime peal as always. "You don't trust me?"

I hesitate—a moment too long—and her smile drops. "Honestly," I say, "I think the less you know, the better."

"Well, did you show Jenessa?"

"Yes—"

"Of course you did." She sighs.

I sit up straight and turn around to face her. "What does that mean?"

She shakes her head. "Maybe it's because you spent more time together in the basement than I did. I always felt like you had some bond that I could never quite access. Some shared secret."

"Lily, that's not—"

"No, it's fine. Whoever you choose to tell about the notes is your business. I understand, really." She adopts a thin-lipped smile. Her hand resumes its circular pattern on her belly.

We sit silently. Music swells from a nearby apartment, opera, as I try to find the words to reassure my little sister. "It's really not about trusting Jenessa so much as I needed a sounding board—one of you—before I knew you came home."

She dips her head, not fully believing me. "All right. Well, you don't have to show me the notes. Can I help you figure this out another way? What theories do you have so far?"

Behind her and through the window, rain begins to patter against the glass. There are less than twenty-four hours before Chet is unleashed. Somewhere within me, I know the killer's plan will shift into its next phase then, as well—whether orchestrated by Chet or someone else I have yet to meet.

I search for my wallet behind a couch pillow. "I'd love to stay and get your thoughts on this stuff because I really haven't made progress alone. But the locksmith should be at my place any minute. Sorry to spring even more bad news on you, with everything you're handling at the moment."

She stands with difficulty, then wraps her arms around me. "I'm glad you told me about Chet. And I'm so thankful you came over. I really needed this."

She pulls back to release me from the hug, but I tighten my grasp at her shoulder blades. "Me too, Lil." I speak into her hair, meaning the words more than I think she knows.

"Marissa."

I turn, expecting to see Lily. But the woman standing on the sidewalk outside Lily's apartment—the one who just spoke my name as though we know each other—brushes long, dark hair back from her face with her index finger. Sheets of red at the tips fade closer to her roots, an ombré design.

"Marissa, you are a vision, aren't you?"

My stomach knots as I check my surroundings. The patio of the Italian restaurant next door is filled with patrons—witnesses. In case something happens. In case this woman tries something.

"Do I know you?" I ask.

She lifts a hand to my face, although she's still six feet away. Her hair shimmers like something out of a shampoo commercial, grazing her hips. "You have his eyes."

Her voice sounds like a five-year-old's, contrasting the loose skin of her neck. She slides her hands into the pockets of low-rise jeans that fit tight across wide hips. "I'm sorry to bother you. I wasn't following you, exactly; I was trying—"

I sidestep her and continue toward my car. The heels she wears *click-clack* behind me.

"Marissa, please."

"Leave me alone!" I whirl on her. "I don't care what you want or why my story resonated with you. Got it?"

Instead of walking away, this woman gasps, appreciatively. "You even sound like him."

I look around for a weapon, a way out, but my car is too far. Running back to Lily's isn't an option. I reach into my bag for my pepper spray and find the slender tube.

"Marissa." She touches my elbow, and I jerk away. "Marissa, we're family. I married Chet in prison after years of letters." She laughs fondly. "So many letters. I'm Karin."

Her words rake across my body. Karin Degrassi. Chet's other visitor this month. "What?"

"I just want to get to know you." She withdraws a photo from the small purse dangling by her side. In it, she and Chet stand face-to-face, holding hands before a man in a black suit. Whereas Chet wore an orange jumper when I met him, in this picture he wears a black T-shirt and jeans with ECHO STATE PRISON stamped on them. This woman, this Karin, wears a formfitting dress. They beam at each other.

The words and sentiments she wields, that she *cares* for the fiend who imprisoned my family and has the balls to call himself my father, are just as dangerous as a serrated knife. Large gray eyes, unnaturally round, like they might fall out of her skull, watch my reaction.

She sighs. "It was the happiest day of my life. He shared that you went to visit him last week."

Pitiful. Embarrassment for her and disgust war within me. I resume walking, cursing myself for using free street parking today instead of paying for a garage nearby.

"Chet is getting out tomorrow, you know," she calls in a singsongy voice. "He wants to see you."

My teeth grind, molar to molar.

"Maybe we could get dinner? The three of us," she adds.

I pause midstep. Take two long strides back toward her that put me within a foot of her deep-V blouse. Cloying perfume engulfs me. "You tell Chet to stay the hell away from me. And my family."

I snatch the photo from her and rip it in two—tear it lengthwise, then turn it over and do it again. She screams, horrified, as I throw the shredded bits in the air; they flutter into the street and slap against the windshield of a passing truck that will carry them somewhere far, far away from me.

Without waiting for a response, I jog in the opposite direction. Restaurant patrons all peer at us. Two people stood up from their tables for a better view.

Not much farther now. A half block.

"He cares for you, you know!" she shouts after me, her voice strained.

I pass a young man with round headphones, bouncing to a beat, oblivious.

"He cares for all of you! And when he gets out, he's coming to be the real father he should have always been. He's a good man!"

A breeze picks up, and I lean into the cool air. I place one foot in front of the other to avoid running back and tearing that woman's throat out. Fury continues to pump through me, and I breathe deeply, try to remind myself that the fight is over and I've already taken flight. I feel much the same way I did after chucking the *Tru Lives* reporter's phone, but this time the remorse is nonexistent. Any person stupid enough to marry Chet, to love a predator she's spent time with only during visiting hours, then to shove it in my face on a downtown street, deserves my outburst and more.

Even if I did just add another public incident to the *Missy Mo: Pissed and All Grown Up* file. Impulsive. Stupid.

For her to presume she'll act as the mediator between Chet and his offspring indicates serious lunacy. Why do some women become infatuated with incarcerated men, let alone those convicted of violent crimes? I've heard it happens, but I never thought Chet could be the object of anyone's affections after what he did to my mothers.

I walk for another minute, then loop back to the front of Lily's building. When I peek around the corner, the brick entry is clear. Did Karin know I was visiting Lily?

What else does she—does Chet—know about us?

A thought surges forward that makes me search the restaurant crowd for that long ombré hair: Could she have left me the Four Alarm note on Chet's behalf? Is Chet reinventing himself, a modern murderer from behind bars, thanks to this woman acting as his proxy?

It's possible her motivation in approaching me was true *family togetherness*. Or she could simply be a distraction. Deliberately misleading me.

Twenty-Four

"I think that should do it." The locksmith slides a narrow pair of pliers back into his belt loop. He wipes his wrist across his forehead, then pats the name tag sewn into his vest. ERROL.

"Someone did a real number on your doorknob," he continues, jiggling the handle on the open door. Behind him, I see Derry Landry pass in the hall for the fourth time. I wonder how long I can avoid giving him the new key. "These housing mass manufacturers always choose the cheapest model," Errol is saying. "But with this new one, you'll be in a better spot."

I wave goodbye to Errol, then shut the door behind me. Safely tucked behind three inches of wood and metal, I survey my apartment in the light of day. The green-and-yellow armchair I bought from a yard sale, the only patterned item I own, catches me as I slip into its worn fabric basin.

My ringtone erupts from on top of the cardboard box—its default trill. I stretch forward to grab it and feel just how tired I am after sleeping in an unfamiliar place last night. And the residual dehydration.

Shia Tua scrolls across the screen. New embarrassment heats my neck, recalling how I barreled into the coffee shop, accusing him of conspiring with the reporter. And we already have a session scheduled for tomorrow. I let the call go to voice mail.

My bed seems to beckon from the floor in the corner of my studio. The idea of taking a sleeping pill and quitting while I'm marginally ahead—thanks, Errol—is tempting.

But my phone rings again, vibrating across the cardboard cube. "Wow, Shia." I reach for it and flip it over, only to see a different contact calling—Oz.

"Hi," I answer, my tone wary. If he wants to strike up another night of romance, I'll need to decline without severing the bridge between us.

"Claire, hey. You hungry?" Noise emanates from the background. He must be in another bar.

"I'm hanging at home tonight. Thanks for calling."

"Claire," he begins, and I can hear his smirk through the phone. "We both know what last night was. You were finally ready to unwind, and I was happy to host. Let's not make this weird."

I roll my eyes, wishing he had video called me to see it. "Sure. Agreed."

"I have some more news on the tunnel murderer. I think you should hear it."

The clock on the kitchen stove reads close to six, as Errol got held up at his last appointment and showed up much later than planned. I've been alone for only a few minutes. The last thing I want to do is venture out again for more shenanigans with Oz, but with less than a day before my two worlds come to a head, I don't see another way. If the *Time to come clean* message means someone else's life may end soon if I don't continue searching, I need to keep going.

Laughter in the background swells as I slowly inhale. "Where are you?"

The Sunday crowd is less drunk than last night. I find Oz at the same spot at the bar, Beijing Suzy's, where we *cheers*ed shot glasses beneath the mounted televisions. Casting a glance toward where the trapdoor sits innocently beneath the dartboard, I weave between tables to him. We exchange awkward pleasantries, and I get the feeling that Oz doesn't usually see a woman again after she spends the night.

I slide into a bar chair. "All right. What is this news?"

Oz flags down the bartender. "Another mule?"

The man nods, cleaning out a glass with a towel, then looks at me. "Same."

Oz throws me a smile. "Let's take a step back. You've been at several crime scenes in the last week."

"Yeah," I reply. "What about it?"

"You're a smart person. You've managed to sneak your way into the right places to get photos for Pauline and get her to pay out more money than she gave our last photographer." The bartender drops off our mugs, and Oz raises his. "What do you think about the killer? I mean, what can we reasonably infer here?"

I uncross my arms from beneath my chest. The impulse to step away from this conversation, to protect what I know and protect myself from any other surprise attacks, wrestles with my need for answers.

"I would say this person has some kind of obsession with enclosed or underground spaces. He has control issues—"

"Issues?" Oz raises one eyebrow. "Elaborate."

I think about what Chet said. "I mean, the killer likes to be in control, likes to control all elements pertaining to his captures and, ultimately, kills. He's probably got a history of—"

"He?" A smile blooms across Oz's pointed chin. "How do we know it's a male?"

I raise my brows. *Suspect Woman* and the notepad from his bedroom were all I thought about on the drive here. Knowing Oz doesn't think Gia is the murderer, I'm still not sure whether that was a note from his police source or his own personal suspicion. The handwriting in his notepad and the scrawl on the binder paper Jenessa received don't appear to match. But any interaction I have with Oz should be with this in mind: he could be involved in this as more than an eager reporter.

"We don't know it's a male. But without more facts, it's safest to assume it is."

"But why, sweet Claire, indeed, would this killer be female? Humor me." Oz seems downright giddy, clasping his hands together on the bar counter. His fingernails catch the overhead lights and gleam as though recently manicured.

"Don't you have some source inside the police? What do they think?"

"They're up to their necks in the same questions."

"Who's your source? Is it Peugeot?"

He wags a finger back and forth like a metronome. "I'll never tell."

"Fine. Female serial killers have commonalities with male serial killers. Both of them usually witness violence at a formative age. But their motivations are what set them apart. What drives female killers is always psychological."

Not only have I grown up spending way too much time exploring the internet's sordid archives; the research I did at the bagel shop after leaving Lily and Bianca added to my arsenal of factoids.

"Always?"

My knee-jerk response—*of course, always*—stops behind my teeth. Right now, the killer may be leaving details from my childhood to implicate me, and it's possible I'm playing into their hands. Rosemary's strained voice booms in my head. *Run. You run away from those crime scenes and that case as fast as you can.*

"I mean, I don't know. The police have no idea why the victims seem to have been killed in such different ways, right? Maybe this guy's got a split personality."

Oz considers my words. He wipes drops of sweat from the side of his glass.

A woman laughs behind me, and I lean closer to Oz. The scent of his shirt tickles my nose; it's sweet yet muted, like my laundry detergent. Once Rosemary, Lily, and I acclimated to the outside, wandering down that fragrant aisle of supermarkets was my favorite thing to do. I would sit on the hard white linoleum floor and breathe in the artificial smells—more appealing than the stifled, stale air that would linger for hours after we cooked dinner in the basement—until Rosemary made me get up, saying it was time to finish our shopping. We weren't ever allowed to wander off by ourselves.

Oz sips his cocktail, maintaining steady eye contact. "So who do you think is the killer?"

I take a drink, too, and buy myself some time to answer. The mule's ginger flavor coats my tongue and reminds me of a soup Rosemary once made, her grandmother's recipe. I loved it—begged her to make it again, but she never did. *Too painful,* she said.

"Whoever chose those tunnels as their headquarters didn't want to answer to anyone. I'd say they prize autonomy and control above all else. Value continuity in a world that feels ever-evolving."

A smile spreads across Oz's clean-shaven mouth. "Sound like anyone you know?"

I stiffen. Has he seen right through my Claire-the-photographer facade? A low thrum of fear purrs in my chest, a feral cat sharpening its claws.

"Sounds like any millennial to my ears."

He laughs, then lifts a pointed finger. "Yes, exactly. Which is why I asked you here and wanted your opinion. I think our murderer is a woman."

"Really? That's so . . . modern of you, Oz." After watching the way he sizes up each bra that passes, I didn't expect him to be so egalitarian.

He offers a shrug. "I know, right? Women can slip in and out of places more easily than men. Plus, the police just confirmed that each victim—while outwardly unrelated—has a massive social media following. The stripper had something like a million Snapchat followers, the insurance salesman has eighty thousand followers on Instagram for his artwork, and the third victim—did you hear about him?"

"No, I didn't know they'd identified him. Only that he'd been burned and died from burns or smoke inhalation."

Oz shakes his head, enjoying my ignorance. "His body was burned after. He died from a gunshot to the chest. He's an advocate for refugees in the Pacific Northwest and has about a hundred thousand followers on Facebook. Each victim had a solid online platform."

"So you're saying that because these people were active on social media, only a woman would be driven to kill them, out of—what? Jealousy? Obsession? Because a man wouldn't care about social media?"

Oz leans back in the chair. "You don't agree?"

I exhale through my nose and look around me. The bar is nearly full of men, but there are two women—the laughing pair—at a table behind us.

"I don't. The facts continue to point to a male, probably white, midthirties, potentially with a history of violence, if we're allowing the textbook markers to guide us. Why do you care anyway? Isn't it all the same to you as a reporter?"

"Didn't hear that, either, did you?" Oz downs his glass. "Police just announced a reward tonight for information that might lead to the killer—or the ringleader if there's more than one. Fifteen grand."

I nod. Seems I'm not the only one in need of extra funds. "That's a good reason."

Throwing enough money on the counter to cover my drink, I stand and finish the rest of my mule. "Thanks for the brainstorming session."

"Where are you going?" His dark eyebrows narrow. "Aren't we hanging out again tonight? I already reserved a round of darts for us." He pats a zippered container on the table.

"Probably a bad idea. I'm a terrible shot."

He removes two darts from the pouch and hands me one. "Humor me."

Grudgingly, I cross the room to the far wall in between a scroll painting of a peacock and a black-and-white photo of chopsticks. After a look beside me to ensure no foot traffic will get caught in my crosshairs, I raise the dart. Close one eye to help my aim. Then lance the dart at the round red target.

It hits the wall beneath the board, then takes a chunk of wall down to the ground with it.

I turn back to Oz. "See?"

Instead of mocking me as I expect, he hands me another dart with a grin. "That was a warm-up."

I laugh outright. Oz Trainor may have gotten attached to someone sleeping in his bed. "No, I shouldn't. I'm going home. See you later."

He nods, disappointment pursing full lips. "Yeah, see you at the next murder."

As I walk back through Chinatown, Oz's logic continues to reverberate in my head. If I incorporate the notes that I've been receiving, the directions I've been given, and the clues that have been planted relating to my life, I've got the following: this murderer, man or woman, is interested in true crimes and, more specifically, my family's trauma. The killer is an able-bodied resident of Portland, and they're intrigued by underground spaces. More urgently, this person knows who I am, where I live, and what I'm trying to hide. They know I have photos of each crime scene. And they wanted me to take pictures of two of the bodies before anyone else was aware.

I pause beneath an awning to peer behind me. Check over my shoulder. Tension knots my neck as the full significance of Oz's good intentions takes shape.

If Oz's source, or anyone else with the police, shares his theory that the killer could be a woman, I'll have gone about this night all wrong. The way I left our conversation, all signs point to the most likely suspect: me.

Twenty-Five

When the Murphy stops making noise I take my hands away from my ears. Twin looks at me with the cover pulled up to her nose but neither of us makes a peep. Her eyes are round and wide like that scared bunny on the Australian Outback cartoon. My heart thumps like the bunny's feet. We both know Mama Rosemary has something different planned than the usual visit.

Mama appears in the doorway. Her nightgown is unbuttoned at the top. "Sweetheart, I need you to come with me."

Twin shakes her head and goes lower under the covers.

Mama walks to her side of the bed. Mama's eyes are big and rounder than I've ever seen. She gets down real close to Twin's ear but I don't breathe so I can hear. "Trust me, baby. I know it's hard. But we have to."

Twin puts her legs out of bed and stands. They walk into the other room and don't look at me. I am froze.

The man makes a happy noise. *Ahhhh.* "Hello there."

"Go ahead, baby." Mama Rosemary's voice is weird. Low and slow. There's a creaking noise from the Murphy and then the man makes another noise a *whooosh* then, "You want more Mars Bars, sweetheart? Come sit on Uncle Chet's lap," then quiet.

Mama Rosemary shouts, "Now, baby!" Sounds come from the other room.

Quick fast noise and a heavy sound—*bang!*—the man grunting he yells out "Ah!" and the big heavy sound again like our cooking pan—*bang bang!* I get nervous wondering what's happening. A box opens—the storage bin?—and the plastic top goes falling to the ground. *Clatter bang.* More grunting and something heavy being kicked. Loud noise.

"Look away, baby!"

Then it's quiet again.

Twin whimpers and Mama Rosemary goes "shhhhh."

There's a noise in the doorway, and I lower the covers. It's Mama. "It's okay, honey. We have to go."

I run into the room and see Twin with tears on her face but she looks normal. Empty like when we're watching television. Like Mama Rosemary when she's staring at the wall.

Mama Rosemary presses my hand into hers. The first room is a mess. The mattress for the Murphy is almost off. One of the man's shoes is on and the other is in the sink and our toy crate is fallen over and puzzle pieces are everywhere. Mama's nightgown is torn on the arm and her skin is all scratched. "Mama Rosemary, you okay?"

She makes a noise in her throat. "Yes, baby." She's shaking.

I look at the man and see his chest go up and down. There's red marks on his neck. "He's asleep?" I whisper.

His arms and legs are tied together like a piggy and he's flat on his tummy. Not a good way to sleep. I step closer to see and Mama stops me with a hand on my back. The rope we've been making during arts and crafts is wrapped around his hands and feet all zigzag.

"Not asleep," she says. "How's your sister?"

"I think she's up," I say. "What happened?"

Twin only picks at her shirt with her fingers.

Mama doesn't answer me. She goes into the second room and her voice is low again. Sweet Lily says something in her baby voice that means she's tired and not feeling good. The bed squeaks and Mama and Sweet Lily come into the first room. Mama wears a backpack I saw her putting our favorite items in today. Sweet Lily takes Mama's hand but Mama snatches it back like she got burned. Red is on her hand. Blood.

"Mama, look!" Twin shouts and I spin and look at the man. But he's still sleeping. I follow Twin's pointing finger to the middle of the rope where it's come loose around his feet. Instead of keeping his legs up like a piggy, his feet start to float to the floor.

"He's coming loose." Twin's mouth shakes and she hugs herself to Mama's leg like she's Sweet Lily's age again.

Mama Rosemary smooths her hair. "I know, honey. We're not going to have as much time as we thought."

"What do you mean?" I ask. Now my mouth is shaky, too. "Not enough time? What do you mean he's coming loose?"

"Hush. We need to get going now."

But Twin pulls away and runs back into the bed room doorway. Her eyes get all big and round and she breathes heavy. "We can't. He'll come get us and be meaner than before. He'll come get us!" Tears wet her face.

I look from Mama Rosemary's bloody hand to Twin's shaking shoulders then to Sweet Lily trying not to put any weight on her bad foot. Splotches on Sweet Lily's cheeks make her paler than usual and her long hair is messed up and knotted.

The rope dangles from the man's feet too loose. Just like when Petey the Penguin captured Bruno the Polar Bear.

"I think I know a way," I say in my naptime voice.

Mama's eyes are soft. Then they get round, too. Then they get skinny and angry. "What way is that exactly?"

I nod. "I can make more rope. Make sure he stays tied up longer and make sure he doesn't go after you."

"No."

"Mama—"

"We're leaving together." She looks around all fast. Her eyes get red but there's no tears. No wetness like my own. Her chin shakes but her face seems hard like when one of us refuses the vitamins she gets for us. She always says, *Baby, do you know what I had to do to get those?* And we always shake our heads because we don't. She won't tell us.

"Mama, Sweet Lily can't run like all of us! She needs help. And that will mean none of us can run away."

Sweet Lily begins to cry, too, and only Twin isn't wiping her cheeks. Instead she's staring at me like she doesn't recognize me.

Mama swoops down and lifts Sweet Lily onto her side—her hip—and looks past me. With her good hand she hoists Sweet Lily up higher but Sweet Lily slips slowly slowly slipping down. Mama hoists her up again onto her hip but Sweet Lily keeps sliding with only Mama's one good hand to hold her in place. She wraps her bad hand around Sweet Lily's leg and blood smears on her little-baby thigh. Mama's face scrunches then she releases Sweet Lily so she can cradle her hand.

I nod again and again. "You said we'll have to run the first few blocks and that the man could be close behind so we had to run fast. We practiced during exercise hour. We practiced our bracelet- and rope-making during arts and crafts to make sure he could be tied up for a while. We practiced geography so we'd know the streets outside and how to get to the big road for help. If someone doesn't stay . . . make sure the others get away safe . . . you said I make rope as good as you, yes?"

Mama Rosemary goes quiet. "We do still have leftover sheet."

"I make rope as good as you, right? You said it."

"I did say that." Her voice is soft. "So you'd make extra rope from the leftover strips and tie it to the rope already around his feet? You don't even know how to make a knot."

"I do too. I knotted all the croissants today."

"Shhh, keep your voice down. Knotting a bracelet is different from a rope around two human feet."

"It's not it's not." I shake my head. "It's the only way! You leave first. I'll make more rope, make a figure eight over feet and hands, knot it, then run out and meet you."

She shakes her head. "We can all do it together."

The man moans. His hands move behind his back grabbing at air and we all freeze.

He stops moving.

"No, Mama," I whisper. "Now is the chance to go, like Mama Nora." I love her and my sisters enough and I'm the best at rope-making just like Petey the Penguin. Maybe better than Mama Rosemary.

I push on her arm to get her to move but she shakes her head again. Then Twin blinks like she just woke up and grabs Mama Rosemary's arm.

"We have to, we have to go. Now!" Twin whisper-yells.

Mama goes for my hand but I step away and Twin pulls Mama harder toward the stairs. Lily holds on to Mama's nightgown and goes, too.

Mama Rosemary looks at the man then the door then the man. He smells like the whiskey Mama doesn't like. She moves faster than I'm ready for and she holds my hand so tight it hurts but I tear away. "No, Mama!"

Twin keeps pulling her up up up the stairs and Sweet Lily follows sucking her thumb. Mama Rosemary's eyes go big and wide at me. "You come right outside after you're done tying, understand? We'll be back to get you with the police. Once you're out, do not come back in here, do you hear me? Wait out front."

"I'm gonna miss you," I whisper. My throat feels like burning and I choke on my cries.

Mama's face is wet. "We're going to see you real soon, baby. Then we'll all go and live together and never worry about bumping into each other again. Okay?"

I pull the sheet from under the storage bin. Sit down against the wall as far away from the man as I can and start tearing more strips.

Mama springs back down and grabs my chin while Twin helps Sweet Lily get up the stairs. She looks me strong in the face and says, "We'll be right outside, darling." Then she touches the end of my nose like always and gives me a kiss.

"You stay on the wall until you're ready to add on to the rope." Excitement makes her scary and I nod fast.

She goes to the door where my sisters are waiting then reads a paper and pushes the buttons on the keypad in just the right order that we never could do before. *Beep beep beep beep beep-beep.* The handle makes a sound then Mama grabs down and pulls. Air comes into the basement all light and clean.

The three of them turn and look at me. Mama speaks again and it sounds like a whisper: "I'll be right back." Her voice shivers like she's cold. She lifts a hand to me then walks through the door. The door stays open but their noises disappear.

Sadness makes me heavy all over. Like a big black blanket that Mama always says isn't real. Worse than I ever felt before. I lean against the wall next to Sweet Lily's drawing of a cow and pretend it's a dream and I'll wake up in between my sisters again.

A cough breaks through my make-believe. The man is waking up. Moving side to side against the ropes. Loosening around his hands and even more around his feet.

I tie the three strips together tuck the knot at my feet and start braiding. Over under. Over under. Over under.

I think back to the Petey the Penguin episode and how it ended. Bruno the Polar Bear got loose and he and Petey became friends. But that won't happen here. Petey was too nice.

Staring at the man as he jerks this way and that I know the truth. I'm not a nice little girl.

Twenty-Six

Four Alarm appears more depressed in the evening shadows, and I hardly recognize it from when I was last here. It's been a week since the body was discovered. The police officers loitering out front are long gone.

The marketing director from the *Post* whose headshot I took said the first person to report a crime often has more to do with it than they let on. What if it's the same thing for the first location of a crime?

A breeze skates across my neck as I stand before the white writing on the window. I check beside me, scan the parked cars, then look toward the corner of the street where it shifts into residential housing.

"Claire?" Topher stares at me from the doorframe. His black hair flops over and across wide-set brown eyes. An apron reaches his knees.

"Hey. Thanks for the quick text reply." I follow him inside.

"Of course. Happy to help. Watch your step; I can't find the *Wet Floor* cone." He points down at the glossy checkered tile. "No one else wanted to come out tonight? Or is the night shift pretty laid-back?"

"Busy day at the station. No one else was free."

He leads me through the dark hallway. Customers lounge in leather booths and on barstools, looking out the window onto the darkened street.

In an itch of paranoia, I turn to the glass and catch a flick of long black hair disappearing from view.

Karin? Has she been following me? Since I went to see Chet in prison or before?

"Claire? We need to move if you want to go down again. I got a table waiting for fresh glasses." Topher peers into the restaurant dining area, looking for someone. "My manager's on break, but I can let her know you're here if you need anything. Detective—what was your last name again?"

"No, that's fine. No need to bother her. There's desk work waiting for me back at the office. I'll be quick." I follow him forward, brainstorming more mundane work phrases to whip out, if needed.

In the cellar, we pass boxes of cutlery, and Topher moves into the opening where the body of the exotic dancer was found. We step over yellow crime scene tape fallen to the ground. The chains have been removed from the wall, and all that remains is a stain on the earth where the victim's blood likely pooled for hours before she was discovered.

"Is there anything I can help you with?" Topher asks, ever the good citizen. His eyes shift nervously from my face to my camera case like it might contain a gun. Little does he know I got rid of my gun before moving here. I didn't like the temptation so close and near my open vodka bottles.

I examine the space, as though weighing his offer. The construction lamps are already lit. "If I could just have a few minutes here, I'll come back up and let you know when I'm through."

Topher nods, then returns to the cellar opening. If he believes that I'm with the police—and is more compliant as a result—all the better.

Alone with my thoughts, the same creeping fear as the first time spools down my back. Chet's basement compound was roomy for most of my childhood. It was only when we turned six or seven, when Lily was becoming more active and Rosemary more unstable, kicking things and drifting into hours of listless depression, that the space began to feel confined. After we got out, I realized that the cereal we had eaten for breakfast every morning tasted sweeter than the store brand we bought, and that the store brand gave me a sugar high whenever I consumed it—the opposite of my experience down below. Sometime after high school, I read about lithium and the sedating effects it can have on children in small doses—as well as its possible long-term damaging health effects. I resented that Rosemary had willfully medicated us, may have stunted Lily's brain development and exacerbated my depression, even knowing it was a preemptive strategy to keep us all sane down there.

Rustling comes from farther in the tunnels. Movement. Footsteps. Shuffling forward. Sweat breaks across my chest. The hair on my forearms rises, and I remember that I'm not a police officer, and I brought only pepper spray. "Who's there?" I call out. "Portland police!"

The movement stops. Then starts again, shuffling, moving forward, coming closer but still outside the sphere of light emanating from the construction lamp.

A rat emerges, trailing a plastic grocery bag caught on its crooked tail. It makes a wide arc around me before zeroing in on the exit into the restaurant.

I gasp out several expletives and clutch my chest. All this slinking around can't be good for my health.

Last night, I dreamed of the day Mama Bethel shared that she was going to have a baby—Lily. I was so excited, I remember jumping up and down, despite the looks of anxiety that flashed across all three women's faces. An early memory, from when I was three or so, it proves that things weren't completely awful for us. What else does Shia know that I'm unaware of?

Without the rat's plastic shuffle, the space feels cavernous, empty, and full of secrets. I take a step backward and land in the brown circle of bloodstain. In a snap of memory, I recall a similar dark stain that we all avoided on the mattress—each of us, except for Lily, because it was hers. The only tangible item she had of her mother, the stain containing the fluids that accompanied her birth.

I creep forward, bending my head slightly beneath the low dirt roof, farther than I saw the police standing when I poked my head into this passageway against Sergeant Peugeot's instructions. The dry-goods cellar and orbs of safety become smaller until my cell phone's flashlight is the only source of light. I hold my breath. Remind myself that I can get out, back up to fresh air and the surface as soon as I want. My eyes adjust to the semidarkness, and bleary shapes become recognizable.

Once, Rosemary refused to succumb to one of Chet's visits, and the next day he turned off the electricity to the basement. It was February. We passed the time by singing songs, making up rhymes, and huddling together for warmth until three days later when the heater kicked back on. I remember, when the batteries on our light-up toys gave out, the darkness was all-consuming. Rosemary stopped talking the last day.

The pathways keep going to the right, curving under the portion of Northwest that was forgotten about. Shovels and police tape are piled together to the side, along with handheld machines, maybe depth gauges. A mound of discarded rocks lies farther ahead.

Except they're too smooth to be rocks. There's a plastic sheet over them, or a tarp.

Inching closer, I wave my phone across the mass, and a sharp patch of white stands stark against the black earth. A hand protruding from the lump.

I stumble backward, stifling the cry that bursts from my mouth. A body. A fourth one.

But there were no new notes today, none on my car or shoved under my door or written on my bathroom mirror, so how could this be happening? Is the killer nearby, still prepping the scene?

I whirl to shine my phone behind me, back toward the brewery. Nothing but semilit ground.

Slowly, I turn toward the body. And listen. Water drips from somewhere in the distance. I'm at least a city block away from the brewery, underground. The only breathing I can discern is my own.

Before I think better of it, I raise my camera to what I thought was a pile of rocks and hit the shutter button. Twice. Three times. A fourth from a higher angle.

Another patch of white reflects the camera's flash. A business card.

I inch closer to the body, ready to recoil at the slightest movement. Nudging the rectangular paper out from under the arm with my shoe, being careful not to touch it directly, I bring my cell phone's flashlight down low and read the two lines of text I spent hours crafting: CL Photography. Headshots. Senior Portraits. Graduations. The business card that I used for all of three weeks before I regretted creating the paper trail.

Scratching reaches my ears. Shuffling. Footsteps.

I grab the card, then turn and sprint to the cellar opening, panic pushing me harder and faster away from the dark. Launching myself up the stairs and into the restaurant, I pause to listen for whether anyone is pursuing me and my breath at fills my ear canals. I cast an eye for the rat, but it's nowhere in sight. Long gone, as I should be.

Topher's voice sounds from somewhere deeper within the restaurant. Instead of seeking him out, I walk toward the front entry as if I were simply a customer who's finished downing my evening beer. A figure blocks the exit. Oz.

"Claire. I thought you were going home."

I stare at him, unsure of how this conversation is supposed to go. Unsure of anything after what I just discovered. There's a fourth body, a business card I made and scattered around a college town—accessible to anyone who visited coffee shops and student dining halls—wedged underneath. The killer has always been one step ahead of me. Returning to a former location, without notifying me, to leave another item from my past.

Oz's features blur in my vision. He waves a hand in front of my face, peers at me with more than concern after I ditched him to return to this crime scene. "What is going on? I received an anonymous tweet telling me to come here."

My muscles clench, preparing to run. Whoever tweeted Oz wanted him to find me here, emerging from below—or simply to find the body and my card together. It's Oz's job to sniff out the truth and alert the public, the authorities, about it.

"I got to go. I just remembered, I have to—" I push past him, then slip on the tile and land hard on my shoulder. The breath gets knocked out of me, and my world becomes the rotating ceiling fan above.

"Whoa, are you okay? Claire? You all right? Man, the floor is all wet. Where the hell is a caution sign?"

Animal noises struggle from my throat. I gasp for air but can't move, can't breathe.

"Oh, hell. Claire, you're okay. Listen, you're going to be fine. The wind. You had the wind knocked out of you. Breathe."

Thanks, genius. I'll try that. The fan's blades rotate in quick turns, mesmerizing to watch from the cold tile that Topher warned me about. Where is Topher?

But I didn't yell—didn't scream. I only fell like deadweight. Like the dead body down in the cellar.

I struggle to my elbows, and a sharp pain shoots down my right side where I landed, sending spots through my vision all over again. *Fuck.* The inhale I manage to take feels like sucking air through a straw. After another meager effort, the animal noises subside and I'm able to breathe.

"Uh. Claire? Your stuff scattered everywhere. I tried to wipe your things off." Oz's voice is flat, strained, and I lift my eyes to his frightened expression. In his right hand, he holds my driver's license and a dish towel. In his left, he holds my camera. Panic tightens my chest—terror—separate from the spill I just took.

"Your ID says 'Marissa Claire Lou,'" he continues. "You've been using your middle name. That much I can understand if you don't like

Marissa. But what is this?" He holds up my camera, turning the square display to face me. The last photo I took glows on the screen: a pale, prostrate body lying beneath a plastic tarp.

"What the hell is this?" he whispers.

I grab my camera and my ID from him. "It's not what it looks like."

"What does it look like, Claire—or Marissa? I'm curious to know."

I sling the camera strap around my neck, avoiding his eyes while I hoist my messenger bag onto my good shoulder. But the engraved label—*MCM*—catches his eye.

Understanding blanches his skin. "Marissa Claire Mo. You're Chet Granger's daughter. Each of the details from the Granger incident report—the penguin . . . the bracelet you were wearing . . . the baby blanket—showed up near these victims. You're the murderer." He takes a step backward. "Our killer is a woman, after all."

I reach out a hand. "No, Oz, that's not—"

"Stay away from me!" he yells.

A pair of men at a table stops their conversation and turns toward the noise. Topher raises his head from behind the bar.

I run.

Bursting through the front doors, I don't slow down until I'm a block away at the corner. Fear strangles my breath, pulsating from every pore, as I look behind me. Oz stands outside the brewery entrance, a hundred yards off. Instead of shock knitting his features, his face is calm, relaxed. Determined. As if he's already decided what he must do next.

Twenty-Seven

In the fifth grade, I was surprised to learn no one really knows why we dream. We theorize that dreams help us work through problems from our waking hours and that dreams help us to store memories—but as my teacher then said, science doesn't yet *know*. I left school that day feeling certain that I did. Dreams were meant to store memories. It was for that reason that I embarked on a sleep strike. Every six months or so, I would dream for several nights in a row that I was back in the basement. I thought if I could stop sleeping, I would interrupt that storage cycle and hopefully remove those memories altogether.

I succeeded in staying awake for three days. I dozed off a few times, but I woke myself up whenever the dreams started.

The next six months came and went with no basement dreams, and I was ecstatic. Empowered and overjoyed. I thought I had excised those bastard nightmares from my mind, and I told my teacher so.

Two years went by before they resumed. The year I turned twelve, I stole my first pack of cigarettes.

After I left Oz staring at me from the doorway of Four Alarm, I dreamed I was running back and forth, touching first one wall of Chet's basement, then the other, increasingly frantic, like a hamster in a cage. I knew I wasn't ever leaving again, and the knowledge fueled my hysteria. When I lifted my hands in the dream, thick red liquid coated my palms, sticky and pungent—blood, dripping in fat drops to the concrete floor. I followed their trail and found the drops formed a pool in which the fourth body lay wrapped in rope made of bedsheets.

Lately, memories or images I'd suppressed from childhood seem to blend with my imagination and create that same sense again—that I'll never get out of the basement. Never be anything but trapped.

Seated at our usual table in Ezra's Brewery, Shia makes notes in that bound journal of his. When he spots me, his mouth shifts into a frown. "Almost thought you wouldn't show. You're late."

"I'm here. My emotional baggage just slowed me down today." I slide into a tall bar-height chair. Shia's head remains bent over a page, but his expression brightens. I rub my shoulder and wince from the deep-purple bruise that was noticeable in the bathroom mirror this morning.

Trying to stop the killer from exposing me has only led me to spending more time with Oz and Topher Cho, the combination of which has outed me in record time. Is that what the intruder's message in my apartment was referencing? It's time to come clean about my family history, to the police department, to the *Portland Post*?

I packed a suitcase last night. Debated leaving town at five in the morning. The same doubts I've had since discovering the windshield note, however, stopped me: What would I do? Where would I go and with what money? With no attractive answers, I woke up, showered on autopilot, then drove here in a daze.

My stomach turns like I might be sick. When I focus on Shia's face again, he's already watching me. "Should we get started?"

I flag down a server and order a plate of tater tots, this establishment's prime offering after beer. The restaurant side is packed with patrons today, all of whom seem to be on their cell phones. Noise carries from the brewery side of the building—the usual raucous shouts. "What do you want to discuss?"

Shia leans forward and hugs his elbows. "I didn't think you'd show. Not because you were late. But because of . . . today."

I place my hands flat on the table and try not to look like I'm craving an aspirin. The lacquered wood tabletop is cool, soothing against my skin. "What do you mean?"

"Claire, look around you. You think this many people normally come to a brewery this early on a Monday? What do you think they're reading on their phones or watching on the TVs right now? What could be so important to them today—and to you?"

The chill returns. It skates across the back of my neck, gliding beneath my ponytail, like a rope. The shouts from the bar seem to shift and morph into clear words that make me wish I'd ordered whiskey instead of tots.

Chet.

Chet Granger.

Chet Granger is free.

Shia dips his head, his eyes never breaking from mine. "That's right, Claire. What day is it?"

I swallow hard, no longer sure how I made it out of bed at all. "Monday. The day of Chet's parole."

"Correct," Shia murmurs.

I gasp—suddenly feeling like I've hit the tile floor again, the wind gone from my chest. "What's happening? What is everyone watching?"

Shia's hand touches mine, but I focus on the scratches carved into the tabletop.

"It's only news coverage at this point. Local stations have been camped out in front of the prison since six this morning. Nothing much has happened, so it's mostly been weather reports. 'Sunny skies the day that Chet Granger is released.' Did you really forget about it?"

The basket of tots arrives, and I grab a handful and swallow, barely chewing. Hunger and anxiety meld together like ravenous mice in my belly. "No. Yes. I don't know. Do we know if he's already out or still signing paperwork or whatever?"

My skin prickles, imagining him walking through the doorway of a restaurant or brewery like this one. Enjoying fresh air and freedom for the first time in years, while assessing how women have changed over time, no doubt considering what crimes he could get away with in this modern age. What statutes may have been legislated since his incarceration and what loopholes will help secure the careful plans he's been making all the while.

"Karin Degrassi, his wife, has been giving interviews." Shia watches me, then writes a note in his book, visible from where I sit—*PTSD undiluted. Does trauma ever really heal? Time heals all wounds or some?*

I take a breath. Using two fingers, I gouge the fat pad of my palm until tears prick my eyes.

My eyes flick toward one of the four flat-screen televisions in the bar area. "Any other news reported this morning?"

Shia shakes his head. "Not that I know of. Why?"

Before I fell asleep last night, I hit "Refresh" on the *Portland Post's* landing page at least thirty times. Waiting. Watching. Knowing that Oz wouldn't sit on what he learned forever.

After I ran out—ran home and locked my new-and-improved dead bolt—he must have gone down to verify for himself whether there was indeed a new body in the tunnels.

Observing my face, Shia stiffens. "What happened?"

He grabs his phone and opens his search browser, then types something I can't make out from across the table. His gaze snaps up to mine. "Another body was found in the tunnels of Four Alarm Brewery. While police previously searched the known passageways, the victim appears to have been moved to this location within the last two days. Police have now sealed off all entrances to the so-called Shanghai Tunnels."

I pull up the same information on my phone, updated this morning at six. All entrances sealed . . . Thinking back on my Saturday night with Oz, the trapdoor entrance to the tunnels was unguarded and accessible to anyone inside Beijing Suzy's.

The *Post* article adds that a brewery employee previously questioned about the murders has been detained again in connection with the latest one. My stomach sinks. Topher let me in after I lied to him about being a photographer with the police. And there's no doubt in my mind he'll offer up every detail to the detectives who interview him—most importantly, that I asked for a self-guided tour. If Oz didn't volunteer right away that I've got a family history of violence and kidnapping of women, he will after learning Topher was misled into allowing me access below.

The words that I spoke to Oz last night return with a sting: *Female serial killers have commonalities with male serial killers. Both of them usually witness violence at a formative age.*

"This is crazy," Shia says, scrolling on his phone. "NWTV suggests they've got an additional source saying the killer isn't the homeless girl but a different woman. Who do you think that is?"

"Who do I think who is? The killer or the source?" I search his face for an accusation.

He peers at me, both eyebrows lifted. "The killer. Women aren't typically serial killers. It's hard to imagine someone who'd have a motive to organize multiple murders like this."

My phone buzzes. Oz's name trails across the square window.

"Hello?" I answer, my voice shaking. My free hand grips the edge of the table, and Shia notices.

"You should know that I'm recording this call." His voice is tremulous, as if he, too, is scared. Scared of what?

"I went to the police early this morning and told them everything that's happened between us. Your photography work for the *Post*, your presence at each crime scene, your returning to the Four Alarm tunnels,

and the photo you took of that dead body. I told them your real name
. . . Marissa . . . and the fact that you are Chet Granger's child and failed
to tell anyone. I made everything about your involvement as a freelance
photographer clear, so that when the police come for you, you won't
take the *Post* down with you."

My mouth falls slack. Oz is scared—of me.

Shia watches my reactions, his eyes unmoving even when a server
spills a tray of fries on the floor.

"Oz—I'm not. You're making a mistake here."

"The hell I am," Oz scoffs, and someone makes a hushing sound in
the background; he's not alone. "I went back through my notes at each
site. At first, I thought maybe the murderer was a rival dancer at The
Stakehouse; then I cross-referenced details from the *Post*'s coverage of
your captivity. I was up all night, hoping to be proven wrong before I
went to the police, but everything in the Granger incident report was
as I remembered. I even confirmed your first meal post-captivity was
croissants, and the third body was found at a French bakery. God knows
what the police will find on your laptop, on top of the photos of the
latest dead body on your camera."

I go to speak, but my words fail me. Everything I feared in receiving the anonymous notes, the way they led me to each successive crime
scene, required that I use clues from my childhood to identify the next
location—obligated me to talk with Shia and recall more—is coming
to a head. The killer would have known I'd save each series of photos,
maintaining a library of evidence to be used against me, true to Oz's
mocking tone. Even as the *Post* incentivized me to take more shots,
always more images, by paying me my first livable wage in years. The
killer must have known about that, too.

"You said it yourself," Oz breathes into the phone. "Serial killers
witness violence at an early age. That's all you, *Missy*."

My mouth goes dry and, instinctively, I search for the nearest exit.

"To think I let you spend the night," he adds. "Hope you enjoy life in prison." The line goes dead.

He hung up on me. How long does it take to triangulate someone's geo-location using cell phone towers? A minute? Longer? Is it longer cell phone to cell phone? Do the police need a warrant to track me?

Practical thoughts torpedo in my brain as I reach across the table and remove a medium-size fry from Shia's plate.

He stares at me, both eyebrows steepled together. "What just happened?"

I chew the greasy treat, then wipe my hands on a paper napkin. "I—I don't know exactly. I think . . . the police are coming for me."

"Are you serious?"

I nod.

"Then you need to leave. Whoever you were speaking with—that Oz guy from the *Post?*—you need to leave."

High-pitched, hysterical laughter tumbles from my throat, halfway past my teeth. I run a hand down my face, then continue to laugh into my palm.

"Claire, I'm serious. You need to leave." Nervous energy rolls off Shia in waves.

"This isn't happening," I say, wiping a tear from my eye. "I'm not—this isn't real." Another round of giggles bursts from me, and I clutch my side against the sudden pinch. "Holy shit, is this happening?"

"Claire. Outside. Follow me outside now. Come on." Shia throws a twenty on the table, then directs me through the restaurant by the elbow. When the sun hits us on the sidewalk, the smile wipes from my face. I feel depleted. Empty. Confused. He leads me to his car, and a dull warning within me says I shouldn't go anywhere with a man I don't actually know—despite opening wide my secrets to him in interviews. I should stop. Go back to the safety of the restaurant and finish the tots.

"Stop." I struggle against his grip on my elbow, but he opens his passenger door and throws me inside. He locks the door from the outside, and even though I can unlock it, I don't. I sit still as he circles the hood and opens the driver's-side door.

Finally, I'll get exactly what I deserve.

He reaches across me, and I flinch when he touches my bare knee. Instead of grabbing me by the shoulders, he retrieves a box hidden beneath a black blanket. A radio scanner. He flicks a button, and the machine powers to life, garbled conversations becoming clearer as Shia manipulates the frequency knobs. When he finds the station he wants, he stares straight ahead, listening. I listen, too, but only understand numbers. Street names. And "Ezra's Brewery and Restaurant."

"What does that mean?" I turn to Shia, all mirth and amusement sucked from my body. I clutch my messenger bag across my legs.

"There's a call out for your arrest." He licks his lips, and a shudder ripples through me before he speaks. "It means you need to run."

Twenty-Eight

"What do I do? Where do I go?" Frenzy elevates my voice. My cheeks flush as sweat breaks across my neck, and I clutch my bag tighter. My laptop and camera, the chief sources of evidence against me, are inside, but how much can be inferred from the photos that the *Post* bought?

The *Portland Post*. The closest bridge to normal I've had in over a year—gone. Pauline must know by now.

If the police are on their way to the restaurant, a separate unit must be en route to my apartment.

Shia grips the steering wheel, looking at something in the road. A man in a blazer and jeans, jaywalking. The man's face drops to his cell phone screen in his hand. My phone pings; Shia's makes the bell chime sound. We each tap on the news alert that popped up, and a string of text appears:

AP News Alert: Convicted of sexual assault and false imprisonment, Chet Granger has been released on parole from Echo State Prison.

The blood drains from my face. I lift my eyes to Shia's wary expression. The stupor that bloomed in my chest carries down my arms and nests in my fingertips. "He's out," I whisper.

Shia resumes staring forward. He turns the key in the ignition and starts the car. "I'll drive you wherever you want to go. But after that, I can't promise anything."

I nod.

"Lay back." He reaches across me—this time I don't flinch—and hits a button on the side of the seat, reclining me click by click.

Leafy green canopies frame my view as Shia drives through downtown, observing every speed limit, stop sign, and traffic signal.

"Where am I going?" he asks after we loop a roundabout for the second time.

I need to regroup. Gather my thoughts and consider next steps. "Drop me off at that coffee shop, Stump City. Your favorite."

He turns right, and we climb a hill. The foliage above becomes thicker, fanning out, so the sunshine only dapples through. Traffic noise diminishes around us, and instead voices seem to multiply as the road levels out. Pedestrians carry on conversations, audible in these narrow streets, maybe taking early lunches or discussing ways to skip town and never be seen again.

Shia pulls to a stop beneath a sign that reads COBBLE YOU UP: SHOE REPAIR.

"We're here," he says, turning to me.

I remain seated, not wanting to move, to be thrust out into a hostile world that's growing more claustrophobic with every minute. "Sorry about . . . Do you have enough to finish your book?"

Shia answers with a sad smile. "The book will be just fine. Worry about you. Once you figure out next steps, stay off the map. Okay?"

The corners of his eyes appear lined in the bright sunshine in a way that wasn't evident in the dim brewery. My first impression of him as another self-serving vulture was a knee-jerk reaction—a fair one, given my history with the media, but not fair to him.

"Do you think I did it? That I could be behind all this?" Although I meant the question to come off casual, nonchalant—not desperate for the affirmation I've been seeking all my life—I hold my breath.

Dark-brown eyes study me. "No, Claire. I don't."

I pull the door handle to exit his car. "Thanks for everything, Shia. I don't know what I would have—"

Stiff white paper pokes from the door's pocket. A rectangular piece of card stock, nearly hidden between a folded map and a receipt. With shaking fingers, I bend to pluck it from the compartment.

My breath catches as I retrieve another of my business cards and bring it to eye level.

After not seeing one for years, believing I had retrieved each of the piles I had left at strategic locations two hours from here, I clutch the second one to cross my path in less than a day. "Shia?"

All color leaches from his face. "I told you. I collected items and information on your family for a long time. This is one of those items I found. I've been hoping to write a book on you. Your story has always given me hope that we don't have to be defined by our upbringings."

Suddenly, my proximity to this man, who has known every part of my childhood, even details previously kept from me, radiates danger. "You set me up," I whisper. "You placed a copy of this card on the fourth victim last night. You're the killer."

"What? Claire, no, I—"

I swing the door open and plant a leg onto the street. I shift my weight to run when Shia grabs me and slams me back into the seat. His grip digs into my arm, his eyes crazed. "Claire, you have to listen to me; I am not a murderer. I only collected the cards for my book, I swear."

Reaching blindly into my bag, I fumble past my wallet and find my pepper spray. Flipping open the cap, I release a cloud into the cab, then bolt from the car. Shia screams behind me, but I don't look back. I run, my bag tucked under my arm, and run harder and faster than I ever have. Down the street, around the corner, until I am six blocks away.

Panting in front of a house's wraparound porch, I slide down between a recycling bin and a garbage can. Try to catch my breath. To digest that I've had the murderer in front of me all along.

Fat tears pour down my cheeks, my first sobs since moving here—another mistake.

I fumble in my bag for cigarettes before remembering I don't have a lighter, don't even own one. My latest form of self-sabotage. New tears trail down my chin as I cover my face with my hands, dig my nails in above my eyebrows. My fingers tremble, vibrate, as the urge swells in me to drag them down to my jaw, to feel the pain of something I can control.

The lies we tell ourselves during stable hours—like *I'm a good person* or *I don't deserve this*—become the lies we bury deep down, too far to access, in times of pain.

My hands relax, stopping just short of drawing blood. Panic gives way to self-loathing.

I should have known. Should have trusted my instincts instead of being tempted by the prospect of money. Stability. A friend.

I wince, reflecting on how desperate I must have been to miss the signs. Shia is the tunnel murderer, an obsessed fan of Chet's just like I initially suspected—the author of the note, just like Jenessa thought. According to the prison's records, he went to visit Chet within the last month, but there's no telling how frequently he's gone over the years.

After waiting five minutes for Shia's silver sedan to pass by searching for me, I stand and return to the boulevard. Shops line the busy street, offering parking at their rears. I find a bench located at the back of a sushi restaurant and open my laptop, hoping for unrestricted Wi-Fi. If there's a warrant out for my arrest, the police might already be tracking my credit cards. And I need to reserve what little cash I have until I figure out next steps.

The network signal lights up as my computer connects. Jackpot. I open my browser.

How the hell did I end up here? Shia's unassuming writer persona was always at odds with the dark-web activity, plus the broad shoulders and the strength of his frame that I thought were window dressing. My arm throbs momentarily, recalling the grip he wielded when I tried to exit his car. He could have overpowered his victims using weapons or strength. And the lack of recurring fingerprints at each crime scene doesn't mean he's the ringleader of a murderous gang; it shows only that he knows how to wear gloves.

I reach into my bag and withdraw the scone I squirreled away at the bookstore yesterday. Despite being squished, the baked good is energizing, grounding when I feel unmoored. My grateful stomach rumbles, and I realize just how hungry I am. There's an apple crammed into an inner pocket, beside the orange I took from the *Portland Post* when I first met with Pauline. I bite into the taut skin with a juicy crunch.

My fingers tremble as I click my bookmark for the *Portland Post* website. In a side bar, the *Post's* social media accounts offer live commentary on Chet's release. I scan the various posts and find several photos taken of Chet leaving prison, looking elated before climbing into a pink Corvette with Karin. A scarf is wrapped around her dark hair, and she wears wide pink sunglasses like the latest iteration of Convertible Barbie. My stomach twists as I scroll down to the final update: Chet is headed toward Portland.

Back on the main landing page, a headline reports the most recent casualty of the tunnel murderer. As of an hour ago, police are pursuing several leads while working to identify the body. The photo I took of Petey the Penguin in front of Four Alarm Brewery sits at the top of the page as the banner image—where it all began.

What is your earliest memory?

Unbidden, Shia's spectral voice fills my ears, pestering me to examine my beginnings. Everything he asked about must have been rooted in framing me. Yet that doesn't mean I was wrong in examining those memories. Right?

Why does something still feel off about the last week? The timeline doesn't add up—how could he have known I'd even see Petey outside Four Alarm? And the killer's notes felt personal, beyond a professional desire on Shia's part to promote the sale of his books.

On the other side of the sushi restaurant, a car honks; then metal crashes against metal. Young female voices erupt in fierce words, too low for me to grasp but clear enough to register their disagreement over who was at fault. Then their dynamic shifts, lightens. One woman admits she was following too closely.

I was following you . . .

My lungs deflate, sucked dry of air, recalling a different voice that spoke those words to me outside a diner I worked at. Certainty snaps like a rubber band down to each of my toes as one of my oldest and original stalkers sparks to mind: Serena Delle.

In a new browser tab, I search for *Serena Delle* and *Eugene*, the college town I moved from and the last city I knew she was living in. A few results from Facebook, dated four years ago, pop up, but when I click the link and access her profile page, it appears they are her most recent posts. Clicking on her "About" section, I'm stopped by one update:

Current city: Portland, Oregon.

She's here.

My fingers fly across my keyboard, and I hope against hope that the sushi restaurant doesn't notice me *click-clack*ing away for free at their back entrance and cut me off. Not now.

I search *Serena Delle* again, this time with the phrase *Portland, Oregon.* The third result shows an address tied to her name. Recalling the TriMet bus pass that Pauline gave me the day I took the marketing department's headshots, I dig through my wallet and find it shoved behind my expired Costco card. According to the TriMet website, the nearest light-rail station is two blocks over. With that as my starting point, I map the fastest route to Serena.

Thirty minutes pass on a rail trolley mostly empty of people, none of them interested in me. A police car speeds by when we pause at an intersection, but I slink farther down the fabric-lined seat. The space between houses lengthens, and yards become larger, now unfenced. A railroad bell rings somewhere nearby. I exit at one of the stations, then follow the map on my phone west on a narrow street with deep ditches flanking each side. At the second-to-last house on the left, the map displays a message, *You have arrived at your destination.*

A pale one-story home spreads across the lot, ranch house–style. Naked saplings with only a handful of buds line the perimeter of the front yard, while empty flowerpots frame a gravel walkway, last summer's contents shriveled and brown. On a metal mailbox atop a wooden post, reflective letters spell out the name *Delle*.

Adrenaline gushes through me. With each step closer to the rusted cross on the front door, I can feel my heart drumming against my ribs.

I hesitate at the threshold. If Serena Delle really has followed me to Portland and has been wreaking havoc in my life the last week, how did she do it so quickly? Or did she move before I did? She pursued me from Arch, where we went to high school together, two hours west to the college town where I worked odd jobs and began my photography business. I thought after the restraining order was filed that she might have moved back to Arch or stayed where she was and succeeded in building her own life. Judging from the way she sent that letter to the *Tru Lives* reporter, she's been keeping tabs on me for longer than I was aware.

If she is behind the murders—with Shia as her partner?—I'd be stupid to come here alone and without a weapon. I withdraw my pepper spray from my messenger bag. The last time I saw Serena, she was wearing a high-waisted flowy dress and her heavy cheeks were flushed.

She showed up at my job, uninvited, and begged me for five minutes outside, where she asked that I reconsider our friendship, swore that she'd misinterpreted me in high school and I was the only friend she had. We had been friends—in middle school. I remember bonding over our mutual dislike of Aaron Carter songs and her father's tendency to hit her mother. As the mayor of Arch, Zeke Delle was untouchable; it was comforting for Serena to meet someone like me, who'd also experienced trauma.

But as I privately battled the depression that reared during adolescence, that came in waves with each photograph I viewed of Rosemary as a twenty-year-old, of Chet as a predatory thirty-five-year-old, and spiraled into days of self-harm, I couldn't handle anyone else's emotional needs. I could barely see straight some days, my vision so blurred with tears and the throbbing heartbeat of wounded skin. I never knew if Serena or anyone else at school recognized the self-destructive behavior. Whether, in leaving dead animals for me to find, she thought she was helping me exorcise some genetic compulsion or if she'd simply developed an affinity for death herself.

All I know is that one day during high school, a dead squirrel showed up beside my car. The next month, there was another. And another. Then two more. Serena and I hadn't spoken in a few years at that point, and I was horrified when I found her depositing the final corpse at my tire. Rather than ask her why, I snatched the body from the ground and threw it at her, splattering her light-blonde hair with squirrel guts and blood. We were both suspended from school for several days.

So why now? Did she and Shia meet somehow, maybe in one of those dark-web forums speculating about my family? When did she graduate from killing small animals to murdering people?

I step forward onto a threadbare welcome mat and lift my fist to the screen door. A cardboard sign beside the doorbell says **BROKEN**, while another one written on faded paper beneath says **NO SOLICITORS**.

I knock twice. I'm not here for anything but a confession.

Footsteps approach from the other side, and the fresh scab on my inner elbow feels like it might spontaneously combust into new embers. I plant my feet to be ready for whatever happens next.

The dead bolt unlocks, and I feel a flash of fear that Shia will be the one to answer, then yank me inside and hold me until the police arrive. The inner door cracks open. A woman stares back at me, full of suspicion from behind the screen.

"Can I help you?" she says. The door opens wider, another six inches, and I meet an older version of Serena Delle. Ash-blonde hair hangs in wisps around a full, lined face, and the same pug nose wrinkles at the sight of me. However, instead of Serena's ghostly blue eyes, this woman examines me with brown eyes. She hunches forward, almost in a bow, in a more exaggerated way than Serena used to shuffle about our high school hallways. She licks thin lips, the kind that might close around a cigarette a dozen times a day.

"Miss? Can I help you?"

No movement comes from behind this woman, and I don't hear a back door slam or feet taking off through the backyard. "I'm . . . I'm looking for Serena. Is she here?"

The woman's face falls. The door opens all the way, although the screen door remains shut. "Were you a friend of hers?"

"What do you mean . . . 'were'?"

"Serena died. Three years ago. She killed herself." The woman bites down on her lip. She stares at the ground, then flicks sharp eyes to mine. "Did you know her?"

My plans out the window, I stammer the truth. "I . . . yes. I did. Back in Arch. I wanted to say hello."

If Serena is dead, and by suicide no less, who sent the *Tru Lives* reporter to talk to me? Who is Shia working with? What the hell is going on?

The woman's face softens. A pink birthmark is visible on her clavicle, similar to the starfish shape that was on Serena's hand. "What's your name, honey?"

"Claire. Claire Lou," I add, not missing a beat.

"Well, Claire," she says, pursing her lips. "You've arrived just a few years too late. Serena could have used a friend out here. Arch wasn't very kind to her growing up, but then you probably know that, having been classmates. I don't know, it's all so hard to tell as a parent . . ." Her voice trails off as a delivery truck rumbles down the street. "I was hoping Serena would get a fresh start in Eugene when she went to U of O. But that seemed to have made things worse."

"I'm sorry to hear that. In high school, Serena kept to herself as far as I knew. But I did learn that Serena had some . . . eccentricities. She left dead animals for a girl, Marissa Mo. Did Serena have some kind of fascination with that family?"

Hearing Serena's mother dismiss the ways her daughter made my life so challenging makes me push for the answers I can never get from Serena now. Why the squirrels? Why the stalking?

The woman glares at me. She doesn't look as certain that I am a kindred spirit, a friend to her beloved, lost child. "Serena had her faults, and you're right, her quirks. There was a lot of pressure on her to be this political prop for her father. But she was a good person. I . . . I never learned what that business was between her and Marissa. I moved up here after her father and I divorced; then she followed about four years ago."

She wipes an eye with a chipped pink nail. "I wish she were here to see you, Claire. Did you want to come inside? I have some juice I could open up. Or a wine cooler."

"That's very kind. Thank you. But I should get going. I'm sorry for your loss," I add genuinely.

When I reach the street, I turn back to find Serena's mother still watching me. She lifts a hand in goodbye, frozen in the doorway. Once

I'm past the sight line of her house, I remove my camera, then take a photo of the trees, the home's rooftop just visible and missing several shingles.

I walk quickly to the light-rail station, hoping a train arrives the moment I do, listening for vengeful footsteps behind me. Now, instead of imagining Serena's heavy gait, my ears strain for the sound of a stranger racing toward me, unhindered, with no intention of stopping.

Twenty-Nine

The second light-rail pulls away from the station, and I wait for the air to clear before inhaling a breath. Without an obvious direction to travel in, I take refuge on a nearby bench. Removed from the stark knowledge that Serena killed herself, and that I may have precipitated her sense of loneliness, the knots in my stomach release, if only by a small margin.

My phone pings. Another news alert from the *Portland Post*. I click on the link, and a video pops up, showing Chet exiting Karin's pink convertible. A box of doughnuts is visible in the back seat. Did they stop by Jenessa's work? Voices shout at Chet, asking him what he is doing there and what he is going to do now that he's on parole.

He turns and faces the camera. His hair is combed and gelled, unlike when I saw him a few days prior, and he appears rested, fresh faced. Fooling a board of prison officials into believing you've learned from your abusive ways will do that.

"I'm simply happy being free for the first time in twenty years," he says with a modest shrug.

I'm just a regular person. Right.

"Now, if you'll excuse me, I need to say hi to someone very special." He turns and walks into the lobby of an apartment building. In the corner, visible through the glass wall and beside a faded chair, a lily of the valley potted flower adds a splash of white and green to the brick wall.

An advertisement for the *Tru Lives* TV show appears, and I dismiss the pop-up to swipe back to the video. I play it again. Again. My eyes pull wider each time I watch Chet take the stairs to Lily's apartment. He found her. But how? She just moved back and I'm sure hasn't completed any public address announcement. Maybe he found Lily after he already found Jenessa? Maybe Karin has been tracking us all down for him.

I navigate to my messages app and find it's empty of unread texts. Neither of my sisters has messaged me in a panic. Maybe Lily isn't home and—it's a little past lunchtime—Jenessa is on break from the doughnut shop. The video would have been filmed fairly recently, then uploaded and published to online news outlets, like the *Post*. There's no telling where Chet is now.

My phone pings again. My heart tightens at the chime in some Pavlovian response. Hovering over the notice bar, this time from a national news outlet, I hesitate, then tap my screen.

AP News Alert: Murderer-rapist Chet Granger released on parole seeks reunion with daughters. Local police issue a warrant for the arrest of the oldest, Marissa Mo, a.k.a. Claire Lou. Have you seen this woman?

Horror snaps through me as my face fills the screen. The photo that Pauline insisted I take for my *Portland Post* badge stares back at me. The closed-mouth smile that I considered professional, if aloof, here appears mysterious—secretive—beneath the paragraph about local police tracking me down.

Casting a glance around me, I scan the faces of other people waiting for the TriMet, for some indication that a call has been placed to the police and I should start running again. The platform remains as calm as when I first arrived.

Run. You run away from those crime scenes and that case as fast as you can. Rosemary was right. It was a trap all along.

Recalling the threat wedged under my doormat, I note that the killer made good on the promised timeline. A body turned up yesterday and threw my world into chaos today, the day of Chet's release. As the murderers, Chet and Karin could have set me up to divert attention away from them, in order to execute some other scheme, but their whereabouts are being closely monitored by the media. Neither one seems to mind.

With Serena Delle long gone from this world, and Chet and his wife roaming the streets of Portland, Rosemary's words take on new significance. Her dismay at my job. Her fears for me. Her darty eyes. Her actions and movements replay in my head like scenes from a movie, as though she gave me the answers; I just didn't know it then. Despite avoiding her for good reason, I trust Rosemary implicitly.

Nora, she's . . . she's had some trouble.

The details found at each crime scene and related to my childhood are too intimate, too accurate to be the work of an onlooker or a stranger. Yes, the penguin toy, the braided bracelet, and Lily's baby blanket were all visible to the outside world. But no one could have known based on photographs how special these items were to me personally. Someone would have needed firsthand insight from Chet's basement or to have been close to sources who did.

Rosemary and Jenessa were trying to warn me in their own ways while protecting someone they loved. Instead of traveling the state, as Jenessa said she was, or emailing plucky updates at Christmastime, according to Rosemary—what if Nora has gone off her medication again and neither one of them wanted to expose her? As Rosemary said, it wasn't their news to share. What if the woman I called Mama Nora has been setting me up?

Rosemary's foreboding returns again. *You handled it differently from Lily or me, and I think better than Jenessa and Nora, too. Nora, she's . . . she's had some trouble. Bad stuff.*

I scroll through my contacts to call Rosemary and verify what she meant, then remember that the police issued a warrant for my arrest. They haven't come screaming down this street yet, but I'll bet I can be tracked by my phone, among a host of other ways. The AP alert they released could be a measly indicator of what's churning off-line. I should only use my phone when I have no other choice.

Shia, during one of our sessions, echoed Rosemary's fear with a similar response. *You're the only one who managed to adjust to outside living, to deal with all the emotional baggage of your past. You made it. Whereas everyone else, all the other women, and Chet included, have struggled to get by.*

A ball forms in my chest, pushing against my ribs. Had Nora envied my supposedly smooth adjustment, watching me grow up, getting updates from Rosemary that would have been scrubbed clean to present a successful front? Jenessa certainly thought that was the case—she accused me of killing my guinea pig, for God's sake. Maybe Nora had planted that idea, bitter that Jenessa's—and even Lily's—turbulent ups and downs were always being unfairly judged against me.

If the world thinks I'm a murderer, her daughter looks far better off by comparison.

It's ridiculous to think something like that could be a competition, and yet it also makes sense. Jenessa considered Rosemary her mother by the time we escaped. Did Nora blame us for their difficult relationship? Did Chet's upcoming release—or maybe just my return to Portland—tip her over the edge of revenge? Rosemary tried to take her daughter. Now, she'd take Rosemary's.

I'm so confused. My nerves are shot, and I feel paranoid, like everyone has a reason to be after me. Shia. Oz. Karin. Nora. The reality is I'm no closer to knowing who the killer is than I was before.

A drop of rain lands on my head. Wetness splashes my forearm and tingles my scars. The air smells thick, ripe with impending thunder.

A train approaches with the chime of a bell. Using the framed map of the waiting area, I find the most direct route to my next stop, knowing the only way forward is to confront Nora. Pose her these questions directly and—if needed—ensure she goes to prison for all the pain she's caused.

⚹

Across the street from a tucked-away road, a trio of boutique shops advertises their wares. Sweat moistens the skin beneath my arms and under my breasts, but the four-block walk in light rain was otherwise subdued. Two unknown numbers called me. Several cars passed me on the side streets I took. No one stopped to arrest me.

The storefronts have changed over time, but Nora's flower shop has always occupied the middle of the three. An OPEN sign hangs in the glass door, while Mrs. Hernandez, the longtime manager who does everything short of owning the place, fixes a bouquet on the counter. Although the area has become more industrial and the foliage thinner, I had to ask directions to this main road only once.

The small home Nora bought with her portion of the settlement sits opposite the shops. White paint on the cottage-style house contrasts the bright blue of the front door. I duck beneath the awning of a cannabis shop and withdraw my camera from my bag. Using my zoom, I search the windowpanes for signs of movement.

The steady flow of traffic breaks, and I jog across the street. At the steps of the front porch, I turn and take a poplar-lined sidewalk to the row of houses behind. Nora's red roof is visible despite a tree with thick branches in a bordering yard, and I sneak up the alleyway, keeping close to the fence. A security camera attached above the next house's gutter is angled toward the front driveway, but I duck down and keep going.

A double layer of tall cedar fencing marks Nora's yard. I hop over it, bracing myself against the flat top. I land between hydrangea bushes, then pause to catch my breath. Listen. Figure out what the hell I do next.

Approaching from the front seemed like an idiot move, but I'm not sure what I planned, sneaking in the back. My fists clench the closer I slink, from flower bed to flower bed. Cramps form in my feet, gripping the soles of my sneakers as I try not to slip on the wet grass. I take the steps up to the back porch, exhaling when the new wooden boards don't creak under my weight.

I press on the handle of the screen door, and it gives without so much as a whine. My mouth waters from dehydration and the tension that flexes every muscle in my body. I wipe my face, try to gather my thoughts.

Someone moves from where I remember the bedrooms are to the right. A bird caws in the neighborhood, louder in its staccato cadence than the low hum of street traffic. No knickknacks or dirty dishes line the kitchen counters, and the circular breakfast table beneath the window is set for two. Tile shines beneath me, the scent of bleach lingering in the air; even the grout has been scrubbed white. Harassment and murder must bring out Nora's homemaking skills.

I move through a narrow hallway to pass a butler's pantry filled with bottles of wine and hard liquor. The sitting room mirrors the kitchen, with everything in order. Above a fireplace—itself clean of soot or wood tinder—sits a mounted flat-screen television, while magazines rest in a stack on a lacquered coffee table. A glass of water occupies a marble coaster. Condensation drips from the glass in the afternoon humidity, a twin to the bead of sweat gliding down my back. A glistening umbrella sits in a bucket beside the front door. She must have just returned home.

Water rushes from down the hall as a toilet flushes. I whirl toward the sound, toward the rooms, and cast around for something sharp. The fireplace poker. I seize it, gearing myself up to confront Nora, to question her. To reveal I know she's tried to frame me for murders she's orchestrated, or committed with Shia, as payback for my role in how her life with Jenessa turned out. I'll demand she turn herself in.

I whip out my phone and prepare to call the cops when a door opens.

Chet steps from the hallway bathroom. He wipes his hands on his jeans, then notices me standing frozen in the front room. A smile spreads across his wrinkled features, revealing yellow teeth.

"Marissa. Just the person I wanted to see next."

Thirty

The man's hair is thin up close. It's straight and brown but shorter on the top of his head. I've never seen the top of his head before. Little black circles stick out of his face, his eyeballs. They remind me of a doll's because they roll back then forward then back. He's quiet for a minute. His cheek was red earlier but now it's purply. I go to work.

I creep up from the wall with my new braided rope wrapped around my arm. Grab the bit of rope that hangs from his feet. He's still tied up like a piggy but his feet and hands are farther apart. I take the dangly rope and my new rope and tie them together in a triple knot. The best kind. Then make a figure eight, over one foot then the other foot, one foot then the other foot. Then I go hands. One hand then the other hand. Over under.

Then I crisscross back again, making sure to wrap around Mama Rosemary's rope for extra Bruno the Polar Bear strength. I sit down on the floor and pull tight.

When I'm all done feet and hands are touching and I'm all hot. My nightgown makes my underarms sticky.

I stand up proud of myself and think how proud Mama Rosemary will be.

My Petey the Penguin toy sits in my corner. Can't leave Petey. I grab his arm—the pasta-stained one—and hug him tight then start toward the stairs. I stay away from the stairs ever since Twin fell and hurt her knee but this time I'm going up up up them.

The man moves reaches for me grabs my ponytail and I jump away but trip and fall flat on the floor and pain all over my ankle. He falls on his side still piggy-tied and I feel his fingers grabbing pulling on my arm to keep me close but I scratch kick move away from him and those hands. I press against the wall and watch his fingers stretch and claw reaching for me still.

I breathe heavy hard and fast. The man is quiet facing the Murphy bed now. His fingers stop moving.

My ankle hurts. I try standing but it hurts too much. It's round now like a ball. Red and bumping like when my head hurts after too much Lith-yum.

The door is open just above the top of the stairs but there's too many steps. I count them. Eight steps.

I try standing again and this time I start to cry because it hurts so bad.

Mama Rosemary will be outside with police soon and I can't go to her.

Hot tears fall down my cheeks but I try not to make a sound. The man's fingers are moving, trying to shake off the ropes but I tied them too tight. I'm proud again then his feet start moving. He starts kicking. Kicking kicking and I get nervous. Worried that he will get free.

Then he goes still.

After a while, I get tired. Bored. I wish Mama Rosemary had turned the television on before she left. My ankle keeps going *bump bump* and it's even bigger now. More tears fall down my face and wet my nightgown.

I wonder where they are. Mama and my sisters. I miss them. But I know they'll come back for me. And we can be a family living together.

I hope we'll share a bed like we do here and not like siblings do on television. I'll be too cold if we sleep separate.

The man looks like he's sleeping again. He hasn't moved in three "Row Row Row Your Boat"s that I sang in my head quiet.

I get sleepy, too. I slide under the bathtub just in case he wakes up before me or he's a liar and only pretending to be asleep. My foot pushes a bunch of puzzle pieces out of the way.

I close my eyes and lay my head on my arms. I prop up my ankle on my other foot. It feels a little better but not so much.

I miss Mama and Twin and Sweet Lily and wish they'd come back already. I close my eyes because I'm tired.

I start to dream of running with my sisters and Mama making pasta in the kitchen. Then someone calls my name and my head hits something hard. The bathtub. New tears come because my head hurts just like when I burned my arm on the stove. I slide out from under the bathtub and rub my hair then push back quick against the wall far away.

The man is still on his tummy. His head flipped over and he's watching me now. He smiles. He is a liar.

"That is your name, isn't it?" he says. "Why don't you untie me, sweetheart? I'll get you more candy. You like Mars Bars, right?"

I don't answer him. Instead I cradle my ankle and think about the way Mama Rosemary smells. How warm her arms are.

I feel so sleepy and the man looks so awake.

Mama Rosemary better hurry back soon I don't know how much longer I can stay awake.

I touch my head again where it hurts most. Something wet. I pull back quick and blood is on my fingers. When I look up, the man sees, too.

He smiles.

Thirty-One

Chet and I stand unspeaking, eyeing each other across the neatly furnished sitting room. Nothing decorates the walls apart from a shelf displaying trinkets from another era. Miniature Russian dolls line up in a row beside a lone wine cork. From down the hall, a buzzer sounds; Nora must be doing laundry.

As the video clip—and the dozen user comments beneath—suggested, Chet appears rested, clean-cut. He regards me with ease now that he's out from behind the six inches of glass in the prison visitor wing. As if he hasn't been locked up the last twenty years for crimes so heinous, only a few twisted individuals can be considered his contemporaries. The tan leather jacket he wears fits his narrow shoulders, as if tailored to his measurements.

With a sickening drop in my stomach, I recognize his tapering frame in my own. Whereas Rosemary's broad shoulders balanced wide hips, I've always been slender to the point of androgynous. Dark eyes the same shade as mine return my stare with an unnerving ability to forgo blinking.

"What are you doing here?" I finally ask. Gripping the fire poker tighter in my fist, I widen my stance. "Shouldn't you and Karin be halfway to Canada by now?"

He lifts thin eyebrows. "Isn't it obvious? I wanted to reconnect. To see all of you. I have no intention of breaking parole, Marissa." His tone is chastising, as though he's deluded himself into believing he has paternal rights.

A shiver rolls across my neck. "You don't get to connect with any of us. You don't get to be here," I hiss.

He takes a step toward me, and I step back, still wielding the poker.

"Didn't Karin tell you?" he begins, lifting both hands palms out. "I tried to make it clear when you came to see me. I only want some sort of relationship with you girls. It's too late for me and Karin to have kids—she found me too late."

I shake my head, feeling my nerves fray, unraveling at the ends. "Bullshit. You're a terror. A sexual predator. What are you doing here?" I repeat.

Chet's appearance at Nora's home, right when I arrive, can mean only one thing. "You're working with her, aren't you?"

Not Nora and Shia. Nora and Chet.

Chet shakes his head. "I think you're not feeling well, Marissa. Is this stress related, from your job? For about three years I immersed myself in Buddhist philosophy, and it's so important to—"

He takes another step closer, and a freeze-frame image of him fills my mind, looming over me as a child with desire in his eyes. Something wild and feral in me rises and shatters my sense of calm, of safety. Being with him in a room again with no prison guards around us—and where is Nora?—saps the bravado that energized my journey from the light-rail station.

"Stay away from me!" I slash at the air with the iron poker, and the asshole actually smiles.

"Marissa, I'm not here to hurt you. I just want to start over with all of you and make amends for what I did."

"Stop calling me that." My arm shakes beneath the poker's weight as I keep it lifted between us. "Make amends? You can never make up for the years of agony you've put us all through. For what you've driven us to." Remembering the look in his eye—"You tried to . . . with me, you wanted to . . ."

But the memory shifts and disappears, and I can't be sure what to say.

"You're sick. I don't believe any of this rehabilitated crap. And now you're here to complete what you began with Nora while still in prison. Where is Karin? Is she hiding somewhere, waiting to jump out, too?"

His eyes narrow to slits. "Karin is making me a welcome-home dinner. I came here alone. What do you mean when you say 'complete what I began'?"

"Don't play coy, Chet. You've been planning this whole network of violence and pain with Nora. You guided her on how to kidnap people, how to imprison them, probably during visits to you. You are godfather to this latest act of murder in this city."

"I never killed anyone—"

"You killed Mama Bethel!" I scream. My breathing comes fast and shallow. "You killed her when you left her alone to give birth in an underground hellhole. I remember how small she was, even though I was barely four years old. She was all belly—the rest of her was gaunt from malnutrition. You did that to her."

He pauses as though actually considering my words. "Hey, you're right, in that I could have done more for her. In hindsight, I *should* have done more for her."

He stands taller as he talks, and I get the impression I'm witnessing some of the speech he gave to the parole examiners.

"But I haven't done anything to anyone in twenty years, Marissa. Think about it. How could I?"

I shake my head. "I don't know. But your coming to Nora's house to see her now is more than telling. Why would you both try to frame me for these murders? Why, when you keep giving me this speech that you want us to be a family?"

Chet hesitates. "Marissa, I don't know what you're talking about. I'm not trying to frame you for anything—least of all these tunnel murders that everyone's upset over. And I didn't come here to see Nora. I'm not allowed to contact my victims while on parole."

I pause. The hair on the back of my neck rises, stands on end. "If you're not here to see Nora, who are you here for?"

Footsteps shuffle toward us from the bedrooms. Long black hair swings forward in the hallway's dim lighting, a curtain that covers rich, tawny skin and a blue T-shirt. The last time I saw Nora years ago, she'd chopped her straight hair to her jaw, sick to death of shampooing the "thick rug," as she called it. The wavy curtain sways; then a gloved hand reaches back and tucks the hair behind her ear. Jenessa fills the doorway before lifting a gun.

"Me." She fires a shot, piercing Chet in the back, and he flies to the floor at my feet.

Wide eyes turn up to my face, pain dilating his pupils into black spheres. With a moan, he drops his head, collapses onto the hardwood.

Trembling, I lift my gaze to my sister's. "Jenessa?"

She stares at Chet, horror stretching her mouth. We look at each other, neither of us knowing what to say. Then she jerks forward, her expression wild. "Claire, you have to go. The police are looking for you. Here, take the gun for protection." She raises it flat in her glove. "Take it."

I reach for it, then pause. The shot continues to ring in my ears. A pool of blood seeps from Chet's body.

"Take it," she says again.

I hesitate, conflicted. Adding my prints to a murder weapon would be a mistake on top of everything else. I wouldn't be able to explain that away. I lift my free hand and find my fingers shaking. "Jenessa. Where is Nora?"

She doesn't flinch. The terror that made her cheeks taut relaxes. In a smooth, collected gesture, she resumes her grip on the gun's handle, then points it at my heart. "Well, if you insist on staying."

"Nora—"

"She's buried. Beneath the hydrangeas out back. Take a seat, Marissa. We have a lot of ground to cover. And we can add Chet to your killing spree another way."

My mind races—my heart beats, cracks, whips against my chest—computing what I should have known and recognized all along. I drop the fireplace poker inside the umbrella bucket.

My sister is the murderer. And as she trains the pistol's barrel on my chest, I realize she's already chosen her next victim.

Thirty-Two

A car alarm howls somewhere on the street, triggered by the reverb from the gunshot. My legs are frozen. Numb. I lift a finger to my cheek. Red comes away. A pool of blood stemming from Chet's torso touches my sneaker. I blink hard, taking in the scene, expecting the edges to blur and remind me that I'm dreaming another nightmare. But everything remains crisp.

Chet is dead—the demon who made me, in more ways than one, who kept me and my family prisoners, and who died believing he could make up for it. Somewhere not so deep inside me, gratification glimmers, content that he'll never have the chance.

"You weren't supposed to come here," Jenessa says, her tone flat.

I take in her brittle mien, the stiff ridge of her upper lip, the gun, and don't reply. Blood drops splatter her blue shirt, blowback from shooting Chet from behind. My own shirt feels thick, warmer than it should. I look down; the same gruesome pinwheel pattern covers my chest.

"Sit down," she commands.

I step over Chet's body in a daze, careful not to track blood in Nora's—Jenessa's?—house. Shock twines through my system as I pat my chest, confirm the bullet didn't travel through Chet's sternum and into my own.

I stumble to a couch cushion. Slide to the back of the seat. Jenessa's face is not one I recognize. Disgust hardens the features I always thought beautiful, if demanding.

After a silent moment, she begins to pace. Walks from one end of the cramped room to the other, then turns and retraces her steps. Her head sways from side to side, and the long black hair she so loves swishes behind her. Back and forth. Back and forth. It's mesmerizing. Allowing me to completely check out from this situation and the danger ready to consume me with its barbed tongue.

She whirls to face me. "You're not supposed to be here. Chet wasn't supposed to be here. Did you two talk beforehand? Did you coordinate this when you visited him in prison?"

I shake my head, my mouth still uncooperative. Light shines through closed shutter slats behind me, making the water glass gleam. A pair of steel scissors lies beyond it.

Jenessa shifts her weight to one foot and tucks the gun beneath her elbow. "I contacted him, too, you know."

I don't say anything, too scared to move.

She nods, pursing her lips together. "Yup. I asked him for tips, tricks, ideas on how to lure people or kidnap them—all hypothetically, of course, so the warden would allow my letter to go through—but he wouldn't give up the goods. He replied to me with some load of crap about me getting help and him seeing the error of his ways. I wanted to go to him in person, to get the real deal from him, but I couldn't risk my plan being linked back to him. His coming here was probably an attempt to reason with me, given that I used Nora's address on the letters. I guess I won't ever know." She glares at his body. "He deserved to die years ago."

"What happened to Nora?" I clear my throat—try to work through some of the fear billowing up as bile. Make sense of everything that's happening. My shoulder aches, and I recall how badly I slipped and fell yesterday at Four Alarm. Was that yesterday?

"You killed Nora," I whisper, unwanted tears filling my eyes. "Why hurt her, after everything we survived?"

Jenessa cocks the gun, then uncocks it. Cocks, then uncocks. She stares at me, as though debating killing me right here and now. "What about me, Marissa—or *Claire* or whatever you're calling yourself these days? What about what she put me through?"

"I know she wasn't a great mom. She had her problems, but she loved you—"

"Do you know how I spent my tenth birthday?" Her jaw works back and forth waiting for a response. "Do you?"

I shake my head.

"She sent me to score drugs for her. Somewhere over the river. Antidepressants, oxycodone, and the same lithium that Chet used to give Rosemary to put in our food and keep us subdued. She said she'd developed a taste for it and couldn't function without it. Know how I spent my eighth birthday, the year after we got out?"

"I don't know."

"Alone. I was alone, as a child, in her apartment, while she blew what was left of her settlement money at the casinos." She spits the words, glaring at me, as if I, too, am to blame. "When I got older, she made me pose for men. Take photos in lingerie and post them online in cybersex chat rooms. I was fourteen."

"That's awful. I'm so sorry," I say slowly and try to remember what I was doing then, why I didn't help. At fourteen, I was dealing with my own self-disgust, surfing the internet archives—likely too self-involved to realize anything was wrong with her. "Why didn't you tell anyone?"

"And be placed in the foster system? No, I don't think so."

"Jenessa, why didn't you tell . . . us? You could have come and lived with us—"

"She never would have allowed it. She knew that's what I wanted all along. She told me over and over that if I did tell, she would clean up her act, and then I'd be returned to her, and it would be worse. She told me how Chet raped her at least once a week, and taking photos for men was nothing in comparison when we needed the money. I confronted her about it, about the abuse she inflicted on me, at the beginning of this year. We were arguing, and my gun went off. It was an accident. I only meant to scare her, to torment her a bit the way that she tormented me for years." She pauses. "I sobbed for an hour in this room."

I don't say anything for a moment, heartbroken and dumbfounded by her confession. I can't imagine Rosemary inflicting a fraction of what she lived—of what we witnessed as children—on me.

"I had no idea. I'm so sorry that happened. Nora was more terrible than I realized. But I also know that, early on at least, she loved . . . well, she tried—"

A snort flies from my sister's nose. "She tried? She left me to *rot* in Chet's basement for another three years after she escaped. You know the day after we got out and she met us at the hospital, she came directly from a date with a man she'd met in a bar? Her supplier, it turned out. She wasn't thinking about me all those years as I had hoped."

Her foot taps an impatient rhythm on the floor, and I watch the gun bounce along with it.

I need to calm her down. What was that song we used to sing as kids?

Jesus, a song isn't going to make her not shoot me.

"The worst part is, by the time we got out, I considered Rosemary to be my mother. I was devastated when I had to go live with Nora."

"I know. I remember."

"Really?" she snaps. "What else do you remember? Watching me struggle through the years, growing up in an unstable home, relying on a woman who could barely care for herself?"

"I had my issues with Rosemary, too. I've been taking care of her since I was eight years old. It wasn't some picnic over in Arch."

"But you and Lily had each other! I had no one!" Her words ring out in the one-story house, seem to boomerang in the tight space. She breathes heavily like she just ran a race and watches me with tented eyebrows.

"I had no one," she repeats, and my heart breaks for her again, knowing it's true.

"So I made my own way," she continues. "Made the bonehead decision to get into drugs, too, and spent too much time in rehab, but I figured my shit out." She sniffs. "After drug running ran its course, I got a few over-the-table jobs. Working at the doughnut shop is what gave me the idea, seeing people take selfies in front of the sign every day."

"What idea?" I'm having trouble stringing together all these bits and pieces she keeps lobbing my way. My senses continue to feel dull, and I know I'm not nearly scared enough observing the wild way she gestures with that loaded pistol. "Why are you telling me all this?"

Chet's body begins to twitch, spasm. More fluid releases from beneath his torso, and I gag watching the pool of blood change color.

"So many people in this city, screaming for attention, available to satisfy a variety of urges. I saw an opportunity. Look at Chet." She nudges the lifeless foot with her boot. "He grabbed Nora to satisfy his need, and I knew he couldn't be the only sick bastard with an unusual thirst."

The warmth drains from my face. "What did you do?"

"I started practicing. After Nora died, I got into her stash of lithium and antipsychotics and found they made me more alert. Ambitious and clearheaded about my goals. Acutely aware that Nora made my life hell growing up, and she was gone, but that the internet would always pick up where she left off.

"All those years of being followed, harassed, and objectified by the media as I got on my feet. I never understood why people sought out that notoriety online. Why some girls post naked photos of themselves, willingly and for free. Why they pursued that social media glittery fame, why the hell anyone would sacrifice their privacy—something I would have killed for even then—just to be famous for five minutes. So I began targeting them. Following these social media whores, going to the locations where they tweeted, or posted they were, and watching them."

My whole frame tenses, prickles at the scene she describes. The poker is out of reach from where I sit on the couch. "What then?"

"I lured them to the Shanghai Tunnels underneath the doughnut shop. Sometimes I got them drunk first. The stripper was sober, so she was harder to convince, but the men were easy. I tied them up. At first I was sloppy—I didn't remember the knots that Rosemary taught us—but I didn't have to keep them for long. The buyers I found on the dark web paid eagerly. Once I had their cash in hand, they were allowed to do what they wanted."

I swallow hard, not sure I want to know more but unable to stop myself from asking. "What did they want?"

She returns a deadpan expression. "To kill someone."

"But . . . I don't understand. You received a note, too. *Time to come clean.*"

"Didn't want you suspecting me."

"That's . . . Jay, how could—this is insane."

"Is it? Or is it nuts that out of all of us, you're the only one who seems okay?" Black eyes bore into mine. "Lily? Pregnant with a limp and alone after her partner abandoned her, a hundred grand in debt from always cutting and running. Rosemary, too terrified to leave her box-infested house; Bethel died a long time ago; and Nora, trust me, is happier buried beneath her plants than she ever was caring for me. And then there's me."

Hearing Jenessa's callous summary of how our family's lives turned out sharpens the hazy filter on my senses. "What about you? You think you have some sob story to tell, that adjusting to freedom was so much more difficult for you than anyone else?"

"I think I got the short end of the stick, yeah, when I was promised a different life. I sacrificed myself for you, for everyone, and that's the thanks that I got."

"What are you talking about? We all made sacrifices." I sit forward on the edge of the seat, my strength and fire returning to me.

"Are you high right now? Or do you really not remember?" Her gaze darts across my face, searching for something. "You don't, do you?"

"What the hell are you talking about, Jenessa? Whatever it is you think I did that makes me so deserving of punishment, just say it!"

She lunges at me. "The day we escaped, Rosemary was set to raise all three of us—together! I was never supposed to go to Nora, and when the police asked, *you* were the one who contradicted Rosemary's story that she gave birth to both you and me, and that Lily was Bethel's child, whom Rosemary was going to formally adopt. Rosemary knew that Nora was mentally and emotionally unfit to be a parent, but you ratted me out. Then when Nora suggested I stay with you all anyway, you hit me so hard, my ear rang for a day. Rosemary said she couldn't allow anyone to live in more violence. She chose you, her biological daughter, and sent me away."

Her words drop like grenades, shattering careful guardrails I'd built up around my memories of those early post-captivity days. "That's not—"

"I stayed behind in the basement. Reinforced the rope and fractured my ankle so that you, Lily, and Rosemary could escape without worrying that Chet would come after you. I sacrificed myself and was abandoned in return," she whispers, now looking past me, through the shutters. "All my life, I wondered what it would have been like being raised by someone who genuinely loved me, who cared for me. And every time something terrible landed on my plate, I remembered that wasn't my path, thanks to you. It was all your fault."

I peer at my sister. Take in the frothing anger on her lips, the unshed tears, and the intensity with which she glares at me. A stranger I thought I knew. "The reason why the fingerprints found at each crime scene have all been different, the modes of killing distinct, is because each killer was a different buyer off the dark web. The clues you planted from our captivity, the messages you left me—they were all meant to frame me as the broker. To finally get your revenge after twenty years."

"A former drug-addict sister would be intriguing, but only if the normal sister wasn't taking perverse photos at each crime scene, some even before the police were alerted to the crime."

My stomach pitches as I realize I did exactly what she wanted. I thought I was potentially preventing another murder while selfishly earning a buck from the *Post*.

"Once the police catch up to you and serve that warrant they've issued for your laptop, it'll be settled. Chet's body will be the icing on the cake, and Nora will be thrown into the mix after I send an anonymous note tipping off the cops. Since you've gone to the trouble of killing perfect strangers, offing two members of your bizarre family won't even raise an eyebrow. Sometimes, people are just born bad."

A sob chokes in my throat, hearing Jenessa voice my lifelong suspicion about myself. "But what about Shia? About Serena Delle? She sent that reporter the letter that gave my whereabouts, but she's dead."

Jenessa taps the gun against her temple. "Think, Marissa. Serena Delle was so depressed that you rejected her over and over again, she jumped into the lazy river in Arch after swallowing horse tranquilizers. It was all over the news, but of course you don't pay attention to anyone else's pain. Another casualty on the list of lives you've ruined."

"That's not fair—"

"Anyone can sign someone's name. I did." She folds her arms, soaking up my pained expression. "I knew you would react all crazy to the reporter and I'd have more evidence of your wild temper. Rosemary wouldn't give up any of those damn boxes that contain your juvenile offenses. Said she couldn't handle parting with them when I offered to clean her house for free."

"They were misdemeanors. Childish forms of acting out. I got into a few fights and stole grocery store makeup. What would they prove?"

"You broke Felix Tempe's nose, then stole makeup to wear at juvenile court when his parents pressed charges."

"He tried to corner me in the girls' bathroom and stick his hand down my—"

"Then, when you finished house arrest, you found him again and broke his leg."

"He . . . he fell down a flight of stairs," I mumble.

"Did he? You were a loose cannon, but somehow you managed to cover it all up. To glide into adulthood without anyone the wiser, get a few jobs, change your name, and that was that. Everyone accepted the trite bullshit you fed them, that you'd been depressed at the time or were desperate for attention from someone other than your therapist. Everyone just looked the other way when it came to you."

I shake my head, try to stay calm. "Jenessa, you're giving me way too much credit. Yes, I was selfish and lashed out at others as a kid, but I was punished for those acts. I didn't get away with anything."

"No skeletons? Except for your guinea pig, whom you force-fed to death. Lily was afraid of you."

"That's a horrible—Lily? I would never hurt—"

"Lily was safe because she was never going to compete with you for the limelight with that limp. Those surgeries for her defect would always mean she played second fiddle to your need to be Rosemary's favorite and everyone's exasperating troublemaker."

A tear splashes the bare skin of my knee, hearing the depth of my sister's hatred for me. "That's not true."

She returns my gaze with cold indifference.

"Whatever you do with me, you'll be looked at next. The police will investigate everyone."

"Sure they will. But with the only conclusive evidence pointing to you, Lily and I won't be given a second glance."

Panic tightens my chest, knowing she's right. "And Shia? Did you plan this whole thing together? Is that why you gave me a story about rejecting being a source for his book, so I wouldn't pair you two as part-ners? Have our interviews all been part of your plan for me?"

A shadow slides down Jenessa's face, wiping clean her smug grin. "I wasn't sure you'd meet with the journalist after I told you to stay away from the media—told you how they ruined my life. But, true to form, you put yourself first. Even after you started working with the *Post* and no longer needed money, I followed you over the last week, watched you provide him with all the details."

Too late, I realize my mistake, and she takes a step closer to me. Cocks, then uncocks, the gun. Cocks. Uncocks. Frenzy casts a red hue on her skin. "But I should be used to your betrayals by now. What mat-ters is you have photos of the dead bodies on your laptop."

The words sting, feel amplified, given everything I've learned in this room. "I still don't understand. How could you have orchestrated all of this by yourself, kidnapped your victims, restrained them, and deposited the bodies in the tunnels alone? Who was your partner?"

Jenessa laughs, then scratches her head with the gun. "You think you have this distrust of men because of Chet or whatever, but you can't imagine I could do all of these things alone because I'm a woman. Well, hate to disappoint you, but I didn't need anyone else, and I had all the tools necessary. Chloroform, chains, restraints, transport dollies. I had the knowledge that each of these idiots deserved what they got."

I shudder at her satisfied expression. "I didn't think you could do it all on your own because I love you. Because I thought you were a good person."

"Sure you did." She waves the gun, then points it at her temple and pretends to shoot herself.

"Jenessa." I breathe deep. "How do you think this ends? You skip town after the police clear you of all involvement, taking the money that your dark-web assassins paid you? It can't be that much for only four victims. What happens then?"

"Actually, it's close to a million dollars. Rich freaks from out of state keep moving here and find that spending their real estate money can be difficult in a sweet city like Portland. The cost of living is so low; the cost of recreation isn't what they're used to, either. Tack on the fifteen grand reward I'm about to get for turning you in, and I'm set up for a little while."

I try to swallow and find my mouth is dry. The puddle around the water glass on the coffee table continues to spread, but I can't move. Can't do anything except stare at this stranger, my sister. She's right. The plan she's just described will work out fine.

I brace myself to whisper the question that matters most. "We're sisters. How could you do this to me?"

She raises the gun and points it at my heart. Cocks. Uncocks. "The same way you betrayed me all those years ago."

I hear another click and shut my eyes.

"Easily."

Thirty-Three

When Shia asked me about my earliest memory, it wasn't Lily's birth announcement or Bethel's pregnant belly that came to mind, not really—it was playing with Jenessa. We would have been around three years old. Nora had us coloring pumpkins that she must have drawn on paper. Jenessa and I reached for the orange crayon at the same time, beginning our first battle of wills.

As kids, we called each other "Twin." From the time we were born to the time we went to live in separate homes. I'm sure the nickname probably came from one of our mothers—*Go play with your twin*—as though we were from the same womb instead of two different women. Siblings are often our first friends. And Jenessa was mine. We were best friends until Lily came along, but even afterward, we were close.

Looking at the grown woman brandishing a gun before me, I don't recognize her anymore, my "twin," or recognize any shred of decency in this husk of a person.

"Here," she says, throwing a pair of workman's gloves in my lap. "Put these on."

I do as I'm told and glance at the fireplace poker again. My eyes land on Chet's body. What might have happened if I hadn't arrived when I did? Did Jenessa intend to kill Chet all along? He kept saying he wasn't there to see Nora but to build bridges between us, to reconnect as a family. Did he speak to Lily?

I stand and plant my feet closer to the poker than is necessary. Jenessa scoffs. "Tut-tut. Outside. Now."

She uses the pistol as a crosswalk attendant might, directing the flow of traffic. "Through the kitchen. Let's go."

"Do you live here?" I ask.

The gun barrel answers with a jab to my back. "Keep walking. For several months, off and on. Nora used my share of the settlement before I turned eighteen to buy this place, so it was only fitting that I take it over when she died."

"You mean when you killed her."

The barrel acts like a battering ram between my shoulder blades. "When you killed her," she corrects.

I wince from the pain still throbbing from my right shoulder but say nothing.

We step out the back door and into the garden. The high wooden fence I first noted upon sneaking up the side makes sense now. The impulse to scream rises in my throat like a cough that won't be contained, but I have no doubt Jenessa would pull the trigger and end this whole debacle. She already has everything she needs from me, all the evidence she could hope for pointed squarely in my direction.

"What are we doing out here?" I ask the flower-bush perimeter. Jenessa's casual chuckle behind me promises nothing good.

A shovel lands next to me on a flower bed Nora must have spent hours cultivating. "Start digging. Under the white hydrangeas."

Nausea turns my stomach. Jenessa said Nora was buried out here. "You want me to—"

"No talking," she snaps. "Or I'll shoot out a kneecap and still make you dig. Your choice."

Neighbors must be able to hear us on a Monday afternoon, right? How is no one coming out to investigate? Unless they're all at work. Or—as a delivery truck passes on the main thoroughfare out front, belching exhaust and leaving a trail of clanging noise—maybe they can't hear us over the street traffic.

With shaking hands, I bend down and grip the shovel. Jenessa can't see my face, so I let the panicked tears fall freely. Images of a lifeless Bethel flash to mind, lying on our blood-soaked mattress after giving birth to Lily. Nora and Rosemary wrapped her in the bedsheets that were ruined and laid her on the floor until Chet agreed to remove the body. Five days later. I didn't want to look, but as a child, I couldn't help it. Or help the recalled images that struck in the middle of the night for years afterward.

The shovel slides into the moist dirt with ease. I lift and remove that hunk of earth, then dig again. Repeat the same movement. Over and over. I wince at each dig, anticipating the moment when I strike a mass that's unquestionably human.

When I turn over my shoulder, Jenessa remains poised against the fence, gun in hand and out of the neighbor's camera's line of sight.

The hole is four feet deep when the shovel hits something soft—softer than rock. I dig around it and discover the outline of a pale forearm, the process of decay well underway.

Rodents long ago burrowed into the skin to take their meal, followed by worms and insects, from the looks of the still-wriggling larvae spread across the ashen flesh. I clap a hand over my mouth, but my stomach won't be quelled. I vomit on all fours into the pile of dirt beside me, retching up the scone and apple.

Nora. All this time, Nora had been struggling with the consequences of her trauma, while trying to raise Jenessa—ultimately, a killer. We should have done more to help Nora, to help them both. They each needed Rosemary, Lily, and me, more than I think anyone was aware. The way I, as a child, treated Jenessa in the past, wronged her, is what's landed me in this position now.

"That's enough," Jenessa says. "Get up. Inside."

Struggling to my feet, I don't question abandoning the task, only partly completed.

She laughs, watching me wipe my mouth; then her smile drops. Her head snaps toward the street. "Get in the house," she hisses.

When I hesitate, she grabs me by my bun of hair and yanks. I cry out, but her grip doesn't lessen, and my only choice is to follow as fast as possible. I trip up the stairs and through the back door, but once we're in the kitchen, she lets go. She raises a finger to her lips in the universal sign for quiet.

"Marissa?" A voice calls from out front, and I stiffen automatically, so close to help.

The cold metal of the gun against my head stifles the urge to answer.

"Marissa, I know you're here. I can see it on my geo-location app, remember? I think I'm having contractions."

Jenessa looks at me; we both recognize Lily's voice at the same time. I plead with my eyes. *Let me go to our younger sister—let me go.* Her jaw pulses in response. "You always were her favorite. She can't even go to the hospital without finding you first. Even though I'm the one who risked everything for us."

"Marissa?" Lily calls again.

Jenessa hesitates, as if considering her options—whether to end me here and now or whether Lily already knows too much by having a record of my whereabouts.

Jesus, Lily. Go to the hospital!

I debate making a run for it, out the back door and scaling the fence, when we both hear it: the doorknob squeaks as it turns counter-clockwise. Lily is coming inside.

Floorboards creak at the front of the house. "Marissa?" she calls; then she gasps, no doubt spotting Chet's body and the small lake of blood around him. Muffled noises come from the other room, as though she's stifling a cry.

Jenessa grips my arm with one hand and presses the gun to my temple with the other. "Not a word," she whispers. The steel is frigid against my flushed cheeks, burning my skin.

Slowly, Lily walks toward the butler's pantry, the old wood announcing each step. Jenessa moves me past a small table and through the other archway into the living room. Floorboards moan beneath us as we step past the fireplace.

Lily whirls back into the front room and sees us. Her eyes pull wide, and her face pales. Her hands fly to her belly in the dress she wears. "What is going on?"

Jenessa stares her down like a dog poised to attack a wounded bird. "What are you doing here, Lily? Don't tell me Chet asked you to meet, too." Jenessa's nails dig into my arm with each word she growls.

Lily glances at the body, then back to us, torn between the two horror stories before her. "He came to my place, but I pretended I wasn't home. What is going on? Why do you have a gun to Marissa's head! Where are we?" Lily's voice jumps an octave. She breathes in through her nose, and her chest rises and falls with a frenzy I haven't seen since we were kids.

I can't see her face, but Jenessa scoffs in my ear. "So you came here, to this address, all on your own. When you've barely contacted me since you've been back for—what—a week?"

Lily hesitates. "We—we spoke yesterday. I've had a lot going on—"

I shake my head an inch to the side, but it's too late. The gun barrel presses harder into my temple. Jenessa's breath is hot on my neck, her own trembling shaking my arm.

"Not so much that you couldn't see Marissa. Right? You want her? Here!" Jenessa flings me across the room, and I shift at the last second to avoid crushing my pregnant sister. Lily falls backward, slumps against the wall, and I knock over a lamp from an end table. The electrical cord tangles at my feet.

Lily moans and clutches her stomach. "Em, I think I'm—I'm having another contraction." She tries to breathe through it on the floor while watching Jenessa, but her eyes clamp shut from the pain.

"How sweet that you two have become—no, remained—so close. Since you grew up together. Since no one separated you when we got out."

"Jenessa, I was a child. I was selfish and stupid and jealous of your relationship with Rosemary. I had no idea what life would be like for you with Nora; I'm sorry." I try to imbue my words with calm, stability—find some way to get both Lily and me out of here alive.

Lily pants below me, the contraction subsiding.

Jenessa hits a button on the wall, and the fireplace surges to life. Flames lick the iron screen before she kicks it aside, sending it clattering against the coffee table. "Wasn't this always your favorite form of self-harm?" she simpers to me. "Come closer, Marissa. If you're too scared to stand near me, why not approach your old friend?"

The burns on my arms seem to light up like an arcade game under her gaze. "You don't know what I went through, either, Jenessa."

"No? Poor little Marissa. *My small-town neighbors think I'm dangerous.* Just looking at you is aggravating. As long as you're walking free, I'll never be seen as more than a broken version of you. The media's favorite fuckup and first person they harass until I can't stomach a full meal from all the stress." Spittle flies from her lips as her volume rises with each word.

"When you began taking photos for the *Post*, I started planting evidence that pointed to you. I wanted to frame you for the murders, make you every bit the pariah I've been all these years. But maybe I was too soft in taking the longer route to get to the same place." Her lips part, baring her teeth, as she raises the gun to my chest once again. "Maybe there's room for one more on my list of victims."

Terror freezes my limbs and cements my feet—my body bracing for what's to come. "Jenessa, please. Let's talk about this. You don't have to—"

A scream rips through the room as Lily shoots up from the ground, launches herself at Jenessa, knocking the gun free and Jenessa to the floor. They scramble for it, but Jenessa grabs the gun and pushes Lily out of the way. Lily screams again—a deep, agonizing sound that claws at my insides.

Jenessa hesitates, seeing Lily in torment, and I reach into my bag and find the orange I took from the *Post*. I launch it at her head and miss, and the fruit knocks a framed painting free from the wall behind. Jenessa startles, and I throw myself toward her and wrap my hands around the gun. I twist the barrel up toward the ceiling, and a shot goes off, sending plaster and dust everywhere; high-pitched ringing erupts in my ear canal.

Jenessa kicks my foot out from under me, and I land on my bad shoulder on the iron screen. I cry out, then roll to my side but still don't release the weapon. Jenessa wrenches it this way and that, but I don't let go. She thrusts my arm into the fire, and a banshee shriek tears from my lungs. Heat boils my hand and wrist; then I feel only cold, adrenaline no doubt flooding my limbs, before the metal begins to boil beneath the blue and yellow flames. I yank my arm back, and the force knocks her off-balance and into the jaws of the blaze. She arches at the last second so that only her long hair singes. The acrid smell instantly fills the room. I snatch the gun from her by the handle and crawl backward to where I knocked over the lamp. Lily lies propped against the couch, away from Chet, clutching her stomach and breathing hard.

A siren wails nearby. Then closer. Closer. Before it slows outside the house.

I look at Jenessa, cradling my hand. The tips of her hair still smoldering, she seems wild, plucked from hell and bent on spilling more blood. Her eyes scan the room, then pause on the coffee table. The scissors on the coffee table.

She lunges for them, and I get to my feet, preparing for her redoubled attack, but she pivots toward Lily. Grabbing her by the arm, she yanks Lily upright, then opens the scissors and presses a blade to Lily's neck. I raise the gun instantly, mirroring her stance. Blue veins visible under Lily's pale skin beat furiously for two.

"Give me the gun," Jenessa says to me, each word a threat. "Or I'll do it." She presses the blade into Lily's throat, but Lily is mute, fear crippling any sound.

I keep the barrel trained on Jenessa's head and try to remember what I learned and never mastered at the gun range. To ignore the orange's juicy insides smeared across the wall and the memory of Oz's face when I threw the dart in the bar and missed the target by feet.

This is not a good idea.

"Marissa. Give me. The gun!" A bead of red appears on Lily's skin. "Now."

Voices travel the walkway leading to the door. The police. Lily's eyes widen to the point of resembling blue discs. Seeing my sister in this state, at the hands of our other sibling, panic swells in me and threatens to take over—shaking my frame and dissolving my strength into sobs—before the emotion shifts. Changes shape. Trembles into the fury I've worked to subdue my whole life.

The sweat on my fingers makes my grip slippery, and I readjust both hands. "You can't do this to us. I won't let you after everything we already survived."

"You deserve to rot in prison for what you did to me. I'm only settling a debt."

Hearing Jenessa speak the words I believed for most of my life—recalling the shame that always surfaced when I thought about the day that we escaped, never realizing that guilt was due to my betrayal of Jenessa—I consider whether she's right.

Consider it, and yet finally know in my bones she's wrong. "I don't deserve prison, Jenessa. I've messed up, and I'm deeply, deeply sorry for hurting you. But this is not how you move forward. How we move forward together."

Footsteps climb the porch steps.

"Marissa. The gun! Now!" Jenessa's voice shakes, but the scissors remain steady on Lily's throat.

I could shoot her. Shoot her and be done with this nightmare, be justified in the act, and no one would judge me for it or say I had bad blood. Everyone would understand.

"Em," Lily whispers. "Please. The baby."

Someone knocks at the front door. "Police! Open up!"

Another moment passes in which no one moves. Then I slowly bend my knees and lower the gun to the floor. Jenessa's eyes fixate on my face. A mixture of stunned and hurt. She watches until I release the gun.

"I always wished you had done that," she says. "Chosen me over yourself."

Wooden splinters explode from the doorway as two police officers crowd inside. "Police! Drop your weapon!"

Jenessa whirls, keeping the blade pressed to Lily's neck. She inches Lily in front of her body, and the younger cop sucks in a breath at seeing Lily's pregnant bulge.

"I said, drop your weapon! You won't get another warning—"

I snatch the gun from the ground, aim for Jenessa's foot, and pull the trigger. A shot goes off, and the police shout something, many things, and train their guns on me. I drop mine and blink hard—again—before I take my eyes from my sisters.

Lily flew forward onto the couch, thrown by Jenessa's momentum, while Jenessa fell sideways into the armchair. She stares at the gaping wound in her thigh, the trail of blood dripping to the ground, before lifting haunted eyes to mine.

She never really left the basement, not in the sense that the rest of us did. Granted, she stayed behind—risked herself in an act of love and generosity beyond her seven years of living. But she's been in a prison of her own ever since, believing what I often struggled with—that she wasn't loved. That she would never be enough.

I toe my messenger bag under the watchful glares of the police officers barking words I don't hear. The scene of my two sisters in such physical and emotional pain is almost too much to bear up close. The intense urge rises in me to withdraw my camera from its case. To angle the lens and position the viewfinder. Instead, I close my eyes and imagine the comforting release.

Click.

Thirty-Four

MISSY

THEN

Outside it's nighttime and hot and I'm so tired and scared but Mama won't let us go home. And this is not how Mama Rosemary described nighttime in the outside. I ask Mama why it's so hot and she doesn't answer.

We should be in bed. Mama should be reading us a story like she always does when we can't sleep. I ask Mama if the man is still in the basement with Jenessa and she doesn't answer again.

We walk fast. Harder than we ever did during exercise hour and I'm carrying Sweet Lily's baby blanket. When I lose my shoe that's too small Mama Rosemary says to leave it. And she says stop asking so many questions.

We pass houses and big tall light-trees too bright for night. I cover my eyes and hold on to Mama's shirt. We walk harder and longer than ever then get to a new road. Mama Rosemary puts Sweet Lily to the ground to rest and Sweet Lily starts to cry. Mama makes soothing noises and picks her back up.

"Mama Rosemary? Is Jenessa okay? Why did we leave? We're supposed to be out front of the house."

"We will be, honey, but we need to get the police first. Jenessa is a good girl. She'll wait out front like I told her. Making the rope will take at least ten minutes, and he won't get free before she does. We're close. We're so close."

"But why, Mama? Why can't we stay? What about Twin?"

"She'll be safe. She's fine, honey. She'll be safe."

"But how do you know?"

Mama doesn't saying nothing. We go left—no, right—on the new street and Mama darts her head back and forth.

"What are you looking for, Mama?"

But she hushes me and looks behind us like she's scared. She mumbles something starts to cry. She says *Alefter Alefter Alefter.*

"Speak up," I say and she shoots me a look. Not mad. But like she's surprised to see me.

She makes a throat-noise and stops crying. "Pouch Street. We're looking for Pouch. Remember geography lessons?"

I nod then start using my eyes, too. Plant-trees are brown in this outside world. Not like the green ones I see in the television or in books. Shadows are everywhere between the tall light-trees. An animal barks. A dog. And I remember that Jenessa's favorite cartoon has a dog in it. A penguin and a sea lion.

Row row row your boat. Gently down the stream.

"Mama Rosemary? Is Twin okay? Are we okay?"

"I hope so, baby. Girls, look!" Mama Rosemary sets Sweet Lily down on the ground again and Sweet Lily leans on her good foot. Dirty cheeks are stripy from tears.

She points with her whole body toward more light-trees. "Do you see it?"

Me and Sweet Lily shake our heads. "No, Mama."

She swings Sweet Lily up into her arms and begins running. I follow her in my one shoe so I gallop like a horse but I'm running. I keep holding the blanket. "Mama, wait for me, Mama Rosemary!" My voice is all high. I couldn't be left here in the dark I can't not like Jenessa all alone with the man.

"Mama!" I scream.

"Hurry up, baby!" she yells back but doesn't stop. Just keeps running running past one light-tree then past another until I see a road that's full of them. And a building. And cars on both left and right. There's a—a train ahead moving as fast as us.

"Hey, Mama Rosemary, a train! Are we gonna get on the train? Are we leaving? Where is it going?" In my favorite show *Mister Rogers* there's a train that takes you to magical places, away from his home.

Then a scary thought slows my feet. Are we gonna go without Jenessa? Without Twin? "Mama, we can't!" I catch up to her. She slowed down now again with Sweet Lily and Sweet Lily walks as quick as she can on her own. "Mama, we need to go back for Twin."

"I know, honey; we will. Almost there."

"No, no, no!" I stomp my foot in the middle of the darkness road in a place with no light-trees. My face gets hot my cheeks start to shake.

"Missy, listen to me." Mama Rosemary gets down real close to my face. She grabs my arms and I think she's gonna hug me but she doesn't. That makes me cry harder.

"Missy, we're so close, baby. We're so close to getting out and home free, but I need you to be a big girl for just a little bit longer, okay?"

"But we are out. And we left our home with Twin inside—"

"I know we did. You're right. I just need you to be brave a few minutes longer, okay? Can you do that?"

A car passes with bright eyeballs and a long tail. Mama Rosemary steps in front of us and waves her arms wild at the car but it doesn't stop. She sniffs then looks behind us at something.

"What, Mama? What is it?"

"We need to keep going." Her voice is low. The one she uses when she's mad. But when she turns and looks at us again her face is shiny. She picks up Sweet Lily and makes a growl noise.

I wipe my chin. My belly feels empty. The veggies and spaghetti we ate for dinner is unhappy. It twists and I think I might throw up like when I got sick when I was five. Then Jenessa got sick because she wanted to sleep with me. I take Mama Rosemary's hand and we keep walking. She takes her hand back to hold Sweet Lily and Sweet Lily curls into her neck like a koala.

"Almost there, girls," Mama Rosemary says again all breath. She walks fast until we are almost at the train and I feel nervous we're going to disappear on it.

There's a building now and she walks on a white part of the road and then up to the door that has a bunch of words on it. I read a little bit and see *pol-ys. Po-lees. Police.*

"We're here, girls." Mama Rosemary looks at us and her face is different than I know it. She's happy but her face is wet again. The most happy I ever saw her.

She pulls on big doors made of glass and pushes us inside. People are everywhere. Strangers and lots of—mans—like the man, and two women.

"You two sit here and don't move a muscle. I mean it." Mama Rosemary points a finger at both me and Sweet Lily and then at two chairs on a wall.

I peek at her through my hands. "It's too bright, Mama." Sweet Lily tucks into me and pulls her hair over her face.

Mama Rosemary looks around. She takes Sweet Lily's baby blanket and puts it over our heads. "There you go. Good girls."

Her voice starts talking to some other voice and when they get going I lift up a corner to see. Mama Rosemary talks to a woman behind a desk and the woman's eyes get real big and she speaks into a—a phone—a telephone. When she puts the phone down she says something to Mama that makes her start crying again.

We get moved into a room with a table and toys and green blankets. All the walls are brown but there's a wall made of glass again with our faces in it. A mirror. Once me and Sweet Lily find a corner we like we sit down and stare around us. It's not home. It's too big.

Mama hugs us both and kisses us. She strokes my hair and I get nervous. "You girls are going to stay here with Officer Chopra. I'm going to go get your sister."

"No, don't leave!" I grip on to Mama Rosemary's arm and make red marks on her skin.

"I'll be back in a few minutes, I promise. Your sister needs me." She strokes my hair again and Sweet Lily's hair waiting for me to say okay. I don't want to.

"Okay. But will you get something for me?"

Mama Rosemary looks at me her eyebrows all high. "We have everything we took with us in the backpack here. Go ahead—you can open it."

I shake my head. "Can you make sure and—and grab Petey the Penguin? I know Jenessa'll want him later and she didn't pack him. I'll carry him until she wants him."

Mama Rosemary's eyes get watery again and her face pinks. "I think she'd appreciate that. I'll be right back."

I watch her walk to the door then turn back and blow us a kiss. When she goes behind the mirror wall she disappears.

Sweet Lily scoots in closer to me her skin so hot from the fever still. It's the first time we've ever been without a mama or Mama Rosemary before in our whole lives. I feel sad but I know she had to go. I feel sad but I know this is what Jenessa is feeling ever since we left.

"Girls? Should we have some juice?" A lady looks at us from the doorway. A real one with wood.

Me and Sweet Lily nod.

The lady gets us cups made out of paper. Inside is pink juice not the orange juice we had at Christmastime but I drink it all. She gives me another. Sweet Lily doesn't want hers so I drink that, too. She goes and lays back down on a blanket in the corner still hot from fever.

"You girls have been so brave this evening," the lady says. "Your mother, too."

"My sister, too. Other sister."

"So I hear." The lady makes a noise in her mouth. "Your whole family has been through a lot."

I gulp back my cup then hold it out for more pink stuff. "Yeah. Then there's Mama Bethel and Mama Nora. But they're gone."

"Who is Mama Bethel?"

I pick at my cup since she's not putting more juice in it. "Sweet Lily's mama. But she died."

"Does that make you sad?"

I think about it. Scrunch my face up to my nose in what Mama Rosemary always says is my sneeze face. "No. Not anymore."

"And Mama Nora? Who is she?"

I don't say anything for a minute. I remember Mama Rosemary saying we don't tell no one about Mama Nora for now. That we keep quiet so we can all be together after.

Then I think about how Mama Rosemary left me and Sweet Lily to go back and get Jenessa. Left us even though I didn't want her to.

And Mama Rosemary always said to tell the truth. "Mama Nora is Jenessa's mama. But she's gone for a long time now."

The lady writes stuff down on paper. She looks at the mirror wall and holds up her thumb. "That's very good, honey. Thank you for telling me. Now what do you want for your first meal out here?"

"Oh! Croissants like my bracelet. See?"

"Very pretty. I think we can do that."

She gives me more juice then I lie down next to Sweet Lily. I hope Mama Rosemary gets back soon with Twin. I can't wait for us to go home. Even though Mama says we're never going back there again. I just want us to be together again. The four of us.

Thirty-Five

A woman in a sleek black dress leads me to a dimly lit room in the back of the restaurant. We pass tables of couples sharing a romantic meal and a few quartets in suits. The city is beautiful from the thirtieth floor through the wall of windows. Lights twinkle along the freeways heading into the suburbs and in the reverse direction toward the city, likely in search of entertainment this Friday night. As I've done.

When Shia first asked me to mark this evening on my calendar, I hesitated. He was welcome to celebrate the launch of his book, do whatever he wanted with it, but the idea of voluntarily embedding myself among the vultures and eager rubberneckers eleven months after the murders struck me as masochistic. Then I remembered my therapist's words and what she termed the "healing process": taking control of our fears and internalizing our agency. We don't have to be subject to anyone's desires or expectations of us; I'm no longer a child or a woman struggling to get on her feet.

The hostess escorts me past a drooping palm frond, behind velvet curtains tied to each side of a wide doorframe, and the noise of conversation rushes my ears. Sergeant Peugeot stands out with his crew cut and striped green-and-beige jacket, stark against the scene of somber colors. I once read somewhere that people mimic the weather in their clothing choices, and it has been a monochromatic winter indeed.

He sees me and dips his head in my direction. The last time I saw him, at Jenessa's sentencing hearing, he was in the back row of the courthouse, a concerned expression stitching his heavy brows together. Despite Peugeot's best efforts at influencing the prosecutor and judge, Jenessa was sentenced to life in prison, with the possibility of parole in twenty years. Just like Chet.

Ironically, for once, Jenessa was not the center of the scandal the whole time. Two millionaires from Silicon Valley and a casino owner from Las Vegas were also given life sentences for taking the tunnel victims' lives.

When I asked Peugeot why he'd made such an effort for my sister, he said that Jenessa was the victim of unusual trauma—we all were. We know so little about the long-term effects of real trauma, he said, and she didn't deserve a life sentence.

After her arrest, Oz and Pauline threatened to sue me for misrepresenting my identity. I felt exposed, foolish for having trusted Oz. Yet when he suggested that he and Pauline could be persuaded not to sue if I agreed to be featured on the front page of the *Post* and in subsequent editorials commenting on Jenessa's trial, my sheepishness turned to contempt. *Screw you,* I'd replied. The look on Oz's face—a woman rejecting him—had been worth giving him more ammunition against me in the articles I knew they would write regardless.

When my therapist asked why I declined, I explained that people would gossip, whether or not I'd misled anyone. There will probably be another book in another twenty years, this one following up on Jenessa's portion of the ordeal, and I shouldn't let the ebb and flow of public interest dictate my life. She gave me a slow clap at that. Said I was making progress.

Shia's book is displayed on a golden platter at the back of the room, surrounded by artfully stacked copies. A blown-up version of the book's cover, with endorsements from other crime biographers splashed across it, occupies an easel beside the table. The title, *Family Ties: The Twentieth*

Anniversary of Portland's House of Horrors, is emblazoned in bronze lettering across a grayscale photograph of Chet's home. A bit dramatic. I told Shia as much, and he said the publisher insisted on the word *horror* being included somehow.

Shia smiles when I catch his eye, but he doesn't leave his conversation. Black curls fall across his forehead, and he brushes the fringe away with awkward fingertips, still not used to the shorter do. An older woman in a stylish pantsuit stands with her back to me, speaking to him. She gestures toward the easel, then sputters a laugh.

Circulate. Enjoy yourself. Just be in the moment and celebrate something you worked hard on. Nobody needs to know. It was easy for Shia to suggest—he wasn't the subject of a four-hundred-page tome on sale at every bookstore. But as the date approached and Jenessa continued to refuse visits from me, the prospect of a party seemed less like corporal punishment and more like an opportunity to move forward.

A slight woman follows behind a child teetering on unsteady, chubby baby legs. They pass below a stage light angled on the books for sale, and Lily's white-blonde crown of hair gleams, braided down to her waist. She waves me over, then scoops Olive up in her arms and plants a loud raspberry kiss on my niece's cheek.

"Hey, glad you could make it," she says.

"Yeah, traffic was a pain. I should have left earlier."

Lily looks over her shoulder, then back to me. "Totally. You missed the crab cakes. We need to get invited to launch events more often."

"Agreed." We could buy crab cakes if we wanted them—as many as we want—but I refrain from pointing out the obvious. Once Shia's publisher accepted the final draft and he sent me my promised portion of the advance, I halved my share between Lily and me—nearly, anyway; I saved twenty grand for Jenessa, for whatever she'd need while in prison: lawyer fees, extra pillows, maybe a standalone gardening bag to place beneath a window.

"Did Mom end up coming?"

A smirk crosses Lily's prim mouth. "'Mom' now? What happened to 'Rosemary'?"

A server passes by with a tray of glasses of white wine, and I grab one. "Therapy is forcing me to accept things about myself and other people, believe it or not. Warts and all."

She raises two eyebrows, impressed. Olive sucks on her fist in Lily's arms. "She said she was going to the bathroom about ten minutes ago. I should make sure she didn't—"

"My two girls!" Rosemary exclaims, joining us. Her hair is curled, and she wears a red dress I've never seen before. "My three girls," she says, nudging Olive's cheek.

"Hey. Thought you might have jumped out the window." I smile so she knows I'm only partly joking.

"Not without my parachute." Rosemary winks, and I can't help marveling at the change in her after only a few months. It turns out that while she did have a hard time being among large groups of people, a consequence of the consistent paranoia she suffered post-captivity, much of it was out of fear of encountering Chet. She always worried he would be released on parole before she was notified. That he'd attack her again, or worse, track her down to ask for her forgiveness. Now he's dead.

For my part, I'd often wondered whether Chet's father, Jameson, might come out of the woodwork once the details about the murders hit the national news circuit. But instead of a ninety-year-old grandfather looking for absolution or a handout, it was his widow who reached out—an eighty-year-old woman who lives on a ranch in Montana. She didn't make any demands but let us know Jameson had no idea about us—or he never confided as much during their fifteen years of marriage. She didn't even know he had a son.

Whether or not the gift of Petey the Penguin came from him or had another explanation, I don't know. I don't need to. Recalling the way that Rosemary recently agreed to donate the boxes of dental gear and training bras taking over her front room, I understand how living in the past is a mistake. I'm through feeling at a disadvantage. I've got the family I need.

Lily sniffs Olive. Olive coos as she grabs at Lily's hair with chubby fingers.

"Uh-oh," Lily says. "Diaper duty. We'll be right back. You two will be okay here."

I nod, knowing Lily didn't mean it as a question. "Of course. Although if it's a two-man job, I'm happy to help out—"

"We'll be fine. I'll take care of her," Rosemary says, looking at me. She gives my elbow a squeeze, and I have to stop myself from flinching at the motherly gesture.

When I confronted Rosemary about the memories that returned to me over the last year, of Chet sitting me on his lap and his growing interest in me, tears formed in her eyes. She said there were so many reasons to get out when we did, but escaping before anything more damaging happened to us kids provided the ultimate push. She said that as the years went by, I seemed to consciously recall less and less, and she didn't want to remind me. It was her suspicion that, unconsciously, I harbored a lot of anger at what happened to me, to all of us. That anger probably manifested in my actions as a teenager in countless ways that neither of us really understood at the time. Knowing Rosemary prioritized my safety when it really mattered began to mend the rift I'd let grow between us. I could see her then—all her faults and strengths and how they composed the woman before me.

The promise of Rosemary taking care of me wets my eyes, and I have to look toward the poster board of Shia's book, away from the warmth of her gaze.

"If you see more bacon-wrapped dates, grab some for me, will you?" Lily swings Olive onto her hip, then heads toward the inky velvet curtains.

Not for the first time, I wonder, watching her leave, how she escaped the crippling self-doubt that both Jenessa and I adopted like a third leg. Probably something to do with her young age at the time of our escape. Memories are more easily blocked or omitted when you can barely sing the alphabet song.

Though Jenessa refuses to see me, Lily has been making monthly visits to the women's prison. Yesterday, she said Jenessa's gunshot, while healed, carries a dull ache and seems worse during poor weather. They barely spent ten minutes together before Jenessa signaled for the guard to take her back to her cell. Still, Lily suspects the visits are good for Jenessa. And baby Olive is becoming pretty popular with the guards.

I turn to Rosemary, my wineglass half-empty. "Do you think Nora would have enjoyed this party?"

She sips her soda, clutching the glass with her hand and navigating the aluminum straw toward her mouth. "Nora, surrounded by free alcohol to celebrate a book about our imprisonment? It would have been hard. But I think she would have been here if you wanted her to be. It's all very strange, being surrounded by people who want to know everything about you."

She takes another drink. I hesitate, knowing how far she's come emotionally herself and what it must have taken for her to drive up to Portland this week. Even if she's happy to stay with Lily and spend time with Olive.

"I didn't mean to . . . I would have understood if you didn't want to join tonight."

Rosemary's eyes widen. "Oh, honey, I know. I wanted to be here for you, promise. Being here is . . . I feel—well, it is hard in a way, being here. But it's also the first time one of us has helped create the narrative that other people were always writing for us. So I'm glad you invited me. I'm enjoying myself."

A server exits the kitchen behind us carrying more bacon-wrapped dates. Rosemary stops him and piles four onto a napkin. She catches my side-eye. "Olive is a growing baby, after all."

I laugh, wondering whether I would have believed my mother capable of joking in public a year ago, whether Nora truly could have also, given the emotional and physical distance between us. Despite any wishful thinking, I do blame Nora—what she did to Jenessa is inexcusable. And at the same time, I pity her. I know what it is to be broken by the past and a life of trauma that never released its clawed grip on your neck.

But playing with my sweet niece, and imagining the world through her child eyes, it's time to let go of the shame I harbored for so long. And which, if I'm being fair, placed me on the same path that Jenessa chose: one of bitterness and self-destruction. We both believed we were damaged goods, flawed on arrival—but she directed that anger toward people who were accepted by the world for their unique traits and passions, while she had been paraded as a caricature. I could understand how that had felt like salt in the wound as we tried to find our identities, away from our origins.

"Hey there." Shia stops by my side. "Pretty good turnout, right?" He extends a hand to Rosemary. "Very pleased to meet you. I'm Shia."

Groups of people eat hors d'oeuvres and sip drinks while discussing Shia's book. A few people, probably with the publisher, comment on specific chapters, but I try not to listen too closely.

"Likewise. I've heard a lot about you," Rosemary adds, giving me a look.

He sucks his teeth. "You could say the same for me, I guess."

Shia and my mother exchange a few more pleasantries, and the image of them chatting over some casserole I made—no, more realistically, a frozen pizza I threw in the oven—enters my head. Shia adjusts his glasses twice during the conversation, and I smile at the nervous tic.

He turns to me. "Any chance you feel like taking a photo together? Not for the book launch. For us."

I shake my head, already feeling my throat constrict with panic. This is exactly what I was hoping to avoid. "No photos for me. I'm low-key tonight, and I don't want to draw attention."

Shia promised me he wouldn't out me or give a speech in my honor or anything.

He draws his eyebrows together. "Are you still worried people are here to judge you? Everyone here supports you. And your family."

I start to protest, and he adds, "No, really. Listen."

Clutching my glass, I take a step away from the wall and eavesdrop on the conversation closest to us, something I've avoided doing since entering this room. I chose to come because I need to practice better, healthier habits. Instead of hearing people's apocalyptic assumptions about me and believing they're correct, I'm working on maintaining a positive self-view—to not be so quick to criticize and break myself down. I threw myself into the lion's den tonight, knowing it might hurt.

". . . I mean, she kind of went off the deep end for a while, right? Dumped coffee on a customer at a restaurant she worked at?" A man with a strong accent and a balding patch on his head gestures to his companion.

I inhale a sharp breath, not sure I'm ready for this—to hear perfect strangers' horrific opinions of me and of the terrible things Jenessa did. Just like my middle school and high school classmates, these people believe I'm latent evil. That a murder spree from one of us was impossible to avoid. I swirl my drink absentmindedly until liquid splashes onto my hand.

Shia peers at me. "Listen."

The same man continues. "But the customer was also stalking her, apparently. Not many people would survive that childhood and come out as well adjusted as they have. Sure, the second oldest went off her nut, but would you have fared better? I'm not sure I would. I mean, I like to think so, but—" The trio breaks into easy laughter.

I meet Shia's gaze. I haven't always been the most trusting. But something about his steady, reassuring nod, and the way in which he passes me a cocktail napkin to wipe the wine I spilled on my shaking hand, makes me think that might be changing.

"Stick around," Shia says. "These people might surprise you. I'm glad you're here, Claire."

He turns and weaves back through the crowd to the glimmering table of books.

"How'd it go? Anyone attack?" Lily returns with a grin, and Olive waves her fist hello. Both ladies look happier now that Olive wears a fresh diaper.

I try to relax. "There was a close call, but no blood was shed." I wince as soon as the words fall out of my idiot mouth. Lily only pats my forearm.

While I might say I don't understand how Jenessa was capable of the things she did, that's a lie; I understand what drove her to these extremes, even if I don't condone them. The trauma that we survived will always be a part of each of us. There's no altering our histories. But the real question is whether we can pivot from these terrible beginnings to lead seminormal lives. To bump into unknowns on the street and not flinch out of fear.

I set my half-full glass on a nearby cocktail table.

As Shia and I lock eyes from across the room, and the memory of his patient interview sessions comes to mind—his easy conversation and the consistent take-out nights that we've come to share on Thursdays—I allow my cheeks to bloom into a smile.

I'm not sure whether I'll ever be capable of leading a seminormal life. To experience an agonizing day and not eye the burning end of a cigarette with a longing to press it against my flesh. But today I don't. And that's a start.

Acknowledgments

Whenever I explore someplace new, I'm on the hunt for its lesser-known features—the activities or monuments that are on the third page of search results and buried beneath a city's flashier attractions. Well, Portland did not disappoint. Many thanks must be extended to this wonderful city for its unique love of coffee, roses, bridges, naked bike rides, breweries, strip clubs, and of course, the Portland Underground, also known as the Portland Shanghai Tunnels. To my friends, thank you for keeping Portland weird and the nicest place around.

This book would not have been written without the thoughtful support of my agent, Jill Marr, whose enthusiasm and wit can't be overrated. Thank you for always knowing the answer, finding the answer, or simply agreeing that the answer can be found in a glass of wine. Much gratitude goes to the team at Sandra Dijkstra Literary Agency for ensuring my t's are crossed and my i's dotted.

Not enough can be said about my editors, Megha Parekh and Caitlin Alexander. Megha, I am so grateful to you for your support of my writing, your passion for diverse books and characters. Thank you for believing in this second book. Caitlin: another one down! Your sharp eyes and ability to dig into all the layers of a story are what keep me sane during the editing process. Thank you for your positivity when I need it most.

Many thanks to the entire Thomas & Mercer team. Sarah Shaw, your patience for my numerous questions is impressive. Thank you for seeking out answers when they're not readily available. Brittany Russell, you are a rock star of publicity; thank you for everything that you do! Lindsey Bragg and Laura Barrett, likewise, I am incredibly lucky to have you both in my corner.

Recognition must also be paid to the talented Jana Foo. Your skill and knowledge of photography were essential to my confidence in this book. Thank you for answering my oddball queries. Any error in this story regarding photography is mine alone.

To Lauren Fisher, my generous sister-in-law and frequenter of breweries. Thank you for brainstorming with me at the beginning of this story.

To Sarah Shekhter, thank you for entertaining my extremely weird questions about the criminal justice system as I strove for plausibility. Any failing there is the result of my own rationale. Likewise, thanks must be paid to Stephanie Kurz for your tireless support.

To my writing friends, Raimey Gallant, Elaine Roth, and Heather Lettieri, I could not get past this first draft without your eyes, helpful texts, and supportive GIFs. Thank you for being the very best in critique partners.

To the Debuts 2020 group: we did it! Heartfelt thanks go to each of you for being the emotional sounding board I needed during our debut year. It's a joy to be on this ride together and a privilege to read your amazing books.

Friends, both near and far, thank you for reading and promoting my work, but mostly thank you for being incredible people. You've each shaped me in your own way and, in that sense, my writing. Enthusiastic gratitude should also go to educators Emily Watson, Maria Russell, Gini Grossenbacher, Maureen Messier, and Craig Howard.

Thanks must be given to my family members, Sue Ma, Greg and Jeannie Cornelius, Erin Cornelius, Ian Cornelius, Liana Marr, Eddie

Mejia, and Kevin Campbell for exploring the Portland Shanghai Tunnels with me. You are a fearless bunch! I probably get all my good qualities from your influence and/or our shared genes.

To my parents and in-laws, thank you for your support. In particular, thank you to Gail Campbell for enthusiastically sharing my writing with the entire state of New Mexico.

Publishing a second book is a dream come true and would not be possible without readers. If you've stuck with me this far—thank you.

Finally, to Caden. Since this book is dedicated to you, I look forward to your thoughts on its pages a very, very long time in the future. You are an absolute gift and make everything better. I am so lucky to be your mama.

And, of course, to Kevin, without whom I'd get no writing done, who is game for a new adventure every day, and whose editorial eye continues to astound: thank you. You're my first reader and favorite brainstormer. The depth of your love and support deserves another photo shoot in the Gorge.

About the Author

Photo © 2019 Jana Foo Photography

Elle Marr is the number one Amazon Charts bestselling author of *The Missing Sister*. She graduated from UC San Diego before moving to France, where she earned a master's degree from the Sorbonne University in Paris. Originally from Sacramento, Elle now lives in Oregon with her husband, son, and one very demanding feline. For more information, visit the author at www.ellemarr.com.